Pei

when you wake and find me gone

Maureen McCarthy, the ninth of ten children, grew up on a farm near Yea in Victoria. After working for a while as an art teacher, Maureen became a full-time scriptwriter and author.

Her novels include *Ganglands*, *Cross My Heart* (shortlisted for the 1993 NSW Premier's Award, the 1994 Victorian Premier's Award, the 1994 SA Festival Award and the 1994 Multicultural Children's Literature Award), *Chain of Hearts* (shortlisted for the Ethel Turner Prize in the 2000 NSW Premier's Literary Awards), *Flash Jack* and the *In Between* series, which was adapted from scripts Maureen co-wrote with Shane Brennan for the SBS TV mini-series. Her bestselling and much-loved book *Queen Kat, Carmel and St Jude Get a Life* was made into a highly successful four-part mini-series produced by Trout Films in association with the Australian Broadcasting Corporation.

Praise for *Queen Kat, Carmel and St Jude Get a Life*:

'Realistic, gutsy and challenging.'
The *Courier Mail* (Brisbane)

'Few books have the power to bring tears of rage or laughter the way this does.'
The *Age*

REJECTED COPY NOT FOR SALE UNDER COPYRIGHT

By the same author

In Between
Ganglands
Cross My Heart
Queen Kat, Carmel and St Jude Get a Life
Chain of Hearts
Flash Jack

maureen
mccarthy

when you wake
and find me gone

Penguin Books

Penguin Books

Published by the Penguin Group
Penguin Books Australia Ltd
250 Camberwell Road
Camberwell, Victoria 3124, Australia
Penguin Books Ltd
80 Strand, London WC2R 0RL, England
Penguin Putnam Inc.
375 Hudson Street, New York, New York 10014, USA
Penguin Books, a division of Pearson Canada
10 Alcorn Avenue, Toronto, Ontario, Canada, M4V 3B2
Penguin Books (N.Z.) Ltd
Cnr Rosedale and Airborne Roads, Albany, Auckland, New Zealand
Penguin Books (South Africa) (Pty) Ltd
24 Sturdee Avenue, Rosebank, Johannesburg 2196, South Africa
Penguin Books India (P) Ltd
11, Community Centre, Panchsheel Park, New Delhi, 110 017, India

First published by Penguin Books Australia, 2002

10 9 8 7 6 5 4 3 2 1

Text copyright © Maureen McCarthy, 2002

The moral right of the author has been asserted

All rights reserved. Without limiting the rights under copyright reserved above,
no part of this publication may be reproduced, stored in or introduced into a retrieval
system, or transmitted, in any form or by any means (electronic, mechanical, photocopying,
recording or otherwise), without the prior written permission of both the copyright owner
and the above publisher of this book.

Design by Marina Messiha, Penguin Design Studio
Cover photograhy by Getty Images
Typeset in 10.5/14pt Bembo by Midland Typesetters, Maryborough, Victoria
Printed and bound in Australia by McPherson's Printing Group, Maryborough, Victoria

National Library of Australia
Cataloguing-in-Publication data:

McCarthy, Maureen, 1953–
When you wake and find me gone.

ISBN 0 14 300031 4.

1. Young women – Fiction. 2. Fathers and daughters –
Fiction. I. Title.

A823.3

www.penguin.com.au

For my son Tom, with love

Sincere thanks to the following people for taking the time to talk with me, and for their interest and insights:

In Ireland
Michael and Kitty Tracy and their daughter Alex, Kathleen O'Halloran, Isobel Reilly, Gerry Boyle, Michelle McCabe, Tommy O'Halloran, Sr Lorna Ridley, Michael Docherty, Col McNally and Deirdre O'Brien.

In Australia
Meg McNena, Liam McCabe, John Stewart, Fr Mal Crawford and Val Noone.

Warm thanks to Ramona Koval for the work room in Kew, to Jane Godwin for her friendship and meticulous attention to detail during the editing process, and to Laura Harris and Julie Watts at Penguin for their continuing support and enthusiasm.

Thanks also to my sister, Patrice McCarthy, in particular for her vivid memories of Belfast in 1981. And a special thanks to my eldest son, Tom, a keen student of Espionage, Terrorism and Global Disorder, at the University of Tasmania.

I read many books and articles about Ireland and the hunger strike of 1981. There are a few that I would particularly like to acknowledge:

Ten Men Dead, the story of the 1981 Irish hunger strike, by David Beresford. Atlantic Monthly Press, New York.

Biting at the Grave, the Irish hunger strikes and the politics of despair, by Padraig O'Malley. Beacon Press, Boston, Massachusetts.

Bobby Sands' Writings from Prison, Mercier Press, Dublin, Ireland.

War as a Way of Life, a Belfast diary, by John Conroy, Heinemann, London.

A Place Apart, by Dervla Murphy. Penguin Books, London.

Killing Rage, by Eamon Collins with Mick McGovern. Granta Books, London.

Part One

CHAPTER ONE

when you wake and find me gone

'Where did you get to last night, Kathleen Mary Therese Quinlan?'

It was Brendan – sarcastic, rude, good-humoured as usual – clattering through the front door with his bike.

Kit winced as the creak and grind of the pedals scraped past her bedroom.

'You invite us to your bloody party,' he roared, 'filled with all those theatre wankers, then you disappear!'

'Would you shut up!' Tamara's sultry voice slid in from the room across the hall. 'Why do you always have to make such a racket?'

'Slackers!' Brendan shouted back cheerfully. 'Time both of you got up.' Then one, two, three further crashes as he pulled the bike down the steps into the old kitchen, dumped his backpack and clattered his way out through the back door to put the bike away. 'If either of you plan moving your arses today,' he went on, 'I'd suggest you take a long hard look inside the fridge. It's, like, growing *mushrooms!* And Quinlan, take note. For all your crap about environmentally friendly rat-killer, the friggin' mice are back in force . . . *and* planning to take over, judging by the size of the pile of crap I swept out of the sink cupboard this morning. By the way, I've done the shopping again.'

The back door slammed shut and there was another series of slams as he threw the shopping into the cupboards. All this was accompanied by a loud off-key rendition of a U2 song.

'You've got to get yourself together
Cause you're stuck in a moment that
You can't get out of . . .'

If it had been an ordinary morning, Kit would have grinned and called out for tea and toast in bed while Brendan was still in full martyr mode. He got like this every so often; acted like she and Tam were a couple of useless bimbos while he managed the really important stuff around the house. It wasn't true and Brendan knew it. The three of them put in in different ways and it mainly evened out. Dishes were done most days. Sort of. Rubbish got put out on Sunday night if someone remembered. Floors were occasionally swept and the shower recess scrubbed when the tiles got too slippery to stand on. But not much else happened, cleaning-wise.

The window-sills, bench-tops and furniture were thick with dust. And the pink nylon curtain in the kitchen, hung some time between the two world wars, had never been washed. But then who with half a brain in their head even looked at curtains, or cared about them? Tam, Kit and Brendan always came back to that point when they rolled home from some party in the middle of the night, suddenly struck with the fact that the old Richmond terrace had a certain charm to it. All the original iron lace-work was there, so too the high-pressed ceilings. It even had stained-glass panels on each side of the window in the bathroom. They all agreed that it could be made to look really fabulous if somebody just put-in-a-bit-of-work. But after ten minutes talk about paint colours and replacing rotting window frames and pulling up the old kitchen lino to sand the floor, and whether the landlord would agree to pay for all or some, they'd lose interest, relieved that yet again they'd got their priorities sorted out.

It *had* been Kit's turn to go to the market, but she didn't see any point in lacerating herself if Brendan decided to go before she'd had a chance to surface. If it had been a normal morning, she would have yelled, 'Hey, thanks a mill, Bren. I swear I'll do it *all* next week: the cooking, the cleaning as well as the shopping. Leave out your shirts too, babe. I'll iron them, no worries. Got any buttons you need sewing on? It'd be a complete joy!' That would have had him chuckling and probably throwing something through the door at her.

But this was no ordinary morning.

Kit was standing, stark naked and nervous, in her room, the phone still in her hands, waiting for the full impact of what she'd just heard to hit her. She shivered slightly in the cool morning air. Waiting and wondering.

Wondering what the hell she would feel when it did hit. And would that match up with what she *should* feel.

Her desk was laid out neatly with books, articles and notes she'd collected for the all-important politics essay she'd planned to begin that afternoon. The one that would get her into Honours the following year, despite the fact that she was a unit short on the requirements. A breeze coming in through the top of the window was making the curtain billow out like a red sail. It was early October but the night before, she'd fancied she could smell summer in the air. Heat from the pavement, scent from the soil and trees in Mrs Boil's garden next door had got into her nostrils.

'Your sister Leonie was in a car accident last night . . . In the Bayton base hospital. Too serious to move. A surgeon has come up from the city to assess her. Maybe operate . . . this afternoon. She's in a coma . . . could die . . . Come home Kathleen . . . come home.'

'Mum, I . . . can't come home. I'm in a play.'

'A play?'

'Remember I told you? The university theatre. I can't let the others down.'

5

'But your sister!'

'I've got the . . . one of the main parts. There's just one more performance tonight and then it's over.'

'Leonie is your only sister, Kathleen.'

'I know, I'll be there just as soon –'

'Couldn't you come on this morning's train and go back this afternoon?'

'I'd be there an hour and I'd have to come straight back.'

'So when will you come?'

'Tomorrow morning. I'll get the eleven a.m.'

'Well . . .' Kit's mother sounded totally strung out, way beyond arguing. 'Just get here as soon as you can, and until then *pray* as hard as you can.'

'Of course I will,' Kit muttered.

Her mother's belief in prayer as a solution for everything from toothache to the state of the world's homeless drove Kit crazy but because she loved her like no one else, she held back. She could picture her standing in the dark hallway of the old house, one hand clutching the phone and the other running anxiously back and forth through her greying hair.

'I will,' Kit said again quickly. 'Did the doctors say anything else, Mum?'

'We're all here now at the hospital waiting for news,' Therese Quinlan whispered, ignoring the question. 'The surgeon is assessing her as we speak.'

'Oh, right.' Of course her mother wouldn't be at home. The house was five kilometres away from the town hospital. Kit had spent quite a bit of time in that hospital during her last year at school when her grandfather was dying so it was easy to picture that room, too. The grey floor, the small chrome chairs and pink walls, the cheap print of a sunset hanging near the door, the smell of carpet cleaner.

6

'So all the boys are there with you, and Dad?' Kit asked, just to fill in time until the shock subsided a little.

'Yes, love. All except Johnny. Damien's just arrived.'

'But Johnny knows, doesn't he?'

'Frank called him an hour ago.'

The boys were Kit's four older brothers. The two who lived nearby were Frank and Pete. Both farmers. They would have been there from the beginning with her mother, their wives as well, probably, and some of their kids. Damien, the family brain, was a psychiatrist who lived in the city. He would've driven up first thing that morning. Kit found herself hoping for her mother's sake that Damien hadn't brought his wife and kids with him. The general level of angst would go up another hundred watts if Lucy and the ultimate-horrors-from-hell had descended as well.

Johnny, the brother nearest to Kit in age, also lived in the city and he was her favourite. Not that she saw much of him these days. He was thirty and in his second year studying to be a priest in a seminary out on the other side of town. In a couple of months he was due to take the first in a series of vows that would have him locked in to that way of life forever.

'Pray that she'll wake soon and' – her mother gave a small involuntary sob that made Kit want to reach across the two hundred kilometres and take her hand to steady her – 'that the surgeon doesn't have to operate. Pray hard for that, Kathleen.'

'Yes, Mum. I will,' Kit said. Her mother had a fear of all things medical. Fear, coupled with a terrible intense fascination. Therese loved hearing about her friends' operations and recounted them in gruesome detail to anyone who'd listen, but the same woman made any excuse not to visit a doctor for a simple check-up herself.

'I don't care what you believe in,' her mother suddenly said sharply. 'Do you hear me? Just *beg* God for Leonie's full recovery.'

'I'll pray for her, Mum. I promise.' Kit meant it, too. Not that she thought God would listen to her in a pink fit. But it was the least she could do. 'Let me know then as soon as you hear.'

'Of course, as soon as there's any news. We'll ring.'

Kit put the phone down. *Leonie.* Her sister. Her only sister was unconscious. Fighting for her life. What did it matter that they hadn't been close for years? Leonie was still her sister. *Please, God . . .*

The truth was that the phone call had woken Kit out of a deep happy sleep. She'd lain there listening to the shrill noise, unable to push away the warm bedclothes to get up and answer it. She'd figured it would be for one of the others, anyway. Brendan had a job in a nearby restaurant and they were always ringing and changing his work roster. Tam's mother often rang on the weekends to check that her precious only daughter's life was on track. Work, love, diet, spirits – the woman was a sponge for every unimportant detail.

So Kit had let the phone ring, waiting for someone else to pick it up, images from the night before shuffling delightfully through her head like a slow waltz.

There had been an impromptu party at Hugh Mitchell's house. He was playing the main role – and he'd invited people back to his place in Collingwood, only a few streets away from Kit's. Everyone had come: all those working on the play, the cast and crew and all the friends and hangers-on. By midnight it was crowded and noisy, the air thick with laughter, smoke and gossip. The two-week season had gone really well. It was just a student production but they'd had good audiences every night and terrific reviews in the university papers. Everyone had been so revved up, talking plans for the coming summer, the next year, what they'd do after the final performance the following night. Then the director, Sebastian Davies, arrived.

Kit had first come across Sebastian at the beginning of the year when he'd given the opening lecture in the third year politics subject she'd enrolled in: *Espionage, Terror and Global Disorder.* Her degree up to this point had been fun more than anything. French and literature and a bit of history – things she was good at and nothing too strenuous. But from the September of the year before – more precisely from September 11th of the year before, when the Twin Towers of the World Trade Centre in New York collapsed – she'd begun to feel stale. Impatient with it all. It had become too easy, too predictable, too *girly*. Shakespeare and Shelley, George Eliot and Walt Whitman, Deconstructing Film. Modern African Novels. Marginalisation in the Post-Colonial World. Blah, blah, blah. And so much of it was in a kind of code language that no ordinary person could understand. After that day in September, Kit had felt that if she heard one more lecturer jaw on about some writer *subverting the text* she'd stand up in the middle of the lecture theatre and scream.

The regular professor for the politics subject had been due back from overseas the following week and so Sebastian Davies had given a two-hour introductory lecture. American imperialism. The Taliban. Islamic fundamentalism. Hezbollah. The PLO. Torture in Iran. The meaning of genocide. His style and presentation, his broad knowledge of world politics and history, had galvanised Kit; it had keyed her right back to the feelings she'd had as she'd watched those extraordinary images on the television the year before. *My god, I know nothing about any of this. This is my world and I know nothing about it.*

She'd walked out of that first lecture in a daze. Yes! This was what she was after. There was a world out there, a real world, and she wanted to know about it.

Three months later, she'd found herself auditioning for the university play and there was Sebastian again: sitting in the director's chair, putting aspiring student actors through their paces, taking notes, being kind and encouraging. Kit had decided to try out for a part just for something to do. Although she had no serious aspirations to act, she decided *what the hell*. Being in a play might just put an extra bit of zing into her life the way the politics unit had. The next day, Sebastian had called to say she had the lead female role. For some reason the news had made her feel insanely pleased. She decided there and then to throw herself into it in the same way she'd thrown herself into her new academic subject. It didn't hurt that the director was the same guy who had impressed her so much at the beginning of the year.

But within the first hour of the first read-through of the play, her world was thrown into complete upheaval. She had her own private blow-up. It was so shocking that until the whole incident was over she didn't exactly know what had happened. Her palms had gone sweaty, her throat constricted. At the same time as feeling she'd die when Sebastian praised her, she was immediately jealous of anyone else he spoke to with any warmth and enthusiasm. Kit had never had such odd and confusing feelings before. Walking home, she'd realised that she'd fallen for a man she didn't know. Someone she'd hardly seen before.

How bloody crazy was it that after nearly three years at university, of never managing to find anyone remotely interesting, she suddenly fell for a man who was right out of her range?

Sebastian was six years older than Kit. He was a politics tutor completing his PhD and involved in student theatre. Relationships between students and staff were frowned on by everybody – including other students – but Kit couldn't help it. Of course during the next few rehearsals she'd tried to let him know. Flirted a bit. Awkwardly, probably. After all, she wasn't used to this kind of thing. Rehearsals progressed and the first performance loomed. Friendly and vaguely warm, Sebastian was the same with everyone. He rarely stayed long at the boozy pizza dinners after late rehearsals, nor did he ask questions about private lives or tell anything of his own.

Every time he left early, giving them all a wave and smile, she died inside. It was like the sun was gone, that there was only murky darkness until next time she saw him. The miserable walk home alone again.

Until last night.

From the moment he'd arrived at the party, Kit could feel his eyes on her. She was wearing a crushed green velvet dress that Tam had picked up for her in an op-shop. A sort of Juliet dress with a wide scooped neck, pulled in tight at the waist, the skirt almost reaching her ankles. Kit's dark wavy hair was down, the front bits pinned back in tiny plaits. Her eyes were bright and she felt, for no reason that she could pinpoint, more confident than she'd been in months.

'Let's dance, Kathleen,' Sebastian said, catching her hand as she'd been heading out to the kitchen to get a drink. 'Tomorrow is our last performance, you know.' He was the one person in her university circle who still called her Kathleen. And when he said it, the old family name took on a sort of sexy undertone that never failed to make her shiver with delight.

'Why now, Sebastian?' Kit replied lamely, laughing, trying to be cool but feeling her heart begin to thud.

He shrugged and refused to let go of her hand. 'Because you want to.' He gave one of his lopsided, breathtakingly innocent grins. 'And because I want to. Isn't that enough?'

And she knew then that he *knew*, and furthermore that it was okay, that there *was* something between them . . .

Kit followed him out onto the lounge-room floor where others were shuffling around, dancing, joking and calling out to each other. He put his arm around her waist and she melted in close as he pulled her towards him. Barely speaking, they danced like that for over an hour. Occasionally, she was aware of others watching. He was the director, after all. He'd never flirted with anyone in the

11

cast before. But what did it matter, really? This was her wildest fantasy coming true. Minute by divine minute!

Sebastian Davies and Kathleen Quinlan. The night before the final performance. Dancing together in front of everyone. Had it really happened?

So as Kit had lain thinking of Sebastian, the phone had kept ringing. Eventually, she'd jumped up to get it. Her love-life was taking off. At last! She was taking off.

She'd picked up the phone.

'*Come home, Kathleen. Come home . . .*'

CHAPTER TWO

By the time she'd finished talking to her mother and put the phone down, there were so many questions Kit knew she should have asked. What was Leonie even doing out in a car on her own at two a.m? Leonie, the eldest in the family, was forty-three and since coming back from overseas two years ago she'd lived a quiet life; she hardly went anywhere. After six years away she'd gone straight back to the country to live with her ageing parents, got herself a job in the local library and basically kept a low profile. So who had she been out with the night before? Was there anyone else involved? Therese had in fact told Kit nothing. Even so, she managed to resist the urge to ring her mother straight back. She sounded so distressed, it would be better to wait a little while.

Kit slipped on her dressing gown, went over to the window and pushed aside the Indian curtain to take a look at the grey concrete backyard.

A perfect pale-blue crisp spring day in Melbourne shone above. October. Waiting for her. Why get into a tizz about it all before she had to? Leonie would be all right. People got over car accidents these days. Doctors could do amazing things.

Kit loved this time of the year. She loved this city. She loved living in this house with Brendan and Tam. And . . . oh, *God*. Kit squeezed her eyes shut and clenched her fists. Now there was Sebastian to think about! It had happened. Last night had made all that she'd been secretly feeling over the last few months legitimate. *I'm in love with him.* She allowed herself to say the words and she couldn't help throwing her head back and laughing silently to herself because they felt just right.

She loved the way Sebastian *cared* about the play, all its themes and tensions. And she loved the way he had his own vision for it but at the same time was genuinely keen to hear everyone else's ideas. She loved, well, everything about him really. The way his thick, badly cut hair fell across his left eyebrow. The way he lifted his right hand when he wanted to make a point, as though mocking himself. Those hands! She'd spent the last fifteen minutes of that first read-through looking at them, imagining them touching her skin. She loved the way he stuttered a bit when he got enthusiastic or excited. The unpretentious Aussie accent, so warm and alive and quick to laugh – unusual for an academic – always trying to find the right words and never quite making it. The shrug, the shake of his head. *You know what I mean!* God, yes, she used to think. *I know what you mean, Sebastian. I do.*

There was a vagueness to him that was endearing. An aloofness, too, a reticence that, because it didn't seem to come from pride or arrogance, gave him a mysterious air.

There were a couple of soft knocks on the door. Kit closed the window and eased herself back into the room.

'Kit, you awake?'

It was Tam, her best friend from the first week she'd landed at uni as a naïve, fresh-faced country girl who barely knew how to catch a tram or gatecrash a college party.

'Can I use your mirror?'

'Sure. Come in.' Kit knew Tam almost certainly didn't want the mirror. She wanted to check out the details of what had happened with Sebastian.

'I'll go get us some tea first, heh?' Tam called through the door.

'Yes please,' Kit called back, sitting down on the bed.

'There's something I've got to show you.' Tam's voice faded away, and Kit heard her footsteps disappear down into the kitchen.

Leonie will be okay. She has to be. My mother is a good woman and her prayers will be answered, even if mine won't.

The door opened and Tamara stood dressed in a low-neck cream lace nightie and dressing gown ensemble. She was holding two cups of steaming tea and smiling. The outfit had a huge ruffle around the hem that stuck out sideways. Kit's breath gave way momentarily. Tam had outdone herself this time. Never before had she found anything quite so bizarre – and tacky.

Tamara's mother was Indonesian and her father a stocky British naval man. Tam took after her mother. She was dark-skinned, short and plumpish with huge brown eyes and a wide mouth. Her skin against the slightly grubby lace in the morning light shone like rich melted chocolate.

'Who rang?' she asked, walking over and handing Kit the tea.

'My mother,' Kit replied, for some reason putting off telling Tam about Leonie. Kit walked around her friend, checking out the costume and taking sips of tea.

'You look bloody crazy, Tam. Where did you get that?'

Tamara's big love in life was scouring op-shops for clothes from the sixties and seventies. She shopped constantly and not just for herself. All Kit's circle was dressed by Tam in one way or another. Her skill was being able to sniff out the right piece of clothing instinctively. Almost every time she managed to delight her friends with her gifts.

Tam did a couple of quick spins, showing how the outfit billowed out behind her as she moved.

15

'I feel like the Queen Mother,' she giggled. 'You like it?'

'Yeah.' Kit began to laugh, 'you look *mad.*'

'Hmmm.' Tamara frowned and considered herself seriously in the mirror. The drawstring under the bust lifted her ample breasts and made them spill out over all the heavy lace. She shook them provocatively then leant over, making a huge cleavage. She pursed her lips.

'Sexy, huh?'

'You look like you've stepped straight off the set of a porno movie.' Kit slumped back onto her bed, hands clasped behind her head.

'So what happened last night?' Tam said quickly, catching Kit's eye in the mirror. 'We saw you leave with your director.'

My director. Kit was embarrassed. Her feelings for Sebastian were so fragile that she didn't want to have to spell them out to anyone. That would be a sure way of making everything wonderful disappear or go wrong.

'Everyone was exceedingly interested,' Tam grinned. 'You okay?'

'Yes,' Kit said warily, thinking that some student circles were as small and nosy as the country town she'd escaped from. She'd told no one except Brendan and Tam about her obsession with Sebastian and she'd sworn them to secrecy. She didn't tell her other best friend, Lou, who lived three houses down. Put simply, Lou had the social judgement of a canary. If Kit had confided in her, then Lou, if ever she met Sebastian, would make a point of telling him every-thing, word for word, convinced the whole time she was doing Kit a huge favour.

'I'm fine, Tam.' Kit hugged herself and giggled. 'I'm really excited actually and,' she grabbed Tam's hand, 'I'm more into him than ever.'

'Yeah?'

'Yep.'

'So has the longest drought in the history of the university broken?'

Kit flushed. Tam was asking if she'd slept with him.

'No, not yet, but I'm working on it.'

'So you're still the sweet maid of Richmond?' Tam mocked, her eyes twinkling.

'Shut up.' Kit put her head under one of the pillows. 'Give me a break, you bitch!'

Tam laughed and sat on the end of the bed, grabbed one of Kit's feet and pretended to look between her toes for fleas.

'You look really stupid in that thing!' Kit pulled her foot away and pointed at Tam's ridiculous outfit. 'How much did you pay for it?'

But Tam only shook her head and kept on laughing. 'Oh Kitty!' she teased, 'Kitty, Kitty! Oh hail virgin queen of the Richmond slums!'

'Shut up, Tam!' Kit said crossly. 'I'm warning you. Just shut up.'

Kit never admitted it to any of them, but her situation *was* beginning to freak her. What if the curse of her family – her family was full of single females – was going to fall on her, too? Even so, she had a dogged stubborn streak that insisted on her own terms in matters of love. *Was it really too much to ask to be in love when I sleep with someone?* Tamara was always falling in and out of relationships. After the sexual side of things was finished, the guys involved mostly went on to become her friends. Kit could see that Tam's way made perfect sense. Tam was looking for a good time and she usually had one. Kit had some great times, too, but at the end of the night she'd end up alone. Often she trudged home with Brendan, arm in arm after a party, joking about being misfits, promising each other that the next time they'd get lucky.

'So,' Tam was over at the mirror again combing her hair, 'tell me all about it. What happened?'

'Nothing *happened*.' Kit lay back on the pillows again. 'That's the thing. Nothing happened. Except . . .' she started laughing, '*everything*.'

'Really?'

'Well, sort of!'

'So tell me. Why did you decide to leave the party when you did?' Tam had to know the ins and outs of everything, and the more sordid the detail the better. 'I mean, what did he say? Where did you go?'

Kit sighed. She knew there was no way she was going to be able to hold out against Tam.

'It's so noisy here,' he'd whispered to her, 'and I'm hungry. Do you want to have a sandwich and coffee somewhere?'

'But it's still early,' Kit's voice had sounded choked even to herself, 'isn't it?'

'You live around here, don't you?'

Ah, so you do know something about me then!

'Yes. Three streets away.'

'I'll take you home, Kathleen,' he smiled. 'We'll stop at a café on the way.'

'Okay,' Kit mumbled, feeling absolutely sick with love and lust and nervousness. 'I'll get my bag.'

They stopped for coffee and talked easily enough. About the play, then the course Kit was doing. He was interested when she told him that she planned to change her major to political science. She didn't tell him about the impact his first lecture had made on her earlier in the year, but she told him she was all set to embark on the big essay that would get her into Honours. He gave her some advice about who to see at the university when it was finished.

It was all easy enough. But not entirely satisfactory. It was bliss sitting there with him but Kit knew she had to somehow *intensify* the situation or he might just slip through her fingers. Suddenly, she was filled with a manic urge to pinch him, just to see if he really *was* sitting across the table from her. Being someone who often went from the gut without thinking things through, she did it. She pinched him hard on the elbow and then again on the soft bit behind his knee.

'Ouch!' he yelped, shocked. 'What the hell . . .' To Kit's relief he immediately laughed when he realised that she'd pinched him for no better reason than she felt like it, and after that they both began joking about everything. It had broken the serious vibe between them. The talk and laughter was full of warm sparks and deep unspoken things. It was entirely satisfactory. Wonderful. Within an hour any sense of how odd it was for them to be sitting there together had dissipated.

They walked back to Kit's house hand-in-hand, and when they got to the gate, Kit took a deep breath and asked him in for coffee. Sebastian had an early start in the morning and thought he'd better be going. But not before he pulled Kit to him and kissed her quickly. Then he said he'd pick her up the following night for the last performance. Maybe they could have a drink together before going on. Did she want to do something afterwards? There would probably be another party, it being the last night and all, but seeing that they'd already been to a great party, maybe they needn't stay long?

Kit smiled to show that she too had had enough of big crowds and noisy parties. Maybe they could go and listen to music some-where, he'd suggested. Would she like that? Kit said she would love it. They said goodbye. Kit walked in through the front door, the kiss still sitting on her mouth flimsy and delicate and somehow alive. She'd been disappointed that he wasn't coming inside, but relieved at the same time because, well, she had the feeling that the night might explode around her if anything else happened.

Tam was laughing by the time Kit had finished.

'What kind of kiss?'

'Tam!'

'Was it slow and lingering, or a short intense *I-gotta-have-you-now* number? Or was it –'

'I'm not going to tell you.'

'I have to know!' Tam grabbed her arm, snorting with laughter. 'Was it *soulful*?'

Kit was laughing, too, in spite of herself, as she searched around for an adequate word. 'It was . . .'

'*What*?' Tam's eyes shone.

'Ardent!' Kit proclaimed.

'Hmmm.' Tam seemed satisfied. 'Ardent will do! Come on,' she said, clapping her hands a couple of times. 'Let's go and tell Brendan.'

Brendan was sitting at the cluttered kitchen table, drinking tea, eating crumpets with honey and reading the paper, his back to the light coming in through the window over the sink. He looked up briefly when Kit and Tam came in, nodded and turned back to his paper.

The girls grinned at each other.

'You still in a huff, Bren?' Kit said, poking him in the back on her way over to the stove. 'About the shopping?'

'No,' he mumbled. 'I'm reading the paper.'

'You don't say.'

Brendan was not handsome, at least by any normal standards. He was six-foot-three and big-boned: one of those heavy guys who seems to fill a room when they enter it. He had a great open ruddy face, with a long, slightly crooked, hooked nose and a square jaw, deep-set green eyes, heavy black eyebrows, and a wide mouth that was always breaking open into a smile or a shout. He played sport well and was a fantastic dancer. He reminded everyone of the French actor Gérard Depardieu, which always pissed him off no end.

'Did the Labels come in last night?'

'Yep,' Brendan muttered.

'Get any sleep?' Tam grinned.

The Labels were Larissa and Mike – a mid-twenties, ultra-glamorous couple who occupied the big front room upstairs adjacent to Brendan's room. They lived quite separate lives to the three students, working long hours in IT jobs, clubbing and eating their way through all the best restaurants in their time off. The big Richmond terrace was really only a cheap convenient stepping-stone – a place to sleep and keep their mountains of clothes before they got around to buying their own home. They hardly ever came down to the kitchen; they never cooked and rarely ate in, and had their own coffee-machine upstairs. But their noisy lovemaking was a great topic of conversation for the other three.

'Wasn't too bad last night,' Brendan said, 'just the usual bang bang of the bed against my wall for half an hour. I only heard "*That's soooo good baby*" once.'

Tam and Kit collapsed into giggles. There was something about the perfect pair upstairs that brought out their worst instincts for character assassination.

'Calvin or Gucci?'

'What do you mean?'

'Who said it?' Tam wanted to know.

'Calvin, of course!' Brendan groaned and turned the newspaper page. '*She* never talks! She just gives out these little fake moans, like she's lost her earring or something.'

Kit and Tam looked at each other and collapsed again.

'God, I've got to get up and record them one night!'

'You're a pervert, Tamara!'

'No, really . . .'

The tall, handsome Michael was nicknamed Calvin because every item of his clothing, down to his underpants and hankies, was manufactured by a major, expensive brand. (Tam and Kit had checked them out on the washing line.) And Larissa – also tall and impossibly perfect in face and figure – was stuck with Gucci after she told Tam that she wouldn't even bother looking at a handbag under three hundred dollars because: 'Well, you couldn't be sure it was real leather, could you?'

Occasionally Kit had twinges of guilt about the way they savaged the Labels so unmercifully behind their backs, but not often enough for her to stop. It was too much fun.

Brendan was the complete opposite of the Labels. This morning he was dressed in a plain windcheater, jeans and elastic-sided boots. His long dark hair was tied back in a wet ponytail. He was the eldest son of a family of Irish immigrants who lived in the housing commission flats in Port Melbourne. His father was killed when Brendan was ten, six weeks after arriving in Melbourne, falling from the scaffolding of a city building-site. Brendan's mother still lived in the commission flat with his five younger siblings and was the scariest woman Kit had ever come across. Loud, tough and shrewd, Nora Delaney saw straight through everybody, and she was not a woman to muck around with pleasantries. After their first meeting, Kit did her best not to be in the woman's presence alone.

Brendan's accent was still there if you listened closely, especially when he was drinking or telling jokes. He was doing his Honours year in engineering and at twenty-five was two years older than Tamara and nearly five years older than Kit.

'The thing I hate about Australian politics now,' he muttered, before turning the page, 'is that the politicians never say anything genuine. They get trained up to deal with interviews.' He looked up. 'Tamara, that outfit is fucking ridiculous. It's bloody obscene. Your tits are hanging out everywhere! Where is a decent man meant to look?'

Tam giggled and went to the back of Brendan's chair, put both plump brown arms around his neck and proceeded to try to strangle him.

'Guess what, dickbrain,' she giggled, 'Kit's got news.'

'I'm a frustrated male, right?' he said, pretending to choke and pulling her arms from around his neck. 'It's not fair to make me think of sex all the time when I'm not getting any!'

'I thought you might have got lucky with that cute little curly-haired number last night?' Kit said cheerfully, going to the sink to wash out the teapot and pinching some of his honey-smeared crumpet on the way. Before leaving the party the night before she'd seen Brendan standing on the back step downing a stubbie and joking with some girl with beautiful heavy blond curls cascading down her back. 'What happened to her?'

'How would I know?'

'So what did happen?' Tam asked, taking a slurp of tea. It really bugged both Kit and Tam that Brendan had no luck with girls. When they'd first moved into the house he'd been living with a very quiet, rather beautiful girl called Margie but within a month Margie had moved out. That had been nearly two years ago and there'd been no one since.

He gave a surly shrug. 'We can't all be lucky,' he said grimly. Then, putting the newspaper down, he turned to Kit. 'Like some people.'

Kit blushed. 'Give me a break, you two,' she said, bringing the teapot over to the table. 'I mean it. Nothing's happened yet.'

'I'm sorry, Kathleen,' Brendan assumed a counsellor pose, a look of deep concern on his face, both hands joined as though in contemplation, 'but it's time to tell Uncle Brendan all about it.'

'Get stuffed!' Kit laughed. 'Come on,' she implored them both, 'let's change the subject, *please*. I don't want to talk about it.'

'But there are questions that must be answered,' Brendan murmured. 'Now tell me, was *safe* sex on the agenda?'

23

Thankfully for Kit, his interrogation was interrupted by a couple of sharp knocks at the back door, then an impatient yell as the door burst open and Kit's other best friend in the world, Lou, more or less fell into the room. She was followed by her huge skinny black-and-white dog, Boy George, who everybody in the world hated, except her.

'Hello, Lou!'

'Hi.'

'How are you?'

'Absolutely fucking terrible!'

Lou slumped heavily onto a chair next to Brendan, her face stitched up into an almighty scowl. She pulled her packet of tobacco and papers from the depths of her tattered shoulder-bag and within a few seconds her thin, yellow-stained fingers had rolled a cigarette. She settled it between her lips and began another hunt through her bag for a light. The dog was, as usual, sniffing around the room's corners and cracks and, when he got a chance, into people's crotches. Kit gave him a quick kick when she felt the dog's inquisitive nose start nuzzling her upper thigh.

'Get the hell out of it,' she snarled, 'or I'll pour boiling water on you.'

Lou gave her a dirty look but didn't say anything because she knew she was on thin ice even letting Boy George inside. The dog always looked half starved even though Lou seemed to spend her entire student allowance on him.

'You're not going to believe this!' Lou groaned, when she at last had her cigarette alight and everyone's attention.

'Try us,' Brendan said, blinking blandly.

'I lost my George Eliot essay!' she declared dramatically. 'The power gave out just as I was on the last paragraph!'

Tam and Kit groaned. Lou was prone to exaggeration and whether or not she'd come to the last paragraph or not they knew exactly what she was after. Tam coughed politely, waved Lou's smoke out of her face and looked away.

'So why didn't you save it?' Brendan was frowning. 'I've got no sympathy.'

'Oh shut up, Mr Perfect!' Tam and Kit immediately sided with Lou. 'Just because you never make a mistake!'

Lou, who barely looked normal at the best of times, being thin and bony, white faced with short, hacked-off dyed red hair, looked totally off the wall this morning. Usually her clothes were fairly nondescript; just old men's jumpers and pants in dark colours, topped with an army coat. (With the black nail polish and the silver rings through her nose and ears it looked weird enough.) But this morning she was wearing a small, black-and-white striped child's dress over the jumper and pants. Popping up out of her elastic-sided cowboy boots were striped football socks which came to her knees. Her face was so blanched, so incredibly unhealthy looking, that Kit found herself thinking that Lou looked exactly as though someone had buried her and dug her up again a week later.

'Can I borrow yours?' Lou asked Kit shamelessly.

'I don't do literature any more, remember.' Kit said sharply. Lou, such a slacker, was always pinching essays. Most of the time Kit didn't mind that much – she changed them so they were unrecognisable – but sometimes it grated.

'Oh shit, why?' Lou snarled. '*Why* did you take that sick, violent subject *Espionage* or whatever it's called. I mean, what has that got to do with anything? You were doing so brilliantly at lit.' She took another deep drag at her smoke and turned away grumpily.

'It's interesting,' Kit snapped back, 'and anyway *Middlemarch* isn't exactly a lot to do with anything either, is it.'

'Well at least Dorothea is a real person,' Lou sniffed, 'not like all this political clap-trap that they make up to get people to watch their stupid political programs and buy newspapers.'

'Actually,' Tam chortled, 'she's not!'

'What do you mean?' Lou tapped her ash into a nearby used cup, a habit Kit and Tam really hated.

'Dorothea,' Tam replied, leaning over to the end of the messy table and pulling an ashtray out from under a pile of somebody's lecture notes and shoving it at Lou, 'is *not* a real person.'

'Never was,' Kit spluttered.

'I love Dorothea!' Lou howled in protest.

'So do we!' Kit shouted back, laughing, 'love her to bits. Always have. She's my idol, my inspiration.'

'So?' Lou yelled back.

'Ah, put a sock in it!' Brendan groaned, getting up to refill his cup. 'It's too early in the morning for one of these kinds of conversations. Just shut up the lot of you.'

Brendan was interested in international politics, too. Since starting this new subject, Kit now competed with him for first read of the paper every morning, peering over each other's shoulders at the World News section, and talking through what was happening in the trouble spots.

'I handed George Eliot in yesterday,' Tamara was saying sharply. 'And I didn't keep a copy.' This was probably a lie, but Kit said nothing. Generous with clothing and presents and her time, Tam was unashamedly tight about a few things and university work was one of them.

'It's due Monday!' Lou shrieked, running her skinny fingers though her hair. 'Are you sure you didn't make a copy?'

'Due dates have never bothered you before,' Brendan said drolly.

Kit grinned and poured herself more tea. Nothing about university was straightforward for Lou. She was always turning up in the wrong venues for lectures, losing reference books and getting exam dates mixed up.

'What am I going to do?' She sighed and then began scratching

26

her scalp violently with both hands as though she had fleas. 'I'm going to fail the subject if I don't get it in on Monday.'

'Listen,' Kit said, 'had you seriously nearly finished it?'

'I was onto the last paragraph.'

'So go home now,' Tam cut in, 'and write it as you remember it.'

'Oh, shit!' Lou moaned, 'give me a break. It's not as though I know it off by heart!'

'So ask for an extension,' Brendan said meanly, 'and bring Boy George along in case the tutor says no.'

Lou sighed, then dragged herself up to the bench under the window to switch the kettle back on. The rest of them watched as she spooned coffee into the glass pot, poured the water and slowly slipped the plunger in, all of it done with an expression of intense concentration as if she was carrying out some highly skilled task.

'That was cool last night,' she mumbled, then turned around to Kit. 'The party, I mean.'

'Yeah,' Kit was surprised, 'it was okay, wasn't it?' This was unusual. Lou never simply *enjoyed* parties.

'Did you meet someone interesting?' Kit teased, knowing the odds of her doing that were pretty remote. Lou met people at football matches (she was a Richmond supporter), outside public toilets, in trains and bus shelters, sometimes at Wicca ceremonies but never at parties or at university.

'I *didn't* like that guy you were dancing with,' Lou went on, ignoring Kit's question.

'Why not?'

'He looked too involved.' Lou stuck her smoke into her mouth, poured steaming coffee into a mug and continued talking, the fag bouncing around her lips. 'He looked like he was going to eat you or something! It's unhealthy to get like that.'

'Right,' Kit said evenly, gulping down tea. How could Lou in a

27

million years start talking about what was healthy when she looked like a week-old cadaver herself?

'Just be careful,' Lou continued ominously, walking back over to the table with her coffee. 'He's dangerous. He looked like he was really hot for you, Kit.'

'Calm down, Lou,' Tam laughed. 'Kit can look after herself.'

'But that's the thing,' Lou said seriously, as though Kit wasn't there. 'I don't think she can.'

'Look, nothing has happened yet,' Kit said quickly. 'So you don't have to worry, okay?' The downside of living so closely with friends was that they were constantly on your back about every detail of your life!

Suddenly the phone rang and at exactly the same moment Boy George rose from where he'd been sitting in the corner of the kitchen and emitted a foul, rotten-meat stink. Kit immediately gagged and Brendan and Tam groaned.

'Get him out of here!' Tam shouted at Lou, who was sitting there as though nothing was happening.

Kit jumped up and opened the door. 'Now, Lou! Get him out!'

'Okay. Okay,' Lou snarled, grabbing Boy George by his collar and pulling him outside, 'don't act like you've never dropped one yourself!'

The phone kept ringing and as Kit sat down again she was momentarily paralysed by a strange sense of inertia. *The phone.* She began praying that it wouldn't be for her. Brendan got up grumpily, noisily pushed his chair back and disappeared into the hallway.

'Where is the friggin' phone?' he shouted.

'Kit's room,' Tam called back.

Kit continued to sit there, not knowing why this sudden chill had got into her back and legs. For a while she'd managed to convince herself that this was just an ordinary Saturday morning. She'd been sitting around in her dressing gown with friends raving on about nothing . . . enjoying herself as though there wasn't this whole other drama happening on the side.

The phone stopped. Kit heard Brendan's voice and then nothing for a few seconds. Brendan came back into the room, holding the phone and Kit suddenly started praying. Give me good news, *please.*

'It's for you,' he said, raising a quizzical eyebrow and holding out the phone.

'Who is it?' Kit said, not getting off her chair. Maybe someone was going to invite her to a party, or try to sell her something. She hoped so.

'Your brother,' Brendan said in a low voice. 'Said it's urgent.' Lou was back inside, minus Boy George who had started whining loudly in the backyard. Tam was flipping through the paper. With the word 'urgent', they immediately focused their attention on Kit.

'Which brother?' Kit said, still not moving.

'Frank.' Brendan motioned impatiently for her to take the phone. 'Come on.'

'Okay. Thanks.' Kit shifted off her chair and stood with her back to them all, holding the phone to her ear like it was something she'd never done before.

'Frank?'

'G'day, love.'

Frank was her oldest brother. He was a farmer, and lived just down the road from Kit's parents with his wife and five kids. Frank had the same gruff friendly voice for everyone.

'Any news?' Kit said, because she could sense the hesitation in his voice.

'Yeah,' he said slowly, 'and not too good. Not real good at all. Mum asked me to ring you.'

'What? What's happened?'

'Not good. Not good at all,' he repeated slowly.

Shit! Come on Frank. What do you mean?

There was a pause and Kit sensed the curious quietness behind her. The three of them were listening.

'So what is it, Frank?' she lowered her voice. 'Is her life in danger or . . .?'

'They're going to have to operate later today. There's a fracture on the lower left side of the skull. Apparently it's dangerous. Blood clots form. They can burst and, well, you know, it's all bloody serious. Can't move her.'

'Hmmm.' Kit didn't know anything about blood clots. She was longing to finish the phone call. 'So when is the operation?'

'In a couple of hours. They're waiting for another surgeon to arrive.'

'Will you ring me when you hear how it went?' she said, knowing there was something more he wanted to tell her. 'I've got to go now, Frank, but will you ring me straight away?'

My poor mother. What the hell did Kit think she was doing raving on to Tam about walks at night and kisses at the gate, making out she had some huge Jane Austen romance happening? A sinking feeling of anxiety descended down her throat, and nestled like a hungry worm just below her ribcage.

'The thing is,' Frank went on slowly as though he hadn't registered what she'd said, 'thing is, she's drifting in and out of consciousness and the doctor said that once he's operated this will probably continue. It'll be some time before we know if it's been successful or not.'

'So can she talk?' Kit cut in.

'Every now and again she sort of *surfaces*,' he said quietly. 'She said your name.'

Kit was shocked. 'What do you mean?'

'Well, just that,' he went on. 'She said something like: "Where's Kathleen?".'

'But . . .' Kit sank to her knees, unable to say anything. She didn't want this. The whole thing suddenly felt like a nightmare, closing her in. She was holed up in the corner of the room, struggling like a rabbit in a trap. She was pulling and scratching with all her might, trying to get away. She and Leonie were not close. The opposite. But she was caught somehow and there was no way she could get away.

'You should come home now,' Frank went on. 'She might recover, but the doctor told us there's also a chance that she won't survive. Either way she's a very sick woman.'

'I can't come today,' Kit said, her voice sounding on the verge of hysteria. 'I told Mum before. I'm in a play.'

'But Leonie wants you,' Frank said simply. Not begging. He was just getting to the point. 'And she might be dying.'

'I can't!' Kit burst out. 'I'll be there tomorrow. I'll leave first thing in the morning.'

'Well,' he sounded bewildered rather than annoyed, 'I don't know what else to say, Kathleen. I mean, Leonie could be dying.'

'I *can't* come today,' Kit shouted, close to tears.

'Well, if you change your mind,' Frank said, 'Johnny is leaving soon.' This calm tone was worse than him yelling at her. 'He'll pick you up, if you let him know. The operation will take a few hours. You could both be here when she wakes up. *If* she wakes up. You ring Johnny if you change your mind, okay?'

'Right,' Kit said through a thick throat. 'Thanks, Frank.'

'You got his number?'

'Yeah.'

'Bye, Kathleen.'

She put the phone down and turned around. The three of them were staring at her.

'My sister's been in a car accident,' she blurted out quickly. 'Very serious. She might die. She's having an operation this afternoon.'

'Which sister?' Lou asked blankly.

31

'I only have one sister,' Kit snapped.

'Okay,' Lou said huffily.

'So, go straight there *now*,' Tamara said, then turned to Brendan. 'She can take your car, can't she?'

'Have it, Kit,' Brendan said quickly. 'Or I'll drive you if you want that.'

'No,' Kit muttered. 'My brother Johnny is going up soon but I can't . . . I've got the play . . .'

'Kit!' Tam was horrified. 'Everyone would understand. Someone will take your place!'

'Actually, there isn't anyone,' Kit shot back defensively.

'What do you mean?'

'There's no one to take my place.'

'There *is* so,' Tamara declared. 'You said last week that some girl in costumes knows the whole thing! She could fill in for you, couldn't she?'

'But she can't act!'

'What complete bullshit.' Tamara never held back when she was angry. It was part of the reason Kit liked her so much. 'This is a student production, Kit. It's not the bloody West End! You know you could get out of it.'

'Look, it's just that . . . I don't want to go up there tonight. Is that okay with you guys or do I have to check out everything I do in my life with you first? I mean this is *my* sister and −'

'It's that guy, isn't it?' Lou jumped in triumphantly. 'You don't want to miss a date with hot boy!'

'Oh shut up, Lou!' Kit shouted, wondering how Lou had got it together to think so clearly for once. 'What would you know? And listen, Tam,' Kit continued, 'you're a single child of a single mother. Both of you are, actually. You don't have any idea what big families are like. The way they suck you in, the way you have to constantly fight just to stay yourself most of the time.'

32

'Hang on,' Brendan cut in, slumping down into a chair. 'All that might be true. But I know if my sister's life was in jeopardy I'd drop everything and –'

'Oh yeah?' Kit sneered. 'Well of course you would, *Saint Brendan*. Saint Brendan of the Port Melbourne Housing Estate. Wow! I'm *sooo* impressed.'

He shrugged and made a brush-off gesture with his hands before standing up again. Kit could tell she'd made him angry.

'Get a grip, Quinlan!' he snarled then pushed past and opened the back door. 'I'm out the back working on my bike if anyone rings, okay?'

They were left looking at each other.

'You're lucky to have a sister, Kit,' Tam was almost whispering, her big brown eyes glistening with tears. 'I don't understand why you wouldn't want to be with her if her life's in danger.'

'Right on!' Lou sniffed with feeling, lighting a fresh cigarette. 'I wish I had a sister.'

'Ah, shit.' Kit shook her head and slammed the door on them. 'What's the point even trying to explain?'

Once in her room, Kit sat against the door and burst into tears, vowing to jump up and strangle anyone who came near her. Especially that great idiot Brendan. How dare he say that! *If my sister's life . . . I'd drop everything . . . blah, blah.*

None of them came to the door for more than an hour. By that time, Kit was wishing someone would.

Kit found herself wondering darkly who the hell these best friends of hers were anyway. She was worlds apart from Tam and Lou. Neither of them understood her or where she'd come from. Face it, she told herself, they were a couple of weirdos she'd picked up in first year when she didn't know anyone. *Tam and Lou.* God, even their names were ridiculous. One dressed like an exotic Middle-Eastern prostitute and the other looked like a half-starved gypsy. What had she been doing with them for nearly three years? It was time she changed her friends as well as her course of study.

Basically, she'd never really forgiven Leonie for what happened when Kit was thirteen years old. It was terrible to admit that she'd held a grudge over all those years but that was the truth. Leonie was the eldest child and Kit was the youngest, with four brothers in between. Leonie had spent all Kit's early childhood living overseas but then had come home when Kit was thirteen. Of course they'd spoken by phone and Leonie wrote and sent photos, but Kit had no memories of her before this time. So when this glamorous older sister turned up out of the blue, Kit was deeply impressed. Leonie seemed so clever and hip, she laughed loudly and told jokes and talked casually of being in places that Kit knew only from her school atlas. It was great just having her around.

Their parents were obviously thrilled, too. And so were the brothers. Everyone in the family treated Leonie like a queen.

Before Leonie came back, Kit had been a quiet, dreamy girl who sunk into the background at home amid all the raucous noise of the boys. How extraordinary for her then, when almost from the first day home Leonie took her under her wing, showing great interest in everything about her life: schoolwork, clothes, opinions.

Her parents were probably a bit worn out by the time Kit came along. Johnny, their youngest boy, was ten when Kit was born. Kit often wondered if her mother thought she'd finished having children after Johnny's birth. After all, she'd had five already. But her mother always told her that she was a 'lovely little surprise'. Even so, Kit would sometimes catch her father with a slightly bemused expression on his face when he looked at her, as though he was trying to remember exactly who she was. He was a big intense man with a short fuse, and not usually contemplative. Kit felt that she had been a surprise for him, and not an entirely welcome one.

It wasn't that her parents were ever mean or neglectful. They loved Kit and were good to her in their own way and she loved them back. But because she was interested in poetry and ideas and books she'd often felt lonely amidst all the football boots and farm work. Her parents certainly didn't have the time, money or inclination to indulge her interests.

But when Leonie arrived home, everything changed. Suddenly Kit became the centre of the family's attention because Leonie decided that she was important.

Leonie made Kit feel it was special to be female, that everything she was interested in and enjoyed was really important. Leonie had a job in the city, so she'd invite Kit down on weekends and take her places: to art galleries, poetry readings, films and plays. Even rock concerts sometimes. Kit was included in almost every aspect of Leonie's interesting life. Kit became the envy of every girl in her class at school. Within a couple of months it was not just that Kit had this fantastic older sister but a best friend as well, who encouraged her to think life was full of all kinds of possibilities. Kit felt that Leonie was opening the world to her. She told her stories of her travels, the jobs she'd had and the people she'd met. She also told Kit constantly that she was beautiful and intelligent and talented.

It wasn't like she'd supplanted their mother – Kit still loved her mum – but it was as if she suddenly had a younger, sparkier, more enthusiastic version all for herself . . .

And then it was over. Just like that. Leonie stayed for around ten months and then she left. There were no explanations, no apologies, no talk about why she had to go back overseas again. Kit's parents were stunned, as were her brothers. *Why?* They wanted to know. But Leonie just kissed everyone goodbye and told Kit she'd see her in a few years.

In a few years? Kit was heartbroken. And when she got over the heartbreak she became angry. And when she got over that she was aware that a piece of steel lay at the bottom of her heart. *No one will ever do that to me again.*

Kit went through the rest of her teenage years without her sister. When Leonie eventually came back again, Kit was nineteen, and deliberately avoided her. Leonie wasn't the same, anyway, and Kit didn't care to find out why. Something had happened in those years away to sap Leonie's special brightness. She was just an ordinary woman now, in her early forties. She'd joined the ranks of the other single females in the family – her father's two sisters were nuns and her mother's three sisters were all unmarried in their fifties. Kit didn't envy Leonie any more. In fact, it stunned her a little to see how dowdy Leonie had become.

Whenever Kit went back home, Leonie tried to catch her alone, wanting personal information about her life. *Who are you going out with? Who do you live with? What will you do when you finish university?* Kit preferred her parents' bland casual interest that was based on trust. As long as she was healthy and going okay at uni, they didn't pry. Nor did they insist that they meet her friends, or that she come home for holidays or meet them for lunch dates in the city. They let her be in a way her cloying inquisitive sister did not. After all, what right did she have, after crashing Kit's thirteen-year-old life to bits, to now try to ingratiate her way back in?

Kit had three more calls from the family that afternoon. One more from Frank, brief and to the point. *'Really think you'll be sorry, love.'* Then a terse one from her mother's sister, Moya. *'Perhaps you don't understand how upset your poor mother is, dear?'* Moya was one of the three unmarried sisters who shared a pretty little house overlooking the main street of Bayton. The other two, Eileen and Det, were favourites of Kit's but she'd always felt wary of Moya. The third phone call was from her mother to say that Leonie was now 'under the knife' and she wanted to make sure that Kit had Johnny's number.

Kit managed to remain firm. Just. She would go home the next day, after the final performance, she told them all calmly. At the end of the phone calls she felt a kind of nascent pride in herself. *This is me*, she kept thinking. *I'm an adult. They can't boss me around. I will do what I think is best.* She had a distinctly weird feeling that, like Leonie, she too was fighting for her life.

CHAPTER THREE

Kit was in her room putting on make-up when the doorbell rang. She looked at her watch and smiled. Just on five o'clock. She loved it when people made an effort to be punctual. She blotted her lipstick on a tissue, took one last peek in the mirror, then stood side-on, pulled her already flat stomach in, and grinned. Sebastian arriving on time would mean they'd be able to have a drink together before the performance. She was wearing tight black pants, high-heeled boots, and a frilly pale-green silk shirt tucked into the waist. Her hair was pulled back into a loose bun. The finishing touch was a black and gold leather belt slung around her hips. Not bad, she told herself. Not bad at all! She looked all right. Damn it, she looked terrific! Her eyes shone back at her as deep and luminous as two blue lilies floating in fading light. All over, her pale skin tingled with excitement. Of course the outfit and make-up would all have to come off for the performance but so what? It would go back on afterwards. And she wanted to make an impression when she opened the door to him.

'Wouldn't be dead for quids,' she whispered to herself, then laughed because it was something her grandfather used to say, often for no other reason than the sun was shining or one of his grandchildren had given him a warm hug. Kit knew exactly what he meant; it was so good, so *bloody* good just being alive. She shivered slightly, thinking of Leonie lying in the hospital bed. Was she still on the operating table? Dying, maybe. Well damn it! It wasn't as though Kit going out for the night was going to change the outcome one way or another.

In the shower she'd had a few misgivings. Did deciding not to go straight home make her a cold, cruel bitch? That was obviously what Tam and Lou thought. Too bad. They'd get over it. And where had Brendan got to? After the hour-long sulk in her bedroom she'd gone looking for him to ask if she could borrow his car the next day, but he wasn't in his room, or out the back.

But getting out of the shower, putting on fresh undies, moisturiser and perfume, Kit felt terrific. She would be twenty-one soon. Maybe she'd have a passionate love affair going by then? A real flesh-and-blood man in her life. Sebastian and Kit an item? She giggled. Now that would be something worth waiting for.

Life got so lonely sometimes. It was the little things about couples that tugged at the heartstrings when you were the one alone. The way their faces lit up when they saw each other in a crowded room. The way they waited for each other after lectures, even if they'd been sitting with other friends. The way they'd glide up and touch each other, and ask details of what the other one had been doing in those hours they'd been apart. The quiet discussions they'd have about what was happening on the weekend. The easy casual assumption that whatever they'd be doing it would happen together. Kit had made good friends, she got on with people but she'd never had someone care about her in that way.

The bell rang again. Kit threw open her bedroom door and bounced along the hallway, her bag already thrown over her shoulder. She took hold of the handle and pulled, deciding not to tell Sebastian about Leonie. Tonight was going to be about other things.

'Hello, Kathleen.'

It was Johnny, her brother.

The disappointment must have shown on her face because Johnny smiled apologetically. 'Sorry to come unannounced. Were you expecting someone else?'

'Yeah,' Kit sighed and motioned him in. He walked past her into the hallway. He wasn't as tall as her other brothers but, as far as Kit was concerned, he was heaps better looking. Johnny was slim and gangly rather than stocky like the others. But he had their colouring; the fair skin, reddy brown hair and hazel eyes that Kit had missed out on.

Johnny was dressed as usual in jeans, a green shirt and sandals. His hair had been recently cut very short, emphasising the skin problems he'd suffered from the time he'd turned fifteen. The marks were still there. Johnny had told her once what a blight that terrible skin had been when he'd been growing up. How it had stopped him going out, how it had made him shy and often depressed, unwilling to believe that any girl would even want to look at him. Even when there were no pimples, the skin on his face and neck was heavily pitted. She cursed whatever it was that had made things so, because her brother was incredibly handsome under that terrible skin. Like Mel Gibson, she often thought fiercely, although that might have been getting a bit carried away. He did have the most beautiful eyes. Eyes that became bright with laughter at the smallest thing. But he wasn't laughing now; he looked deadly serious.

'Can we talk somewhere in private?' he asked.

'Yeah,' she sighed. 'My room, I guess.'

One day! she thought angrily. *That's all I'm after. One day. One evening.* Then she'd be up there doing her duty, sitting at her sister's bedside with the rest of them. She could picture them all in that horrible little hospital waiting-room. Mumbling and crying.

40

Praying. All those bloody aunts would have the rosary beads out for sure. When in doubt say a decade of the rosary. Yeah, right! None of them knew anything. They had no idea what city life was like. They didn't know how hard it was just keeping afloat. Sometimes she felt like one of those little buoys bobbing along on top of the water, people around her going down: freaking out and dropping out, failing courses and taking drugs, getting pregnant, getting depressed and . . . Her family knew Johnny would be the hardest one to say no to and so they'd sent him. Damn them! But she'd come this far so she'd travel a bit further if necessary. Something important was taking place in her own life and for once she wasn't going to ignore it. Too bad if they thought she was a heartless bitch.

'Johnny,' she began, 'I've told them I can't come until tomorrow. I mean it.'

'Okay,' he said, shifting slightly. She could tell that he was uncomfortable in this role they'd given him of coming to fetch her. About to offer him a quick coffee, she was surprised when he suddenly took her arm firmly.

'Which one is your room?' he asked.

Kit took a hard look at her brother. He was behaving strangely.

'Johnny, please understand,' she began again, feeling close to tears, 'my being there tonight is not going to make any difference. There is something important going on here with someone I really like. Look, I just can't leave tonight, okay?'

Then she had a sudden flash that he was here on another mission altogether. A chill went down her legs.

'She hasn't died, has she?' Kit whispered.

To her relief, Johnny shook his head. 'No. She's still in the operation. Been over four hours already.'

'So you're going up there now?'

He nodded, still holding her elbow. She edged over to her bedroom door and kicked it open.

41

'Come in here. I'm afraid I don't have much time. I'm expecting someone any minute.'

'Okay.'

Right then, the front door opened and Brendan burst in with his fifteen-year-old brother Rory who often stayed over on weekends. Brendan nodded politely to them both and, putting one hand on the back of his brother's neck, proceeded to push past.

Rory was difficult. A real wild boy. He had a shifty, impatient, pissed-off air about him. But right now Kit loved him. Maybe they could all stand around having a breezy conversation until Sebastian showed up. Then she could make her apologies and do a flit.

'Brendan, have you met my brother Johnny?' she began. 'And this is Rory.'

'G'day, Rory.' Johnny was always a natural with kids. 'How's it going?'

'Not bad, thanks.' The kid looked up from under a frowning brow.

'Good to meet you, Brendan,' Johnny smiled. 'I'm sorry, but I have to speak to Kit before I take off to the country.'

'Oh, sure,' Brendan was moving away too, his hand still on his brother's neck. 'Any news on your sister?' he called back at them.

'Not yet,' Johnny said, almost pushing Kit into the bedroom. 'We're still waiting.'

Once inside the room, he shut the door behind them.

Kit went to the window and slammed it shut. She would have to hear him out. He was her brother after all, and he'd come especially to convince her.

'Kathleen,' Johnny began, leaning one thin hand on the marble mantelpiece and looking down as though into a fire.

'I have something important to tell you.'

Kit's heart did a dive. He was going to beg her and it was going to be terrible having to refuse. Even so, one ear was listening for the front doorbell. She looked at her watch. Ten past five. If only Sebastian would come, she'd be able to get away. From her brother, Brendan and Tam, from this house and –

'This is something that you should have been told already,' Johnny went on, 'but no one wanted to be the one. Well, anyway, here I am.' He hesitated. He turned around to face her with an apologetic half smile. 'Do you have any idea what I'm talking about?'

Kit shook her head, puzzled.

'Any inkling of what I'm going to tell you?'

She shook her head again.

He opened his mouth, about to speak, and then shut it. He walked over to her, took her hand and led her to the bed in the middle of the room.

'Come over here,' he said. 'Sit down.'

'Johnny, what is it?' Kit laughed, genuinely mystified. 'Is this about Leonie?'

'Yes,' he said abruptly. 'It is.' He was really agitated, rubbing her hand between his two cold thin ones.

'Spill the beans,' she said. 'Tell me, whatever it is.'

'Well, it's like this,' Johnny said, still massaging her hands. 'I don't know how else to say it. Leonie is not your sister. She's . . . your mother.'

Leonie is not your sister. She's your mother.

Right. Try that one again.

Leonie is not your sister. She's . . . your mother?

Everything in the room seemed to rush about and then just as suddenly it all became absolutely still.

'What do you mean?' Kit asked, feeling so strange – not cold exactly but as though she might be getting slowly smaller. She took him by the wrist and held on hard to keep herself there. There was a sort of prickliness creeping down her back. Her clothes felt big, as if she was being lost in them. She was slowly shrinking away.

43

'Well, Leonie had you when she was twenty-four,' Johnny said. His voice was grave and his face troubled. 'And she was single. So she gave the baby, she gave *you*, to Mum and Dad.'

'Gave me to . . . Mum and Dad?' Kit repeated wonderingly.

'Yes.' Johnny went on more quickly. 'She couldn't keep you herself and she didn't want to give you away to strangers. So she called Mum and Dad over to where she was living and they took you back with them.'

'They took me back. Back where?'

'Back to Australia.'

'Oh, right,' she breathed softly. 'I mean, where was she living?'

'Overseas.' Johnny sounded so strained and miserable. 'She had you overseas. Oh hell, Kit,' he put his arm around her, 'this must be bloody awful for you. Leonie was going to tell you when you were about thirteen, then didn't. Then she was going to write to you when you were eighteen and she didn't. Somehow it never seemed to be the right time for her. I know Mum and Dad were determined that you know when you turned twenty-one. They said they were going to tell you themselves if Leonie didn't.' He squeezed her shoulders again. 'Now this accident has happened. I'm really sorry that you have to be told now. But everyone thinks it's important that you know.'

'So where?' Kit gulped. Why had her voice become so faint? 'Where was I born?'

'Ireland. Northern Ireland, actually. Belfast.'

'*Belfast.*' Kit shook her head. 'I don't think so, Johnny.' The words rushed out of her mouth like water through a rusty pipe. 'Leonie never talked to me about Ireland or Belfast! It was all about Paris and London and what a great time she had there and all the people that she met and —'

'Well, that's where Mum and Dad went to get you,' Johnny cut her off bluntly. 'From a hospital in Belfast. Leonie had been living in Ireland for some time.'

'But how old was I?'

'Just a week or two, I think,' Johnny sighed. 'Ask them all about it when you see them. But I think as soon as she had you, they went over to get you and bring you home.'

Kit nodded slowly.

'So she gave me away?'

'To Mum and Dad,' he said encouragingly. 'To the best people in the world as far as she was concerned.'

'But they're not *my* mum and dad,' Kit said wonderingly.

'No.'

'So,' Kit looked at him intently, 'you're not my brother.'

'No,' he said quietly, one arm still around her shoulders, his face turned into hers, looking at her with such concern that she almost started crying.

'My uncle.' Every muscle in her face had become locked somehow. 'You're my uncle?'

'That's right.'

'Ah well, Johnny . . .' and at this point tears did suddenly fill her eyes and spill over. 'You are the nicest uncle anyone could ever have. And that's for sure.'

He held her tightly as a few deep sobs racked though her.

'I dunno about that,' he said quietly.

'Nah,' Kit was gasping. 'You are. The best, Johnny. The best uncle ever.'

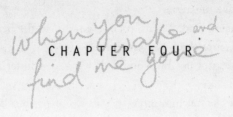

CHAPTER FOUR

It hadn't taken Kit long to get her things together. Within an hour she and Johnny were on the freeway heading home.

Johnny had gone out to the kitchen to tell the others she was going while Kit had packed her things. She'd managed to yell goodbye from the front door but they'd rushed up the hallway and hugged her anyway. They hadn't said much which was just as well because Kit felt she would have had nothing to say back. She'd had the distinct feeling that she was leaving everything behind – her friends and fun; study; Sebastian.

'I'll tell work,' Tam had said. 'Wally will understand.'

'Oh, thanks.'

'And I'll tell everyone else,' Lou had yelled.

Oh shit. Kit had closed her eyes. It was all finished somehow. She knew she shouldn't be thinking like that, that it was a ridiculous thought. But that's how it felt; finished. Absolutely.

Now, Kit sat back and watched the suburbs roll past, unwinding the window every now and then and sticking her head out to cool her face. Her initial weepiness had left her with a headache and hot cheeks. She was glad for the long ride in the car, figuring that it might be exactly what she needed to haul herself back together again.

Johnny, bless him, mostly kept quiet. He drove the ten-year-old Holden fast but well, gripping the steering wheel and leaning forward, frowning. It made Kit smile. Johnny got like that: intense and frustrated at the same time.

It was evening. In between bouts of self-pity and bewilderment, Kit found herself marvelling that after all that had happened, the beautiful day was still out there.

Summer's coming, she thought to herself; summer and swimming at the Richmond baths. Catching the tram with Tam down to St Kilda beach. Summer and bright drinks in long glasses (she loved Bloody Marys with mint) after a shift at the pub where she and Tam worked. Summer and light clothes, and going home for Christmas.

Home.

Her mood simply wouldn't settle for more than half a minute. It was as though she had a mini ocean inside her. Everything was crashing furiously against jagged rocks one moment, impossible to control or contain, and the next it would calm right down into smooth lapping waves. Flat and green and chilly. Under it all was a feeling that she couldn't put her finger on. A raw, anxious, nervy feeling that had her clenching her fists and biting her lip before she became aware she was doing it.

'Do you know where it happened? The accident, I mean?' she asked, suddenly realising she knew nothing. 'Was anyone else hurt?'

Johnny shook his head. 'No. She was on her own, apparently travelling back from the city on the old highway. Don't know why. Funny that she should choose the long route. Anyway, the crash happened just near Muirdale on that bend as you come into the town.'

Kit nodded, although she only had a vague idea of the spot he was talking about. Since the dual freeway had been built she'd forgotten the older, prettier but more treacherous road.

47

'Anyway, she failed to take the bend,' Johnny went on. 'Her car rolled and she ended up upside-down about twenty-five metres off the side of the road. No other car was involved. She must have fallen asleep.'

'What time was this?'

'They think it happened a bit after two this morning.'

'What was she in the city for?'

'An old friend from overseas was in town,' Johnny said. 'They'd arranged to meet up. Mum said that she'd seemed quite excited, although she didn't say much.'

'Strange she didn't stay somewhere,' Kit murmured. 'I mean, if she was going to have a late night.'

'Well, that's what we can't work out,' Jimmy frowned. 'Apparently she had arranged to stay at Bernadette's place.'

'So why didn't she?'

Johnny shrugged. Kit pictured Leonie's oldest friend, Bernadette, with her plump smiling face and easy ways, and felt sad that she'd lost touch with her. The worst thing about falling out with Leonie was losing touch with some of those friends that Kit had enjoyed so much when she'd been thirteen.

'So Bernie was definitely expecting Leonie to turn up?'

'Oh, yeah,' Johnny said, 'she'd left the key out. Made up the spare bed. Was expecting to see her for breakfast in the morning. Instead she gets a phone call to say she's been in this terrible accident.'

They stopped for coffee at the half-way point, and sat like two strangers on the plastic chairs outside the little roadside café, staring around them.

'Nothing has changed, you know,' Johnny said after a while. 'I mean, of course it's different, but in all the important things, nothing has changed.'

Kit hadn't the energy to argue. What was more important than who your mother was? Suddenly, her mother was not her mother any more. Somebody else was. Somebody she didn't even like very much. Her sister was her mother. Her father was now her grandfather. Her brothers were her uncles. As far as she was concerned, *that* amounted to everything changing and there was no point denying it.

My mother is very ill . . . maybe dying.

She said the words to herself, trying to make them sink in but they remained on the surface, like the little flecks of dust and grit that floated on the dam at home.

'Does everyone know about this?' she asked on their way back to the car.

He nodded.

'I mean do the aunts and all the boys?'

'Yeah,' Johnny said uncomfortably. 'They all know.'

'What about neighbours and relations?'

'It was never spoken about much,' he said. 'As far as I know, Mum acted from the start like you were hers and people just accepted it.'

Kit nodded slowly. Everyone knew this secret about her. She was the only one who wasn't in on it.

'There must have been talk, though? I mean you can't just turn up with a baby without being pregnant.'

'You can in the country,' Johnny said mildly. 'Mum apparently never went out much in the last few months of her pregnancies. Then there was the trip overseas and, well, people had to accept it.'

'Would all the kids I went to school with have known about it?'

Johnny shook his head. 'Any gossip would have died away by that stage.' He smiled. 'Can't imagine that kids would be able to keep it quiet if they knew, could you?'

Kit nodded without meeting his eyes. She was already thinking of something else.

Sebastian had come to pick her up earlier, at exactly quarter past five. Tam must have opened the front door and shown him to her room because there were quiet murmurs before two polite knocks. Kit hadn't even heard the bell.

The door pushed open and Sebastian's face appeared around it. Kit, who was sitting on the bed with Johnny's arm around her, looked up in horror. Within the space of about ten minutes she'd forgotten all about him.

'Oh, I'm sorry,' Sebastian said. 'I'll come back. I didn't realise –'

'No!' Kit's voice called him back. 'I can't go tonight,' she explained hoarsely. 'Go without me.'

Sebastian stepped into the room. 'Well, okay,' he said, immediately edgy. 'So I'll see you at the performance then?'

'No,' Kit said, 'I can't go tonight. You'll have to contact Linda.'

'What do you mean?' he said, his voice steely. 'At this late stage? That's not fair on Linda. On anybody, actually.'

Through the fog of incomprehension, Kit could tell that he was pissed-off. She watched his hands curling up into tight fists and she thought about how she'd fantasised about his fingers on her neck, playing softly down her backbone. And then last night it had happened. It had almost happened. But all that was now way back in the distant past. The stuff of another person's life altogether.

'Something has happened,' Kit said, sounding bleak and half-dead to herself. 'I have to go home.'

'Home?' he repeated.

'My sister. I mean,' she corrected herself angrily, 'my *mother* is in hospital. She's been in an accident.'

'I'm sorry,' he said curtly, his eyes flickering over Johnny suspiciously as though he might be the guilty party, the instigator of this disturbing turn of events. 'So, there's absolutely no chance of you performing tonight?'

'No.'

'Well, I'm very sorry about your mother,' he said formally, 'but you'll understand that I have to go and try and organise tonight? The play, I mean.'

'Of course,' she whispered. Without another word, Sebastian turned around very neatly, like a dancer, in one swift twist of his body, and made for the door. It had closed behind him before Kit realised that she could have explained more. She hadn't even introduced Johnny. Sebastian probably thought he was some boyfriend or . . . Oh, God! How could she have let him walk out without at least trying to explain the situation?

By eight that evening, they were at last nearing the town.

'How you doing?' Johnny asked. They'd been quiet for over an hour, him concentrating on driving and Kit curled up at the other end of the front seat, her face half out the open window.

'Okay, thanks.' Kit suddenly turned to her brother. 'So who the bloody hell is my father? I mean, if Leonie is my mother, then what about my real father?'

Johnny shrugged. 'I was wondering that, too, and wondering when you'd ask.' He smiled. 'Sorry, I don't know. I don't know if anyone knows. Except Leonie, of course.'

'Well . . .' Kit smiled back, feeling her spirits rise with Johnny's grin. 'I just hope she lives long enough to tell me.'

There was an uneasy silence as her flippant tone bounced around in the air between them.

'I just hope she *lives*,' Johnny said softly, a gentle rebuke, the grin well and truly gone.

Kit sat back in her seat, shamed by his genuine feeling for his sister. The truth was, she didn't care much about Leonie. When it came down to it, life would be easier if Leonie just fell off the face of the earth. It wasn't all Kit felt, but the thought was definitely there, part of the strange mix of emotions that were churning away inside her. And it made her wonder at herself. What sort of person feels ambivalent about their mother being involved in a terrible car accident? *Shit!* Maybe she'd been hanging around with Tam and Lou for too long. They were such cool cats with their weird clothes, their goofy opinions and their odd collection of lovers. Maybe she, Kit, had lost sight of the normal emotions, of all the things that mattered. Then she remembered both Tam and Lou's response to the news of the accident and was shamed all over again. They had offered normal human sympathy and concern. And she had shut them out.

Kit tried to imagine what she'd say to Leonie if and when she regained consciousness.

'So you're my mother! Well, isn't that something!'

Is that why you turned into such a dreary boring snoop of late? Is that why you think that I owe you some kind of explanation for my life?

She ran her fingers through her hair and swatted at an insect that fluttered about the cabin of the car. Those kinds of imaginary conversations were useless. There was no point to them at all.

The outskirts of the town were sedate and quiet in the fading light. Small neat houses edged either side of the main road that led into the town centre. There was no one much about, just an old couple walking their dog and a few kids on the nature-strip as Johnny's car glided slowly past. Kit wound the window right down and stared out at the pie shop corner where she and Marie Bateson, her best friend at school, got caught by the Phys Ed teacher with cigarettes when they were in year nine. Then at the first set of traffic lights, the intersection where Johnny was knocked off his bike when he was fourteen. Kit had only been four but she remembered the drama of that day and the way Johnny had had to hobble around for weeks with his leg in plaster.

This was Kit's home town and it never failed to give her a twinge of delight. Her pleasure was in the familiar things, all of the landmarks that conjured up memories of her younger self. But the feeling was coupled with an equally deep sense of relief that she'd left it all behind, that now she was shooting her way into a new life.

Johnny turned a hard left off the main road which led out to the family farm.

'Where are we going?' Kit said sharply.

'We might as well go straight to the hospital,' he replied. 'Every-one will be there.'

Kit's heart sank. She wished they could go out to the farm and just be by themselves for a while before the rest of the family got back. It would be too much at the hospital. Too many family members. Too much angst. How would they all treat her now? *Now that they knew that she knew?* She wished that this terrible fluttering in her stomach would subside. They'd all want her to cry and get soppy about Leonie, *her* mother, lying there in hospital.

Would she have to stand staring at Leonie and fake undying love? *Shit!*

'Only a few minutes now, kiddo,' Johnny said, picking up speed.

The Bayton base hospital was a four-storey cream brick monstrosity built in the mid-sixties, with four wings branching out from a central point. It was one of the biggest hospitals in rural Victoria, servicing a broad group of surrounding towns and districts. There were a few dozen cars in the visitors' car-park when they pulled in, so Kit figured that it must be visiting hours. Johnny seemed to know what to do. Kit got out, slammed her door shut and followed him over to the main entrance without a word.

'They'll put her in intensive care after the operation,' Johnny mumbled as he studied the map in the main foyer, 'so that's on the fourth floor.' They headed to the lifts.

'Maybe we shouldn't go up right now,' Kit said, panic rearing up in her belly. 'I mean, there'll be too many people already. It isn't likely that they'd let lots of people into a ward where someone's really sick. I mean if she's just come out of an operation . . .'

'Mum told me there's a little waiting room right next to the intensive-care ward,' Johnny replied calmly. 'That's where everyone will be.'

'Oh,' Kit gulped. The lift doors glided shut and she closed her eyes briefly after catching sight of her reflection. Who was that young woman in the green silk shirt, with flushed cheeks and huge blue eyes, staring back at her. Beautiful? Almost. But anxious, too. Anxious and . . . lost. The girl in the reflection looked like she'd arrived somewhere after a long trip and the people who were to meet her hadn't turned up. What was she going to do?

Kit took a quick glimpse at her family through the glass window of the door before Johnny pushed it open.

Brothers, mother, father and aunts. They were all sitting on chairs around the wall, eyes glazed over or shut, each seemingly alone with their thoughts. Perhaps they were praying . . . She took a deep breath and followed Johnny.

'G'day everyone,' Johnny said. 'Any news?'

'Oh!' A relieved smile flooded Therese's exhausted face. 'Johnny and Kathleen! Oh, thanks be to God! You got here safely.' She stood up to welcome them.

'Hi, Mum,' Kit fell into her mother's warm hug. 'Any news yet?'

'Nothing yet. We're waiting for the doctor to come.'

There were lines around Therese's mouth that Kit had never noticed before, and shadows under her eyes. Old woman's lines. But lines didn't just appear overnight, did they?

'Good to see you.' Her father's hug was brief. 'She's been out of the operation for about an hour now,' he said stiffly. 'The surgeon will be along soon to speak to us.'

'Good, er, so you don't know if it was a success or . . .'

'We don't know anything yet.'

'Have you seen her?'

'Mum and I sat with her for a while. She's unconscious, of course. All bandaged up and, well, you'll go in, won't you?'

'Yes.' Kit had a sudden flash that this was how it had always been with her father. He'd always been preoccupied when he was with her. Was it about her not being his child?

My mother and father, she reminded herself quickly, *who are really my grandparents.* Kit looked over to the three brothers who were standing awkwardly, blinking as though waking from sleep, ready to greet her too. *My uncles.* And an aunt over in one corner, one of her mother's sisters, *now my great aunt.* The few nephews and nieces, who were looking up from where they'd been squatting on the floor playing cards, were now *cousins.* She smiled and waved at them, wondering if her own face showed any confusion.

'G'day, Frank.'

'Good to see you.' The eldest brother was dressed in short-sleeved checked shirt, his big farmer's forearms displayed beneath. He put one hand on Kit's shoulder before bending low to peck her cheek. 'Knew you'd do the right thing in the end,' he muttered.

Kit stilled herself against the familiar intrusive, authoritative tone. He'd always been maddeningly sure of himself. Confident about telling everyone what they should do. *Especially* his baby sister. *Shit!* Kit thought angrily, *I'm so glad I don't live here.* She turned to Frank's overweight wife Julie.

'Good to see you, Kathleen,' her sister-in-law said soberly. 'Sorry about the circumstances.'

'I know. It's terrible, isn't it?'

Had Frank and Julie always looked like this? So heavy and florid-faced? Since going to study in the city, Kit had missed a lot. Her mother told her things, wrote letters, tried to keep her up with

55

everyone's lives. But she hadn't been that interested. Now she was here, in the midst of them all, things felt slightly out of kilter. She *did* know that Frank and Julie were having a hard time keeping their farm afloat financially. She knew that in spite of the extra fencing work he took on, with five children they were struggling. Her mother had been deeply worried when she'd told Kit of the latest abysmal grain prices Frank got a month ago. 'How are they going to survive, Kathleen? With all those children, tell me, how will they survive?' Kit, on her way out to the first dress-rehearsal for the play, made the right noises but really the dire predictions weren't getting to her at all. Farmers were always complaining about something: the weather, grain and stock prices, the government. They survived, didn't they? Frank was his parent's stalwart, the eldest son and apple of their eyes. Plain and unhurried in his views, he was utterly trustworthy, utterly dependable and, to Kit anyway, utterly boring.

'So did it take you long? The trip up?' Julie asked politely.

'Not really,' Kit shrugged, 'just the usual trip, you know.' She hated tedious conversations about how long the trip from the city took. Discussions about road journeys and in-depth ruminations on the weather were what these people revelled in. She floundered around in her head for something quick to say that would steer Julie off course.

'So how long have you been here?'

'Oh, we've all been here since this morning, right through the afternoon.' Julie looked around timidly for confirmation. 'Just waiting for news.' Everyone nodded sadly. Kit wondered if they were trying to make her feel guilty, because it was working. Now she was here she could hardly imagine her own response that morning.

'Mum and Dad got the word about eight,' Julie added in a reverential whisper, 'so as soon as we heard we came straight over.'

Kit always found Julie too needy to take seriously. Too willing to talk on endlessly about anything at all just so there wouldn't be two seconds silence. She was oddly moved now to find her sister-in-law quiet and subdued; her big soft face, which still contained a little of her youthful prettiness, looked so utterly wretched with worry.

'The operation went for over seven hours,' Julie added. 'We thought it would never end.'

'Really,' Kit muttered. 'Seven hours!'

Pete was big like Frank but not as commanding or sure in his manner. His small neat wife, Trish, smiled awkwardly at Kit before pecking her cheek, giving nothing away as usual. While Julie, so warm and bubbly, so utterly transparent, made everyone feel easy, Trish was watchful and cool. It made people suspicious. Trish and Pete had one child, a quiet semi-autistic boy named Kevin who took up a lot of Trish's time.

'So where is Kevin?' Kit looked over at the kids who were playing cards in the corner.

'He's being looked after,' Trish said quickly. 'A neighbour. He wouldn't be able to cope with any of this.'

'Of course not.' At least Trish never dumped her strange little kid on other people. Not like Frank and Julie. Wherever they went their noisy brood of five went with them. They were good-natured kids but when boredom or tiredness hit they'd erupt en masse like active volcanoes. Frank and Julie smacked and yelled and threatened but rarely did anything sensible like take them home or insist they go to bed or stay outside to let off steam.

'So did they expect the operation to take so long?'

'No,' Frank answered. 'We were told about three hours.'

'Does that mean they found something unusual?'

'We don't know yet.'

Kit's third brother, Damien, looked so citified next to Frank and Pete that it made her smile as she put her face next to his for a quick kiss.

'Hello, Dame!' The smell of him! Some kind of strong fancy after-shave that was more like perfume filled her nostrils. He was much slimmer than his older brothers; and dressed in designer jeans and white T-shirt under a well-cut linen jacket, he looked a different species altogether. His face was tanned from a recent holiday in Noosa and his shiny black slip-on shoes, casual in the city context, looked fancy enough for ballroom dancing. Damien looked like a successful eastern suburbs shrink, which was exactly what he was.

'So you okay, Kathleen?' he asked, taking her arm in that overly caring way that she hated.

Kit knew he was referring to the news about herself. She decided not to be led onto that subject. Not right now, in front of everyone.

'I'm okay.'

Damien was probably put out that he hadn't been asked to tell the news. He would *love* showing off his counselling skills to the rest of the family.

'Lucy not here?' she asked coolly.

'No, she's got something big happening at work,' Damien replied intimately with a sly little we'll-talk-about-this-later smile. 'But she'll be up just as soon as she can. With the kids, of course.'

'Right.'

Tell them to stay right where they are, Kit was tempted to shout, knowing that everyone else in the room would be silently scream-ing the same thing. Damien's wife Lucy was a pain: finicky, bossy, and mean, despite being a highly successful professional. She was in charge of some mental health department in a big hospital and never tired of letting everyone know just how important her job was and how brilliantly she did it. If you didn't know she held down an important job, you'd be tempted to describe her as a very *thick* woman with no saving graces apart from her ability to occasionally shut up – something no one else in the family was very good at.

58

She wasn't even particularly good-looking. She was one of those thin-hipped, blond-tipped, perfectly dressed, frozen-faced, thirty-something professionals you see everywhere. Kit often wondered how Damien, who, apart from his boring need to impress, was really a warm-hearted fellow, had ended up with her. It was a source of wonderment for the whole family, actually.

The children – Oliver, a boy of eleven, and Zoe, a girl of eight – were out of control. Both parents were psychiatrists and the kids couldn't be taken anywhere without destroying any room they were in within the first ten minutes.

'Well, it will be good to see them all,' Kit said, completely unconvincingly. 'How are they going anyway?' she added to make up for her half-hearted tone.

'You mean at school?' Damian asked.

'Yeah.' Kit shrugged. *School would do.*

'Well they're both doing very well academically. But, you know, neither of them have had very good teachers this year and –'

That's right, blame the teachers! Kit wanted to scream.

'They're not actually getting on too well with their peers at the moment, but I guess that will pass,' her brother went on gamely as though trying to convince himself. 'That kind of thing usually sorts itself out.'

'Oh yeah,' Kit mumbled.

If Lucy even smiled it was reported back along the family grapevine as a major happening. Nobody liked her, not even Therese who tried very hard to like everybody. Kit was the only one in the family who knew that her mother had secretly said a novena to Our Lady of Fatima in the hope that things might improve between her son's wife and herself. Nothing had improved, so Kit guessed that the Blessed Virgin had had more serious things on her plate.

'Kathleen, dear!'

Therese's elder sister Moya waited until Johnny and Kit had greeted the others before she got up. Moya was an immaculately turned-out lady in her late fifties, dressed in a pink linen skirt, freshly ironed printed silk blouse, stockings and heels. Her hair, a subtly dyed strawberry blond colour, was done up in a sleek french roll with not one stray hair in sight. This was a marked contrast to her younger sister, Therese. Kit hated the way her mother never took care of herself; the way she let her hair grow out at least an inch before it occurred to her to get the colour re-done. She never got it cut properly either. And those shapeless, bright, cheap no-nonsense smocks she wore were terrible. Her mother was actually a nice-looking woman. When she tried, she looked just as nice as her three older sisters in spite of having had six kids to their none. *Five kids, actually*, Kit reminded herself. *Five kids and me.*

'So, Aunty Moya,' Kit said, trying without much success to take the false expression from her own voice, 'how are you?' Moya always made her feel young, foolish and very badly dressed. 'And where's Aunty Eileen and Det?'

'They're in sitting with Leonie now,' Moya whispered, taking Kit by both shoulders and pushing her soft powdery cheek up against Kit's, holding it there meaningfully for way too long. 'Only two allowed in at a time.'

Kit nodded and groaned inside. Her aunt had always fancied herself centre stage, and this accident was a chance for her to shine.

'What terrible circumstances these are!' Moya went on in her low throaty actress voice, edging Kit away from everyone else as though she'd been waiting all her life for this private conversation. She stared meaningfully into Kit's eyes. 'We're all sick with worry about you too, dear. All you've been through. When you go in to see poor Leonie, you'll be so *very* glad you came today.'

Thanks Moya! Thanks so much for reminding me of my bad attitude and for telling me how I'll feel in the future.

Like Damien, Moya was dying to get her teeth into the whole business of Kit's strange beginnings. But Kit smiled back blankly. She wasn't going to give any of them the satisfaction just yet.

'I'm okay, Moya. It's Leonie we have to worry about.'

'Oh *I know*!' Moya breathed. 'You're *so* right, dear.'

There was a tap at the door. A pretty young nurse entered followed by a short portly man in a dark suit.

'Mr and Mrs Quinlan?' The nurse's stern voice seemed incongruous with her girlish looks. Kit's parents nodded nervously and took a step forward. They looked vulnerable, like children who'd been caught doing something wrong. 'This is Mr Peter Elliot, the surgeon who operated on your daughter.'

'Oh.' Kit's mother's face drained of colour. She tottered towards the man as though about to embrace him. Kit's father reached out and held her back. 'Oh, doctor!' Therese breathed again. 'How is she?'

The doctor nodded and shook their hands formally without replying. Kit tried to still the fluttering in her own stomach.

'So you are all Miss Quinlan's family?' the doctor asked sternly, glaring suspiciously around as though there might be an interloper in the room. *What does it matter to you?* Kit glowered back, noting that the rest were all nodding their heads like good little children.

Johnny was suddenly beside her, clutching her elbow tightly. 'Cool it,' he said softly. 'It'll be okay.'

'It is important for only close family members to hear the news first,' the doctor said, his voice dropping in volume, making him seem less stern. 'These things are always a terrible shock for everyone. It's only right that close family should be the first to hear.'

Kit nodded when his big, rather beautiful brown eyes rested on her for a moment. She noted a sudden change in herself. She too was keen and eager to please him. There was this stupid feeling that her good behavior might improve Leonie's outcome.

'Your daughter has sustained a very serious injury to the brain, Mr and Mrs Quinlan,' he said, looking only at Kit's mother and father and speaking very slowly. 'And at this stage we don't know if she will survive it.'

There was a small gasp from Julie, then a couple of sobs. Aunty Moya moved over to Julie's side to comfort her. Someone grunted something that sounded like a prayer. The surgeon waited, like a teacher, for everyone's full attention.

'Once we opened the wound,' he continued, 'we saw that her condition was more serious than we'd originally thought. Not only has the skull been fractured and compressed in two places, but the casing that surrounds the brain has been punctured.' He held his two small fat hands together in the shape of a brain. 'She has lost a lot of blood. Twice during the operation we thought we'd lost her . . . however . . .' He stopped for breath, obviously trying to think of the best way to put the next bit of information, 'towards the end of the operation we had a couple of quite hopeful signs.'

'Yes?' Therese whispered.

'Very hopeful signs,' the doctor went on. 'To put it simply, once we took a number of bone fragments from the brain tissue there was definite movement in the right leg and arm, and this means,' he looked around slowly as though checking that he still had everyone's undivided attention, '*if* she survives the next crucial few days, then there is a good chance she will be able to learn to walk again, and possibly have partial movement of the right hand. But injuries to the brain such as those sustained by your daughter often end up with the patient not being able to walk, talk or use their hands. They survive, but in a severely handicapped state.'

'A quadriplegic,' Aunty Moya mumbled.

'That's right,' the doctor said, 'or a paraplegic – someone with minimal movement. But should she survive the shock of the next forty-eight hours, then there is a good chance of a partial recovery . . .'

He stopped and then continued even more slowly, emphasising every word. 'There will be a long rehabilitation. Years. There will be memory loss. Whole sections of her life will be missing for some time. Perhaps forever. There has been extensive damage to the brain.' He hesitated again, about to go on, but then stopped himself. 'Any questions at this stage?'

No one said anything. Kit felt nauseous. She'd been thinking that Leonie was either going to live or die. Secretly, she'd assumed that Leonie would recover. She hadn't considered any other possibility. *A quadriplegic!* And her memory? *What if she's forgotten who I am? Who my father is? What if she doesn't survive these next two days and I'm left forever in the dark about it all?*

'Now, I know this has been a terrible shock,' the doctor gave a small encouraging smile, 'but please hang on to the fact that we have real hope for your daughter's survival. Believe me, I often have to give worse reports to families.'

The man gave a deep weary sigh and rubbed his eye with one of his plump fists. 'I'm sorry, it's been a long day. Let me repeat, if your daughter survives the next forty-eight hours then she has a good chance of partial recovery.'

'Oh, thank you, doctor!' Therese was the first to exclaim. 'Thank you for all you've done.'

When the doctor left, they all found their tongues. Therese was highly agitated, alternatively weeping and laughing and throwing her hands in the air as she went over all the possibilities with Moya. Kit couldn't quite pick up on what they were saying, but it was something about the miracle of prayer. Frank and his father couldn't keep still. They walked up and down the room, throwing loud comments out to each other.

'Sounds hopeful,' said Damien.

'She's got to get through the next two days,' Frank said sceptically.

'Quiet, everybody.' Gerard's voice boomed out across the top of everyone. 'We've heard the news. Only one thing now. We must *pray* for Leonie to survive these next forty-eight hours.'

'That's right,' Therese agreed, wiping her eyes.

'Anyone got rosary beads?' Gerard demanded.

Kit took a quick desperate look at Johnny. Kneeling down in this small horrible room with all these relatives was not high on her list of priorities but everyone, especially poor Therese, looked so stressed out, she couldn't object.

There was silence while Moya rummaged through her handbag, eventually holding up a large set of mother-of-pearl beads.

'Lovely, Moya,' Therese murmured.

'From my 1972 visit to the Holy Land,' Moya whispered.

'All right,' Gerard went on firmly, in the same tone he would use if he were organising a cattle sale, 'will you lead, Moya?'

'Yes, of course.' Moya was pleased to be asked, then she looked over at Johnny coyly. 'Or perhaps Johnny should?'

'No, no, Aunty Moya,' Johnny said quickly. 'You, please.'

She immediately knelt down where she was. 'In the name of the Father,' she began, 'the first joyful mystery —'

Just then, a nurse pushed the door open, 'Just wanted to let you all know there's a coffee machine down the hall and —' her voice died away when she saw that half the family were kneeling. She smiled nervously and went out again.

Johnny decided to use the interruption to his advantage.

'Hang on, everyone,' he said, grabbing Kit by the arm. 'Kathleen and I are going in to see Leonie.'

There was a disapproving silence as the rest of the family watched him leading Kit to the door.

'Excuse us,' Johnny pushed Kit out and then turned around before exiting himself. 'Kathleen needs to go and see her *mother*,' he said meaningfully.

'Thanks!' Kit groaned, once they were away from the door. She leant up against the corridor and, collapsing into nervous laughter, let herself slide down into a squatting position. 'Johnny, I could bottle you.'

He grinned and squatted down next to her.

'I don't think I could have lasted through the rosary.'

'Me neither,' Johnny said, 'but listen, I actually do think you should go and see her.'

Kit covered her face with both hands. 'Okay,' she mumbled, 'if you say so.'

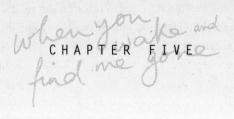

CHAPTER FIVE

As soon as the door slid shut behind her, Kit was in another world. Outside the confines of this room were all the normal things: family, relationships, ambitions and secret dreads, favourite foods and fantasies and . . . none of them mattered here. She had entered the mute desperate world of slow time. Time that was marked out in seconds and the soft clicking sounds of machines. The world of hard shiny surfaces, pulled blinds, blipping screens, bodies. The world of life and death.

And the world of waiting.

She took a few steps in and stopped, overwhelmed. Life as it was lived in this room was just a slender thread. A single silver wavering thread that might break any second.

Johnny waited for her to move first. There were four beds in the ward but only two were occupied. In the one to her right was a man – the short thick bush of silver grey hair above the gaunt closed face made Kit feel queasy. Above him on a counter were two small television screens, green pulsating lines racing along them like gunshot.

Sitting beside the bed was a middle-aged woman dressed almost totally in black. Both hands were clasped around a bar of the chrome side-railing on the bed, and she was staring into the face of the unconscious man, as though willing him to open his eyes.

The other two beds seemed spooky in their flat white stillness. Someone has died, Kit thought. Here, right in this room. They've been in these beds and now they've been carted away.

On the left, up near the window, was Leonie. She lay on her back. Her head, bound in a thick white bandage, was elevated a little by a pillow. Her face and neck, above the cotton hospital gown, were exposed. A thin tube ran into her left nostril. It was taped to the side of her face with two thin plasters. Both arms were tied down loosely at her sides, with separate drips running into veins inside each of her elbows. A nurse was replacing a plastic bag at the side of the bed. She smiled as they approached.

'Well,' she said, 'it's a big family.'

'Yes.'

'Very quiet now,' the nurse commanded softly, 'she's in a critical state.'

Kit and Johnny stood silently as though in church, and looked at Leonie. Calm, breathtakingly calm. Apart from the tubes and drips, she might have been lightly asleep. She looked clean – not a drop of blood on her – and peaceful, quite beautiful really. Any lines had been smoothed away. There was no tension at all around her eyes or mouth. She was forty-five but looked almost like a child.

'So how is she?' Johnny asked the nurse.

'Stable,' the nurse replied. 'But early days yet. You've spoken to the doctor?'

'Yes,' Johnny whispered anxiously, as though he didn't want the nurse to leave. 'How often do you check her?'

'Every quarter hour,' the nurse said matter-of-factly. 'It's just a waiting game now. Everything is being done that can be.' She looked over at Kit briefly, her face softening with a smile. 'Don't be afraid. Take her hand. Talk to her. They can sometimes hear, you know. Especially when they start coming out of it.'

Kit nodded dumbly, frozen where she stood and unable to respond further. The nurse left the room, her soft rubber soles hardly making a sound.

Kit turned away. It was terrible, utterly terrible and she didn't understand it at all but instead of being filled with sympathy, all she could feel was a terrible rage. She felt as though it was going to explode if she stood there gawking at the prone body a moment longer. She walked to the window and looked out, trying to calm down. It was frightening. She wanted to walk over to that bed and slap Leonie's calm face, take her by the shoulders and shake her. Pull out all the needles and drips, unwind the bandage from her damaged head and let her lie there and take her chances.

After all, you let me take my chances didn't you? You coward.

Not enough guts for an abortion, nor the guts to look after a baby herself. And not enough courage to give up her baby for adoption, either. She didn't want her baby but she made sure she never had to experience the sorrow of giving her away to strangers. After dumping Kit on her parents she could go straight back to her old life, knowing she could see her child whenever she felt like it. Not very often, as it turned out. She could have it both ways, couldn't she? All ways, in fact. She could see her child grow up without the responsibility of ever being her mother.

Then, as the years went by and her baby bonded with the rest of her family, she still couldn't find the guts to tell the truth.

You deserve to die!

Kit's breathing had gone shallow. She was trembling. *Get out!* she wanted to scream. *Everyone get out. Leave me alone with this bitch. I'll show her.* She jerked with shock when she felt her brother's hand on her shoulder.

'Come on, Kathleen,' he said quietly. 'Let's go home.'

The atmosphere on the drive out to the family farm was subdued. Kit had no idea if Johnny had sensed her mood or not. The anger had dissipated as she'd come outside anyway, sucked from her like debris up into a vacuum bag. Now she just felt limp. Exhausted.

The evening had turned chilly but when they turned off the main road onto the dirt track which led up to the house, Kit opened the car window. The familiar smells of peppermint and sugar gums were comforting. Home, she kept thinking. *Home.* Or it was, until today. The thought nagged at her even though she knew it was crazy. No one in the family had ever treated her like an outsider. Even amidst all the drama of Leonie's accident, Kit was totally accepted and loved. *And yet . . .*

At two or three hundred metres from the big white weatherboard house, the dogs rushed out to meet the car, barking like mad things.

'So,' Johnny pulled up in front of the house, noting the lack of lights, 'here we are. The first back.'

'Thank God,' Kit muttered. 'How long will they stay at the hospital?'

'Dunno. They'll have to come home at some stage tonight.'

After their session with Leonie in intensive care, Johnny had told his parents that he was taking Kit home to sleep. Kit bent to pat the dogs and whisper hello before following Johnny through the wrought-iron gate, past her mother's roses to the front door.

Johnny turned on the light and Kit smiled weakly. God, it was all here. The huge kitchen almost sung with everyone who'd recently left it. Her father's newspapers were all over the table, his work overalls dropped in a heap. Her mother must have been in the middle of making a cake when she got the news that morning because the mixture was still sitting in a heavy bowl on the table along with a rusty tin filled with eggs caked in dirt − obviously recently collected − and a split open bag of oranges.

There were work-boots by the door, a clutter of unwashed dishes in the sink and a compact of cheap make-up sitting on the window-sill. Kit shivered and walked over to see if she could scratch the fire to life, but the coals weren't even warm. She closed the door, went over to the table and took a dip of the cake mixture with her finger.

'I'm hungry,' she said.

'Hmmm, let's see.' Johnny was already at the fridge getting out bread, cheese and tomatoes. 'Will I make us something?'

'I'll do it.' Kit pushed him away. 'You go light the fire.'

'Sexist,' he grinned and then did as he was told.

The open fireplace was up the other end of the room and it was filled with ash and a half burnt log. As she sliced the cheese, Kit watched Johnny scraping it out and setting a new one. She was mesmerised by the sureness of his movements. He and Sebastian were alike in a way. They were both serious but they had a certain quiet spontaneity about them too, which was attractive.

'Toasted sangers okay for you, Johnno?'

'Sure.' He was laying the kindling carefully along the crumpled paper. 'Anything.'

'So, where are you going to drop yourself tonight, kiddo?' he asked, reaching for the matches on the mantelpiece.

'In my room,' Kit said in surprise. 'Why?'

'Well, there'll be a lot of people and noise.' Johnny was kneeling on the hearth concentrating on the fire. 'I mean over the next few days. Lucy and the kids and all the rest will arrive tomorrow. I mean if you want some sleep you might be better off out in the bungalow.'

'Leonie's room?' Kit shuddered. 'God, I don't think so!'

He laughed, surprised. 'Why not? Take it from me, it'll be a circus here by the end of the week.' He stopped a moment as though struck by a new thought. 'Whatever happens.'

As if she would, as if she *could* sleep in Leonie's room! God, she was still shaken from the little episode in the hospital. What if

70

Leonie died in the night and her ghost came roaming around the bungalow after her daughter. Blaming Kit. *You wanted me dead so I died.* Kit shuddered as she opened the cupboard, searching for plates for the sandwiches. Get a grip, she told herself. Get a bloody grip on yourself. She suddenly wished Brendan was around. He wasn't kind and understanding like Johnny. He'd yell for her to pull her head in if she went on with this kind of crap. And they'd both end up cracking up with laughter. She would have liked to talk to someone about how she felt, vent some inner spleen and confusion. But not Johnny. Johnny didn't deserve her evil thoughts.

It was a big, rambling house. The central four rooms were over a hundred years old but had been added to over the years. A hallway and four extra bedrooms built in the sixties were the main addition. The small one, right next to the kitchen, had been Kit's.

Another addition had been a bungalow built at the back of the house for Gerard's mother. When she died, it gradually became filled with all the assorted junk that families accumulate over time. But then Leonie came back from overseas and the bungalow was revived. Gerard and Frank converted it for Leonie and she declared herself delighted. She was living with her family, but had a little privacy at the same time.

When the sandwiches were ready and the tea made, Kit turned off the big fluorescent light and brought over a tray to Johnny, who was sitting in an armchair in front of the fire. He'd pulled a chair across for her, too, but she decided to park herself on the floor, leaning her back against his chair, letting her legs stretch out in front of her towards the flames. They began to eat hungrily. She found herself smiling in the semi-darkness. Who else would she be able to sit with so quietly and comfortably? Johnny was special. *Brother? Uncle? What did it matter?*

Johnny would make a wonderful priest. He'd bring such commitment and intelligence to it. He was a good listener and so caring.

71

Kit felt a surge of pride just imagining how people would love him and rely on him. But at the same time she couldn't bear the idea of him resigning himself to such a selfless, lonely life. She'd never seen Johnny look really happy, and she longed to. She'd never heard him roaring with laughter, nor seen him tipsy or flinging himself around a dance-floor. Kit munched her food, thinking that if she was being absolutely honest then she wanted to see her favourite brother lose it completely. It would have thrilled her to learn that Johnny had been found out on the pavement at six in the morning as drunk as a skunk, his arm around some sexy blonde, reciting all that poetry he knew by heart. She loved him to bits but he was thirty and she doubted that he'd ever done a truly impulsive thing in his life. She'd bet a million bucks he'd never been in love, for example. Had he ever even had a proper girlfriend? She couldn't remember.

'So who was it who came around today?' Johnny interrupted her thoughts. 'The one you told that you couldn't do the play. Is he your boyfriend?'

'I don't have a boyfriend,' Kit said shortly. 'I've never had a boyfriend.' She turned to him with a grim smile. 'I'm destined to end up like the aunts. A nice old single dame who plays cards, and, I don't know, what else do they do?'

'Knit?' Johnny laughed.

'And embroider,' Kit groaned. 'I'll take that up.'

'But you've *had* boyfriends,' Johnny said, perplexed. 'What about that Gary?'

'Oh, give me a break, Johnny!' Kit remembered the sports jock she went out with during her last year at school. 'Okay, I went out with him a bit years ago and I've been out with a few guys since then . . .'

'Oh, so we are talking about staying *in* with someone, are we?' Johnny teased, 'rather than going *out* with him.'

'Well, of course,' Kit smiled. 'I'm nearly twenty-one. Not sixteen. I don't want to just go on bloody dates all my life!'

Suddenly, she remembered the girlfriend that Johnny had brought home once. During his first year at university. Valerie. The family had been stunned at first. 'Couldn't he get someone who looked even vaguely normal?' they'd grumbled. The girl was a cripple. She'd had some disease when she was young and one leg was much thinner and shorter than the other. She was also the plainest girl that they had ever seen. Skinny and small, her poor little body was like a twelve-year-old's, but hunched over and sort of bent. Her thin wispy brown hair stood up on her head like rodent fluff, and her hands, so white and delicate, were as tiny as chicken feet. She wore thick round glasses and she stuttered. But Valerie had been the only girl in college who hadn't been invited to the mid-year ball. She was not so much shunned as ignored by everyone. So Johnny had invited her. Of course. And they'd gone out for a few months after that, to meals and films and seemed to have developed a real closeness that ended only when she moved with her family to The States.

Actually, it didn't take long to forget Valerie's plainness and various disabilities. Once everyone got to know her she turned out to be lovely: clever, with a quietly wicked wit. Kit's family felt ashamed that it had taken them so long to see what had been so obvious to Johnny straight away. But on the other hand the whole thing was so . . . *Johnny*. But did it have to be like that? Was he destined always to support and save and bolster others? After all, he was a gorgeous guy. All her friends thought he was handsome and sweet with a good sense of humour. Why couldn't he have a bit of what everyone else took for granted?

Johnny put his plate down and threw his arms back into a huge stretch.

'I should come home more often,' he said contentedly. 'I love this place.'

They looked around at the familiar worn furniture: the piano in the corner, the kitchen chairs set haphazardly around the table up the other end of the room.

'Even those terrible floral curtains look okay in this light,' Kit agreed. 'Remember when Mum came home with them?'

'Shit. Yes!' Johnny was laughing. 'Moya went berserk. So did Leonie. She came home from overseas about then. And she told poor old Mum that they reminded her of chuck!'

The curtains were gaudy; huge patches of bright colour against a white background. Therese had bought them at a sale and in spite of everyone else's disapproval declared them perfect for the family room.

'We don't even notice them now,' Kit sighed. 'Somehow they've worn their way into the room and they look right.'

'Leonie was telling me only last week how much she missed home when she was overseas all those years,' Johnny said dreamily.

Kit took a sip of her drink and turned her face to the fire. *And did she ever wake up and wonder how her daughter was going?*

'Have I said something wrong?' Johnny's hand was on her shoulder.

'No, of course not,' Kit said gruffly. She was glad of the darkness because she could wipe away the splash of tears running down her cheeks without him seeing. It was just self-pity, really. That time when she'd learnt that her big sister was off again, after all the attention and fun. And she wouldn't be back. Not for ages.

'You playing your flute at all these days?' Johnny asked casually.

'No'. Kit grimaced in the dark. Her parents had bought her a beautiful flute at the beginning of her last year at school. They'd got it secondhand but it was a quality instrument and had cost quite a lot of money. Right through secondary school, Kit had been a keen flautist. She'd loved her teacher and practised incessantly. Then when she'd got an A+ in her exam at the end of the year, everyone thought she'd choose music as her major. But she decided not to and gradually let the flute slide to the point where she didn't play for weeks on end. Last time she'd come home, she'd been unable to even find the thing.

'Don't tell anyone this, Johnny,' she said slowly, 'but I don't know where my flute is. It must be somewhere around but I've got no idea where.'

'You think someone has stolen it?'

'I don't know,' Kit shrugged. 'The last time I remember playing was here. Remember Aunty Moya's birthday? I'd brought it home for that and forgot to bring it back, and now it's gone.'

'You always kept it on top of the piano when you were home.'

'I know.' Kit sighed and got up, brushing the crumbs from her legs. 'Listen, I've been thinking. I will go and check out that room,' she mumbled quickly. 'It might do.'

Kit had no idea what to expect when she opened the door to the bungalow. A mess of Leonie's personal stuff maybe, clothing draped over chairs, books and magazines lying about, maybe a pinboard with notes and photos.

A little photo of Kit? Oh yeah. Fat chance. All the bits and pieces that accumulate around one adult woman: that's what she'd expected. She'd come out to have a snoop really, a vague idea of having a poke through Leonie's things before someone else did – one of the aunts or maybe the dreaded Lucy and her two bratty kids.

But there was no mess, no clutter whatsoever. What greeted her was a room stark and neat: a bed, made up with a yellow chenille bedspread, a desk under the window with nothing but a few pencils on it, a grey wicker chair and a small empty bookcase. Nothing hung on any wall, not a print or a mirror or a photo. There wasn't a vase or piece of pottery, or any ornament at all to be seen. It looked like a hotel room or a hospital ward. *Worse.* This was so stark Kit felt sure it was saying something. But what exactly?

People used to make jokes about all the stuff Leonie collected – all her clothes, the bits and pieces of pottery and sculpture that her arty friends had given her, all her books. Kit wondered if she'd got

75

it wrong and perhaps Leonie had parked all her things somewhere else. Maybe she'd moved out of this room and dumped her stuff into one of her brother's rooms for some reason? But that didn't make sense. Why would she?

Kit slid open the built-in robes and saw that all Leonie's clothes were there, on hangers and under plastic, her half-dozen pairs of shoes lined like soldiers at the bottom of the cupboard. She pushed open the door into the small bathroom. All very neat in there, too: just a couple of folded towels on the rack and a plastic container of handcream on the basin. Next to the mirror was a big square map of Ireland. Kit frowned, staring at the map, a small chill passing through her. She moved closer. *Ireland.* It was a relatively new print of an old map, depicting the four provinces of Ulster, Connaught, Munster and Leinster. Kit's eyes searched out Belfast and she wondered whether you were meant to feel anything when you looked at the place of your birth on a map. *Did she feel something?* Well, curiosity, she supposed. And a certain disbelief. How odd, to think that she might have other relations over there. Could her father still be alive? Was he Australian or Irish? She tried to think back on conversations she'd had with Leonie when she'd been a kid. Had Leonie even mentioned Belfast? Surely she'd remember it if she had. Kit moved back to the main room and closed the door abruptly. She shut her eyes.

This was so strange.

Normally she would hate a room like this – for its cool neatness, its lack of personality, its lack of warmth and ease. And she did hate it. But somehow the bareness of it was freeing, too, soothing her troubled spirit. She knew that she wanted to stay in this room, although she couldn't quite work out why. Only that she felt calmed by the odd emptiness that Leonie had left. She quickly went in to tell Johnny what she'd decided and to get herself some fresh sheets and towels before the others got home.

CHAPTER SIX

The next day was mayhem, just as Johnny had predicted. As soon as the news was out, it seemed as though a well-oiled network of neighbours, family and friends had suddenly lurched into life. The phone rang constantly with offers of help. People dropped off casseroles and flowers. Visitors dropped in 'for a minute' and stayed all day. Cars went in relays to the hospital and came back with tiny snippets of news that were repeated by somebody every ten minutes.

'The surgeon is pleased with her blood pressure.'

'She was stable right through the night.'

'Nurse said by Wednesday we'll know.'

Asleep in the bungalow, Kit missed out on the morning dramas. As soon as her head hit the soft pillow on the strange bed at around midnight she fell into a thick dreamless sleep. Then as morning came, although she heard the noises of her family, the cars coming and going, the sounds of children calling, she couldn't seem to wake up properly.

'Kathleen! Are you awake? Long distance!'

Kit sat up with a start. She threw back the bedclothes and

jumped out of bed. Feeling dizzy, she scrambled around for her clothes before realising that she didn't actually have to be dressed to greet her mother at the door. She pulled a big cardigan over her nightie.

'Thanks,' she said, taking the phone. Therese looked brighter this morning.

Kit put her hand over the mouthpiece. 'Did you get any sleep, Mum?'

'Oh yes, love, a few hours.'

'And is she . . . did anything happen or –'

'She had a peaceful night,' Therese said. 'Johnny said he'd take you in soon.'

'Oh, okay,' Kit nodded. 'Thanks.' How could she tell her mother that she dreaded going into that ward again.

'Hello?' Kit spoke into the phone warily, hoping it wasn't one of her old girlfriends from school who'd just heard about Leonie's accident and wanted to commiserate for an hour.

'Kit, it's Tam. How's your sister?' Tam spoke breathlessly as though she'd just come in from a run.

'Hi, Tam. She's had the operation and now we're just waiting for her to regain consciousness.'

'God, it must be terrible.' There was real sympathy in Tam's voice. 'Listen, I'm sorry about yesterday.' She gave a short apologetic groan. 'You know me. I'm a pain. Did your brother talk you into going up there or –'

'No. It's okay, Tam,' Kit replied quickly. 'I went off the deep end too. Sorry.'

There was a moment of awkwardness where they both waited for the other to speak. Kit decided to plunge in; after all, this was her best friend.

'Actually, Tam, it's more complicated. I found out, yesterday, that Leonie is not my sister but my mother.'

'*What?*' Tam was speechless as she digested this information. 'No shit?'

Kit smiled, a wash of warmth for her friend flooding her head.

'You *must* be having me on!'

'No, I'm not.' Kit managed to keep her voice even, wanting to cry and laugh at the same time. She and Tam shared most things. But it was usually Tam with the big news items.

'Jeez!' Tam said. 'Amazing. Wait till I tell Lou! Brendan will go bananas. God, how do you *feel*? What about your real, I mean your other mother?'

'She's my grandmother.'

'*No shit?*'

Kit laughed. 'It feels like I've been away a week instead of half a day and a night.'

'Well, no wonder!' Tam was virtually shouting. 'No bloody wonder! You must feel like you've lived a bloody *lifetime* up there in twenty-four hours!'

Kit was secretly delighted with Tam's response. She found many people far too cool. Their whole aim in life seemed to be to try and give the impression that they weren't shocked, appalled, flabbergasted, delighted or absolutely dismayed by whatever was going on. Tam's shrieks of disbelief reminded Kit why she liked her so much. Tam got right into whatever was going on, one hundred per cent.

'Kit, I've got something to tell you,' Tam said slowly, 'but I feel a bit strange now.'

'What?'

'I *think* I should tell you,' Tam said slowly. 'I guess I should.'

'Tam,' Kit demanded, 'come on! What is it?'

'Gucci told me this morning that Leonie came around here the night before last. When we were at the party.'

'To our house?' It was Kit's turn to be stunned. Since Leonie had

79

come back from overseas, Kit had made a point of never inviting her over. Sometimes she'd agree to meet her in a café for coffee but an invitation to the Richmond house was never extended, even though Kit knew that Leonie would have killed for one. It was partly punishment for being rejected years ago, but it was also about Kit's determination to have her own life apart from her family, *especially her sister*. Although it was never put into words, Kit felt sure Leonie understood this. So it was hard now to imagine why she thought it would be okay to come unannounced.

'Why didn't Gucci tell me?' Kit asked.

'She was going to tell you yesterday but she couldn't find you and I told her you'd left for the farm. Apparently the Labels were home having one of their rare *groovy* nights in. Probably because we were out. Anyway, they said that there was a strange woman at the door asking for you. And she was really agitated . . .'

'Agitated?' Kit repeated sharply. 'What do you mean?'

'Well, just nervous I guess,' Tam said slowly, 'although Gucci used the word *abusive* but hey, anyone who spoke above a sweet little whisper would be abusive to her. When they told her that you weren't home she demanded to know where you were. And then she told Gucci, and I quote, *"that your big sister Leonie called"*.'

'God, how weird!' Kit was blown away by this news. 'What time?'

'They said about midnight. Gucci was all put out about it when she told me. God! I tell you I let her have it.'

'What did you say?'

'I told her to stick it!' Tam continued, 'because that same person, your sister, mother, whatever, has now been in a terrible accident. You should have seen Gucci's face drop. She went all quiet and then, wait for this, she *apologised*.'

'Wow!' Kit's mouth fell open. 'Gucci baby apologising!'

'Yeah, well,' Tam groaned, 'those two are such emotional cripples.

Oh Kit, I *wish wish wish* they'd move out! We could get somebody really good up there.'

Kit and Tam were always having fantasies about how fabulous it would be when the Labels moved out, but changing house dynamics wasn't on her mind right then.

'So Leonie was upset?' Kit said in a small voice.

'Well yes, apparently. She walked off to her car in a real state,' Tam said and then added awkwardly, 'so what do you think?'

'No idea,' Kit sighed.

'How are your family taking it?' Tam asked.

'Well, you know. Bad, I suppose.' Kit walked over to the window and stared out into the backyard. Someone was just arriving. Therese was rushing out along the path to welcome them. Two kids and a dog and . . . oh no. It was Lucy, Oliver and Zoe. 'Shit, Tam, it's actually a nightmare. I don't know what to think or do. Tell me something about our place. Anything happening? How are Lou and Brendan?'

'Haven't seen either of them today,' Tam said shortly, 'but Brendan said last night he was going to ring you.'

'Tell him I'm hanging out to hear from him.'

'Who's your father then, Kit?' Tam asked suddenly.

'I don't know, but I was born in Ireland. Belfast.'

'That's where she had you?'

'Apparently,' Kit sighed. 'I'm sleeping in her room out the back of the house and there's this big map of Ireland on the wall. It's the only bit of decoration. It felt so weird just looking at it, knowing that's where I was born. I've always felt so Australian.'

'So he'd be Irish, probably?'

'I don't know.'

'Shame it's not Dublin.'

'Yeah,' Kit gave a dry laugh. 'That's what I thought. Dublin would be cool. Be good if he was a muso or –'

'Yeah, a fiddle player!'

'Or what about a writer?'

'Yeah, Roddy Doyle or someone like that.'

'What about the Corrs' manager or something?'

'Yeah. Rich and sort of *arty* . . . would be good.'

'A big rich Celtic tiger would do!'

They both laughed.

'What's Belfast got?'

'I don't know.' Kit thought for a moment. 'Well, there's a *war*, that's been going on forever. I don't know much about it. I'll have to ask Brendan.'

'Actually, my father was stationed in Belfast years ago,' Tam said thoughtfully. 'When he was in the army.'

Kit had only met Tam's father once and she didn't like him. He was a pompous little man. Tam didn't seem to like him much either. He'd left her and her mother for another woman when Tam was a teenager and went back to England with her to live.

'Hey, they might have known each other,' Kit joked. 'My mother and your father. When was he there?'

'I dunno,' Tam sighed, 'he got out of the army when I was about eight.'

'We might be sisters, Tam!' Kit chortled. 'You never know!'

'Yeah, right,' Tam groaned. 'And I'm going to be elected Prime Minister tomorrow, Loony Lou will finally get her degree with Honours and the Labels will give up their jobs and go and work in Africa for the general good of mankind.'

'Calvin will start getting his undies in the supermarket!' Kit giggled. 'In the specials department. You know those bright little six-packs? And he'll go a whole week without the gym or looking at himself in the mirror.' She sighed, becoming serious. 'I don't have a sister any more.'

'Take heart,' Tam said promptly, 'you got two mothers now, babe.'

'One would do, actually.'

'How are you going to find out?' Tam asked. 'I mean about all this stuff.'

'I'll ask my family,' Kit replied, 'but I'm not sure they know anything either.'

'She'd better wake up then,' Tam said grimly. 'Your *real* mother, I mean. She owes you.'

About to say goodbye, Kit was hit with a longing to hang on. Tam felt like the one link back to her other, real life in the city.

'Tam, did you hear how the play went last night? It was the last night, you know.'

Tam hesitated. 'No, sorry. I didn't.'

'You didn't hear *anything*?'

'Not a thing.'

There was a couple of moments silence.

'Of course it *is* all over the papers this morning. I suppose I better not keep it from you.'

'What?'

'Oh, just how much better the production is without you.'

'Bitch!' Kit laughed.

'Yeah, they're all saying it. Front page. Big headlines. Thank God that Quinlan no-talent has gone missing. Now this show is going to be a real hit.'

'Thanks, Tam.'

'You're welcome!'

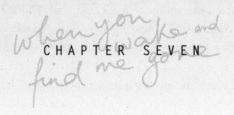

CHAPTER SEVEN

Kit managed to get out of seeing Leonie that day. She went to the hospital with Johnny in the afternoon but chickened out at the front steps.

'Johnny, I don't think I can do this,' she said. 'You go in. I'll wait.'

'You want to talk?' he asked kindly, putting his arm around her.

'No, I just don't feel too good.' She actually did feel queasy. 'I'll wait for you over at the park.'

'Okay then.'

He was about to go when she held him back. 'Johnny, did you ever hear anything about why Leonie left to live overseas again? You know, when I was thirteen. Why did she leave so suddenly?'

Johnny began walking with her across the road to the park. 'I heard nothing at the time,' he said slowly. 'None of us knew. But later, Mum said that it was something about her not feeling up to being a mother. That she'd come home to give it a go. Then she found that she couldn't.'

Kit jerked free of Johnny. Arms folded tightly across her chest, she lifted her face to the sky.

'What a complete bitch,' she said hoarsely.

Johnny was staring at his feet, frowning deeply.

'You go now, Johnny,' Kit said.

'Are you sure?'

'Of course,' Kit replied, turning away and mumbling to herself, 'as long as I don't have to go into that ward again.'

Kit bought a drink and sat under a tree in the park. She was glad to be on her own. Why had Leonie come to see her the other night and why had she been upset? Why hadn't she stayed the night with Bernadette like she'd planned? Kit picked at the grass, her brain trying to tease out the possibilities, but she didn't know enough about Leonie's life for any of her scenarios to make much sense.

The last time she'd seen Leonie had been about a month before the accident. Leonie was going to be down in the city for a library conference and wanted to arrange lunch. Kit had said she was too busy for lunch, which wasn't true, but would meet her for coffee later that afternoon.

Leonie was nervous. Kit could tell by the way she played with the menu and it gave Kit a mean sense of power.

Still a nice-looking woman, Leonie was slim and fair-skinned, but her clothes didn't suit her – neither colour nor style. And she did nothing with her lovely hair except scrape it back into a pigtail. Her only jewelry was a cheap watch and her face was completely bare of make-up. Kit thought of the way the aunts tut-tutted about Leonie and found herself thinking that they had a point.

'You can't afford to let yourself go in your thirties,' Moya always sniffed, '*if* you want to look reasonable in your forties.'

'I can't stay long, Kit muttered. Got to get back to rehearsals.'

'How is the play coming along?'

'Good.'

'You enjoy acting?' Leonie seemed sceptical so Kit couldn't resist the temptation to lay it on thick.

'Oh, yes. Love it! Might apply for drama school after my degree.'

'You used to be such a shy little girl.'

Kit winced. She hated Leonie even mentioning her as a little girl. And anyway, Kit had never been seriously keen on acting. Her interest in the play was totally with Sebastian.

Once, the year earlier, Kit had tried to talk to Leonie about that time when she was thirteen. She'd thought it might clear the air and that afterwards they could move on, into some kind of more honest relationship. But Leonie hadn't wanted to hear it. She'd listened to Kit's account of what it felt like to be dropped so suddenly by the older sister you adored. But all the time Kit was talking, Leonie had had this slightly dazed look on her face. Kit had bumbled on, feeling like a complete idiot but determined to finish what she'd started, knowing all the while that it wasn't going to work.

Leonie's response, when it came, had been completely false and inadequate.

'Oh, I am sorry! Did you really feel like that? Goodness. I had no idea. It was a very difficult time for me.'

Yeah? Well, me too.

Kit had tried to be honest and it had been shoved back in her face.

'So am I going to get an invite to the play?'

'The cast is allowed six freebies each,' Kit said. 'Mine have already been allocated.'

'So you've given Mum and Dad theirs?'

'No.' Kit hadn't even thought about inviting her parents.

'Surely you're inviting them?'

'They won't come!' Kit said forcefully.

'How do you know?'

'They never go to plays.'

'They'd come to yours! And the aunts, too! They'd love it. God, Kathleen. I can't believe you . . . they'd . . . *we'd all* love it! So who have your tickets gone to?'

'Friends,' Kit said defensively. 'Good friends.'

'You're lucky to have six *good* friends,' Leonie said coolly.

'Are you telling me you don't have six good friends?' Kit snapped before taking a sip of her coffee.

Leonie stopped playing with the menu for a moment. 'Well,' she began softly, then gave a quick smile. 'Yep, I admit it. I don't have six good friends.'

'What about overseas?' Kit said, realising at the same time that she probably didn't have six good friends herself.

'I had friends overseas,' Leonie said thoughtfully, 'good friends, I suppose.'

'Do you keep in contact?' Kit said.

'With one or two.'

'Why only a couple?' Kit thought she should use the opportunity to extract some information out of Leonie. 'And what about here? In Australia?'

'Well there's just Bernadette here, really,' Leonie said, a little defensively. 'She's always been my best friend. Although her job makes it difficult.' Bernadette worked for an airline and was often away.

'No one else?'

'Oh, you know,' Leonie waved one hand dismissively, 'things change. I was away a long time. And I was involved with things back then that I'm not involved with now. None of it's worth talking about.'

If only Kit had put Leonie on the spot, pushed her further to explain things. Maybe it would have all come out. Johnny said she'd planned to tell.

Kit lay on her back and looked up into the dappled light filtering through the leaves, heat from the ground rising up into her bones.

Ireland. How would it be to have a baby in a strange land? At what stage had Therese and Gerard been told? How had they felt going over there to fetch a baby; their granddaughter? She tried to imagine it; Leonie in bed, handing a swaddled baby over to her parents. Would Leonie be upset, or just glad to be rid of it? Would they have to sign papers? Did Leonie choose her name? What did her parents say before walking out with the baby?

Half asleep now, her mind was suddenly filled with an image of Sebastian; moving quickly around the stage, organising people. It was as vivid as a piece of music humming in her head. The last dress-rehearsal. He'd touched her arm and told her to move a few paces to the right so the audience would see her when she turned to make her speech. His fingers had been cool and firm, up close she could see that his hair needed a wash and that his eyes, normally so bright, looked tired. But those eyes had met her own for an instant. And his smile had been warm and . . . interested. Maybe that had been the moment for him. Maybe it was then that he'd realised she meant something to him? Maybe he'd gone home that night and decided to wait until the play had run its season before doing anything about it. A sob rose in Kit's throat. She didn't want to end up another Moya, or Eileen or Det. Or her own mother, when it came down to it. Much as she loved them all, she wanted something different. Would she ever feel his mouth again, on her own, and that rich warm feeling rushing up from her knees, making her weak. Would they ever share a bed, make cups of tea in the morning for each other? Read the paper together. She should ring him, explain things . . . But that didn't seem possible somehow. Not now. She sat up quickly and the image faded away. This other business would have to come first. She would try to pin Therese down and see what she knew.

CHAPTER EIGHT

Kit despaired of ever finding a quiet moment with Therese. The next day visitors came and went, meals were prepared and eaten and phone calls were made and taken. Tears were shed. With Therese in the middle of it all. The mood was up. Hadn't Leonie lasted the forty-eight hours without her condition deteriorating? The doctor had seen her parents that afternoon and said how delighted he was that she'd survived the crucial period. She was already showing early signs of waking from the coma. Her eyelids were fluttering. She mumbled words sometimes and she was moving a little: all good signs. He was now hopeful that it was only a matter of days before she woke, but cautioned them about not expecting too much too soon.

Therese seemed incapable of extricating herself from the heart of this family drama. Watching for an opportunity, Kit realised that her mother's endless cooking, making pots of tea, taking phone calls and talking, was about preserving for herself some kind of surface normality. A terrible fear for the wellbeing of her eldest child lurked just below Therese's skin. She had to live at this frenetic pace just to keep the panic at bay.

After breakfast on the third day, Kit at last got her chance.

Therese had come out with the scrap can to feed the hens and Kit, having retreated to the bungalow an hour before, spied her mother through the window.

'Mum,' she said, walking over. 'Can I ask you something?'

Therese nodded tensely and then went back to feeding the hens. Kit had a sense of her battening down the hatches in readiness for something difficult. She decided to push straight in before Therese had time to work out a hedging strategy.

'I want to know about you taking me when I was a baby.'

Bending down and fiddling with the wire of the hens' shed, Therese gave a small gasp. Kit didn't know if it was a reaction to her own words or if she'd hurt herself on the wire.

'Well, Johnny told you, didn't he?'

'Yeah, he told me the –'

'So what else do you want to know?' Therese stood up straight and looked at Kit, acting like things were already obvious, all out in the open with nothing to worry about.

'Everything,' Kit said. This was ridiculous. Wasn't it enough that they'd kept her in the dark for so long? 'I want to know about you going to Ireland to get me. When did you know you were going to take me home? And I want to know about Leonie over there. What was she doing? Who was my father?'

Therese looked out across the paddock. The sun was already bright in the sky. Another lovely spring day.

'We didn't know anything about Leonie's life over there,' she said quietly. 'We had no idea what she was doing or who she was with. And she wouldn't tell us when we got there.'

'Did she ask you to take me?'

'Yes.'

'What, she rang you?'

'Yes. In the middle of the night. We didn't even know she was pregnant.'

'You're kidding! You had no time to prepare?'

'None.'

'What was your reaction?'

'I said yes immediately.' Therese turned to Kit, tears spilling from her eyes. 'I didn't even ask Gerard, because I knew in my bones he'd feel the same. Our daughter's child? Of course we said yes. And we've never regretted it,' she added forcefully, almost angrily. 'Not for a moment.'

Kit was momentarily stunned. All the irritation was washed away with those words. The generosity of it. Not to even have to talk it over. It rang true. They were generous people. Anything they had they were quick to lend or give away. She put out her hand, touching Therese's arm, suddenly wanting to fall into her arms and thank her, tell her that she was one of a rare breed of truly beautiful people. But there was something about Therese's stance, rigid and defiant, as though she still had important things to say.

'We didn't approve of her not telling you,' she went on stiffly. 'There is nothing but trouble in hiding things like that. But it was up to her. Can you see that? It was up to Leonie to tell you. And now . . .'

Therese turned away, her face in her hand, suddenly weeping again. Kit rushed forward and put both arms tightly around her.

'Mum,' she mumbled into Therese's hair, holding her fiercely, 'God, Mum, I just need to know. That's all! You were, you *are* the best bloody mother anyone could have. The best parents.'

'But I'd like to know, too,' Therese said through her tears, hugging her back. 'I'd like to know who your father was.'

'Well, isn't it on my birth certificate?'

'No, it isn't.'

'Where is my birth certificate? Why haven't I ever seen it?' Kit thought for a moment. 'Didn't I need it to enrol at uni?'

'Leonie was very keen that you didn't see it, love, before she told you herself. So we sent it on to the university. Remember?'

Kit looked away. 'Was she ever going to tell me?'

Therese took a deep breath. 'She said only last week that she was planning to tell you before your twenty-first birthday. But that she couldn't work out the best way. Whether to write it all down for you or tell you to your face. She seemed very concerned about it.'

'What did you say?'

'Well, I couldn't work out why she seemed so weighed down by it all. My advice was to just give a simple explanation and then let you ask questions, but she dismissed that. Acted as though that wasn't possible. I couldn't see why not, I –'

'Because she'd left it so long!' Kit cut in sharply, 'because she was so gutless!'

Therese's shoulders slumped. 'Try not to be hard about it, Kathleen,' she said softly. 'Leonie always had to do things her own way.'

'I know,' Kit shrugged impatiently. Just because Leonie's life was in danger didn't make her action, or lack of action, any the better. It annoyed Kit to think that Leonie was now the focus of everyone's sympathy and attention when by rights it should be herself. She was the wronged party and yet it was she who was being asked to be understanding and sympathetic.

Therese reached out and took Kit's hand. 'You must be patient, Kathleen,' she said. 'If, by the grace of God, she does recover, give her time to do it in her own way.'

'But I'm sick of Leonie's way, Mum!' Kit said hotly. 'Seems to me everything has always been her way!'

'I mean it, Kathleen.' Therese would not release Kit's hand. 'If she recovers then we must, you must, let her find her own way of telling you. I would hate her to be harassed or badgered about any of this.'

'God, Mum, as if I would!'

'So you will promise?'

'I promise, Mum.'

CHAPTER NINE

Kit was washing up the lunch dishes when her father came looking for her. She was finding life back in the bosom of her family tough going. Johnny had had to go back to Melbourne for a couple of days and she'd wanted to go with him but couldn't think of a reasonable excuse. After all it was *her* mother so critically ill, no one else's.

Then there was the open curiosity about herself. '*Oh, so she knows now*', she'd heard Aunty Ruth, her father's sister, whisper to Julie. '*So how is she taking it?*' It was humiliating to think that all these old biddies had known this huge secret about her. The sympathetic looks and kind comments were irritating in the extreme. Not one for housework usually, Kit found herself jumping up after every meal to clear away and wash up, just so she didn't have to sit talking with everyone.

'Ah, there you are, Kathleen.' Her father's gruff voice pulled her out of her reverie.

'Yep, here I am, Dad.'

'Can I have a word?'

Kit nodded and picked up a tea-towel to begin drying. Gerard

93

had obviously just come back from town. He was dressed in his good clothes.

'You've been at the hospital?'

'Yes.' Gerard stood there awkwardly, looking at her as if he didn't quite know how to carry out some unpleasant but necessary task. It made Kit feel, as always, jittery and vaguely guilty. Maybe he was going to chastise her for not sitting with Leonie for long hours like the others did, but she forced herself to stop jumping the gun.

'So how is she today?'

'Much the same,' he said matter-of-factly. 'She's alive, and hasn't gone downhill since yesterday.'

At times Kit really appreciated her father's taciturn nature. It sure beat all the gushing emotion and wild speculation the others went on with.

'But she's starting to show signs of coming to,' Kit said, 'didn't the doctor say that?'

'Yes . . .' Her father seemed distracted. 'So we can only hope and pray.'

Kit placed the towel down on the bench and leant up against one of the counters. She looked her father in the eye. What did he want? He was a big man in his sixties. The clear light-blue eyes shone like two glass marbles in the middle of his worn, leathery face. He often made her feel like this: a foolish girl who must be told things for her own good.

He took a brief look around. There was no one else in the room. 'Now, this has been a shock for you,' he began very formally, looking at some point just behind her right shoulder. 'Learning that you are Leonie's child.'

Kit nodded and swallowed.

I'm glad I'm not yours, you great big thick hick, she thought and then immediately felt ashamed. After all, he'd been a good father. Good enough, anyway.

'I want you to know that whatever happens to Leonie, your mother − that is Therese − and I, consider you our daughter, and always have. When we're dead, everything we own will be divided equally between you and our other children.'

'Well, thanks, Dad.' Kit was touched. She could see he was doing his best. She took a deep breath. 'Dad, do you know *anything* about the time Leonie had me? I asked Mum this morning. Do you know anything at all about my *actual* father?'

Gerard stopped, his face stiffening. 'Leonie wouldn't say,' he said shortly. 'But he was some kind of good-for-nothing.'

Kit was shocked. 'Why do you say that?' Gerard usually only used that term for drunkards and wife-beaters.

'No doubt about it,' he said. 'Left the poor girl to deal with everything on her own.'

'But maybe she wanted to do it like that?' Kit said quickly. 'She might have left him?' For some reason it was important for Kit that Gerard didn't dismiss her real father so completely. Not before they knew something about him, anyway.

'No, no,' Gerard shook his head, and then, as though he'd only just remembered a minor detail, 'he was in jail at the time of your birth.'

'Jail?'

'Yes, that's right. In jail.' He looked at her kindly. 'So you see, he was some kind of no-hoper.'

'*You're sure?*' Kit felt devastated.

'Yes, he was serving time,' her father said matter-of-factly. 'One of the nurses told me. I didn't bother telling Therese. It would only have made it worse for her.'

'What for?'

'How do you mean?'

'What was he in jail for?'

Gerard shrugged, as though all criminal activity was in essence the same. 'I wouldn't go chasing up that side of things, Kathleen,' he said.

95

'You've turned out a lovely girl in spite of him. Clever, too. There's no need to be running after no-hopers . . .'

That night, Kit's sleep was light, punctuated by dreams so vivid that she woke up exhausted.

In the dream she remembered clearly, she was in a car with Sebastian and they were running away together. Except that he was now her father. He kept asking her if she felt okay about running away with him because they would probably get into a lot of trouble when they got caught. In a high state of sexual excitement, Kit didn't care at all. Just go, *go*, she kept saying, I don't care! She was longing for him, and scared at the same time. But when he pulled the car off the highway down a dirt track, under some trees and bent over to kiss her, she was overwhelmed.

Kit woke up hot and breathless, right at the soft delicious edgy moment before a deep thundering climax, only to have it slide away from her . . . She shut her eyes and tried to bring the dream back, fury and disappointment overwhelming her. The bungalow was airless, stale with old memories and worn out hopes. If only she *was* in a car with Sebastian now, on that highway with his hands caressing her skin, his tongue probing her mouth, the whole bulk of him climbing over her, moving in, getting right down into her deep secret places! Then she could live, *live*! The rest of it, this life that she was meant to go on living, felt like slow suffocation.

She threw the blankets off and groaned. *Why?* Why did she have to be lying alone in this poxy single bed? In this ugly little room? Her thoughts going around in circles about a mother she didn't like and a father she didn't know.

She could hear the morning noises of the children out in the garden. Her cousins.

Kit got up slowly and looked carefully around the room. Maybe

96

she could find some clues to Leonie. It might be worth a search. The built-in cupboards had to be the most obvious place. Kit dragged over the wicker chair and climbed up. The long top shelf above the hanging clothes was filled with boxes of clothes and books, some photos and prints, all fairly neatly packed up but dusty. Kit took every box and case down and methodically went through the lot. Nothing.

But the search wasn't completely wasted. Just as she was about to give up, to her great surprise she found her flute right at the bottom of a drawer full of Leonie's jumpers. *So who the hell had put it there?* Kit pulled out the slightly battered black case excitedly and clicked it open. A rush of relief went through her when she saw that the instrument was still in perfect condition, lying comfortably in the faded red velvet-lined cavities. She took it over to the table and carefully removed the three pieces, fitting them together, her fingers caressing the smooth tubing and knobbly bits of silver with pleasure. Only three years before she'd done this every day. How familiar she'd been with each piece then. How she'd loved the whole business of opening the case, setting out her music, loosening up her fingers with scales. She realised she'd been worried, thinking maybe she'd lost it, or been careless enough to let it get stolen.

Kit moistened her lips with her tongue, lifted the instrument, fitted her fingers over the keys and blew a long, low note. She said a silent prayer of thanks as a familiar tingle of delight rippled up her neck. Yes. Maybe finding her instrument after all this time was a sign that she should begin practising again. She tried to remember one of the pieces she'd learnt for her exam but her fingers seemed to belong to someone much slower and clumsier than herself. Still she persisted, reverting to childish pieces and easy scales, quite lost to everything around her as she haltingly found her way back into the sound and feel of her instrument again. Underneath the pleasure she was perplexed and annoyed. Had

Leonie hidden her flute in a bottom drawer? *Why would she do that?*

'Kathleen! Phone call.'

Someone was calling from inside the house. Why couldn't they bring the phone out to her? Kit pulled a jumper on over her nightie and stuffed her feet into a pair of slippers. Never mind. One way or another she would find things out. Even if she did have to badger and harass. Too bad. She had a right. The thought gave her comfort as she trudged out on the path to the house.

It was Tam again.

'Brendan said to tell you he's tried phoning you heaps of times but can't get through.'

'That would be right,' Kit sniffed. 'The phone's always engaged here.'

'So how are you?'

'Oh, you know.'

'No I don't. That's why I asked. You sound like you're going to explode. What's happened?'

'Nothing,' Kit said sourly.

'What about your sister?'

'She's alive,' Kit muttered.

'And?'

'They think she's going to come out of it soon.'

'That's good. Then you can ask her everything.'

'Yeah,' Kit said huffily. 'That's what I thought, but it doesn't work like that, Tam. She'll take ages to fully regain consciousness. Then she might have to learn to talk again. She won't remember things, some things she might never remember . . .' Kit brightened suddenly. 'Anything happening back there?'

'Lots, actually,' Tam said.

'What?'

'Well, do you want the good news or the bad news first?'

'Bad,' Kit said immediately. 'I need something to look forward to.'

Tam laughed. 'Okay, Lou's band has been invited to play in Adelaide for a month. She's leaving next week.'

'You're kidding me! *Lou's* band?'

'Lou's band,' Tam repeated.

'You can't mean it! They're, like, the *worst* band in the world. Who's invited them?'

'I dunno, but someone has got them gigs every night over there. Lou is super elated and, wait for it, she's getting back into Wicca again.'

'No!' Kit groaned. Lou had been a witch of sorts the year before for a couple of months. She'd driven them all mad with her moon ceremonies and spells.

'Yep, she's putting spells on the Kombi van for a safe trip and she wants your brother to bless the trip with special holy water.'

'Oh God!' Kit had to laugh. 'I didn't think witches approved of the church.'

'Typical Lou,' Tam giggled. 'She can't even get who she's meant to hate right! What *is* holy water exactly, Kit?'

'Some other time, Tam,' Kit groaned. 'But tell me, why is this bad news for us? It's not as though we have to listen to them if they're in Adelaide.'

'You're going to hate me for this, Kit.'

'What?'

'She got me at a bad moment. I was feeling lonely . . .' Tam sighed and rushed the rest out. 'They won't let her take Boy George. So she asked me, asked *us*, to mind him.'

'Tam, you didn't!' Kit exploded. 'You hate him more than anyone!'

'I know I do,' Tam wailed, 'and I'm convinced I'm going to kill him without actually meaning to. It's terrible. I dreamt last night I pushed him into a deep freeze, alive! What if I kill Boy George in my sleep or something?'

'You'd be doing everyone a favour,' Kit said sharply. 'So that mutt is going to be in our house full-time for –'

'A month,' Tam finished the sentence. 'But you know Lou. It might be shorter, or –'

'Longer!' they said in unison and then both laughed.

'Not inside, though,' Tam said. 'We won't let him inside.'

'If he comes inside I'll kill him,' Kit quickly agreed. 'Seriously though, Tam, wasn't there someone else she could park him with?' Kit thought of the huge unpleasant animal cooped up in the backyard. 'I mean he's going to have to be taken for walks and fed. And who's going to clean up the shit?'

'Me and Brendan. And you, babe. Except I haven't told Brendan yet. Would you tell him?'

'Tam, I'm up here! Going crazy. How would I be able to tell him?'

'Phone?' Tam said in a small voice. And for some reason this made them both break into a fresh bout of hysterical laughter. At the end of it Kit felt better than she had in days.

'So what's the good news?' she asked at last.

'I met a man last week,' Tam said. 'Totally gorgeous.'

'You're always meeting men.'

'This is different,' Tam said seriously. 'This is *it*.'

Kit laughed. 'So tell me about him.'

'Only if you promise not to be judgemental.'

Kit waited. Tam never spoke like this about guys she was going with. She never took her relationships seriously. It was all fun and good times and as soon as that stopped she dumped them.

'Well, he's twelve years older than me,' Tam said. 'And he's been married, twice.'

'Twice,' Kit murmured. 'Hell.'

'Don't be judgemental!' Tam snapped.

100

'But Tam, that makes him, like, thirty-five!' Kit said, 'and you're only twenty-three.'

'Surprising as it may seem, I have worked that out, Kit,' Tam said tartly.

'It's a big difference,' Kit said. 'Has he got any kids?'

'Yes.'

'Oh, *Tam*! How many?'

'Three,' Tam said uneasily. 'But he never sees them.'

'Never?' This set alarm bells ringing for Kit, more than the age difference and the two marriages. 'Is that supposed to be a good thing? Doesn't he *want* to see them?'

'Both the ex-wives are real bitches, apparently.' Tam was defensive. 'They won't let him see his kids. He wants to and everything.'

Kit said nothing.

'Thing is, Kit,' Tam went on breathlessly, 'Lou's having a big farewell party next Friday night. Is there any chance you can come back for it? Sorry if this sounds insensitive, with your sister — sorry, I mean your mother, being so ill and everything. But it wouldn't be the same without you.'

'Oh, *God*! You don't know how much I want to come!'

'Do you think you will?'

'Yeah,' Kit sighed. 'If I possibly can.'

'Thing is, honey,' Tam said, 'I took the liberty of inviting Sebastian.'

'What!' Kit whispered, stunned. 'You didn't!'

'Yeah, I ran into him at uni,' Tam giggled. 'In the admin building. He didn't remember me, so I introduced myself. I told him about you being holed up there. He said he'd get in touch with you.'

'Jesus, Tam,' Kit was nearly wetting herself. 'He didn't!'

'Yep,' Tam giggled. 'So I said you'd probably be down for the party. Then I invited him. He took down the address and said he'd do his best to be there.'

'You are a true friend, Tamara Diamond Price.'

'I know. I know.'

'I'll just have to think of a way of getting away from here.'

'You said it, babe.'

CHAPTER TEN

Kit was making her way out to the car with Therese and Gerard for a hospital visit when the police pulled up. Johnny was due back that evening and Kit had decided that she would ask him to help her with an excuse to get away for the party.

The police were local men. The driver, well into his fifties, got out and began a friendly chat with Gerard and Therese, inquiring about Leonie's progress and commenting on the rain they'd had the night before. Meanwhile, the younger man was lifting a couple of cases from the back seat. One was a normal sized suitcase, the other a small battered briefcase with a zip opening.

'In your sister's car at the time of the accident,' he explained to Kit. 'You mind signing this?'

'Oh, okay.' Kit signed the form and took the cases from him.

'There were a whole lot of scattered papers at the scene,' the policeman told her. 'Handwritten stuff. Was your sister studying?'

Kit shook her head, suddenly mute with anticipation as his words took hold. *Maybe Leonie had been writing something about . . .*

'So where are they?' she asked, as casually as she could. 'The papers, I mean.'

'We had to destroy a lot of it,' he went on. 'Some of it was covered in dirt and oil, and,' he lowered his voice respectfully, 'blood.'

Kit nodded, hope rushing out of her like air from a balloon. The man pointed to the smaller of the bags. 'I think one of the young fellows saved some bits and pieces,' he said. 'In there.'

Kit tried to remain calm. 'Thanks.'

'I'll just put these away,' she called to her parents. They nodded and continued their conversation with the older cop.

Kit put the large case down at the door to the bungalow and, hands trembling, began unzipping the small one.

But the man was right. It was mostly scraps: shopping lists; a few addresses and phone numbers; notes to herself about coming events and silly little doodles. Kit was bitterly disappointed, until she saw a thick exercise book in another compartment of the case. She immediately opened the first page, holding her breath. It was filled with Leonie's big loose scrawl in black ink. Kit would know that writing anywhere. She flipped on through the rest of the notebook, her mood diving between elation and disappointment. It was all so scrappy. But at least a hundred pages had been filled.

Slumping down onto the bed she went back to the first page again.

I am trying to put things in order, the first line read.

Kit stopped, staring at the words. A sense of dread came over her. Do I really want to get into all this, she wondered. Why not wait until Leonie regained consciousness? If she wanted to build a relationship with her new mother, then surely it would be better done in an honest open way. Which meant not sneaking into Leonie's private papers beforehand.

But of course she couldn't help it.

'Kathleen!' It was her father calling and he sounded irritated. 'What's holding you up?'

She heard the friendly shouts of goodbye, the police car turn around and head off back down the track, a quick beep of the horn.

'Coming, Dad!' she yelled. 'I'll just be a minute!'

Her eyes skimmed down through the first page of Leonie's handwriting. There were whole sections crossed out and individual words circled with exclamations and question marks in red. It was obviously a first draft of something.

I am trying to put things in order, so they make sense for you. Some of it isn't pretty. Bloody terrifying, when I look back. But I refuse to lie. (I've done enough of that.)

I've kept accounts. Sort of. Rough ones of myself and my friends so you can see for yourself. Decide what you make of me: your mother. I've written to people. Asked them to send on all the letters and photos, the articles and notes from me and others. Once they start coming in, I'll pin some explanations onto the bits and pieces that don't make sense, hoping you'll be able to follow my tracks.

I don't want to gloss over any of it. These bits and pieces will tell you more about what it was really like than me simply explaining things in retrospect. But I'll try and do that, too.

Above all, I don't want to make excuses. I hate it when people say, 'Well, things were different then.'

Things are always different! There are always choices to be made. People always have to decide if they are going to stand by and watch or if they are going to jump in and get their hands dirty. That's what happened to me. I jumped in with the best of intentions and I got burnt. Badly, as it happened.

But then I burnt other people, too, as you will see.

I want to beg you; please don't judge me too harshly. At the same time I know you must judge as you see fit. All I ask is that you read everything, think about everything, before you decide.

You were born in the year of the hunger strike (1981) in Belfast. I don't know whether I should start there or not. I don't know how much you know. I've tried to get some idea about your attitudes to politics but you don't give away much. I can only assume you know nothing about what they call the Troubles. Anyway, my pregnancy was finally confirmed the day Raymond McCreesh died. I knew before that, of course, but I'd put off going to the doctor. What a year. What a crazy culmination of events. How can I begin?

The morning I went into labour with you, a bomb went off in the city. Three killed. I helped put it there.

I resented getting up onto the delivery table. I hated the whole experience. Not because of the pain, that was bad enough. But it just seemed like a waste of time. I should have been somewhere else. I felt vaguely humiliated to be where I was. I just wanted to get it over with and get out of there.

The hospital was the Royal Victoria, at the end of Falls Road. The best accident and emergency department in the world. Even the Yanks used to come to learn how to deal with the aftermath of terrorist shootings, bombs and mass disaster. My friend Annie was a nurse there and she wanted to be with me when you were born. It was her day off, and she was desperate to come and help. But I said no. I thought that if I didn't have any witnesses then it would be easier to forget.

This is harsh and hurtful, I know. But I'm not going to coat things with sentimentality. I'm trying to tell it the way it was.

Then you were born and they put you in my arms. I could tell they were trying to make me feel something. But all I saw was this little screwed up thing with black hair. Tiny.

'She's beautiful,' the nurse said, 'isn't she?'

I didn't answer. I suppose part of me could see that you were beautiful but I was already thinking of what was happening outside. They'd got Eamon a few weeks before and I couldn't think of anything else. I couldn't wait to get out of that place. I didn't want to play at being mummy while my friends were in danger. While my friends were dying. Declan had died by then. On the run down in County Armagh. Shot in *the back trying to get away. I know I was scared stiff that they'd have Pete and Robbie by the end of the day. But the hospital wouldn't let me out. I was bleeding too much and anyway there was all the paper-work about the adoption.*

Mum came in first. She looked so worried. And then when she saw you she just sat down and cried. I think I cried, too. Out of relief. I could see straight away that she loved you. She kept saying over and over again, 'Oh, the poor wee girl! The poor wee girl! (Just like they do in the North.) I remember wondering at the time if it might be genetic! I'd never known Mum to say 'wee' at home, have you? But her people came from up in Donegal way and it's the way they speak up there. Did you know that?

'Oh, we'll love her, Leonie,' she said. 'Don't you fear. She'll be well loved.'

Dad didn't say much. He looked around the ward. 'What are you involved in?' he said at last. I wouldn't answer him. 'Where is the father?' he said next. Once again, I wouldn't answer.

I never thanked Mum and Dad. Not properly. I was so relieved to see them come in, then within half an hour I was dying for them to leave. To take you off my hands.

The horn sounded again. Kit put the notebook into a folder then stuffed the lot into the black briefcase. She felt giddy walking to the door.

. . . a bomb . . . three killed . . . I helped put it there . . .

She would wait until she was alone. She needed absolute privacy to even take the words in.

Kit walked up to the car, trying to think clearly. She must contact Bernadette. Find out about this friend from overseas who Leonie had gone down to the city to meet. Maybe they'd had some kind of fight. Maybe the accident hadn't been an accident at all. Anything was possible . . .

CHAPTER ELEVEN

Brendan found his sweatshirt among the pile of clothes in the back room, pulled it on and let himself out into the cool night air. One good thing about working nights at Magic Pizza was the walk home. There wasn't much traffic around and the darkness was soothing after the noisy bustle of the café.

He let himself in through the front door and switched on the hall light. No one was in the front lounge or the kitchen. Within a week, their house had changed from a warm busy place into a blasted morgue. Kit had gone home to the country. Tamara was spending all her time over at her new boyfriend's place. Brendan had met the guy three times and each time disliked him more. Not that he'd said anything to Tam. Anyone could see she was smitten. Anyway, he knew that people had to work these things out for themselves. Brendan shook his head as he opened the fridge door. It never ceased to amaze him how women could be so stupid about guys. They refused to see what was patently obvious. He hadn't needed to be told by Tam that the guy had pissed off on two families already, or that he'd been inside for three months for battery with intent. No, that information was written all over his sharp little mug. The tight mouth, the wary flick of his sludge-coloured eyes, the way he kept clenching his fists when Brendan was in the room, like he was considering a punch-up any second. Some guys walking the streets should be back in the jungle and the fact that Tam's new man was one of them didn't give Brendan much pleasure.

He grinned to himself as he pulled a half finished carton of orange juice out of the fridge and took a couple of gulps. He'd last seen Lou two days ago. She'd shaved the front of her hair back so she had this enormous spooky forehead. And there were new silver studs around her mouth and eyebrows. The trip was obviously providing focus for a complete image overhaul. Brendan took another longer gulp of juice, noting the footsteps above him, the flushing of a toilet and then the click of high-heeled shoes walking back through to the front again. Gucci must be up there alone. He'd seen her other half, Calvin, speeding off in his little convertible just as he got home. Funny. She seemed to be home quite a bit lately.

Ah, God! He fell down into one of the kitchen chairs and looked around. He was tired as hell but he didn't feel like going to bed. Everything was pissing him off. There was all the stuff with Rory for starters. Fourteen years old and the kid was getting into one fix after another. Things were getting serious. The school had him on a good behavior bond. If he messed up one more time, he was going to be suspended. But the worst of it was that his mother seemed to be relying on Brendan to kick his brother back into shape.

He got up and hunted around the cupboards. Time to eat, but there was nothing much around. In the end he settled on some dry biscuits and a tin of smoked oysters. A couple of tomatoes sitting in the fruit basket and a wedge of cheese that had seen better days were added to the pile. He began to systematically build some sandwiches. There were his exam results, too. That had pissed him off. He'd passed, of course. Even got a few Second Class Honours. But he should have done better. His tutor had been disappointed in his results. He'd be lucky to scrape into Masters now when only a year ago he was hitting the top of his year in all his subjects. Maybe it was all this stuff with Rory. *And* all the bloody time he had to waste doing stupid things for his mother.

Nora Delaney was virtually illiterate. Brendan had to write letters for her, fill in forms, and explain all manner of other stuff that would have been easy if she could read above first grade standard. Brendan loved his mother fiercely but she could never say a simple *thank you*. He knew she *was* grateful but actually expressing it would bring out the fact that she relied on him totally, and Nora had always been a proud woman.

Brendan took the plate and juice and sat on the back step, light from the kitchen behind him spreading a yellow glow over the concrete and tin fence. The backyard looked better at night. You didn't see the squalor of the kicked-in rubbish bins, the rusted fence or the sad, half-dead geraniums that Tam had planted then forgotten to water. He began to eat his supper looking dolefully up at Mrs Boil's tom cat, Bruce, who was sitting on the fence staring down at him suspiciously.

Mrs Boil was a widow, with eyes as sharp as her cat's. The lifestyles of the student households surrounding her were of endless interest. She often sat on her front verandah in a wicker chair, back as straight as an iron bar, watching everyone coming and going, never missing a beat.

Brendan grinned. Big Bruce was probably thinking: What kind of idiot would sit on a stone step outside in the cold when he could be sitting on a cushioned chair inside? In the end you had to give it to cats. Their view of life was pretty cool. Sympathy was simply not their forté. Old Bruce the battler. Just looking at the torn off left ear and the patchy fur made Brendan feel he had some kind of kindred spirit living right nearby.

He got up slowly, shut the door on Bruce and lumbered towards

110

the stairs. At least he could sleep in in the morning. Then the phone rang. Brendan groaned and slowly retraced his steps.

'It's me, Brendan.'

'Kit!' He hadn't allowed himself to even think how much he'd missed Kit over the last week. 'How's it going up there?'

'Okay,' she hesitated. 'Sorry you couldn't get through.'

'How's your sister?' Brendan began. 'Er, sorry, I mean your mother?'

They both laughed, and the tension eased.

'So you heard?' Kit said.

'Yeah.'

'She's doing okay, apparently,' Kit said, and then quickly, her voice low, 'but Brendan, where were you born?'

'Ireland.'

'Yeah, but where?'

'The North,' he said shortly. 'Derry. What do you want to know for?'

'Shit! I didn't know that! What was it like? Can you remember it? Were you *involved*?'

'In what?'

'All the Troubles?'

'I was ten when I left there, Kit.'

'Yeah, but what about your family? Were your mother or father involved at all?'

'Of course,' Brendan said. 'Everyone was involved.'

'Can you remember much?'

'Ah, shit. What do you want to know for?'

'Well, that's where I was born, too!' she burst out. 'In the North, anyway. In a hospital in Belfast. Didn't Tam tell you?'

'I haven't seen Tam for days.'

Brendan didn't understand why, but even the mention of the place where he'd spent his first years made him want to heave. No,

111

he hadn't known Kit had been born in the North. Tam had just said Ireland and he'd assumed Dublin or some little picturesque place on the west coast.

'So who was your old man then?' he asked calmly, but his voice sounded like an echo, as if someone else might have been asking the question.

'That's what I want to know!' Kit was almost yelling. 'Do you remember the hunger strike?'

Brendan opened his mouth to speak, but found that he couldn't. His heart seemed to lurch into a new rhythm: faster, stronger, like he was running towards some place. But no . . . he was trying to escape. This was completely ridiculous. Tears were welling in his eyes.

'Brendan? You there?'

'Yeah. I remember the hunger strike.'

'You sound weird, Bren. What's the matter?'

'I can't really talk about it now, okay?' he said, his voice thick.

'*Not* okay!' she shouted down the phone at him. 'Why not? I need to know stuff. I'm reading all this crap my mother wrote, and I don't understand any of it!'

Kit's outrage broke the strange knot inside Brendan. All the plugs that kept him intact were being pulled out one by one, and whatever it was that was essentially *him*, was running out through the holes. The thick skin he'd built up over himself was just sliding away and letting it happen.

He began to laugh, but at the same time tears were splashing down his cheeks.

'And Bobby Sands?' Kit went on.

'I went to Bobby Sands' funeral,' he managed to get out. 'I was five years old. It's my earliest memory. I sat on my father's shoulders, all the way down Falls Road, to the Milltown Cemetery. The crowd was huge. One-hundred-thousand people followed the coffin.

Everyone was quiet, except for the people crying. They put these screens up to shield the unionists from chucking rocks at us. He went sixty-six days without food . . .'

He stopped. How come all this stuff was still inside him?

'So, you were there?' Kit said.

Brendan didn't answer. He was back there, riding on his father's broad shoulders. Feeling the breeze in his face. Flicks of hard rain on his cheeks, making his father's hair flatten down across his head. The pain and the anguish and the pride flowing around him. Only five, but he could feel it. Thick as honey but not sweet. Not sweet at all. Bitter and old as centuries.

'Tell me about it, Bren,' she said gently.

'I can't, Quinlan,' he muttered. 'It was like, he was, he was giving his life for us.' Brendan struggled for words. 'That's what it felt like. It was like being at *the crucifixion*. It just went on and on. By the end of it ten of them had done it. Ten dead. It was just *terrible*. It was fantastic.'

Brendan pulled his hanky from his jeans and wiped his dripping nose. Shit. She asks him a couple of questions and he falls to pieces.

'So do you think your mother was involved?' he asked.

'I know she was.'

'How do you know?'

'I've found some stuff she'd written. Brendan, I'm desperate to find out about my father, but there's all this political stuff, too. I know my father was in jail when I was born, but she talks about guys in the *movement*? They're her friends. What does that mean?'

'The Republican movement,' he said.

'Oh,' Kit was thoughtful. 'Is that the IRA then?'

'Probably.'

'Oh shit,' Kit said. 'All the stuff they do. The killing. The bombing. Jeez, Brendan. It's hard reading this. I don't know what to make of it.'

113

'I reckon they're heroes.'

'Who? The IRA?'

'Yeah.'

Brendan remembered again. He was seven or eight this time, and too scared to speak. All of them – Brendan, his sisters, his mother – sitting around the tea table, with fresh white bread, jam and a cup of sweet milky tea each, listening to his father. Big Joe Delaney was a heavy man, bulky, but he could move fast and hit hard. He had thick red hands with fingers like sausages, and a hard impatient voice. He didn't like small talk. He knew what was what.

'All of them?'

'Well . . .'

'Brendan! How can you say that? I mean what if there was . . . I'm not sure about any of this.'

'Kit, I can't talk about this stuff now.'

'Okay,' she sighed, then her voice brightened. 'I'm coming down for Lou's party.'

'Great!' The great black insect weighing Brendan down began to crawl away. 'It'll be great to see you. We can talk more then. Okay?'

'I'm relying on you, Bren. I mean *seriously* relying on you. Did Tam tell you she ran into Sebastian at uni?'

'No.'

'She's asked him, too! Said he's coming. God, I'm so nervous. I can't miss it.'

'Okay. Well, I'll see you then.'

CHAPTER TWELVE

It was my job to watch. To drive our volunteers places. And wait for them. I had a legitimate job as well, as a librarian in a girls' school. So it was ages before anyone caught on.

But all this is jumping the gun, as Dad would say. I have to go back to when I was first involved. Tell you why I got involved. I'm doing this for myself as much as for you. I want to understand the shift that happens. The one that happened to me, anyway. One day you're a sympathetic observer, then the next, well, the next day you're part of it. You're willing to die for it.

And you're willing to kill for it.

So what happens?

This is so hard to think about. Please bear with me, Kathleen. Forgive me.

I came to the North because I was chasing someone. His name was Tom. We'd met in Paris. Now isn't the time to go into detailed descriptions of Tom – that humourless, arrogant, skinny goat of a man. I followed him from Paris to Belfast and I got myself a job in a school there. In the library. And I found a tiny bedsitter near the university. I was twenty-two. The soldiers on the street didn't worry me, nor did the road-blocks, bombings, shootings and beatings that were on the news every night and in the papers in the morning. I blocked it out, like everyone else who wasn't directly involved. And the cold. That first year I hardly noticed that terrible grey Belfast blackness that sets in by November and doesn't lift for months. None of it worried me. I had my man.

I had no idea who Tom was, really. Nor where he'd come from. He refused to bring me home to meet his family in Portadown. I was terribly hurt about this initially. I think for a few months there I wanted to marry him! Have babies and everything. Then I heard about his family from someone else and I understood. They were bigoted Unionists who would have slit their throats (or mine) before having me in their house. So I didn't push it after that.

Oddly enough, Tom, in spite of all his faults, was not a bigot. He'd travelled overseas and it had given him a distaste for sectarianism of any kind.

I know why I fell for him. There is nothing so attractive as someone who knows their own mind, especially when you don't know yours! Put that with someone on a mission and, hey, you've got the most attractive man in the world. Women, poor silly sods that we are, fall at their feet!

On some primitive, unconscious level we must think that all that confidence is going to protect us. What a joke! Protection is the last thing on their minds.

Tom taught me to despise my femaleness. His inadequacies as a person were revered as commendable traits in the circles we moved in, and I went along with it. Coldness, rigidity, a sort of disdain for the ordinary, even as he professed to be making works of art for 'the people'. My emotionalism, my love of pretty clothes and 'girl talk' was evidence of my inferior brain. It didn't take long for me to fall into line, to repress my natural joy at being young and interested in all that life had to offer and join him in his contempt of me. Isn't it funny the way

116

men can do that to women sometimes! They need our femaleness; our gaiety, our gentleness, the soft yielding warmth of our bodies, then turn around and despise us for those very same things.

Anyway, Tom was nothing. A no-talent parasite I was lucky to get rid of when I did. I write of him only to explain how and why I ended up in Belfast.

I suppose it was a few months after Tom and I were finished that I made the shift – the one I was talking about earlier. Maybe that's why I'm harping on about him. He was the beginning. 'Leonie's bad beginning', some would say. There were so many other good people, your father among them. Yes, I will write of him. But not now.

Forgive me, Kathleen. Forgive me for everything.

I think most people are waiting around for something to happen to them. For a while we're duped. We think that meaning is going to come and hit us, smack bang in the head. So we wait around for all to be revealed. We look at others and think that they must have the secret. Why else do they smile so much? But all that happens is that time passes. Our days are little stones cast out of our pockets into the bottom of a river. One after another. And at the end – just a pile of stones. Until you do something, it stays like that – a pile of stones.

Well, I decided to do something.

I can remember when I first noticed her. Nuala Boylan. A tall thin girl of sixteen with long dark hair and white skin in her last year of school. Eyes like two oval cut-out pieces of summer sky. But she wasn't pretty. She was far too intense to be called pretty.

The details are important. So I'll try to paint a picture of what happened. To her and to me.

Sister Lorna was holding a small senior class. History, I think it was. The builders were renovating the senior school, section by section and so sometimes classes had to be held in the library. Sister Lorna was a nice old bird. She had lots of spark and good humour. Probably not so old, either. When I think of it, she probably wouldn't have been more *than fifty. But to me (and of course to you now) that seemed ancient.*

It was the end of class and she was taking up work, checking names off a list. Was there anyone who hadn't done this last important essay? One girl stood up and to my surprise the others groaned as though this was what they all expected and wasn't it just so boring.

'Why not, Nuala Boylan?' Sister demanded, her bright brown eyes flashing furiously in the plump rosy face.

'I wasn't allowed out to the library, Sister,' the girl answered quietly, her face white and grave.

'And just how far is the library from your home, Miss?'

Although these scenes about homework happened every day, this time I found myself stopping to watch. I thought the nun was being deliberately obtuse; anyone could tell that this girl was telling the truth.

'Just down the street, Sister,' Nuala Boylan answered. I said her name to myself. Nuala. There was something about her, some steady flame inside her that I felt drawn to. She was refusing to be shamed by the nun's blustering but at the same time she was quietly well-mannered.

'Well, you're a big girl,' the nun said. 'I find it hard to believe that you couldn't have gone down the street, after your dinner.'

'There was a bomb-scare in our street last night, Sister,' the girl replied. 'No one was allowed out for five hours.'

The nun sighed as if this was just the latest lame excuse from someone who was too lazy to do her work.

'Well, dear, there are no bomb-scares around here,' she said. The other girls tittered. 'So you can stay back after school next Thursday and finish it in this library.'

This Catholic school took girls from all over the city. It was a selective school and so only the very brightest were accepted. The vast bulk of them came from the more well-off areas, areas that were not directly involved with the war. It's hard to believe, but in spite of the roadblocks, the armed British soldiers in the streets, the almost daily accounts in the papers of sectarian shootings and terrorist

118

activity, the war (for that is what it was) was rarely even mentioned in the school, except perhaps in morning prayers.

'Let us pray for peace in our city. For the leaders on both sides to work out their differences with open hearts,' the head nun would piously intone at the beginning of Friday morning assembly. And everyone would bow their heads and say 'Amen'. And that was the end of it. Even in the staffroom, the talk was all about the weather, and the holidays and who was going where, and who was seen going out with whom. The war was not happening in these people's lives. It was happening over there, in West Belfast, the Falls area and the Shankill, and in other, poorer parts of the city that most of these girls never went to. Shootings and beatings, knee-cappings and murders were happening only two kilometres away. My interest was caught because this girl seemed to be living right in the middle of it.

I watched the girls file out chattering together and then noticed that Nuala had stayed back. She disappeared behind the bookshelves at the far end of the room.

When I went over, I was shocked to find Nuala hunched up in the corner, sobbing her heart out. I hesitated. Not because I didn't want to comfort her, I did. But she seemed so contained there. Like it was her own private space. I didn't want to intrude. Eventually she looked up. Startled, she immediately stopped crying, got to her feet, and wiped her eyes and nose.

'Sorry, Miss,' she mumbled, picking up her bag and positioning it over her arm, 'I'm going now.'

'It's okay,' I said, moving closer. 'Don't let Sister Lorna upset you.' I smiled, trying to make light of the nun's attitude.

Nuala didn't answer. She was fumbling around in her bag for a fresh tissue.

'She doesn't mean it,' I continued stupidly, pulling some fresh tissues from my sleeve and handing them to her. I don't know why I

119

felt I should stick up for the nun and make light of this girl's tears but that's what I did.

Nuala blew her nose. 'It's not her,' she said quietly. 'I don't care about her.'

'Oh?' I said, surprised. 'So what is it?'

The girl shot me a look of angry impatience and I felt myself wilt. It was such an adult look, filled with irritation, and not one I was used to getting from sixteen-year-old students. I was miffed at first and a bit torn. Should I pull rank and act like a teacher or simply treat the girl as an equal? To my credit I decided on the latter. Mainly, I have to say, because I was curious.

'Where do you come from?' I asked.

'Lower Falls,' she said, moving to the door.

'Can I give you a ride home then?' I asked. I thought, what the hell, why not? I didn't know West Belfast at all. It was less than a couple of kilometres from the central business district and although I'd been living in the city for close on a year I'd only driven through once. My friend Annie took me on a tour not long after I'd arrived. Small narrow streets, rows and rows of tenement houses. Crowded and poor. Only ten minutes passing through and I found the heavy army presence so oppressive that I actually felt guilty of some crime, which was so ridiculous. I wondered, in my privileged, middle-class way, how people could possibly live there. Why didn't they just move out? As if they had a choice!

'I don't think so!' Nuala actually laughed. A bit nastily. Once again, so adult; as though she knew all sorts of things that I didn't. 'It would be more trouble than it's worth.'

'How do you mean?'

'Roadblocks are extra bad at the moment.'

'Why is that?'

She shrugged. 'The usual,' she began, then stopped and looked at me. What do you want to know for? she seemed to be saying. I stared

120

back at her. It was a very odd moment, the two of us in the corner of the library, each willing the other to look away first.

'They lifted our Martin last night,' she whispered.

'They?'

'The Brits,' she snapped angrily.

'And Martin is?'

'My brother.' She was weeping again, but this time not bothering to cover her face, the tears gushing from her eyes, and every now and again she'd take a furious swipe at them with her fist. 'And they pulled our house apart again. With Mammy sick and all . . .'

'What were they looking for?' I asked blandly.

The poor girl was in such a state that my first instinct was to draw her to me, but of course I didn't. She didn't even want to talk to me. Who was I? Only another teacher. Someone with a funny accent from a different world altogether. But she needed to spill her guts to somebody. Maybe my Australian accent made her feel a little freer to talk.

'Guns,' she muttered, 'and explosives.'

'Did they find any?'

'Of course not!' she fumed. 'They knew they wouldn't. They were just picking on us. Making things difficult because of Daddy.'

'What does he do?'

'Oh, he has men around and . . .' She flushed and hesitated.

'Men?'

'We've got a poster in the front window supporting the prisoners in Long Kesh,' she said quickly. 'So they pick on us all the time.'

'Are there other people they pick on?'

'Oh, of course,' she said furiously. 'They're always stopping us in the street, abusing us!'

'So they pulled your house apart last night?'

'We were up for four hours in the kitchen. They broke down our front door, pulled every board off our bedroom wall. They smashed Mammy's holy pictures and her little statue of the Virgin she got when her sister died. Laughing all the time . . . and Pearse and Kevin, they're the twins, they're only nine. My brothers. They started screaming and Kevin wet his pants and they wouldn't let him go to the bathroom for ages to clean up. It's our house! But they made him stay in his pyjamas for an hour or more getting cold and then they . . .'

She couldn't go on. Her teeth were chattering and she was trembling all over. I realised that the girl was completely traumatised. It was so weird to think of her standing up in class only half an hour before, having to explain about something as ordinary as homework.

'Martin is artistic,' she was almost screaming at me, blotting her eyes with the handful of tissues. 'He shouldn't have to suffer for what Daddy does!'

'No,' I murmured, 'he shouldn't.' I was wondering all the time what exactly Daddy did.

'He was getting his folio ready for his A Levels,' she gasped. 'Beautiful drawings. And they . . .' she slumped down onto the carpet again, sobbing, 'they tore them all to pieces! Now he's got nothing. It's all he wanted, to get into the tech school and do Commercial Art.'

'No!' I was genuinely outraged by this. I don't quite know why but I'd pictured an older brother, well into his twenties. I suppose underneath I thought that this brother was guilty of something too. Otherwise why would the army be after him? But if he was doing his A levels he wouldn't have been more than seventeen.

'He's my twin,' she explained.

'Was Martin involved at all with anything?' I asked gently, sitting down next to the girl, putting my arm around her. 'Any unlawful stuff?'

She shrugged me off. 'No!' she yelled.

'Okay,' I said, trying to calm her.

'Just because he's a young fellow from the Falls, everyone assumes he's involved but he isn't. He hates the Brits like the rest of us, but he's never been involved. Daddy let him alone a long time ago when Declan got caught.'

'Who's Declan?'

'My other brother,' she whispered. 'The eldest.' She covered her face with her hands. 'But he's dead now.'

So that's how it all began for me. After Tom, I had space in my life. Gradually Nuala Boylan and her family began to fill it.

I took her home that night. We had tea and toast at a little café first. There had been seven children in the family. Now there were six. One other older son had left to marry and now lived in America. Her mother was a cleaner in the Royal Victoria hospital. A lot of the caring of the three younger children fell to Nuala and to a lesser extent Martin. Her mother's health had deteriorated over the last few years. I couldn't get out of her exactly what was wrong, except that there was a problem with her nerves and she had to take pills. Nuala did the shopping for the family supper, cooked it, made sure they ate, then supervised them until her mother came home from work.

All this was wrung out of the girl with enormous difficulty. Having broken down in front of me, she was now suspicious that I might be going to do some kind of number on her. But she needed to talk, too. So the conversation was sporadic. Big silences of sipping our tea, then it would all spill out as though she was unable to help herself.

We went through three checkpoints on our way into the Falls. The whole area was a ghetto, barricaded in with huge steel fences and concrete roadblocks. It was almost completely dark and the soldiers looked in my boot and back seat with a torch. They shone the torches in our faces too, which I found threatening. Nuala sat next to me, staring ahead grimly as though none of it was happening. They checked my identity and asked why I was in the area.

'I suppose you're used to all this,' I said lightly, as I turned into her street.

'I'll never get used to it,' she snapped, her eyes blazing with hatred. 'Never! I'm Irish. This is my country!'

123

Her house was grey brick, the fifth one along in a row of identical houses in a small street just off from a main road. She didn't ask me in. In one sense I was relieved. I didn't want to stay on this bleak narrow street any longer than I had to, but I was curious, too. I would have liked to go inside if only to see how you fitted seven people into such a tiny place. But Nuala was thanking me and leaving before it came to that. I had the feeling that she regretted having confided in me, and that she would try to put as much distance between us as she could.

But I was wrong. The next day she sought me out in the library, her manner a lot brighter. Martin was free, she told me. They'd only held him a few hours. He was back home.

'Fantastic,' I said. 'Your mother will be pleased.'

'We all are,' she said. For the first time she looked like who she was: a young girl.

'What normally happens?' I asked. 'I mean, what were you afraid would happen to him?'

'Sometimes they get held for days,' she said. 'Then they pin stuff on them and make them sign false confessions. But Martin is okay now. We're all telling him to keep his head down. He's got to get through his exams.'

'What about the drawings?' I asked tentatively, not wanting to spoil her mood. But I'd woken up in the middle of the night thinking about the soldiers ripping up the boy's artwork.

'Ah, well,' she shrugged philosophically. 'That's the way it goes. He's going to concentrate on his exams now, build up his folio and try again next year.'

We talked a lot after that. She would sometimes wait for me after school. I knew she liked talking to me, and that she was lonely. We both were, actually. We were both fish out of water in that school. I couldn't seem to make friends on the staff, although everyone was polite enough. I don't know that Nuala liked me that much, but I was somebody who believed her when she spoke about her life. Someone

124

who was interested. She told me that when she'd tried to explain to her classmates what happened in her neighbourhood they usually laughed.

'That doesn't really go on!' they'd jeer. 'That's the Provos' propaganda!'

'Pull the other one!'

'My mammy said half of it is made up.'

But by that stage I'd begun to read Irish history. The more I read, the more I wondered how the school could be so complacent. These present day Troubles had begun hundreds of years before! Irish history was a wild, intoxicating story of great injustice, great bravery. Of martyrs and fighters. Cowards and infiltrators. Of savage repression and heroic rebellion. Of a people stripped of their lands, their religion and their language, yet still refusing to submit. And now the fight continued right into the end of the twentieth century in this tiny Northern province – the last outpost of the British empire. The more I read, the more the present-day life around me seemed imbued with history. I became like one of those converts to a new religion. I couldn't believe that others around me didn't find it as fascinating as I did. I probably bored everybody senseless.

It's only in Australia that we think that history doesn't matter. We think that everything more or less started when we were born, or at best when our grandparents were kids! Well, in that place, things were different. History was everywhere. I don't mean statues or ceremonies, or museums, but in the way people think and the way they live.

I think my interest thrilled Nuala. I began reading the papers again. Properly. There were hundreds of Republicans in jail at this time, 'on the blanket' – refusing to wear prison uniforms or do prison work until they regained their status as political prisoners. They wanted to live separately from the other prisoners, and to conduct educational classes. These were the ones Nuala and her family were supporting with their posters. The lengths these guys went to were totally bizarre or heroic, depending on your point of view. They refused to speak to the guards, to wash or do work, and they covered their prison cells with their own filth. I'd read the accounts of it before but had discounted it as too revolting to even think about. But with Nuala I began to see it as part of a continuum of revolt; action rooted in a sense of history. I became interested. Sympathetic. Why did political status mean so much to them? What were they fighting for really?

The more I read, the more I saw Nuala and her family not as simple people battling the odds but representative of a whole class of Irish people who had been repressed for generations.

Then the crisis happened. Nuala's father was charged with conspiracy to murder and the next day her mother was taken to hospital, seriously ill. Nuala came to tell me on the Friday that she would not be back at school the next week. There would be no point her sitting the exams because she wouldn't be able to study. I went to the head nun and begged for some kind of help for the girl. Surely there was something that could be done for her? Sister Paul was outwardly sympathetic but I could tell she had already made up her mind.

'This kind of thing happens to our girls from time to time,' she said shortly. 'The school can't take responsibility.'

'There must be some way she can stay at school,' I protested.

'We don't condone the kind of political activity her father is accused of,' she countered.

This made me furious. Whatever happened to innocent until proven guilty?

'I'm not saying that you should, Sister,' I said. 'Merely that the girl shouldn't suffer for what the father does.'

'Those kinds of attitudes do tend to get passed on,' the nun said, 'from one generation to the next. If you see what I mean.'

'Well, no,' I said, forcing myself to be polite. 'What do you mean, Sister?' But I knew of course. They didn't really want girls in the school whose fathers were criminals.

'The girl would be welcome back the next year if her circumstances change,' was the final decision.

Well, that's when I decided that I would pitch in. I thought I might as well, there was nothing else going on in my life. I was twenty-three, but I felt so old. So finished. No one loved me and I had no one to love.

I went to see Nuala the following Monday after school. I told her to get back into her uniform the next day, that I would move into her house and take over her mother's duties – all the shopping, cooking and caring for the little ones after school – so that she and her brother could get to the library and sit their exams. If no one wanted me, then at least I could be useful.

Big hearted of me, wasn't it? You can't imagine how unpopular it made me with the teachers at school. How suspicious they were! I think from the time she heard, the head nun was looking for a way to kick me out. I made sure I kept my head down and became conscientious. I knew I really needed the job if I was going to help Nuala.

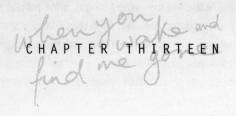

CHAPTER THIRTEEN

Relief flooded through Kit's body as she felt the train pull away from the station. It was early morning and as she looked out and waved to Johnny, she felt excited. *Away, away, away.* Rivulets of water ran helter-skelter down the window near where she sat. Blasts of wind made them spread into weird horizontal lines and splotches over the glass, making a fresh spurt of good humour rise inside Kit all over again. *Wild.* Spring rain. She loved the train; she loved the enforced idleness and privacy of the three hours it took to get down to the city. She could withdraw into herself, let her mind wander.

God knows, she had enough to think about. She looked about her, pleased that so far she was virtually alone. There were only half a dozen other people in the carriage. She fumbled in her overnight bag and drew out the exercise book. She wanted to read over Leonie's stuff again in peace, and work out some basic questions to ask Brendan.

Bernadette had rung from Sydney the night before and seemed relieved when Kit told her she now knew that Leonie was her mother.

'Kathleen, at last!' she'd exclaimed. 'I'm so glad. It was silly to wait so long. I think Leonie was scared, or something.'

'Yes,' Kit had replied shortly.

'So I imagine it was a shock,' Bernadette had continued kindly.

'Well, yes,' Kit had said, 'but do you know who Leonie was meeting on the night of the accident?'

'Darling, I don't. If only I'd asked. All I know is that it was someone from overseas. A friend. She was going out with them to dinner and then coming back to stay at my place. I was going to catch up with her the following night.'

'Do you know if it was a male or female?'

'I assumed it was a female friend, but I couldn't swear to it.'

'And my . . . father?'

'Yes . . .'

'Do you know anything about him?'

'I don't really. No.'

'You don't know his name?'

'I'm sorry, darling. She never told me anything.'

'Eamon? Would she have spoken to you about an Eamon or a Declan or . . .' Kit thought back to the bits and pieces of Leonie's writing, 'a Pearse at all?'

'I don't remember those names,' she'd said, 'and I think I would remember if she had. But Kathleen?'

'Yes.'

'I'll think about all this some more. I'll let you know if I remember anything.'

'Thanks, Bernadette. It's just that I'd like . . . I *need* to know.'

'Of course you do.'

'Did you ever ask her?'

'About your father?'

'Yes.'

'I did, but she never said much. She implied that . . . oh, darling this might be painful for you.'

'Please tell me.'

'That it was an unimportant affair. That they weren't really all that close.'

'Oh.' Kit had felt suddenly beaten.

'But that might have just been her way of fobbing me off,' Bernadette had said. 'Knowing Leonie, I'm sure that he would have meant a lot to her.'

'Yes, well . . .' Kit hadn't felt so strongly herself. 'Maybe you're right.'

After ten days, Kit had been dying to get back to the city. She was tired of the sympathetic looks from her family whenever she came into a room. 'She's taking it so well,' she heard Aunty Eileen whisper to a neighbour who'd come with a batch of scones. 'It almost makes you wonder if it's properly registered yet.'

A day early, too. What luck. The arrangement had been that she'd leave on the day of the party. But then Brendan had called and said that Tam was in some kind of trouble, that he really didn't want to talk about it on the phone but could she come as soon as possible.

So Kit had announced to her family that her best friend was in trouble, and that she had to go *that very day*. She caught the look that passed between her parents and aunts and nearly exploded. *Did they want her to stay up here forever!* Damn it, she had a life and she had a right to get back to it – at least for a bit.

'What friend's trouble could be more important than your own poor mother's condition?' Moya had whispered to her over the washing-up, but this only made Kit more determined to go. Moya was such a control freak. Anyway, she really did have to go to uni and fix things up for next year. She had to see Wally at the pub, too, and explain the situation in person. Just phoning him wouldn't be right. Then there was the party, and she wanted to see Lou before she left. And there was Sebastian too, of course.

Two days earlier, Leonie had smiled. Up till then no one knew if she understood them as they held her hand and spoke gentle words while she lay in her hospital bed. The stimulation did her good, the nurses explained. Who knew quite what she actually heard?

In spite of the nurses' assurances, Kit knew that over the last few days her parents had become dispirited with Leonie's lack of response. The family's hopes had been raised with her survival through the first critical period, but this next stage seemed to be taking so long. Even the surgeon was a little baffled; all the signs were that Leonie was on the brink of regaining consciousness, but, although her eyes would open sometimes, she didn't seem able to focus, and she gave no indication that she understood anything. She was still in intensive care but some of the tubes had gone. She gave no sign of recognition to those standing around her bedside.

Until two days ago.

Kit had come in later than the rest of her family. Only two visitors were meant to be at her bedside at a time but by this stage the nurses had eased up a little. The family was so big and as there were no other patients in the ward, the tacit agreement was that a crowd around her bed, as long as they were reasonably subdued, would do no harm. They were all taking a turn to talk to Leonie, who'd been sat up a little higher on her pillows.

As soon as Kit moved in amongst her relatives, Leonie's eyes focused on her. Everyone noticed and moved back, waiting with bated breath. Something was going on behind the eyes. Kit was pushed forward.

'Here's Kathleen, darling,' Therese said gently, stroking Leonie's arm with one hand and pulling Kit nearer to the bed with the other. 'See, here's your little girl.'

Leonie frowned, her eyes still focusing intently on Kit. Then Leonie's mouth began to move and a few incoherent sounds emerged.

'Take her hand,' Therese whispered sharply to Kit. 'Sit here now, Kathleen, and talk to her.'

Awkwardly, Kit did as she was told.

'Hi, Leonie,' she managed. 'It's me, Kathleen. How are you feeling?'

That was when Leonie smiled. A watery, innocent, simple smile, like a baby's. Then it disappeared and Leonie closed her eyes and began to toss about the bed in a distressed state, shaking her head. Still holding her hand, Kit felt the pressure of Leonie's fingers around her own.

'She's squeezing my hand, Mum,' Kit whispered, her voice trembling. 'See here . . .' she pointed at the hand that was holding Leonie's, 'see, she's squeezing my fingers.'

'Oh, thank God,' Therese whispered, kneeling down by the bed. 'She's coming back to us.' Tears were streaming down her exhausted face. 'Thanks be to God!'

That night Kit got stuck into Gerard's sherry when everyone else was in bed. Sitting by the fire on her own in the semi-darkness, her mood turned maudlin. It was nearly midnight when she rang Brendan. Thankfully, he was home.

'Promise me something, Brendan,' she said as soon as he answered the phone.

'Anything,' he said quickly, and a rush of gratitude filled her head like a quick shower of summer rain. Brendan wasn't someone who insisted on chit-chat or preliminaries before getting down to the nitty-gritty and she loved that about him.

'When we're old and –'

'Oh, here we go . . .'

'No, I mean it.' Kit was half laughing and half crying. She knew he would be able to hear the drunken slur in her voice but didn't care. 'And our marriages have failed – I mean yours because you're such a mean stubborn bastard and me, well, I won't be married. So anyway, let's get together. So we don't have to live alone. We'll get a couple of granny flats next to each other and be companions on the journey to death.'

'Oh Jesus, Quinlan. You are sad. How many have you had?'

'Four glasses.'

'Four glasses of what?'

'Sherry.'

Brendan groaned.

'Sorry,' Kit went on, 'but I really do mean this. I don't want to live my old age alone.'

'Okay, it's a date,' Brendan laughed, 'but just for your information, Quinlan, I'm gunna have a fantastic life. I'm gunna have a great marriage. I'm gunna have four kids and –'

'Four?'

'Yeah,' he said, 'and I'm gunna be a brilliant engineer. One smart bastard . . .'

'What if your wife doesn't want four kids?'

'Well, three would do, at a pinch.'

'What are you saying to me?' Kit sniffed. 'You're going to leave me alone? I'm just going to be sitting out my time with no hubby, no kids, no job. I can't get on with people, Brendan. Even my mother, er, grandmother, she's like the nicest person on the earth and she's driving me nuts!'

'Stop calling her your grandmother,' Brendan said sharply.

'Well, she is!'

'Look, she's your mum in the real sense. She fed you and she looked after you, didn't she?'

Kit was now sobbing in drunken self-pity. 'In the *real* sense, she isn't my mum!' she shot back. 'My mum is in hospital. About to croak it. She's a liar! And a murderer. I told you about that stuff I read, didn't I?'

'Yeah, you told me,' Brendan cut in. 'Get a grip, Quinlan. And don't talk about things you don't understand.'

'Okay,' Kit sniffed again. 'I'll go now.'

'Go to bed, Kit.'

'Love you, Brendan.'

'Yeah,' he said softly. 'Okay.'

'Anything happening there I should know about?'

'Nothing, except I've got my brother with me. He caught sight of Gucci today and reckons I should start shagging her ASAP!'

'God!' Kit gave a sudden squeal. 'I can just imagine,' she laughed, 'she's a fourteen-year-old boy's fantasy!'

'You're not wrong.'

CHAPTER FOURTEEN

Brendan's mother had been on the phone at nine that morning.

'Rory's done a flit,' she snapped. 'The school's just rung. Didn't turn up yesterday and he's not there this morning. They wanted to know if he's home sick. I told them no way, he's –'

'You got any idea where he is?' Brendan cut in.

'How would I? He went off this morning at eight as usual, dressed for school.'

'Okay.'

Brendan was heartily sick of hearing about Rory. He wanted to tell his mother to forget about the little bastard and concentrate on the girls. Brendan's sisters were good kids and doing well at school. 'So what do you want me to do?' he muttered sourly.

'Can you come over?' He could hear the worry in her voice. 'Help me find him.'

'Right now?' he sighed.

'What's the matter?' she snapped impatiently. 'It's after nine.'

'Nothing, Mum,' he snarled, 'but I didn't get to bed until three.'

'Well, whose fault is that?'

'I was working,' Brendan said, 'at the café.'

'Oh.' Nora's tone changed a little but she remained defensive. 'I'm just sick with worry,' she said. 'These bloody drug-dealers are like blowflies around here now.' She gave an outraged snort. 'They're bloody brazen! In the laundries, in the bloody stairwells. You should see them. Nance Mallard's daughter is on it now. Selling herself, you know. And Ken –'

'Yeah, I know all about it, Mum. I used to live there, remember.'

'It's much worse now.'

'I know.' Everyone knew it was worse at the flats now. Every year it got worse.

'Did you give him a belting like I told you last week?' she snapped suddenly.

'No.' Brendan closed his eyes. It really cut him that whenever his mother felt powerless she reverted to violent solutions. If someone snubbed her in a shop, then she was going to 'punch their head in'. If someone tried to edge their way into the flower-arranging group at the local church (where she'd been in charge for the last ten years) then she would quick as lightning threaten to 'deck' them. She never followed through on any of her threats. The tough talk was just her way of coping.

'Well, you know it's just what he needs.'

'I'll be right over, okay?'

'Right, see you then.' She slammed the phone down.

Brendan walked into the bathroom and turned on the shower. The truth was, she treated him like a free taxi service. As he soaped himself he began to whistle 'It's a Beautiful Day'. Low at first. But by the time he was out, drying himself with the thin, damp towel, he'd cheered himself right up, singing loudly and whistling like a train.

'It's a beautiful day. Don't let it get away.'

When he walked out with the towel around his middle, Gucci was bouncing down the stairs to work. Brendan muttered a greeting then noticed that her eyes were all red and puffy.

'Hi,' she said in a small voice.

'G'day,' Brendan said gruffly, embarrassed to be caught in only a towel and singing at the top of his voice. He'd thought she'd have left for work by now. 'How's it going?'

'Okay,' she said gamely. 'You in tonight?'

'Er, yeah,' he stammered at last. 'Think so. I'm not working.'

'I just thought,' she took a gulp, 'we could eat together. We seem to be the only ones left around here lately.'

'Oh, right,' Brendan nodded, acting as if this was a normal suggestion. In fact, he'd lived ten months with the Labels and had never so much as had a cup of coffee with either of them. 'Okay, you're on.' He grinned suddenly. 'What will we have?'

'Snags!' she said immediately, with a slightly coy smile. 'There's a great butcher right near where I work. I'll pick some up.'

'Sounds good,' Brendan called, walking off towards his room. 'I'll get some salad stuff.' It was bad enough being caught half naked in front of Gucci, without hanging about all day talking to her.

He found his brother with assorted mates down near the Calder Bridge pathway. The mates all looked like deadbeats and they seemed a lot older than Rory. They were on something, too. Brendan hoped it was just the weed.

He grabbed Rory and hauled him off to the car. The kid grumbled and sulked but he didn't run and Brendan told himself that meant things hadn't got right out of hand. Brendan started the car and pulled out onto the freeway, all the time trying to work out what to say. Nothing came to mind. Let that little bugger explain himself. But Rory didn't say a word. He was sitting as far away from Brendan as he could, looking out the window, playing dumb.

'The old lady is fuming,' Brendan said.

Nothing. Rory didn't even grunt.

'So you don't like school at the moment?'

137

'What do you think?'

Brendan shrugged. He'd always liked school himself. Sure, in the younger grades it was hard-going with those big classes, the bullies and the mucking around. But once you got to year ten and the teachers knew you were serious, they helped. He'd had some great teachers. The worst thing about school for Brendan had been types like Rory: tough and aggressive and bent on destroying every class.

'I thought it was getting better for you,' he said calmly.

There was a pause.

'I haven't done the work,' Rory said in a slightly less aggressive voice. 'I'm way behind. I won't be able to catch up.'

'Bullshit, Rory! You're smart. If you want to, you can. You've been going these last few weeks, haven't you?'

Rory nodded and sighed.

'Come on.' Brendan felt completely inadequate to the task of getting his younger brother on track again. 'You see those deadbeats around who don't finish school. What have they got? You want to work in Coles all your life?'

Rory shrugged listlessly, staring straight ahead, but Brendan could tell he was listening and it gave him heart. 'You want to end up dealing? What a great life that'd be!'

'What are you talking about?' the kid muttered.

'Come on! I'm not a fool. Who were those guys back there?'

'Just guys.'

'Yeah, right! So what were you taking?'

'I didn't have anything.' Rory gave an angry snort. 'Didn't have no money.'

'But you've bought from them before, right?'

'Just a bit of weed,' the kid muttered. 'Hey, where we going now?' he asked suddenly.

Brendan sighed. 'You wanna come home with me?'

138

'Yeah.'

'All right, then.' Brendan would have much rather dumped Rory and got back to Richmond for an afternoon nap. 'Only if you swear you'll go to school tomorrow and you'll stay there.'

'Yeah, okay.'

Brendan didn't believe him for a minute. But he didn't want to have to deal with his angry mother, so the Richmond house seemed the next best option.

The afternoon turned out okay in the end. They rang Nora as soon as they got home and after she'd given Rory a loud piece of her mind, Brendan agreed to ring Rory's school and make an appointment for the next day with the Principal, to beg for another chance.

Then he spent two hours helping Rory with his maths. The kid was reluctant at first but after a while he settled down and agreed to do a whole set from his text book.

Brendan went out and bought some bread and cheese and made them some sandwiches down in the kitchen. When he brought them upstairs, he was surprised to see that Rory had continued working while he'd been away. All is not yet lost, he thought wryly. After explaining a new set of problems in the next chapter, Brendan left him to it. He lay down on his bed with an engineering text-book and promptly went to sleep.

It was after six when he was woken by a strange female voice calling out to him.

'Brendan! You up there?'

He sat up with a start. Rory was still at the desk, but playing the computer now. He turned around and grinned at Brendan.

'Good dream?' Rory smirked, and then proudly, 'I finished both sets.'

'Good.' Brendan yawned. 'Who was that?'

'You up there, Brendan?' The voice came again. Then he

twigged. It was Gucci! He groaned, remembering the meal, and the fact that he'd promised a salad.

'Yeah,' he called back, jumping off the bed and going to the door. 'I'm here. Fell asleep.'

She was standing at the bottom of the stairs looking up with those great big green eyes, the blond hair up in an untidy knot.

'You want to eat soon?' she said.

'Er, yeah. Whenever. But I forgot the salad.'

'No worries,' she smiled. 'I picked up some stuff. It won't exactly be gourmet.'

'Oh damn!' Brendan made a horrified face. She laughed. Then he remembered Rory.

'I got my brother here, too.'

'There'll be plenty,' she said easily and turned around, disappearing back into the kitchen.

Brendan grinned as he splashed cold water onto his face. Tam and Kit would be in hysterics if they knew he was about to eat a meal with Gucci. Did this constitute eating with the enemy?

It was good to see the old table set properly, with cutlery and glasses. The sky-blue tablecloth made the room come alive. It sure beat eating biscuits on his own again. Brendan smiled at Gucci who was standing at the stove testing the potatoes, then introduced his brother.

'Larissa, this is my brother, Rory.'

'Hi, Rory!' She turned around and smiled. 'Pleased to meet you.'

'Yeah, hi,' Rory mumbled.

'This is all right.' Brendan waved at the nicely set table. 'Thanks.'

'Yeah, well, I get sick of eating out.'

Gucci looked totally amazing as usual, in blue silk cargo pants and matching sleeveless top. She seemed cheerful enough, too. Certainly no mention was made of whatever had been making her cry that morning. She asked Rory a few questions about school, which he answered politely – Brendan could see that her looks had immediately put Rory in deep thrall – and then proceeded to tell them a couple of funny stories of her own school days at a boarding school in Sydney. Not all that funny, actually. But Brendan and Rory smiled, made the right noises and tucked in gratefully.

In fact, they had a nice meal together. Having Rory there somehow took any awkwardness away. The meal – potatoes in their skins, some fancy sausages, bread and salad – went down very well with the bottle of red that Brendan had brought down from his room, deciding at the last moment that it would be tight of him not to contribute something.

When Gucci went out to answer the phone towards the end of the meal, Rory turned to Brendan with real awe in his voice.

'Who *is* she?' he whispered.

'She lives upstairs with her boyfriend,' Brendan replied, reaching for a crusty white roll and spreading on thick butter. 'Haven't you seen her before?'

'Jeez,' Rory shook his head in amazement, 'why can't you get a girlfriend like that?'

Brendan laughed.

'She's like a friggin' model!' the kid continued. 'Better!'

'Yeah, well,' Brendan took a bite and followed it with a deep gulp of wine, 'not all of us are lucky, heh?'

'Why don't you hit on her while the boyfriend's out?'

'God, Rory,' Brendan laughed, 'what movies have you been watching lately?'

'Nah,' Rory shook his head, frowning, 'you're in with a chance, you know.'

'Yeah, well,' Brendan said gruffly, 'just keep your imagination for your schoolwork, heh?'

'I reckon she's hot for ya!' the kid proclaimed with a sudden grin. 'Why do you think she cooked this meal and everything?'

'Didn't you hear her? She didn't feel like eating out.'

'Someone like that,' Rory went on, 'you'd be mad not to try to give her one. She'd probably go like a rabbit!'

'Watch your mouth.' Brendan cuffed his brother over the ear, then stood up to clear the plates. 'Or you might find yourself in deep trouble.'

'Already am,' Rory said cheekily. 'I'm in a lot of trouble already, aren't I?'

Brendan had started washing up when Gucci came back into the room. She seemed surprised that the meal was finished, but sat down, poured herself another glass of wine, and lit up a cigarette.

'So how's the city job going?' he asked.

'It's okay,' she said, pinning two clumps of her beautiful long hair back from her face with a couple of clips from the pocket of her trousers. 'Bit sick of it, actually. Looking for a new challenge.'

'In the same area?' Brendan wasn't really interested, but thought he might as well make a bit of polite conversation.

'I might go overseas,' she said, then turned and smiled at Rory. 'You look a bit like Tom Cruise. Has anyone ever told you that?'

Rory shook his head, blushing deeply. Seeing his embarrassment made Brendan and Gucci laugh.

'Go Rory!' Brendan shouted. In fact, the kid *was* good looking. His features were strong; straight nose, nice wide smile, even teeth, and the heavily lidded brown eyes gave his face a sort of dozy, sexy attractiveness.

'Shut up.'

'It's true,' she said sweetly. 'Ever thought of being an actor?'

'Nah.'

Brendan looked at his brother, thinking that it was good to see the smart-mouthed little bastard flummoxed for once.

When the kitchen was more or less in order, Gucci went upstairs, and Brendan decided to hit the books for a few hours. He

142

left Rory in the front room watching television but had only been at his desk for half an hour when he heard the phone ring.

'It's for you,' Rory called up. 'Hey, Brendan!'

Brendan snapped the huge text book shut and got up grumpily. He went to the phone.

'It's Tam, Bren.'

'What's the matter?' Brendan could hear the tears in her voice.

'I . . .' But she couldn't speak. She was gasping and gulping for air. 'Can you come and get me?' she finally managed.

'Where are you?'

'I'm on Chapel Street,' she managed to whisper. On the corner of Commercial Road.'

'Okay,' Brendan sighed, 'I'll be there. You've had a fight or something?'

'And Brendan?' Tam said, ignoring the question, 'I think I'm going to have to go to hospital or see a doctor or –'

'Shit, Tam!'

'I know, I know,' she stifled a sob. 'Don't say anything. Just come and pick me up.'

CHAPTER FIFTEEN

when you wake and find me gone

Kit pushed the front door open.

'Hello!' she called into the empty hallway, 'I'm back!'

No answer. Dropping her bag, she let the door slam and went down the hall towards the kitchen, making as much noise as she could.

'Come on!' she called, then under her breath, 'be home, you mongrels! *Please* be home.'

Where were they? Kit looked at her watch. Just on midday. Brendan could be at work, but what about Tam? Surely Brendan had told her that Kit was coming back a day early especially for her. Kit went back up the hall, collected her bag and went into her room.

She shut the door behind her and looked around. Everything was just as she'd left it, down to the one dead rose in the Vegemite jar on her dressing table. Closing her eyes, she crushed the dry petals in her fingers. This was her room, her bed with the faded pink doona cover and saggy pillows, her little chest of drawers that Brendan had found for her at an auction. The long mirror with flecked gold wooden edges had been a birthday present from Tam.

Kit unzipped her bag on the bed. Along with all the clothes and shoes, she took out Leonie's exercise book and dumped it on her side table.

It was ridiculous, but the book seemed alive in some way. Almost menacing. It lay there like a flat squat animal, loose pages spilling out like bared teeth. Kit had a sudden urge to pick it up and throw it as far away as she could. Down some chute maybe, where all that mish-mash of memory and excuse and half-hearted pleas for understanding could be minced up into tiny pieces. What, after all, did she care about unhappy schoolgirls in Ireland twenty years ago? Or families going crazy because of army harassment? When it came down to it, what Leonie did over there had nothing to do with her. That scratchy, almost incomprehensible scrawl of her mother's had told her nothing about what she really wanted to know. It was only a rough draft – not in any way finished or worked out. Just a whole lot of stuff that confused her utterly. It was disconcerting reading Leonie's private thoughts, and it made Kit feel guilty. She had no real right to them and yet she couldn't stop herself.

Kit gingerly picked up the book again, crawled onto the bed and lay there awhile, hands behind her head and legs crossed, staring at the ceiling, the book on her stomach. *I was in limbo*, Leonie had written. *Worse, I felt old . . . finished. I had no one to love . . .*

The words touched Kit. She tried to imagine Leonie at twenty-four, with her long red hair and white skin. What had she been looking for, to go there in the first place? Why had she gone to make a life so far away from home?

I had no one to love . . .

Kit slowly opened the exercise book, a sudden rush of tears spilling down her face. She brushed them away with one fist, then licked her fingers, tasting the salt. Well, they had something in common, didn't they.

145

So how did you meet him? I hear you asking. Was it love at first sight? Was he a fellow teacher? Did you meet in a pub?

This might be hard to believe, but the first time I looked into your father's eyes, he was holding a gun to my head.

But first, let me explain.

I moved into the Falls Road house with Nuala Boylan. The father was in jail, the mother in hospital. I got permission from both of them to move in for a while to help out, but they didn't seem particularly grateful. The mother just nodded warily in her hospital bed, as though it was quite on the cards that I would pull some kind of swifty on her but that she was beyond caring. And the father, well, I didn't see him, but wrote him a letter and a message came back via some strange man that he gave his assent. The aunt down the road was glad for me to be there. She had five of her own and could well do without feeding her sister's children.

Once ensconced in the house, I took my cue from Nuala and her brother Martin. It was just as I expected: making meals, supervising the young kids, getting them up in the morning. As soon as school finished in the afternoon, I hurried to my car and went back into the sectioned-off part of the city. After a while the soldiers got to know me and although they didn't approve of me being there, they waved me on through the road-checks. I couldn't be rude to the soldiers because I felt sorry for them; they were such young fellows and they seemed scared stiff. But my friendliness was frowned on by the locals. If I hadn't been a weird foreigner who was doing a kind deed for one of their neighbours, then it wouldn't have been tolerated.

The people hated the soldiers and for the most part it was vice-versa. I never saw one local give a nod, much less a kind word or a smile to a soldier. On my second day I watched a kid of ten tell a young soldier on patrol to 'go fuck himself' when the guy held out five quid and asked him in a kindly fashion to go buy him a packet of cigarettes and keep the change. It wasn't so much the words the kid used, or the fact that he'd refused, that shocked me. It was his face. That kind of stony, hate-filled expression is terrible to see on anyone and on one so young, it's frightening. But I got used to it. Most of the children around had similar faces. That soldier would have got used to it, too. He must have been new to the job to even ask. It was a war and the children had to take up their parents' mantle. So they threw stones at the soldiers and screamed abuse at the saracens, the tanks that lumbered down the streets at all hours. Sometimes I could see that it was akin to sport for the younger kids. A destructive, sometimes deadly sport, but nevertheless more exciting than watching football on telly, because they were part of it.

Some welfare money came in, and the neighbours were good, but I ended up spending a fair bit of my own money as well. The younger children were suspicious, naturally. And resentful. They didn't want this strange woman with a weird accent taking over from their mammy. I made the usual mistakes: cooking healthy food, and then having to throw it out when they wouldn't eat it. Another was trying to get them to turn the telly off when there was homework to do. All that was quickly rectified. I learnt to fit in with them rather than the other way around.

When I first moved in, I used to look out the window as the soldiers moved past the house. They were so near. Everything was near. The people next door, the shop down the road, the street outside, the army and the police. It was all on a smaller scale than what I was used to. The soldiers passed in four-man patrols at all times of the day or night; watchful, wary, fully armed, always alert to the possibility that there might be a sniper on a roof, or a bomb in some rubbish bin on the footpath. They stopped pedestrians in the street, usually young men, frisking them, asking for names and identification. Where were they going, what were they doing, who were they going to be doing it with? The same young man might be stopped three times on his way down to the city. They might take him away and question him for hours. Within a

147

week, I understood that the resentment amongst the population was huge and bitter and occasionally bubbled over into violence that was not planned and didn't usually go anywhere.

Occasionally, one of the soldiers would park himself against the Boylan house, keeping cover for the others on his patrol who were edging their way along the street. It was an odd thing to look out the front window and see a soldier using our railing as support as he aimed his weapon at pedestrians on the other side of the street.

But of course they weren't the only ones with guns. They weren't the only ones making people fearful, either.

There had been an incident just before I arrived that was still sending shockwaves around the community. A Catholic mother of ten had come out of her house to help a young British soldier who was lying on the road bleeding to death from a sniper's bullet. She knelt down and tried to stem the bleeding before the army arrived with their ambulance. Later that night, she was taken away by Provos and shot dead for her disloyalty.

It's hard now to describe how tough it was, but the fear and hostility and repression in the streets was palpable at times.

One evening, Nuala told me how she felt. She was sitting up in bed reading Crime and Punishment, for school I think. I sat down on the end of her bed and we got talking about the characters, and what the book was all about. Eventually we got onto the subject of fear.

'I'm dead scared most of the time,' she admitted slowly, staring over at her sleeping younger sister in the nearby bed. 'I was always afraid of my dad. Now he's gone I'm afraid of the Brits and shit-scared of the police as well.'

I nodded. I didn't know much about her father but she had every reason to be scared of the other two: the Brits and the RUC. The first were the ones who were continually ransacking her house, they'd taken her father off, and they were on the streets with their rifles every day, supposedly protecting but really harassing the local population. The

RUC, or Royal Ulster Constabulary, was Northern Ireland's police force, made up almost completely of Protestants, with a shocking reputation of bigotry towards the Catholic population.

'Anyone else?' I said, looking at her thin girlish frame, the red around her eyes, wishing I could take some of that anxiety away.

'Yeah,' she smiled nervously. 'I'm terrified of the UVF and the UFF, and the other Protestant paramilitaries.'

'Me, too.' I smiled at her. By then I knew that these groups – the Ulster Volunteer Force and the Ulster Freedom Fighters – sometimes came into the Catholic areas and simply bashed, knifed or shot anyone they saw, before fading quickly into their own communities. Worse, sometimes they took people away and tortured them before killing them. They'd picked up a girl only months before; just picked her out of a Catholic pub at random, then raped and mutilated her before eventually killing her. Bad as the army and police were to people like Nuala, the UVF and the UFF were worse, because their hatred was so intense and completely irrational. And they were hardly ever caught.

'And?' I looked at Nuala, expecting that next she would say that she was afraid of losing both her parents. That her mother might die in hospital and her father, if he was found guilty, might languish in jail for a long time. And then what would happen?

'And I'm afraid of the Provos, too,' she muttered grimly. 'Some of them are mad bastards, so they are.'

I'm going off on tangents again. Where was I? Ah yes, meeting your father, that first time.

It was about eleven at night and I was switching the lights off downstairs, looking forward to getting up to my room to bed. There had been a lot of army activity the night before. A raid had had most of the street up from around three a.m. I'd lain nervously in bed, thinking it was going to be our house next. But they hadn't come to our door, and I'd gone off to work in the morning, red-eyed with tiredness, knowing nothing about what the raid had been for. Nuala told me when I got in that afternoon that there'd been a march down Falls Road in support of prisoners' rights early that day; only a few hundred had turned up – mainly housewives. Although it had gone off peacefully enough, the foreign press had been there, and CNN's pictures were going out around the world. The raid was a way for the army to get their own back. The whole conflict was full of tit-for-tat reprisals like this, both petty and huge.

But this night was peaceful, the street outside quiet. I turned the last light off and stood in the kitchen for a moment. Martin had opened up to me a little over tea, when I'd been able to help him with his schoolwork. Like Nuala, he was quiet but he was not as nervy as his sister and he smiled more easily. I liked him. His coarse sandy hair, the spotty skin and skinny frame, made me think of my own brothers back home. He'd told me a little about his hopes and dreams. They were, well, like a lot of kids his age, I suppose. To get an education and a good job, in graphic design, and eventually to get a fast motor bike and travel the world. Given his circumstances, those hopes were unrealistic. Unemployment inside the Catholic area of the Falls was huge and the percentage who made it to university was miniscule. It was very hard to leave that area at all. People stayed, for generations. Still, I was pleased that Martin had dreams. So many of the kids around didn't – you could see it in their faces.

By eleven the kids were asleep, and I suppose I stood there in the dark enjoying the feeling of having them all safe under my care. I remember thinking that the nuns who'd taught me back home would be proud if they ever got to hear what I'd done for this family. These two older kids were clever and they would get to university against the longest odds because I'd come to help. It's embarrassing having to admit it, but the fact was, I was standing there in the kitchen congratulating myself!

I heard something at the back of the house but decided to ignore it.

The army hardly ever went to the same street two nights in a row. I was beginning to think like a local by this stage. So I went to go upstairs. On the landing, I stopped. There were definite banging noises. I was already in my nightie, so I went up to the bedroom and picked up my dressing gown, putting it on as I ran back down to see what the commotion was.

When I pushed aside the curtain from the kitchen window I saw three dark figures standing in the yard, one of them bent over the lock of our back door. Fear raced up my spine. I stiffened and stood there trying to calm myself. Accounts of the Protestant paramilitaries who broke into the Catholic districts at night were terrifying. Any Catholic would do. Any Catholic house. They killed randomly, the terror caused by unpredictability a deliberate part of their campaign. This was Pat Boylan's house. He was inside now on charges of conspiring to murder. My God! What if they were coming for his family in reprisal! There was the sound of muffled voices and the scraping of metal on metal. They were trying to break the lock. What could I do?

Oddly enough, it was the younger children who came to mind. They were still innocents, in spite of the fact that they threw stones at British tanks and hurled abuse at the soldiers. They still knew how to laugh and when I told them stories about home, about the horses we had, and the cows and my brothers and parents, they were as wide-eyed and curious as any nine-year-olds.

I suppose I was beginning to love them. And it was this that galvanised my courage. I couldn't bear them to be victimised by some bloody Unionist thug. I would have to take a chance that I'd be able to deal with whoever it was.

So, trembling and completely terrified, I opened the door.

'What do you want?' I hissed at the three men.

They stood back. They were in shadow, but two of them auto-matically brought their hands up to their faces in an attempt to hide themselves. They were dressed in old jeans and ragged coats; two of them needed a shave.

151

'Who are you?' one of them said in surprise. He was younger than the others, and had a mean, pinched little face.

I had a feeling that they hadn't expected anyone to be home.

'Who are you?' I demanded. Their surprise gave me confidence, I suppose. I thought I might be able to bluff my way out of any trouble. I felt that my Australian accent gave me a sort of immunity in the situation. They couldn't immediately pigeon-hole me or assume anything. Of course at that stage I had no idea who I was dealing with.

'Oh shite!' another man, taller and more heavily built, muttered. He seemed to be remembering something. Then he looked at the others. 'I forgot about her.'

'What do you mean?' I said, a little hysterically. 'Please clear off, the lot of you.'

'Miss,' he said quietly, politely, 'I'm sorry, but we're going to have to come in.'

'No,' I said emphatically. 'There are children in this house and I don't want . . .' I closed the door. Or tried to.

Suddenly it flew right open, I was shoved to one side and the three of them pushed past me into the kitchen. The light suddenly went on and I could see them. The older man waved the other two on into the next room. Then he pulled a gun out of his jacket pocket.

'Provisional IRA,' he said, putting the gun to my head, 'don't cause trouble and you won't get any.'

I resisted the urge to scream because I had a sudden shocking image of my brains being splattered over the wall. I stood very still, although at the same time I couldn't really feel my legs. I took a quick look into his face. His blue eyes were really startlingly bright, like two pools of glass. I had a couple of seconds of complete disbelief. But my body knew, even if my mind was in denial. Feeling came back to my legs, they began to shake a little. My body could feel the metal against my head. I nodded dumbly, trembling all over.

I looked over to the living room where the other two men were

152

discussing something quietly. The man with the gun was standing close to me at that stage, the short metallic pistol lightly touching my right temple.

'I've never had anyone point a gun at me before,' I whispered in a voice that seemed to belong to somebody else. 'Would you really pull the trigger?'

I can't believe that I said those pathetic words, but it's the truth. Something like them, anyhow.

'Ma'am,' he said quietly, 'believe me. If I had to, I would.'

In the living room, the other two walked up and down. Every now and again one of them would jump as if he was testing the floorboards. Just as I'd worked out that they must be looking for something, the door between us was slammed shut.

'Got it,' a muffled voice said.

'So hurry,' the man who was holding the gun at my head called urgently. 'We should be out of here already.'

I figured that they must have been lifting floorboards. Finally the door opened again and the two men appeared, one of them with a small wooden box under his arm. The gun was lowered from my head. The men with the box went out the back door and the older man, hesitated. I thought maybe he might be going to warn me not to say anything or threaten me further. Instead, he apologised.

'I'm really, really sorry about tonight,' he said, quite sincerely. 'It was a terrible mistake forgetting about you being here.'

'So did you think the house was empty?' I said quietly, then added sarcastically, 'or did you think it was okay to break in with only the children to frighten?'

'We knew the children slept upstairs,' he said. 'We thought we'd wait till they were asleep, so we wouldn't frighten them.'

'Wait till they were asleep before you came in and stole what you wanted,' I said bitterly. God, I was furious now. Now that the gun wasn't at my head, I had a sudden surge of energy. I felt like taking him on with my fists. *'Have you any idea how frightening it is for children to be woken in the night. How frightening it is for anyone . . .'*

My voice cracked. This annoyed me and so to ward off tears I spoke more harshly than I intended. *'I hate you people. You're as bad as the Brits, coming into people's houses and stealing.'*

'We weren't stealing,' he said softly. 'We had full permission from Pat Boylan whose house this is.'

'Is that so?'

'Yes, it is so.'

'So what was it that you took from here?'

That simple question made him smile. And that smile was my undoing. He looked impossibly boyish and, well, so unaffectedly handsome and good-natured, that my anger dissipated. Not that I intended letting him know it.

'Miss Quinlan,' he said, his blue eyes twinkling like stars, 'do you take me for a fool?'

'How do you know my name?' I said.

'Oh sweet mother of God, everybody knows your name,' he said, laughing again when he saw my surprise. 'I know where you teach and I even know the town you come from in Australia!'

'You don't!' I laughed in disbelief. 'You're kidding me.'

His laughter stopped abruptly, and he stared into my face. 'I also know you are doing a fantastic job here, and that everyone appreciates it very much. Pat was worried sick about how his wee ones would get on, with the mammy sick and all. He sends his regards, by the way.'

'Right.' What else could I say? 'Thanks.'

CHAPTER SIXTEEN

Kit was in the kitchen filling the kettle when she heard the front door open. It was Tam, sashaying down the hall towards her room, humming an old Beatles song.

'*Something in the way she moves . . .*'

'Tam!' Kit called, 'is that you?'

'Kit! You're back!' Tam yelled. 'When?'

'Just before.'

They met in the hallway, just outside Tam's room, staring at each other for a few moments, convulsed with nervous laughter. 'Come and give me a hug, Quinlan,' Tam said softly. 'I've been missing you heaps.'

Kit stepped forward and threw her arms around her friend. Something felt different, but Kit couldn't put her finger on it.

'Listen,' said Kit, 'I want to know everything.'

'Me too.'

'Brendan said you were in some kind of trouble?'

'Oh, Brendan!' Tam waved one hand as though exasperated. 'I'm okay. You needed an excuse to get away. Come on, let's go have something to eat.'

It wasn't until an hour later that Kit understood what had happened to Tam. They sat in the kitchen drinking tea and eating sandwiches from the cut roast lamb and homemade chutney that Therese had given Kit to bring back. They skated around the topic of Robbie, talking of everything else: Brendan, Lou, work and all Kit's family stuff. Kit thought Tam seemed subdued, and was being coy about the new boyfriend, but she let it pass. There was no need to push for everything at once. Brendan's lunch shift finished at three and she suggested that they walk down to the restaurant together and meet him.

'I'll just run and change my top,' Tam said.

Kit picked up her bag and popped her head around the door of Tam's room.

'I'll wait for you on the –'

Kit stopped mid sentence, completely stunned. Tam was standing in just a white singlet, staring at herself in the mirror. Her upper arms and chest were covered in deep black and purple bruises. Appalled, Kit came into the room. Tam simply stood there, expressionless, letting Kit look at her.

'It's bad, huh?' Tam said at last.

'Did this guy, this new guy, do this?'

Tam nodded dully.

'Tam!' Kit was almost speechless with anger. *'Why?'* She took her friend's hand, tears beginning in her eyes. 'How come? Tell me how, why?'

Tam shook herself free. 'Don't say anything,' she said quietly. 'It's over now.'

'Over?'

'I told him last night,' Tam said. 'It's over.'

'You don't love him any more?'

'Whatever,' Tam was defensive. 'It's over, anyhow.'

'I should think so!'

'Don't give me a lecture, Kit. I've been an idiot,' Tam said, slipping on a long sleeved T-shirt, wincing a little as she settled it against her bruised skin.

'*You've* been an idiot? What about him?'

'Yeah, well . . .' Tam seemed exhausted, cut off and sad.

'Does Brendan know about this?'

'Yeah.' Tam took Kit's arm, walking her to the door. 'He knows.'

The following night, after trying on three different outfits, Kit decided on a dress she'd pulled from Leonie's things at the last minute before coming back to the city. It was a lovely fitted dress that she'd tried on in the bungalow at home. It was made of tapestry-like material; thick and rich, in red and gold colours that really brought out the deep blue of Kit's eyes and made her skin glow. The shape of it on the hanger was a bit old-fashioned, but as soon as she put it on, Kit knew it was right. She'd resisted wearing it at first. What did it mean to be pinching your mother's clothes? Did it make her a thief or just a complete weirdo? There was something vaguely creepy about it: Leonie lying in hospital and her daughter down in the city making merry in her clothes.

Then she'd decided, what the hell. She needed to look great for this party.

She stared at her bare face in the mirror, holding her hair up at the back with one hand and twisting her head about to see the effect from all angles. Would she pin it up or let it hang loose? What would *he* like? Pinning it up would make her seem older, more sophisticated. Then again, all through the rehearsals she'd worn it down. Down made her look younger, friendlier, more *accessible?* She shuddered and let her hair drop. Maybe he was attracted to young students who wore jeans and tight short T-shirts with their navels showing. She'd never been one of those. Her bum was too big, her personality too sharp. Maybe she should try a totally different look altogether. She began to pin up her hair frantically. It was ten o'clock. Sounds from the party down the street could already be heard. Tam was waiting for her in the kitchen. They'd decided earlier that they would walk down to the party together. Make an impact. Kit wished she felt as light-hearted now. The phone rang and she could hear Tam answering it.

Hair up and lipstick on, Kit suddenly slumped down on the bath. What a weird day. It felt like it had been going on forever. Part of her didn't want to go to the party now that the time had arrived. What was she doing back here anyway, when the rest of her family were supporting Leonie? *Her mother!* What if Leonie was waiting for her to come back so she could smile again? The thought made Kit shudder and want to crawl into bed, forget about everything until she could catch the first train back.

It didn't help that Tam was in some kind of strange mental space. She wouldn't talk about what had happened between her and Robbie. And bloody Brendan! What had got into him? After an initial hug and a few quick questions he'd gone out for hours and then when he came back he'd thrown himself into Lou's party preparations. She'd been wanting to catch him all day, to show him those pages of Leonie's and ask him questions. Every time she tried to talk properly to him he was friendly enough, but distant. If she didn't know better, if she didn't really know Brendan, she'd think he was trying to avoid her.

Kit had got stuck into baking the cakes she'd promised Lou. She thought that it was odd the way a week or two could make this kind of difference. All the dynamics had changed. They were out of sync with each other.

She laughed to herself as she sat on the bath, picturing Mrs Boil earlier that afternoon, standing on her front verandah, staring suspiciously at the steady stream of human traffic going to and from both the houses.

'Just organising a drug haul, Mrs Boil,' Brendan had called cheerily, holding up the box of glasses he was carrying over to Lou's.

Kit had had a few minutes with Brendan in the late afternoon before Lou rolled up with her list of instructions for dealing with Boy George. But their conversation had made her feel more dislocated than ever.

'So it all takes off again tonight, heh?' Brendan had sauntered in from outside. 'The love affair of the decade?'

Kit had just washed her hair. She was sitting on the back step drying it with a towel. The four chocolate cakes were cooling on the table. She looked up from under her hair quizzically.

'You and lover man,' he added, slurping from a cup of coffee left on the table. 'Sebastian baby?'

'Well, I don't know.' Kit took a quick look at Brendan, put out by his sarcastic tone. 'I hope so. But he might not even turn up.'

'He'll turn up, Quinlan.'

'What makes you so sure?'

'For a girl like you!' Brendan gave her a cheesy smile. 'He'd be out of his mind not to.'

She followed him upstairs, but he went into his room.

'Brendan, have you got a minute?'

Her hair was dripping around her shoulders.

'For you Kathleen,' he called from inside the room, 'I've got hours!'

'No, seriously,' said Kit when he came to the doorway. 'I've got this one thing that my mother wrote. I've got heaps, actually, but this one is worrying me. I need a few pointers.' She held out the page for him to take.

'What is it?'

'I found it amongst her papers. Remember I told you I found

them? I just wanted to show you this bit. There's other stuff too, but it can wait till after the party and everything.'

Brendan nodded, took the page and was about to close the door. Kit jammed her foot in it.

'What's going on with you, Brendan?' she snapped.

He frowned down at the paper in his hand but said nothing. About to launch into an are-you-trying-to-avoid-me number, Kit decided to change tack.

'Do you know anything about what happened to Tam?' she asked. Have you met the *shit* who . . .?'

Brendan shook his head then held his hands out in mock surrender, giving one of his slow deliberate smiles.

'Which one first, Quinlan? This stuff of your mother's or Tam?'

'Oh, you're a bastard!' she flushed immediately, embarrassed now. 'No use talking to you, is there? You're in one of your bloody moods.'

'I'm not in a mood. I'll read this and then I'll come and chew the fat with you about Tam. Is that what you want?'

'Okay.' Kit smiled sheepishly, folded her arms and leant against the wall. 'But I need to know something first.'

'What?'

'You and me?'

'What?'

'I mean, are we still mates and everything?' Kit blew out. This was going badly. 'Sorry. I'm confused,' she joked in her best Oprah confessional tone, 'I really need to know if I figure in your life.'

Brendan shook his head. 'You still figure in my life,' he mumbled grudgingly. There was an awkward silence between them before the door downstairs slammed loudly.

'Yahoo!' It was Lou. 'Anyone home?'

'Yeah!' Brendan shouted, 'I'll just be a minute.'

'Well, hurry! I'm so completely stressed I think my head is going to explode.'

160

Brendan and Kit looked at each other and laughed.

'I mean it, Brendan. I'm in a state of severe overload.'

'So what's new?' Brendan shouted back, slipping his jumper off and throwing it, along with the page of Leonie's scrawl that Kit had given him, onto the bed. 'I thought your fuses had blown years ago!'

'Listen, dickhead Delaney, I've got Boy George here,' Lou yelled as she came up the stairs, 'and I swear he knows something is up. He knows I'm bailing out on him. Oh God, it's you! *Kit!* You're back!'

'Hi ya Lou.' Kit skipped down the top stairs and into the skinny arms of her friend, who was dressed in party-mode. She was wearing a vile, skin-tight, purple lurex pantsuit; silver, gold and purple eye make-up, and silver rings running up her ears, around her neck and along her arms. The end of her dreads were dyed green. Kit couldn't help thinking that she looked like some weird tropical spider on a David Attenborough nature program.

'So you're off tomorrow?'

'Yeah.' Lou seemed agitated. 'But I gotta get you three together. There are things you need to know about Boy George. He's got this whole *other side* to him that you guys don't even know about yet. How's your sister by the way?'

Kit made a so-so gesture with one hand while she ran the other hand over the top of the newly shaved part of Lou's head.

'She's getting there,' Kit said. 'This is nice.'

'So what are you doing here?' Lou asked, frowning. 'I mean if she's coming out of the coma, shouldn't you be there sucking her toes or something?'

Kit shrugged.

'Tam told me all that far-out stuff about her being your mother and all,' Lou went on breathlessly, 'but I decided it was way too *weird*. As far as I'm concerned if she couldn't come clean when you were a kid, then she's your sister and that's the way you should treat her. Don't let her lay any heavy stuff on you.'

'I had to come back to see you off on your big trip,' Kit said, ignoring Lou's comments about Leonie.

'Good.' Lou linked arms with her, the bangles on her arms clanging like chimes. 'Glad you did. Now let's get Brendan and Tam and we'll have the meeting.'

'Meeting?'

'I have a list of requirements for Boy George's welfare while I'm gone,' Lou said haughtily. 'Come on. Some of it is very serious.'

Kit rolled her eyes at Brendan who'd come up behind them.

'Whatever you say, Lou.'

They sat at the kitchen table and watched Lou stick a list of instructions to the fridge. There were general headings like Walks and Food, Behavior in the Car, Dealing with Dog Poo, then at the bottom of the page: 'Boy George has a feminine side. Please respect this.'

Brendan, Tam and Kit went into paroxysms of laughter.

'Listen, Lou, if there is one dog on this earth who *doesn't* have a feminine side, it's Boy George!' Brendan snorted.

In the end Kit went to the party alone. Brendan was called over to Port Melbourne by his mother, and Tam pulled out at the last minute, saying she had to wait for a call from her mother, but she'd come after that.

Kit's heart was pounding even before she made it to the open front door. What if Sebastian was here already? What would she say? Then again, what if he wasn't? What if he didn't turn up at all? She made herself walk through the wrought-iron gate and up the stone stairs and into the throng of people congregating around the doorway. The party was in full swing. There were lots of people she knew. Even so, she was nervous. Inside the wide hallway, groups of people stood drinking, yelling and laughing above the loud music. She wove her way through, smiling and occasionally kissing someone hello. Above her, a mirror-ball sprinkled flashes of light onto the blood-red walls and she had a sudden spurt of empathy for Leonie's fear all those years ago. The gun at her head, and the realisation that her brains might be splattered over the nearby walls any second. *What a horrible thing to do to someone.* Kit shivered. *And the one who did that was my father. Do I really want to meet him?* She knew her fear of meeting up with Sebastian was childish in comparison. But that didn't stop the squirming in her stomach.

Kit made her way down to the big main room just off the kitchen. He wasn't there. He hadn't come. People were sitting about on sofas and in dark corners, clutching drinks, chatting quietly; the music down this end of the house was more muted and conducive to talk. The whiff of dope hung about, making the air heavy and sweet. She waved to Lou who was on the other side of the room, offering food from two enormous plates.

'Lou, do you want me to cut the cakes?' Kit called. 'Hand them around?' She'd brought her offerings down earlier, iced and decorated with Smarties.

'Two have gone already,' Lou laughed, coming up to her. 'Where have you been?'

'I was waiting for Tam but . . . she's coming soon. Did you meet Tam's boyfriend?'

'Nah,' Lou giggled, pleasantly off her head on some chemical or other. 'He's top secret. But he's coming tonight.'

Before Kit could comment, Lou motioned around the crowded party excitedly. 'Everyone looks so cool, don't they?'

'Yeah. But Lou, I thought Tam had broken up with him?'

'No, he's coming tonight,' Lou said again. 'Tam told me this afternoon.' Lou suddenly threw her arm around Kit's shoulders, hugging her tightly.

'I'm going to miss you.'

'It's only three weeks, Lou.' Kit hugged her back. 'You look after yourself, heh? Don't get lost over there.' Lou was always losing her way around Melbourne. The idea of her at large in another city was verging on scary.

'I'll be right,' she said gamely. 'Just care for Boy George, *please!*'

'We will.' Kit pulled away from her friend, laughing, 'I promise to respect him in every way.'

'Good,' Lou said ruefully. 'He's very special, you know.'

'Oh Lou,' Kit laughed. 'I know he is. One in a million. Absolutely.'

Kit made her way out of the kitchen, past a group who were sitting passing joints at the table. She got herself a drink from the punch bowl which was already half empty, thinking about how boring, how *absolutely* boring stoned people were. She took a sip, almost gagged and then took another. The stuff was lethal but the burning feeling that immediately hit her gut steadied her.

She stood against the wall, sipping the drink. Suddenly the whole scene around her seemed unbelievably tacky and stupid, absolutely boring and infantile.

I want to be somewhere else. Neither Sebastian nor Brendan nor Tam had shown up. She wanted to run back home, curl up in her bed and read over Leonie's pages again. She wanted to look for clues about her father, to lie there and try to imagine him. Did he even know she existed?

But it *was* Lou's party, and she wouldn't be around for a few weeks. Kit owed Lou that much loyalty at least, and well, it was only midnight. Sebastian still might show.

She wandered into the backyard. It was dark out there and cool, with only a bare bulb illuminating the concrete paving and tin shed.

He hadn't come. Why would he? A party with a whole lot of undergraduates? Really, what could be more tedious for someone like him. She was bored herself. A deep chill settled like a chunk of ice under her rib cage as she looked up into the night sky. *I want to be somewhere else. I want to be someone different. I want to find my father. I want to know if he's alive, at least. Sit with him maybe, ask him things. I want to find out why he went to jail, and if he still thinks it's okay to hold a gun at someone's head. I want to know why, if, he left my mother.* A sob rose in her throat and spilled out her mouth with a dull choking sound.

What now? Who am I? What do I do now?

She wandered back inside to find that Tam had arrived with a guy who looked like a younger version of Clint Eastwood. His broad shoulders looked like those of a weightlifter. He stood out in the crowd of thin, young, long-haired students, mostly dressed untidily in loose casual clothes and runners. There was something about him, a kind of aloofness that caught Kit's attention immediately. *He thinks he's too good for this,* Kit thought angrily, forgetting that she'd been thinking exactly the same thing only minutes before. She watched them, her curiosity quickening. They stood in the corner, holding hands. Occasionally he turned to glance in a detached way at the revellers around them, smiling vaguely as if he wasn't quite sure where he was.

People greeted Tam and stopped to talk, but although she smiled and talked back, she clung to the guy the whole time. It was so unlike Tam.

Kit finished her glass of punch, and feeling almost weightless, she pushed her way through the crowd and reached Tam. That punch was strong. It had made her feel loose and furious.

'Hi there, Robbie. I'm Kit.' She held out her hand.

He stared at her, without taking her hand, pretending he hadn't seen it.

She shut her eyes for a moment, tottering slightly, but continuing to hold her hand out, thinking, *I will keep holding it out until this arrogant shit takes it.*

'Kit!' Tam hadn't noticed the outstretched hand and seemed genuinely relieved to see her, 'Where have you been?' She nudged the guy, giggling nervously. 'Robbie, this is my best friend, Kit.'

Leaning forward, he then took her hand but after a brief hard squeeze dropped it suddenly, staring into her face the whole time. *He's playing power-games with me and we've only just met.*

'Kit,' he said soberly. 'I've heard about you.'

'Have you?' Kit laughed sarcastically. She could see the alarm in Tam's eyes, but couldn't stop herself. 'That's *sooo* funny, Robbie, because Tam hasn't told me a thing about you.'

'Is that right?' His voice was stony but she knew it would take more than this to unsettle him. She wasn't even registering as a blip on his internal computer screen. But Kit wanted blood. She knew he sensed her desire to get at him in some way and she was glad.

Suddenly, someone turned off the music. Another light went on. Around them, people were moving back and muttering. With a flash, Kit remembered that she was meant to be making a speech, wishing the band good luck for their tour. God, what would she say? She and Brendan had been going to do a little number together but Brendan hadn't shown. People were backing away from the middle of the room. Someone yelled out that they wanted to hear Lou make a speech. Then thankfully some other guy was in the middle of the floor calling everyone to attention, cracking jokes.

'Well, initially, she did talk about you,' Kit went on loudly. 'I heard about the ex-wives and the kids that you don't see, but then Tam stopped talking. I wondered why, Robbie. Until I saw all the bruises down her arms, I wondered why she didn't want to talk about you any more.'

'Kit!' Tam's face dropped in absolute shock. 'Stop it.'

Around them, people were listening, Kit could tell. Tam pulled Robbie's arm and glared at Kit.

166

'Shut up,' she said furiously, then to Robbie, 'Come on! Let's go, please.'

But Robbie wasn't moving. Arms folded across his chest, he was trying to stare Kit down.

Feeling more reckless than she'd ever felt in her life, Kit stared back into his face. *Who was this little shit gangster anyway?* Her own mother had had a gun pointed at her head and had still managed to stay upright. *I will not be intimidated by this guy.* She felt a surge of wildness rise in her. No one could touch her now. She could've jumped off a roof, or killed someone without blinking.

'I want to say something to you,' she whispered hoarsely, aware that everyone in the room was looking at them. She was euphoric. This was better than acting. These were her own lines, in her own life.

'You touch her again and you'll be sorry, you hear me!' Kit moved forward and poked Robbie's chest.

When he made no reaction, she did it again. His chest was as hard as a brick and his eyes never wavered from her own, but she didn't care. 'You touch her and I'll . . . I'll . . .' She stopped, closed her eyes and felt herself spin a little. *What would she do?* She opened her eyes and saw that he was waiting. Everyone was waiting for her to finish the sentence. A flicker of mockery sparkled in his eyes. He was thinking the same thing. What in the world would she ever be able to do to him?

'I've got brothers,' she ranted wildly. 'Big brothers. Country boys. Four of them. And they've got friends, too. They deal with little shits like you every day! They're really good with cricket bats! If you get my drift, Robbie?'

'So you're threatening me?' he asked, blandly amused now. But she noticed the faint tic around the edge of his mouth. He'd been caught off-guard. It elated her. She *had* unsettled him.

'Yes. I'm threatening you, shithead!'

167

He nodded, said nothing. Then, in answer to Tam's insistent pulls, he shrugged and followed Tam out of the room.

'I mean it!' Kit shouted after him.

She watched them disappear down the hallway to the front door. When she turned back to the room, she was surrounded by baffled faces.

Should she feel ashamed or victorious? The euphoric high came rushing back. Hadn't she spoken the truth after all? Hadn't she said what any right-minded person would think when they saw those bruises? What were best friends for?

'Did you want to speak now, Kit?' the guy who'd been cracking jokes asked.

'Oh, sure!' Kit shrugged off the image of Tam's distraught expression and ran over to the middle of the room.

'On behalf of everyone here I want to wish Lou and the rest of the band the very best of luck for their tour. I just know they are going to set that place alight!'

Although she only spoke for a few minutes, Kit's impromptu speech went over well. The adrenaline pumping through her made her witty and confident. She had the whole crowd laughing and clapping. Lou came forward and accepted the present a few of her friends had pitched in to buy – a fake-gold framed, blown-up photo of Boy George at the beach, looking windswept and heroic with a piece of wood between his teeth.

'Just in case you get lonely at night,' Kit quipped. 'You'll be able to pull out your torch and see he's still with you!'

Lou was thrilled and promised that it would have pride of place in the Kombi van alongside her spells and stage make-up.

After the speeches, the band began to play. Some people stayed to dance, and others moved off to other rooms to talk. The whole incident with Tam and Robbie seemed forgotten. No one mentioned it as Kit edged her way out of the room, back into the kitchen, although there were some who gave her strange looks. Did these people think she was crazy? Kit wondered herself if it had even happened. Somehow it seemed too out of line, too bizarre. She got herself another glass of the punch and went out into the backyard.

Someone had switched off the bulb outside. Kit stood sipping her drink in the darkness, trying to collect her thoughts.

Then she heard a cough behind her.

'Hello there,' a soft male voice said.

Kit jerked around. All she could see was the party crowd through the window.

'Is that you, Kathleen?'

It was him. Sebastian. How long had he been standing there? She was embarrassed. Had he seen her let fly at Robbie? What would he think? Her courageous stand on her friend's behalf suddenly seemed like a badly managed childish bungle.

'It's me,' she said.

'So what are you doing out here?' He seemed amused as he walked over.

'Just looking at the sky,' she mumbled. 'Er, when did you get here?'

'Just now. I heard the last part of your speech.'

'Did you?' She wanted to ask which speech but didn't dare.

'Yes, you did well. Lou seems like a real character.'

'Would you like a drink or something?'

He shook his head. They looked at each other awkwardly. Then he took her elbow lightly and led her to the one garden seat. One of the slats was missing, and it was cold, but Kit was glad that he didn't want to go inside.

'So how are things?' he said. 'You had an accident in the family. If I remember, it was your mother? I'm sorry that I didn't call you and find out how things were going.'

'Oh no,' she smiled, not knowing where to begin. 'It's me who should apologise. Did the last performance go off all right?'

'It was fine. We missed you, of course. Is your mother recovering?'

'Well, yes,' Kit said, not quite knowing how to explain Leonie's progress without going into a lot of detail. The truth was, his polite, gentle manner was somehow more scary than if he'd been openly uninterested. She could feel the aloofness in him that had always been part of his attraction. But now it seemed terrifying. She felt an enormous gap between them that might never be bridged. And yet he'd come. And that meant he wanted to see her, didn't it? Should she tell him about it all? About being born in Ireland, her real mother giving her away . . . Would that make her more *interesting*? Maybe then he'd give her one of his warm smiles and suggest that they go off together to dance. Or for coffee and a sandwich like last time . . . God, it was embarrassing now that he was here, thinking about the way she'd longed for him over the last couple of weeks. The fantasies she'd had.

'She's improving,' Kit muttered shyly.

'That's great to hear.' He was smiling at her again in that perfectly acceptable, friendly, dispassionate way. 'Look, I'm afraid I can't stay long tonight. I have to pick my own mother up from the airport at five a.m. tomorrow.'

'Five a.m.!' Kit acted amused, although deep down she was devastated. 'Where has she been?'

He'd come out of politeness, that was all. Within an hour he would be back in his own life and she'd never see him again. She meant nothing to him.

'She's been in a conference in South America.'

'A conference,' Kit repeated, trying to stay calm, trying not to be intimidated. She didn't know any mothers who went on conferences. 'What does she do?' Her own mother stayed at home and looked after the family. Then with a jolt Kit remembered, her real mother was a car accident victim with a weird, violent past. Someone who had got herself involved in another country's politics. Her real mother was a bloody terrorist! Kit suddenly wanted to burst out laughing and tell him. Surely that was just as interesting as someone who went to conferences?

'She's a professor of psychology,' Sebastian said proudly. 'She's been on a study tour for the last three months.'

'Psychology?' Kit said dully. 'So what was that like? I mean having a mother who —'

'Could analyse me?' Sebastian cut in with a laugh. 'A bit tough, actually. I was glad to leave home when I did.'

'Was your father one too?'

'No, he died when I was very young.' Sebastian took her hand in a brotherly way. 'But tell me about your mother's accident.'

Kit hesitated before taking a deep breath. 'The thing is, Sebastian, when the accident happened, my life became a whole lot more complicated . . .'

'Oh?' he said. 'In what way?'

Once she started, Kit couldn't stop. She had the feeling that someone had turned a tap on inside her mouth. Worst of all, it was not having the desired effect. She could see that even as she continued talking, he was not drawing closer to her. He was interested, but in an impersonal, academic way. He'd let go of her hand, and was sitting back, frowning thoughtfully like a cool professional. He seemed to become more and more remote. Finally it was all out, about Leonie being her mother, about her father being in the IRA, about the intimations that her mother had been involved in violence. Then she stopped, and the quietness between them was terrible.

'The thing is, I know nothing about the situation there,' Kit finished in a small voice.

'Well, there are some fundamental historical facts that you

should understand. But any book on Northern Ireland will give you the background. Have you done any reading at all?'

'You mean apart from my mother's papers?' Kit gulped, feeling foolish. Why hadn't she at least gone to the library to check out a book or two?

'You do need some basic historical knowledge to make sense of it,' he said again softly, leaning back and looking up at the night sky, both arms stretched out along the back of the seat. Kit had a sudden longing for those arms to encircle her. Perhaps she could just shift in her seat, get closer, pretend she was cold. She wished all over again that she hadn't brought the topic up. He was acting like a politics lecturer and that was the last thing she wanted. The idea of pinching him like she did on their first date came and went. Somehow she didn't have that kind of confidence any more.

'What are some of these events I should know about?' she asked, unable to stop herself from sounding like a student.

'The present situation goes back a long way,' Sebastian sighed. He sounded slightly bored and Kit panicked as she saw him look surreptitiously at his watch. It was after midnight. He would be going soon.

'Eight hundred years, really.' He smiled at her and she immediately felt relieved. 'At least. You could go back to the 1200s, but probably the key time to start would be the plantation of Ulster back in the 1600s.'

'The plantation of Ulster?' she repeated.

'Put simply, the Irish had always given the British trouble. The plantation was a deliberate policy to undercut Irish rebelliousness by importing or planting English people, mainly Scots, to live there,' he explained quickly. 'The indigenous Irish were put off their lands and made to go west to the poorer country. Queen Elizabeth wanted Protestantism to flourish, and it did in the rich northern lands of Ulster. But at the expense of those who'd lived there previously. Much of the underlying resentment can be traced back to that time . . .'

'Four hundred years?' Kit said with a laugh. 'You're telling me that to understand what my mother got involved in, I have to go back to the 1600s?'

'Sure.' He snapped his fingers. 'Four hundred years is nothing in historical terms.'

'And apart from that time?'

'Well, there's the formation of the Orange Order in the 1790s,' he went on mildly. 'That's the Protestant ruling elite whose real purpose was to keep the Catholic Irish population in their place.'

'Their place being?'

'Well, let's say,' Sebastian said quietly, 'at the bottom of the heap. Not in government, anyway. After the defeat of the Catholic King Charles in 1790, the penal laws were introduced, which meant all kinds of gross discrimination against the Irish Catholic population. They weren't allowed to vote, own land, speak their language or practise their religion. Those laws were eventually repealed but they reverberated right through into the next two centuries.'

He turned to look at her and her heart dived, because she could tell he was seeing her as just another ignorant student. 'You need to understand those laws,' he went on, 'and understand that the same kind of discrimination was still being played out, albeit at perhaps a less obvious level, at the time your mother is writing about.'

Kit tried to think of something intelligent to say. The weird thing was that part of her was intensely interested. But she didn't want to be given study pointers by a man she was wildly in love with. Sitting in the dark with him explaining what she should study was so far from how she'd imagined their next meeting that she wanted to scream out in protest, or burst into tears.

'How come you know all this?' she cut in shyly, miserably. 'I mean I know your thing is politics but . . .'

'My *thing*.' He smiled indulgently.

'Well, you didn't mention Northern Ireland in the first lecture I went to at the beginning of the year.'

'Which lecture?'

'You gave the introduction to my unit Espionage, Terrorism and Global Disorder.'

'So I did.' He laughed. 'In place of Prof Gleeson if I remember. So I didn't mention Ireland?'

'No.' Kit's despair deepened. She was almost at the point of letting on how impressed she'd been with him that day. How his lecture had galvanised her desire to study politics. But she managed to hold back, knowing it would make her seem young and even more naïve and unknowing.

'Well,' he began again in lecturer-mode, 'the conflict there is long running, but small by comparison to many others . . .' He turned to her. 'Ireland is very interesting, though. Your mother's story sounds interesting. If you need any help –'

'Well, thanks.' She tried to sound enthusiastic. 'I don't know anything really.'

He elbowed her in the ribs playfully. 'You really must start reading!'

'I will,' she replied. Sebastian stretched out again and looked at his watch.

'Have to go soon,' he said.

Kit was on the verge of grabbing his arm and begging him. *Please, please don't go.* A lot could happen between now and five a.m. They could stay awake together until then. They could travel out to the airport together. What could she do or say to make him stay? Her mind raced from one scenario to another, each one more unlikely than the last.

But he was off again. Spouting about the subject that she wished she hadn't brought up.

174

'Then of course there's the Easter Rising in 1916, the civil war and the formal partition of Ireland, which incidentally at the time hardly anyone wanted, not even the Protestant population, but,' he waved his hand, 'it was agreed to as a kind of temporary measure and has been the cause of a lot of trouble since. Then there's the growth of the civil rights movement in the late 1960s, and the slide into violence after August 1969 . . . which is really the beginning of your mother's time.'

He stood and did up his coat.

'So they're the main areas I should take a long look at?' Kit said shyly, reluctantly standing too.

'Oh, Kathleen,' Sebastian smiled, 'there's so much more really. Take the famine in the 1840s. That had a devastating effect on the Irish.'

'Yes, I've heard about that,' Kit said meekly, kicking herself for being so ignorant.

'So when are you going to get going on all this?' he said, taking her elbow lightly, too lightly, moving her towards the door in his friendly cool way. 'Maybe you should do your Honours essay on this instead of . . . what were you going to write on? Sorry, I've forgotten.'

'African independent states,' she muttered, only just able to remember herself. 'Come out through the backyard if you like,' she added, pointing to the back gate. 'Save you walking through the party.'

They went through the old iron gate that led onto a cobbled laneway and walked along in silence to where his car was parked in the main street. He unlocked the car and turned to her before opening the door.

'I'll dig up some books for you, to get you started.'

Kit's mood lifted. 'I'd appreciate that,' she said softly. 'I need to know all kinds of stuff. I don't even know why the British army were there in the first place.'

'Look, as far as I'm concerned, maintaining Protestant supremacy was *the* only real reason the state of Northern Ireland existed,' he said, slicing the air with his hand as though he was in the middle of the lecture. 'So you'd have to agree that the state itself is an immoral concept. Like South Africa under Apartheid. And the British army sent in initially to protect the Catholic population was defending that state.' He leant down to peck her cheek. 'I'll look up those books for you,' he said in a more friendly fashion. 'Perhaps you could drop around some time?'

'Yes. That would be great. But I don't have your address.'

He pulled out his wallet and gave her a card.

Kit took it. This meant she was definitely going to see him again! She squinted at the card but it was too dark to read it.

'Give me a few days,' he said, 'and I'll dig out whatever I've got.'

'Thanks,' Kit smiled, buoyed up. She had his address. He began to open the car door and Kit was hit with a desperate need for them to end on a more familiar note.

'So, should I be proud of my *new* parents?' she said flirtatiously, holding onto the door as he got in. It was the first thing that had come into her head.

He stared up at her thoughtfully, as though he was waiting for her to explain herself.

'I mean, at least they're on the right side,' she laughed nervously, 'fighting the British.'

'Oh, Kathleen,' he sighed, shaking his head. 'You have a lot to learn, haven't you?'

Kit gulped. 'How do you mean?'

'Well, no,' he said, quietly, 'I don't approve of your parents. The IRA is mostly made up of irrational fanatics who believe in their own mythology to the point where nothing else matters. Bully boys, with their punishment beatings and knee-cappings. They ruin the very lives they maintain they are trying to save.'

176

'Oh.' Kit stood rigidly, completely stunned. 'But I thought –'

'Their so-called war of liberation,' he cut in, 'has been a long drawn-out blight on Ireland. It has not advanced in any real way the cause of Catholics in the north . . .'

'But . . .' Kit didn't know what to say. She was humiliated and outraged at the same time. She didn't know enough to argue with him. But she did know he was talking about her parents. Suddenly, she felt the need to defend them. This mother who she didn't like. This father who she didn't know. Who was Sebastian to tell her that they were nothing but irrational fanatics? If only Brendan was here. He'd be able to say something.

'Well, I'll think about what you've said.'

She stood looking down as he started the car, wishing he'd just go now and let her be. But he was winding down the window.

'Of course the Protestant paramilitary groups are worse, if any-thing,' he said. 'Vicious sectarian bastards. But anyway, you'll find all this out. See you soon.'

'Yes. See you.'

The car was off. Kit returned to the house through the back gate, then changed her mind when she saw the crowd still partying. She hadn't brought a bag, only her coat. She could pick that up tomorrow. She rushed back out the gate and into the laneway.

Walk, she told herself. Just walk. It was the only way for her to calm the conflicting thoughts battering around her brain. Kit crossed the road and set off towards the city, within a few minutes wishing that she had fetched her coat after all. The night was cool, and the dress she'd pinched from her mother's wardrobe was by no means adequate.

CHAPTER SEVENTEEN

when you wake and find me gone

When Kit got back to the house two hours later, she was relieved to find the front window had been left unlocked. It was three a.m. and she'd forgotten her key. Although the hallway light was on, she didn't dare knock on the front door. What if Tam was in there with Robbie? The idea of facing either of them at this point was too much like a nightmare. *Tomorrow,* she told herself, she would face everything. If apologies were called for, then she would apologise. If explanations were needed, then she would give those too.

She hauled up the window, feeling exhausted, freezing and freaked out.

Slipping off her shoes and pulling up her dress, she threw one leg over, straddling the window for a moment before allowing herself to slide into the front lounge room. She would sneak up the stairs and lock herself in her room.

At the bottom of the stairs she heard noises from Tam's room. Kit stopped when she realised that it was Tam crying. A lump rose in Kit's throat: a mixture of guilt and concern. Tam rarely cried. The quiet sobs sounded intimate and warm. Kit tip-toed to Tam's door. She was about to open it, when a man's voice intruded over the sobs. It was the gentle, soothing and consoling voice of Robbie – so utterly repulsive to Kit. That cocky self-assured bastard who had bruised her friend so badly. Kit miserably turned away. No way in a million years could she face him tonight. *If ever.* She went to the kitchen for a glass of water.

The yellow light in the kitchen revealed a worse mess than usual. Someone had cooked an elaborate meal. There were dirty dishes strewn around the table, and pots and pans cluttering the sink. The place smelt of spicy meat, tomatoes and fried onions. Kit shuddered as she saw a mouse skip across the stove and out through a hole in the bench. Damn. They were always a problem if the place got too messy. Who hadn't cleaned up? She went to the sink and filled a glass.

Kit had switched off the kitchen light and was about to tip-toe back out to the hallway, when she heard a noise. Footsteps were coming down the hall towards the kitchen. Kit froze. What if it was Robbie? Without thinking, she picked up the breadknife lying on the table and crouched in the far corner, on the other side of the fridge. Fear began to jolt through her. He might have heard her come in and be on his way to get his own back. She had humiliated him, or tried to. People like Robbie didn't just sit back and take that. Kit tried to steel herself for the worst as the footsteps drew closer. This was it. Just let him try getting heavy with her. She would defend herself. She opened her mouth, ready to scream. The light was switched on. Kit blinked. It was only . . . *Brendan*!

'Quinlan!' he said gruffly, staring at her still crouched near the fridge, the knife in her hands. 'What the hell are you doing?'

'Oh, it's *you*,' she muttered. 'I was just going to bed.' She put the knife back onto the table as casually as she could manage. 'I'm pretty wrecked, actually.'

'With a knife?' Brendan grinned. 'You're going to bed with a knife?'

179

'Well, no, I . . .' Kit thought that it might be best to change the subject. 'I didn't see you at the party.'

'Well, I got there eventually,' Brendan answered laconically. He was at the sink gulping down water. 'But apparently I missed the best part.'

'Oh, that.' Kit was trying to sound jocular but it didn't quite come off.

'It's okay, Kit,' he said dryly, switching on the kettle and washing a cup. 'You don't have to laugh. Apparently it wasn't all that funny, especially for Tam.'

'Who told you?' she asked. 'Did you see Tam or something?'

'Quinlan, have you ever heard of minding your own business?' Brendan asked, cheerfully ignoring her question. He went to the fridge and got out a stubbie. 'Who made all these friggin dishes?' He burped, waving at the mess around them, and then groaned. 'And why didn't they wash up?'

'The mice are back,' Kit declared.

'They've never really left us, you know,' Brendan said sombrely.

Kit looked up and they both suddenly dissolved into silent laughter.

'Jeez, Kit!' Brendan shook his head, trying to free himself from the madness of it. 'Why *do* stuff like that?'

'She's our friend,' Kit said vehemently, wiping the tears away with the back of her hand. 'I had to say something.'

'She's a grown woman of twenty-three. Maybe she gets off on it.'

'What crap,' Kit shot back angrily. 'No one likes being beaten up.'

'You sure of that, are you?' Brendan said. 'Listen, why don't you go to bed. You look like shit.'

'Thanks.' Kit didn't move. She wanted to fight with Brendan and at the same time she wanted to hug him.

'My mother had four kids by the time she was twenty-three,' Brendan said suddenly.

'Did she?'

Kit tried to picture the terrifying Nora surrounded by babies and toddlers. Then it hit her that it was at around that age that Leonie had her. She tried to imagine herself in a couple of years with a baby. She wouldn't know how to feed it, or hold it. What if it cried all the time? Maybe that's how Leonie had felt. That a baby would just be impossible.

Me. I'd be just impossible.

Kit's head felt like a mass of crossed wires, pulled too tight, on the verge of snapping. It probably meant she'd have one of her bad headaches before the night was over.

'So did the man show?' Brendan asked suddenly. 'Lover boy?'

'He showed.'

Brendan raised one eyebrow calmly. 'What happened?'

'He told me that my parents were irrational fanatics.'

'He would,' Brendan said coldly, reaching for the paper and opening it at the TV section.

'Why do you say that?'

'That type always thinks like that.'

'You've met him once, Brendan. You don't know him.'

'I know him,' Brendan said darkly. 'You only need to meet someone once to know what drives them. So did you two hit it off?'

Kit sighed, 'No, we didn't hit it off.'

'What happened?'

'In the morning, Bren,' Kit said. 'I'll tell you then.'

'Okay.'

'I gotta talk to you about all this stuff.'

'What stuff?'

'My mother. Ireland. All that stuff.'

'I'll be here.'

She got up slowly and took a quick look at him sitting there moodily. A rush of love swept through her like flame through long

181

dry grass. His tousled hair. The dry, dependable take on everything. That nose. He looked up and caught her smiling at him.

'What are you looking at?'

'Nothing.'

They stared at each other, both of them lost for a couple of moments.

'Shit, Quinlan, I forgot. Your brother Johnny rang.'

'Any news?'

'No. No panic. He said to ring in the morning.'

'Okay.' Kit stretched, and moved to the door. 'How's Rory?'

'Don't ask,' Brendan sighed. 'Don't even ask.'

Before getting into bed, Kit took the precaution of pulling her heavy chair in front of the door. If that bullying bastard in there with Tam wanted to try anything then she would hear the scraping of the chair first. At least it would give her a chance to scream.

But she fell asleep quickly. Her dreams, anxious and muddled, were full of long arduous searches for something or someone she didn't know. She'd felt confused the whole time. And yet it seemed imperative that she keep searching. When she eventually woke around midday, confused and disorientated, she still couldn't pin-point what or who she'd been searching for.

But her sleep was deep. She heard neither Robbie leave the house nor Larissa come in. She certainly never heard anything of what happened to Brendan not long after she went to bed.

After Kit's head hit the pillow, Brendan decided to follow suit. He'd been miserable driving back from Port Melbourne, then felt worse after he'd stopped off for a quick drink at Lou's party and heard about Kit's performance with Robbie. What the hell did she think she could achieve with that sort of scene? Yet he was amused, too, and he admired her fierceness. He hadn't been able to find her at the party, so he figured that she and Sebastian had left together. What a pleasant surprise then, when he'd burst into the kitchen to find her there, on her own, looking as though she'd had a terrible night.

He switched on his bedside lamp, threw off his clothes, fell into bed and pulled up the blankets.

Sebastian had called Kit's parents fanatics for their involvement in the Republican movement. Well, Brendan could tell her something about all that. After all, he'd lived it and all that guy had was theories.

There was a tap at his door.

'Brendan?'

'Yeah.' Brendan didn't immediately recognise the voice.

'It's Larissa. Can I come in?'

'Yeah,' Brendan called back, completely flummoxed. What the hell! It was nearly four a.m. About to jump up to open the door he remembered that he had no clothes on. 'Come in,' he said, embarrassed. 'Did you want to borrow something?'

When she came in, it seemed to Brendan as if an angel had entered his room. She was in a long white silk nightie and her hair was hanging loose about her face and shoulders like a halo. He'd forgotten to close the front curtains so in the moonlight he could see her well. The beauty of her slim shapely figure put a lump in his throat.

'I heard you come to bed,' she whispered, standing just inside the door. 'I couldn't sleep, so I wondered if I could come in for a talk.'

Brendan was stunned. 'Yeah, well, I was about to go to sleep but . . .' He laughed. 'Larissa! It's nearly four o'clock!'

'Yes, I know,' she laughed too. 'Can I sit on your bed?'

'Sure,' Brendan sat up. 'You cold?' When she nodded, he pulled off one of his blankets and helped wrap it around her shoulders. 'So has something happened?' he asked awkwardly.

'You could say that,' she said with a sigh.

'Fire away.'

183

'Mike and I have finally broken up. He left last week. You probably didn't notice – he's coming back for his things next weekend. And just today . . . I can hardly believe this . . . I lost my job.'

'You didn't!'

'Yep, the whole company has closed down. We all lost our jobs.'

'You're kidding me!'

'Nope.' She shook her head and smiled sadly. Her gorgeous hair seemed like spun gold, swaying and bouncing in the moonlight as she flipped it back with one hand. 'We were called together after lunch. Told we had an hour to get out.'

'So the company has gone under?'

'Yep. The shareholders pulled the plug.' Larissa gave a small laugh. 'There's just the managing director left to mop up the mess.'

Brendan hadn't meant to embrace her. It was intended as a friendly hug of sympathy. In fact that's exactly what it had been, until Larissa had answered his brotherly arm around the shoulders with a cuddle of her own. When she moved closer and pushed her silk covered breast against him and burst into tears, what could he do but hold her? The skin of her arms felt soft and when he pushed his face in her hair, it made him think of the sea and of sweet warm days at the Port Melbourne baths with his first girlfriend when he'd been sixteen.

He hadn't been the first one to think about kissing, either. Well maybe he *thought* about it, but he certainly didn't do anything. After all, perhaps she really had come to him for sympathy. What a bastard he'd be if he took advantage of her vulnerability. He'd actually pulled away a bit, searching under his pillow for a hanky to dry her tears, when she'd lifted her face up to his and kissed him on the mouth with her soft sweet wet lips. Shocked but immediately aroused, he'd tried to hold back. Then she did it again.

'Can I come in there with you?' she whispered, when she felt him kissing her back. 'Just for a little while?'

Brendan held back the covers for her. Oh, jeez. The smell of her. The feel of her. Within a minute she was pulling off the silk nightie and Brendan was finding out about the shape and feel of a woman again, after such a long time. Shit, he'd been so closed down. Why had he let himself get like that? This was, well there was no other word for it. This was *fantastic!*

They slept for maybe five or six hours. Brendan woke to bright sun pouring through the windows. They were lying in his bed like two spoons in a drawer. His big hand was cupping her right breast and their legs were entwined. How was this crazy situation going to pan out now it was morning? And he hadn't even thought *condom*, much less used one. He groaned quietly to himself. Shit, this whole thing might be going to get very complicated.

Then he remembered the way women thought about things. Sex affected them differently. As soon as it was over, they sometimes had *expectations*. Shit, what if she was after a full-on relationship? Him and Gucci? No way. What if she wanted some kind of commitment. What if she started asking what she should wear and whether these shoes were right with that dress and what if she wanted him to take cute little trips around the supermarket together on Saturday mornings. What if she thought they were an item now? Brendan shifted uncomfortably and propped himself up on his elbows. She was waking up. He was going to have to get this over with, straight away. Even if she cried, slapped his face, walked out in a huff, never spoke to him again, he had to do it. It was only fair to come clean right now.

But she beat him to it.

'Brendan, I really like you,' Larissa said softly. 'But you do understand this, don't you?'

'Er, understand what?'

'Well,' she giggled and continued stroking his chest, 'I hope you understand I was just using your lovely body?'

Brendan laughed. 'Were you?' he said wonderingly. 'Well, I can't say I object, actually.'

'I like you,' she said, 'I always have. Compared to those two bitches downstairs you're just great.'

'Hmmm.' Brendan gulped. *Jesus, I'm not getting into that territory.*

'Don't worry, I know you're friendly with them,' she went on. 'That's okay. But I've just broken up with Mike and I don't want another relationship right now. Is that okay with you?'

Brendan gave her a hug. 'That's *fine* with me. You don't have to say any more, and we can both forget this happened. Is that what you want?'

'I don't want to forget about it,' she said coyly. 'I had a great time last night.'

'Yeah, me too.'

'Well,' she giggled, 'we can do it again any old time we please!'

'Okay,' he said shyly.

'Just as long as you know that I'm not your girlfriend and I don't consider you my boyfriend.'

'We're just friends, right?' he said slowly.

'Is that okay with you?' she asked seriously. 'I mean is it okay with you to have no serious expectations?'

'Yes,' he said. 'That's fine.'

Satisfied that she'd made her point and that he understood, Larissa immediately changed the mood. She gave a little squeal of glee then jumped astride him, pushing his arms back above his head, pretending to hold him prisoner.

'I'm going to have my way with you,' she said playfully, 'so watch out!'

'Well, I don't know about that.'

'Oh yes you do!'

Within about fifteen seconds he was inside her again and he could hardly believe how good it felt.

CHAPTER EIGHTEEN

Kit woke to loud knocking on the front door. She looked at the clock. Nearly midday.

The knocking continued.

'Damn,' Tam cursed from the room across the hall and Kit groaned as the night before came flooding back. Why had she bull-dozed her way into Tam's scene like that? Brendan was right. It wasn't her business. What would she say to Tam? She heard voices, both Lou and Tam, and then shuffling noises as the two of them walked past her door with the dog. Kit hid her head under the blankets as she remembered this was the day Boy George was coming to stay.

She had to go to the toilet. She wanted a cup of tea, and she wanted to ring home and check with her family that everything was all right. But all those things would have to wait. More than anything she *didn't* want to come face to face with Tam or Robbie. Not just yet, anyway.

So she picked up the exercise book from the bedside table to take her mind off more pressing physical needs, keeping her ear out for when quietness descended on the kitchen.

187

He had wild blue eyes and black curly hair that unless it was cut very short, shot out from his head like wire springs. Just like yours. When mum sent over the photos of you as a little girl, and I saw that wild hair on you, my breath always gave way and my heart would snag in my chest and I would simply have to sit down for a while and rock myself. What have I done? I used to moan. And what am I doing?

When Mum and Dad left with you only about a week old, it finally hit me. I'd had a baby and I'd given her away. My friend Annie drove us all out to the airport. I was in the back next to Mum, who was holding you. Dad was in the front next to Annie. No one spoke, apart from the little things. Where will we get a park? It looks like more rain. I hardly dared look at you in Mum's arms. I didn't trust myself. But when I did take a glimpse, there was just this sweet little face with a whole lot of black hair that shot straight up like a paintbrush, eyes and fists clamped shut like you didn't want to know what was happening. I think mum was crying but I can't be sure. I felt like I was made of stone when I said goodbye to them.

When they'd gone and Annie and I got back to where I lived in Andersonstown, Annie ran me a bath. And I sat in there for about three hours, howling my eyes out, letting the great mess inside just burst open. She left me alone. When I got out of the bath she made me some tea. I sat at the little table and wrote about how I was feeling. Then, when I'd finished, I thought I would keep it for you. I wish I could find that letter because I really let my heart speak that day. I hadn't allowed myself to do that for a long time. And afterwards, when you'd gone, when I started doing more stuff for the movement, I closed myself down. For years. But just for that hour, I let loose.

So what did it say? That's the worst of it, I can't recall! But I remember deciding that I'd keep it for you. I packed it into an envelope and wrote on the outside, 'When you wake and find me gone . . .'

I knew it wouldn't be appropriate to write 'For my darling daughter', or 'For sweet Kathleen', or anything like that. So it was just, 'When you wake and find me gone.' That's all I can remember.

But you know, Kathleen, I've searched and searched for that letter. My only explanation is that someone has taken it. Sometimes I lie awake at night going over and over that line. In a way it haunts me.

When you wake and find me gone.

The sun came out for Lou's departure and in the end the small group who'd gathered to wave goodbye turned into an impromptu street party. Music blared out from a front window, wine in plastic cups and a plate of leftover sandwiches appeared via one of Lou's house-mates. Once it became obvious that everyone was welcome, two Vietnamese families from the block of flats opposite brought over spring rolls and glasses of lemonade, offering them around as they looked in wonder at Lou's newly painted bright-red van. The band's name, 'Pawsound', was painted on both sides in huge gold lettering. Even Mrs Boil, as curious and dignified as ever, donated a parcel of sandwiches for the trip, wishing Lou the best as she handed it over. To Brendan's amusement, Mrs Boil then began quizzing him on his exam results and just what kind of trouble his little brother was getting into.

By the time the two vehicles, a drab grey Holden and Lou's Kombi complete with streamers and balloons, were loaded up and finally lumbered off, the mood was raucous. Everyone was waving and yelling 'good luck' 'break a leg' and 'make sure you come back!'

Kit stood on the footpath, a little apart from the others, trying not to appear as desperate and weird as she felt. When the Kombi disappeared around the corner, she looked over to where Tam was pulling hard on the leash, trying to keep Boy George from jumping on a man passing by. Kit took a deep breath and walked over.

'You want me to take him for a bit?' she asked.

'Nah, it's okay.' Tam didn't look at her.

'I'm sorry about last night,' Kit said simply.

'Well, then I guess I should say it's okay.'

'But it's not really, is it?' Kit said miserably.

Tam shrugged.

They began walking back to the house, the dog straining at the leash. Brendan was in the front doorway, talking to Gucci who was on her way out. Why were that Barbie doll and her stupid Ken boyfriend still living in their house? Why didn't they just go and buy some swanky apartment on Southbank? It maddened Kit to see the perfect blonde in all her up-market gym gear, smiling coyly at Brendan, running one hand through her long hair as though she was on a film set. What in the hell did they have to talk about anyway? Kit dodged around them and went inside.

'Oh, Kit,' Brendan called after her, 'you want to talk about all that stuff soon?'

'What?' she snapped.

'The Irish stuff.' He grinned at her sullen mood. 'You hung over or something?'

'No,' Kit turned away. 'Yeah, I want to talk. If you've got time.'

'Sure.'

But they didn't get a chance. The phone was ringing. It was Johnny, for Kit.

'Leonie seems to have had a bit of a relapse. Are you coming back soon?'

'Yeah,' Kit said, immediately panicking. *She can't die. Not now. She's got to wake and tell me stuff.* 'Tomorrow, probably. Just have to get my job and uni sorted out.'

'Good.' Johnny sounded relieved. 'It'll be good for her to see you.'

'What do the doctors say?'

'Apparently there are often these little setbacks.

'Shit.'

They're scanning her again today, in case there's a clot or something.'

'A clot?'

'On the brain.'

'Oh. Well, I'll be there tomorrow.'

It was while she was waiting for the kettle to boil, standing alone on the greasy lino in her bare feet, that Kit decided what she had to do. She looked up at the ceiling. Two spindly spiders were creeping around the light-fitting. One was beginning to descend down the cord towards the bulb. It was such a fine delicate wispy thing, just going about its business. It struck her that that was all anyone could be expected to do; go about their own business. When it came down to it, that was what she had to do, too.

She would defer university for next year. She wouldn't have the big important essay done anyway. Besides that, she'd lost all interest in African independent states. She'd go and see Wally. Get as much work as he would give her. Save her money, then go to Ireland and find her father. She'd organise her passport right away. Leonie would wake up properly soon and would tell her his name. If not, she'd find it somewhere else. Do some detective work. Her birth would be registered at the hospital, surely? She'd get on the Internet and find stuff out. The adoption papers would have some information. Something told her that Gerard knew more than he was letting on. He must know the name. She would quiz him.

When Kit had the name and the money for the fare, then she would go and find him. Simple, really. Why had she thought it was more complicated than that?

CHAPTER NINETEEN

Kit stopped in the doorway of the day ward. It was a large bright room with only one other patient, down the other end watching a small television. Leonie was propped up on pillows facing the window. She was lying on top of the bed, her bare white feet poking out the end of a long light-blue gown. Det and Eileen were sitting on either side of her, talking quietly. Kit was shocked by Leonie's smallness, by the bare shaven head and the two long, slightly crooked red scars that crossed at the back of her skull. She looked as thin and fragile as a concentration camp victim. Somehow she seemed so much more ill than when she'd been lying completely unconscious with her head bound in a white bandage the day after the accident.

When the aunts caught sight of Kit and Johnny, they waved.

'Oh, good!' Det called in a loud whisper. 'Kathleen, you made it. And you look beautiful as usual.'

Det gave her a kiss. 'You always say nice things,' smiled Kit. 'It's good to see you . . . all.'

'And don't you look lovely, Kathleen?' Eileen, like her sister, was always quick to pay compliments. 'Love you in pink.' She leant down to Leonie, speaking slowly and loudly. 'Here's Kathleen at last to see you, darling.'

Kit moved nearer and bent down to kiss Leonie awkwardly.

'Hey there,' she said. 'How are you?'

Leonie didn't smile, but her eyes, huge and luminous in her thin face, flickered wide open as if they recognised the voice, then they fastened immediately on Kit's face, looking deeply mesmerised. One hand, so thin and small now, lifted and trembled a little. Kit noticed that the other one was pushed uselessly across Leonie's stomach.

Kit cleared her throat and looked up at the aunts for help. But they were both edging away.

'It's good to see you,' Kit managed at last. 'I've been down in the city seeing about uni, and other things.'

Leonie continued to stare at her, giving no indication that she'd heard or understood. Johnny moved off and Kit panicked, wondering how long she was expected to sit there. What else could she talk about? God, what were you meant to say to someone who just stared at you? Everyone said stimulation was important. Kit knew she should start talking but everything she thought of to say seemed ridiculous. She continued to sit there holding Leonie's hand, feeling absurdly self-conscious. Kit's mind began to wander. Seeing Leonie like this made her think seriously of her own good health for the first time in her life – the fact that she could run and move and shout. When she got back to the farm she would take a long walk down by the creek, past all the places she'd loved when she'd been younger, and she would run and shout and –

'Kathleen,' Leonie whispered.

The word came out very slowly, as though it took all her strength. Kit, who'd been staring out the window, turned back in shock. The voice, hoarse and whispery, was still in the room, sitting in the air between them.

'What, Leonie?' Kit said numbly. Things Leonie had written in the exercise book came to mind and Kit felt oddly nauseous. *A bomb. I helped put it there.* It was so hard to imagine this sick woman having anything to do with a bomb. *Had she meant to kill those people? And what would the rest of the family say if they knew?*

'Tell me about my father, Leonie,' she said quietly. 'Please.'

Leonie, lying back on her pillows, stared at Kit blankly, her eyes huge glassy brown pools in the sunlight streaming in through the window.

'I'm sorry,' Kit stumbled on quickly, 'but I just need to know his name.'

Leonie continued to stare at her.

'I know you're so sick, but . . .' a sob caught unexpectedly in Kit's throat, 'I have to know.'

Leonie made a low noise, then turned her head away. Anger jolted through Kit. She wanted to lean over and shake the fragile body in front of her.

'You have to, Leonie,' she whispered again.

Leonie jerked up in the bed suddenly, her eyes shut. She began shaking her head in great distress. Kit moved away in alarm. Leonie seemed to be having some kind of fit. Her legs under the light gown were jerking involuntarily and her mouth began to grimace fiercely, especially on one side as though she might be in pain.

A nurse came into the room and Kit, ashamed that she had probably been the cause of this sudden attack, motioned her over.

'I'm sorry, I think I upset her,' Kit mumbled in a small voice.

'Don't worry, dear,' said the nurse, putting an arm around Leonie's twitching shoulders. 'It's okay. These little fits are very common with head injuries. It takes a while to get the drugs sorted out.' She then proceeded to take both of Leonie's hands in her own, and push her back gently onto the pillows.

'Come on now, Leonie,' the nurse continued calmly. 'It's okay

194

now.' She turned to Kit with a smile. 'She's had a lot of visitors today. Might be time for a rest.'

That night there was a call from Ireland. Everyone else was already in bed and Kit picked it up.

'Is that Leonie Quinlan's place?' The accent was sharp Northern Irish, surprisingly clear – and very brusque.

'It is.' Kit's heart began to beat wildly.

'It's Annie Ryan here. I'm ringing from Belfast. To whom am I speaking?'

'I'm Kathleen,' Kit answered automatically. 'Leonie's sister.' About to correct herself and tell the woman that she was Leonie's daughter, Kit didn't get a chance.

'I've only just heard,' Annie continued sharply, 'about the accident. I can't believe it. How is she?'

'She survived the operation and she's starting to get better.' Kit guiltily remembered the relapse. 'Er, slowly,' she added.

'My God, I just can't believe it!' the woman said again. 'I had dinner with her and she was so well and full of plans. To think it happened that very night. I'm absolutely shattered!'

There was something about this woman that grated on Kit. It was a sort of bossy, queen-bee manner. Then it hit her. This must be the overseas friend Leonie had met up with the night of the accident! *Annie!* Maybe it was Annie the nurse. The one who wanted to help Leonie when she was having the baby. *Having me!* Annie the good friend who'd driven Therese and Gerard to the airport all those years ago. If anyone knew anything about Leonie and her father, then it might be this woman.

'So it was you she had dinner with? Over here, I mean in Australia, in Melbourne?'

'Yes,' Annie said coolly, 'yes, we had dinner and I was off the next day to a conference in Singapore as it happens. I only got home a

195

few days ago. Oh, I do feel terrible that I've only just found out.'

'Sorry, but we didn't know any of her overseas friends,' Kit said defensively. 'We had no names to call.'

'They told me head injuries?' Annie said, ignoring Kit's apology. 'And I believe there was a long operation?'

'Yes.'

'So is she conscious?'

'Yes, partly.'

'Partly?' Annie snapped. 'What do you mean? Does she recognise people?'

'Well,' Kit said hurriedly, 'she's more conscious some times than others. The doctors think she's coming out of it.'

Annie gave an exasperated sigh. Kit didn't know if it was because of her own inadequate explanation or not.

'What else do the doctors say?'

Kit tried to collect her thoughts. She knew she should keep answering questions to keep this woman on-side, but who the hell was she to be so rude? Kit wanted some questions of her own answered. Leonie had been upset about something the night she'd had dinner with this woman. She'd come around to the Richmond house in some kind of emotional state, according to Gucci.

'There will be a long convalescence,' she said, then, before the woman could ask anything else, 'So are you a nurse?'

The woman hesitated. 'I used to be a nurse.'

'And you knew Leonie back in 1981, at the time of the hunger strike?'

'I did.'

'So you know that I'm actually her daughter?'

Annie didn't reply. Kit felt herself shrink inside as each silent moment moved on to the next. Kit knew she should play things more carefully but it was difficult trying to quell her curiosity.

'You know who my father is then?' Kit went on more carefully.

196

'You know about the circumstances of my birth. Could I talk to you about it?' The words were rushing from her. 'Not now if you don't want to, but please, could I have your number? I could ring you back and –'

'I don't think that would be a good idea.'

'Why not?'

'All this is for Leonie to tell you.'

'But she can't speak,' Kit cried, 'and she hasn't said a word about it all my life! And I'm nearly twenty-one!'

'I know how old you are. Don't think that date isn't etched on my mind forever!'

'She's lost her memory,' Kit went on, 'and she might never get it back. You've got to help me!'

'Listen, Kathleen,' Annie said coldly and slowly, 'and listen carefully. I don't have to do anything.'

'Oh.' Kit felt suddenly foolish, on the point of tears. *What have I said to antagonise her?* 'But please, would you?' She was begging now. 'I'm just asking you if you would.'

'I'll think about it. I'll ring you back.'

'When?'

'Soon. Maybe. Meanwhile, may I have the name and number of Leonie's doctor?'

Kit searched through the numbers pinned to the wall near the phone. 'Here it is.' She gave out the number.

'Good,' Annie muttered. 'I need to speak to someone sensible about Leonie.'

Kit opened her mouth, too shocked by the insult to speak. She would have liked to punch her! Annie must have realised how her last comment sounded because she immediately tried to soften it. 'Er, I mean someone who'll be able to talk specifics about her medical condition,' she added hurriedly.

'Right.'

'Thanks for your help, Kathleen.'

'Okay.'

'Goodbye.'

'Bye.'

Kit hung up. She made herself a cup of cocoa and sat down, trying to work out what to do next. The trouble was, she desperately wanted that horrible woman to ring back.

CHAPTER TWENTY

After three days back at the farm, Kit returned to the city, using the job at the pub as her excuse. Even so, no one could understand her leaving. What did she need a job for? Her parents would give her money if she needed it. Wasn't it more important to be there to help Leonie recover? She would be sorry later if . . .

But no one could bring themselves to speak the words.

If Leonie didn't make it. If Leonie died.

Eventually, Kit had to tell them of her plan to defer university, save and go overseas to find her father. The whole family seemed to collapse in shock. Damien was called in, to talk her 'through the issues', but really to talk her out of it. Why go off on a wild-goose chase after some man who had shown no interest in her whatsoever? Especially when her own mother was right here and needing her desperately? Kit said nothing. What did he know, what did any of them know, about this deep longing for answers? It might be months before Leonie would be able to speak properly again, if ever. And what if she didn't want to talk about it. Or if she couldn't remember? Kit needed to know about her beginnings. Leonie would be here when she came back.

And if she wasn't?

Well, Kit was prepared to risk it.

She knew her family were all desperate to see her and Leonie become a proper mother and daughter now that the big secret was out. Involved, loving, close. Kit shuddered thinking about how much she *didn't* want that. Of course she hoped that Leonie would get better. But that didn't mean that she wanted their relationship to change. Leonie could have all that close warm cuddly stuff with Therese and Gerard, *and* the brothers *and* the aunts *and* friends like Bernadette. There were heaps of people for Leonie to be close to. Kit didn't want a new relationship with Leonie – just information about her former life and, of course, about her father.

Kit had been washing up sourly when Sebastian arrived the day after she got back. They weren't her dishes and there were so many of them, and the scraps of food had congealed and stuck, making them hard to clean. The front door must have been left open because she heard no ring or knock, just a cheery 'Hello! Anyone home?' Kit caught sight of herself in the mirror above the sink. She'd worked late the night before, and had only just got up. She hadn't combed her hair. She hadn't even had a shower. She looked terrible and felt worse . . .

It was Sebastian. He walked into the kitchen, holding a big bright plastic bag under one arm.

'Hi there,' he said, stopping at the doorway. 'Sorry, but the front door was wide open. I did knock.'

'Oh.' Kit smiled nervously. 'I didn't hear anything.'

They both stood there looking awkwardly at each other, then started speaking at the same time.

'Thought I might as well bring these around today,' he said, dumping the plastic bag on the table.

'So you picked up your mother then?'

'Sorry . . .'

'No, sorry. You first.'

'Yes, I picked up my mother. She's still jet-lagged,' he chuckled. 'She's a bloody awful pain when she's tired. Anyway,' he waved at the bag on the table, 'I went through my books and pulled a few out for you.'

'Oh, thanks.' Kit moved over to the table and pulled the books out of the bag, staring stupidly at the covers. If only she had something intelligent to say! But all she could think of was that she hadn't brushed her teeth or had a shower and that if he came close he'd smell her for sure.

'So which one first?'

He looked older than when she'd last seen him – more lined and weary. World-worn. But noticing all that didn't make her blood slow down any or the slight shake in her hands subside.

'Well,' he picked up a couple and set them aside, 'these two are general texts so you could start here.' He grinned suddenly. 'Any chance of a cup of coffee?'

Kit smiled, feeling relieved but almost light-headed with nerves. 'Please sit down. I'll make a pot.'

Kit knew before she opened the lid that there would be no coffee left. Of course. No one had been shopping. Everything was against her. Mice, dirty dishes, no coffee, unexpected special visitors when she looked like crap. Why hadn't she just crawled back into bed that morning and waited for the day to be over?

'Sorry,' she said, showing him the empty tin. 'What about tea?'

'I hate tea,' he said emphatically.

Kit must have looked worried because he suddenly smiled to show he was joking. 'Why don't we go out for a coffee?'

Kit's mood lifted at the prospect of getting away from the house, and those books on the table.

'Could you give me two minutes to have a shower?'

'Sure.'

They found themselves a table overlooking the footpath in Shambles, the nearest café to Kit's house. The short walk, the warm sunshine and the breeze put colour into Kit's cheeks. She told herself that everything was all right now. Within five minutes she'd managed to shower, clean her teeth, dress in jeans and a bright pink shirt. Her hair, now brushed and shining, was pinned back with two clips on each side of her head. Surely it had to mean something that he'd come?

'Your mother's story is interesting,' Sebastain began evenly, stirring sugar into his coffee. 'I'd like to know more.'

'Yeah, well,' Kit murmured, watching his lovely fingers, mesmerised by their dexterity and fine shape, 'me too.'

'I hope I wasn't too bossy the other night,' he added, looking up at her with one of his sweet attentive smiles, 'I tend to get a bit preachy when I'm interested in something.'

'No, no.' She melted inside at his lopsided smile, accepting his masked apology with relief. He had been a bit preachy but at least he knew it. 'What you said was interesting.' She stopped herself from going on because she was desperate not to get onto politics again. 'It's just that I'm so unfamiliar with the issues.'

'So you'll have a read of those books?' he asked cautiously.

'Oh, yes. For sure. I will.'

'And I promise I won't tell you what to think,' he grinned and she smiled back shyly.

It was pleasant enough sitting there together as the weak sunshine poured in. Pleasant enough and totally unsatisfactory. He wanted to know when the party had finally ended and she asked him more about his mother. But when the coffees were finished they both got up and paid for their own. There didn't seem any point in lingering.

'I might ring you when I've read a bit,' Kit suggested tentatively.

'Oh yes. Please do. I'll look forward to it.'

They walked back up to the street and parted on the pavement outside her house. He planted a brief kiss on her cheek. Kit waved then hurried back inside and burst into tears. Nothing was turning out right for her. She adored Sebastian. He'd come around, out of the blue, to see her, and she . . . *she hadn't known what to say*. She'd stuffed up completely.

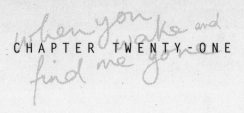

CHAPTER TWENTY-ONE

After spending the rest of the day by herself, at nine that evening Kit lay down on her bed, fully clothed, pulled a rug over her and picked up one of Sebastian's books. She flipped through the pages.

There were a lot of black-and-white photos alongside small squares of text. She stopped at one and read the caption underneath: *Protesters in Derry*. Brendan's city. *1973. Bloody Sunday.* There were bodies on the ground – a priest bending over one – a crowd of onlookers surrounding them. Kit stared at each face intently. *Any one of these men could be my father.* She felt excited, imbued with new energy. She'd always loved her university work. She loved looking things up, understanding things from the inside out. It was what she was good at. She would find him; once she got over there and put her mind to it. She was good at research. *So why had she become intimidated by Sebastian?* She closed the book. She, Kit Quinlan, was one of the brightest students in her year. She was a bit younger than Sebastian, and that was all. As soon as she felt she had a basic grip on it all, she'd go around and see him. They'd sit on his couch and discuss it and this time she would know what he was talking about. She'd be able to argue with him.

She lay back down on her pillows, letting the book slide as she tried to imagine his house, his lounge room. It would be comfortable, maybe a bit messy. Long windows, and vases of flowers, books and coffee cups everywhere. She giggled suddenly. No teapot! He'd invite her to dinner. They'd have a glass of wine maybe and then start holding hands. Things would be cooking on the stove. This time it wouldn't matter that they were talking politics because they would be equals, and close. So close. But as her mind relaxed, things became confused. Whose lounge room was she in again? Sebastian's or her fathers? Was that soft evening light streaming in through the tall windows Irish or Australian? Which one was she looking for? Which one did she want most? Who was she nestling up to on the couch? Her father or her lover?

A click at the front door woke Kit a few hours later. She looked at the clock. Midnight. She switched on the light and pushed off the blanket.

Kit got up and tiptoed out into the hall to the bathroom and splashed her face with water. It must have been Tam who'd just come in. Kit hesitated, then summoned up her courage and gently tapped on Tam's door. There was no answer.

'Tam?' Kit whispered, 'you there?' She pushed the door open and immediately froze. The bedside lamp was on and Robbie was there, in jeans and bare chested, leaning up against the back wall, one foot raised flat against it, smirking. He was waiting. *For her?* His well-muscled torso gleamed in the soft yellow light. He was holding one of the long pink feathers Tam had stuck in the side of her dressing table, running it back and forth through his thumb and forefinger as if he was about to perform some kind of erotic dance. Kit stood like a rabbit caught in headlights, staring at him. He didn't move, just kept looking at her, the feather moving rhythmically through his hands.

'I was looking for Tam,' Kit mumbled.

'Well . . .' He waved one arm around to indicate he was alone, then laughed at her confusion. 'As you can see, she ain't here.'

Kit slowly backed out again, carefully shutting the door. She stood in the hallway.

What the hell was he doing in there?

She tried to calm herself as she walked back to her room. She sat on the bed. There was only a hallway between them. *God, calm down!* He was Tam's boyfriend and so he had a right to be in her bedroom, didn't he? She remembered Tam mentioning in passing that she was going out with her mother and would be late in. So he had let himself into the house. That meant he had his own key.

Kit climbed back under the covers and lay there, rigid as a steel pole. If only Brendan was home or if Tam would come in, then Robbie being there wouldn't seem so creepy. He hated her, she knew it. She could see it in his eyes. She shuddered. There was no way she'd be able to go to sleep with him under the same roof.

Kit sat up again and pulled on her jacket. Damn it, there was no way she'd stay in the house with that creep! She would go down to Lou's and sleep in her bed.

Kit picked up her bag. At that moment there were three soft taps on her door, and a man's muffled voice.

'Kit.' The low whisper sent a flutter of panic into her gut. *Who was it?* Was it him? She didn't dare answer.

'Are you awake?' the voice said.

Without replying, hardly even thinking, Kit ran for the window. She opened it and threw one leg over, slipping her whole body after it quickly. She hurt her knee in the process and banged her head but she didn't care. She ran for the old back gate and slipped the bolt across, stepped out onto the cobbled laneway and began walking towards the street. She wanted to be away from that house. Away from that creep. If only she had the money to buy her ticket

206

for Ireland now. Was there someone she knew who'd lend it to her? She'd already hit on Johnny for it but he, although willing, had no money.

What had Robbie come knocking on her door for? What did he want?

Kit didn't plan to end up at Sebastian's. Not consciously anyway. She rushed off down the street, feeling furiously righteous. She had to leave her own house because of that guy! Kit hurried past Lou's without even slowing down, even though minutes before she'd told herself that's where she was headed. She walked fast and steady down Victoria Street and past the lights of the cafés and bars. What would she do now? Where would she go?

She didn't even have to take the card out to check the address. She knew the street and it wasn't that far. It was at the edge of a park in Clifton Hill only a couple of kilometres away. She told herself that she'd just go and check out the house, then head home again. Brendan would be there by the time she got back, probably even Tam.

Kit stood at the edge of the park, staring over at his house. His car was out the front. It was a small Victorian weatherboard with lace-work on the verandah and a red front door. On either side were two much grander double-storied brick terraces. What did the light in the high window above his door mean? That he was up? Perhaps working late? Would he like a visitor? She stood for a few moments practising her smile and a few variations of what to say.

'Hi there. I was just passing. Thought I'd call in for a few minutes. A quick cup of coffee maybe?'

Kit walked towards the red door, knowing that if she didn't do it straight away she never would, not daring to admit to herself that she was desperate and that he would know that. Who, after all, would be *just passing* after midnight? It was a ridiculous thing to do.

The truth was, she wanted to build on that kiss of however many weeks ago. She was hoping that as soon as he saw her he might remember it too, pull her into his arms, tell her that he'd been longing for her, kiss her, lead her off to his bedroom. Lie her down. Make love to her. And that would make all the bullshit about this real father that she'd never known just slide away. Her brother Damien was right, this father had never shown any interest in her so why would that change even if she did go over there? She and Sebastian would kiss and laugh about the awkwardness between them earlier that day in the café. They would fall onto the bed, serious at first, then they'd tumble around, rolling and giggling in each other's arms, smelling each other's sweat, sliding in and out of each other's bodies. She shuddered with longing . . . Everything would be perfect. She just had to pick up the knocker and let it go. *Crash*.

She wanted to stay the night with him. That's why she'd come.

The steady beat of footsteps came down the hallway. The door opened and it was him, squinting down at her in distracted surprise. He was dressed in jeans and an old loose jumper with holes in one elbow and strands of wool unravelling at the neck, a pen and small note-book in one hand.

He stood blinking on the doorstep. 'Er, *hello*,' he said at last, smiling a little. 'How are you?' He was very polite but not pleased. Kit smiled nervously, immediately forgetting what she'd coached herself to say.

'Fine, thanks. How are you?'

'You want to come in?'

'Yes. Okay. Thanks.'

Heart thudding, she followed him down the long narrow hallway, through a pretty stained-glass door and into the lounge room. It was perfect. Smaller than she'd imagined, but soft yellow light from two old-fashioned standard lamps oozed warmth and coziness. Over against the far wall was a messy table and four straight chairs. Well-packed bookcases lined the two long walls.

Perfect, except for the fact that he already had a guest. She was sitting on one of the chairs, a couple of note-pads on her lap and piles of paper at her feet. Thick straight dark hair swung around her pretty face.

She had to be a guest, because she was wearing high heels and a rather expensive leather bag sat next to her on the couch. She was looking questioningly at Kit.

'We were just doing a bit of work,' Sebastian smiled vaguely. 'Kathleen, I'd like you to meet Sara.'

Kit nodded and gulped. Sara stared at her coolly through deep round hazel eyes.

'Well, hello,' Sara said, not bothering to get up, hold out her hand or keep the surprise out of her voice. 'Nice to meet you, Kathleen.' She looked at the tiny silver watch on her wrist and laughed softly. 'Well!'

Kit felt herself shrink inside. Here was a cool sophisticated woman, probably in her late twenties, the gold pen poised between her fingers as if she was in the middle of writing a very important sentence. She had a thick silver necklace at her throat with some kind of blue stone set into it. There were matching stones in her ears. Kit's hopes plummeted. *How can I possibly compete with you?*

'Nice to meet you, too,' Kit mumbled, feeling the heat rush to her face, thanking God for the low light.

'Why don't you sit down?' Sebastian waved at the chair opposite Sara that he'd obviously been sitting in himself.

There were dishes on the table. And empty wine glasses. These two had just had a intimate dinner. Kit's mind began to race. Maybe this woman was his *wife*! She looked for the telltale wedding ring on the woman's hand but the long olive-skinned fingers flipping so confidently through the note-book on her lap were covered in rings of all shapes and sizes and so it was impossible to tell if one of them signified a wedding.

'So what are you working on?' Kit asked shyly.

Sebastian, standing at the doorway into the kitchen, held up his hand. 'Just before we get onto that,' he said, running his hand through his hair, 'a cup of something, Kathleen?'

'Well, I don't want to interrupt.' Kit looked from him back to his friend. *Why had she come?*

'Not at all,' he said kindly, but without any real enthusiasm. 'Coffee? We were just about to have some, weren't we, Sara?'

'Hmmm. That would be lovely,' Sara murmured. She was looking down at her notes, frowning, letting Kit know that in fact it wasn't all right to interrupt like this. That turning up after midnight for a visit was not done. Kit would have liked a glass of wine. Something to settle her nerves. But she didn't dare ask.

'Coffee would be good,' she said, brightly.

They sat on opposite sides of the fireplace, Sara fiddling with her notes and Kit trying to appear relaxed. She could hear Sebastian whistling in the kitchen as he organised cups.

'So you're working on something big?' Kit asked in desperation.

The woman looked up, as though surprised that Kit had spoken. 'Yes, I'm doing a book, actually,' she said with that same appraising, knowing smile.

'What about?'

'Resistance groups in Indonesia.'

'Oh,' Kit nodded and looked away. So she was in his field. Probably a PhD student, too. 'That must be interesting.'

The woman nodded and began to organise her notes into three different piles on the floor. Whoever she was, Kit thought grimly – wife, lover, colleague – she was pretty sure of her place in this room. Kit looked around, longing to go out and join Sebastian in the kitchen. How long would coffee take? This was such a big mistake.

A shag on the rock, that's how she felt. The expression bumped around in her mind. *A shag on a rock.* The last time she'd used it Tam had fallen about laughing. *Oh God. Tam, where are you now?* In the kitchen the kettle began to whine. When it stopped, Sebastian hummed a tune. Both women sat there listening to him and the sound of water being poured into cups.

'Don't worry,' Sara said, leaning towards Kit conspiratorially. 'Many women fall in love with him. You're not the only one.'

Kit stared at the woman. Were Kit's feelings so obvious? Oh shit. How bloody *appalling!*

'Just then, Sebastian came in holding a tray with three steaming cups and a plate of sweet biscuits. He settled the tray on a small table near one of the chairs.

'Kit was in the play, Sara,' he said, handing her a cup. Then he turned to Kit, smiling warmly, holding out a cup for her. 'She's a damned good actor, too. Do you want sugar?'

Kit shook her head and stood up without meeting his eyes.

'Really?' Sara's eyes flashed mockingly at Kit across his head. 'So have you done any acting since then?'

'Sebastian, I've just realised I can't stay,' Kit said, ignoring the question, and feigning a sort of breathless girl-in-a-hurry stance.

'Oh?'

'I actually have to be somewhere else. I didn't realise the time,' Kit gushed on. 'Sorry, and thanks.'

'Well, that *was* a fleeting visit,' he said awkwardly to her turned back.

'Yes, well thanks, anyway.'

'Good to meet you, Kathleen.' Sara's cool voice called after Kit as she rushed down the hallway to the front door, but Kit didn't answer. She didn't even turn to say goodbye to Sebastian properly.

'Bye then. See you,' she said over her shoulder as she darted out the door.

'Do you want a ride home?' he called after her, real concern in his voice now. 'It's very late.'

'No thanks.'

'It would be no trouble.'

Kit hated him and she hated the woman. She hated her life and she didn't have any idea what she was going to do with the rest of it.

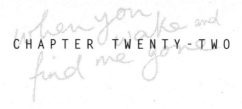

CHAPTER TWENTY-TWO

By the time Kit got back home it was after one in the morning and she'd calmed down. Traipsing though the streets at night often did that for her. There had been a shower of rain earlier and the roads were gleaming like giant licorice straps under the pink and yellow lights from the clubs and bars along Victoria Street. She passed a number of crowds on the footpaths. Further on, there was a group trying to line dance on the edge of the busy road.

Cities were best at night. All the monotony and shabbiness of the power lines and miles of concrete, the stink of car fumes, faded away when the sun went down. In the darkness, they took on a splendour that Kit had never quite learnt to take for granted. Sometimes beauty hung out just beneath the surface of the oddest, plainest, most mundane things.

So who was that woman anyway? Sebastian hadn't acted as though he'd been caught out with a wife or girlfriend. Maybe she was a colleague with secret designs of her own? Oh, shit! Kit found herself laughing aloud. It was so typical of her, to go off half-cocked. It would have made much more sense to hang around to find out about his relationship to that woman instead of heading off blindly into the night.

Kit rounded the corner of her street, in time to see Gucci arriving home in a taxi and (blessing upon blessing!) Robbie leaving in his little silver-grey Saab. Kit stood watching from the far end of the street as he embraced Tam, then got into the car. Tam stood on the footpath waving him off before walking back into the house. Now she might be able to catch Tam for a talk. Kit walked on quickly towards the house, fishing in her pocket for her key.

But when Kit opened the door into the kitchen, it was just Brendan, sitting at the table, tucking into a plate of baked beans on toast.

Kit smiled. 'Hiya, Bren!'

Brendan nodded and went back to his food. He was often terse and undemonstrative when he was tired. In a way Kit was now relieved she'd missed Tam. It was way too late for a big heart-to-heart. Besides, she hadn't seen Brendan since she'd got back from the country.

'You been working?' she asked, walking over to the sink for a cup.

'Yep,' he said. 'Since midday.'

'Over twelve hours!'

'I've been here for a while. I knocked on your door.'

Oh, so it wasn't Robbie.

Kit gave Brendan's broad shoulders a quick squeeze. 'Apart from being shit-tired, how are you?'

'Okay,' he said, still without looking up from his food.

'What about Rory?'

'He's been kicked out of school.'

'No!' Kit slumped down in a chair opposite Brendan, then leant over and took a piece of toast from the side of his plate. Brendan gave no indication that he noticed her doing this or cared one way or the other.

'Why?'

'Dealing,' Brendan muttered.

'Shit!' Kit said, munching the toast. 'I didn't think they were allowed to kick kids out of school at his age. How old is he?'

'Fourteen.'

'So will he be allowed back next year?'

'Yeah, if he behaves.' Brendan pushed away the plate, giving a tired groan. 'He's going to stay here for a week, if you and Tam don't mind.'

'Of course not. But you must be getting a bit sick of it all.'

They were silent for a few moments. Kit got up and made tea. She poured two cups and brought them over to the table, handing him one.

'Sorry I haven't been around,' she said lightly, 'to help out.'

'It's okay. You're busy too. How's your mother, by the way?'

'Okay, but she's had a couple of these fits. Everyone's worried that she's going to, you know, get worse.'

'It's common,' Brendan said quickly. 'With head injuries.'

Kit sipped her tea. It was wonderfully hot and strong. She leant over and spooned in extra sugar.

'Trust you to know!'

'What?'

'That fits are common with head injuries.'

'Hmmm,' Brendan shrugged. Kit looked at him, trying to gauge his mood. Definitely down, but something else was going on, too.

'We still haven't talked about Ireland properly, Brendan,' she said at last. 'That page I gave you of Leonie's. When are we going to be able to catch up? I haven't told you my plans or anything.'

'What plans?'

'I'm going to defer uni next year. To get over there somehow.'

Brendan frowned and nodded slowly.

'Glad you find it so exciting,' Kit rolled her eyes.

Brendan pushed the cup away impatiently, then got up, irritated. He went over and opened the back door, letting in a cool draught of night air. He leant against the door with his back to her.

'I don't want to talk about Ireland,' he said moodily.

'Why not? You said you would.'

'Well, I will,' Brendan sighed. 'I mean, I will if you want.'

'Brendan, what is going on with you?' Kit burst out. 'You're not making sense lately.'

'There's something I've got to tell you,' he said. 'Something I've got to say.'

'What?'

There was a moment before he spoke.

'That . . . I . . . love you,' Brendan said slowly, still with his back to her. 'I know it will seem stupid, after all this time.'

Kit laughed, almost got up to hug him, but there was something about that big turned back and serious profile that stopped her.

'Well,' she said, still laughing, 'I love you, too. You're my best . . .' She hesitated, instinctively knowing it might not be what he wanted to hear. 'My best friend,' she finished in a small voice.

Brendan turned around quickly. 'I don't mean it like that,' he said angrily. 'I mean I really love you. Like I'm *in love* with you.'

Kit was shocked by the flare of temper. She felt awkward. *What was he saying?*

The room grew still. The silence between them was uncomfortable. It seemed thick and full of something strong and bitter. And yet there was sweetness in it, too. Right in this room. Sweetness. But she didn't know how to find it. She was unconnected to the moment somehow, as though she was being dragged away from everything she'd ever known. It was almost frightening.

'I don't think so, Brendan,' she said eventually. 'You've been having a rotten time lately, what with Rory and stuff. Maybe you've got things mixed up and – '

216

'Don't patronise me!' Brendan flew back at her. 'Actually, I've been having a rather *good* time lately for your information!' He stopped himself. When he spoke again his voice was softer. 'I know how I feel and I'm not expecting you to do anything about it. I know you think of me as a friend and that you're in love with that tosser Sebastian. But I've just got to tell you because I'm going mad.'

'Brendan, come on . . .'

'It is real, okay?' he went on sharply. 'Just tell me you understand that, at least.'

Kit jumped up. 'I don't have to tell you anything! And I *don't* have to tell you what I believe or don't believe.' To her amazement, she was suddenly crying. Full of rage, and crying. She stood helplessly, wringing her hands, tears pouring down her cheeks.

'I don't fucking need this, Brendan!' she gasped through her tears. 'I need a bloody friend! Tam won't talk to me and – '

'Ever thought why not?' he yelled.

'Okay, I said some stupid things to that *shithead* of a boyfriend! Big deal. I also said I was sorry. I thought the three of us were mates. Real friends. So a bit of crap happens and we're at each other's throats. Or . . .' she pointed at him menacingly, 'thinking crazy stuff!'

'This is not crazy stuff, Kit! That's what I'm trying to tell you. I've felt like this for months. I just hadn't admitted it to myself. I didn't let on because . . .'

'All this bloody stuff happening with my family,' Kit went on, putting her hands over her ears, refusing to listen. 'My sister, who I don't even like, turns out to be my bloody mother! And I've got no father.'

'Nor have I!' Brendan yelled. 'So what? I don't whinge about it all day.'

'I tell you I could do with a friend,' Kit said again. 'I don't want a boyfriend.' But the words hung in the air. Because of course, that's what she did want. But she wasn't going to admit that to Brendan. Kit ran from the room, letting the door slam behind her.

She threw off her clothes and fell naked into bed, pulling the doona up around her chin, letting Sebastian's books scatter to the floor. What did she care? She had six hours at the most before she had to get up again, and she was damned if that idiot out in the kitchen was going to stop her sleeping. Wally wanted her at the pub at nine in the morning and she would be there. She was going overseas. And she had to save. She needed all the work she could get. Kit switched off the lamp and lay there, watching tiny dots of pink light flicker in through her window onto the opposite wall. How in the world was she going to be able to sleep? Robbie, Sebastian and now Brendan. Was this really ordinary life? *Her ordinary life?* More likely a crap soap opera that some idiot had dropped her into. She tried to tell herself that Brendan must have been overtired, or drunk, and that in the morning he'd be sensible, and they'd be able to resume their easy ordinary friendship.

But Brendan wasn't someone who would say something like that for fun. He was old-fashioned in that way. She'd seen him drunk. He might fall over, or slur his words a bit, even go to the bathroom and be sick, but he never ever said stupid stuff that he didn't mean. He never said things he had to apologise for in the morning.

The trouble was, it wasn't even true to tell herself that she'd never thought of Brendan as more than a friend. When she'd first moved into the house two years before, and he'd been living there with Margie, Kit had been attracted to Brendan. But all that was years ago! She squirmed with the humiliation of having to admit that she had initially tried to model her awkward, country-girl self on Margie, Brendan's slinky girlfriend. Kit had wanted to work out how she might attract a guy *just like Brendan*.

But so what? Time had passed and so much had happened. She'd met lots of other people. Made friends. She'd started to shine with her university work. She'd grown up. Then Sebastian had made his entrance and she'd fallen for him. Madly, deeply . . . Living together, she and Brendan knew each other warts and all. They were housemates who'd become close friends and that was it.

Kit shut her eyes tightly in the dark. *Why* was it that nothing seemed to happen at the right time in her life?

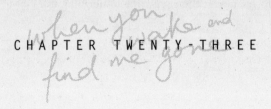

CHAPTER TWENTY-THREE

Brendan lay awake for ages, utterly dejected, wondering what the hell he'd do next.

Kit had obviously never considered him. Never would, either. What went against him was not only that nerdy weed Sebastian. The real problem was that Brendan and Kit got on so well. They could talk for hours. They made each other laugh and they both loved arguing. When they were in a room together, it came alive. Other people noticed that spark. Tam, Lou and other friends often commented on the way Kit and Brendan were always at each other, joking and arguing, telling stories. The truth was, it felt like she was his other half. And the weird thing was, she'd admitted as much to him, a few times. But had he taken it as his cue? Had he had the guts to take the initiative and respond back then? No way! Weak coward that he was. One time he particularly remembered because it was just before Kit got involved in the play . . .

They'd been walking home together from some party on a frosty night in the middle of last winter, her hand in the crook of his arm. It was about three a.m. They were walking into the wind, gasping with the cold, laughing like lunatics. It felt to Brendan then as though it had all happened already, as though the preliminaries had been gone through and now they were together. They'd been talking earlier about Africa. About what had been happening in Zaire. She'd been reading a bit of the history of the place and he'd been telling her what he knew about the present situation, then she'd stopped right in the middle of the road and pulled him up with her.

'Ah, Bren,' she'd said wistfully, still clutching his arm but looking up at the stars, 'I don't know that I'll ever love anyone the way I love you.'

He hadn't been able to answer, hardly believed he'd heard the words. But he'd slipped his arm around her waist, pulled her nearer and kissed the top of her head, a jolt of joy in his chest bobbing around, melting, running like sweet dark chocolate through his whole body.

'Of course I wouldn't say that to you during the day,' she'd added. 'You might think I was a complete loser.' They'd both chuckled. The empty street had suddenly come to life around them. Breathing with promise. This was it, this is what everything else was building up to. The moment didn't have a beginning and it didn't end. It was an impossibly difficult maths problem just unknotting itself on the page before his eyes. Hidden laws rose to the surface and played themselves out, making perfect sense. That's how it would be with him and Kit.

But within minutes they'd reached the front door. Lou and Tam and at least a dozen others had been sitting around drinking and listening to loud music and the magical moment had disappeared, as flimsy and as hard to grasp as smoke.

So why hadn't he grabbed the chance then, out on that frosty street? Told her that's how he felt, too. That being great friends was good but it wasn't good enough. The two of them could be so much more. God, he couldn't believe how completely thick he'd been.

221

The trouble was that they *got on*. Everyone knew that women never fancied guys who they could talk to, or guys who obviously liked them. They liked mean bastards who treated them like shit. Or mysterious elusive guys (like that cool nancy-boy Sebastian) who never hung about long enough for any woman to get to know them. Then there were the rich guys of course. You could be a complete bastard as well as a piece of crap to look at and still pull a girl if you had money.

The worst thing about being in love with someone you shared a house with was that if you came clean and she didn't feel the same way, then everything would be ruined; the easy joking camaraderie would just disappear. That, more than anything, was what had held him back. He hadn't wanted to wreck this really happy situation between the three of them.

Brendan sighed and turned over again. God, it had killed him at that party watching her dance with Sebastian.

And what the hell had been going on these last few nights with Gucci? Crazy stuff. Crazy and mad and very bad timing.

You're an engineer, Brendan told himself. Timing is crucial to so many calculations. How come you've messed everything up so badly? The whole thing would be funny if it wasn't so damned sad!

CHAPTER TWENTY-FOUR

when you wake and find me gone

Whatever it was about Brendan's declaration that had given Kit a smidgen of joy the night before disappeared into a cloud of anger the next day. She was at the pub clearing tables when Tam approached her, asking what time she finished, because Boy George had to be taken for a walk and Tam wouldn't be home till late. This was the first day back that Kit had worked the same shift as Tam. All morning they'd kept a polite distance from each other. The lunchtime crowd had been particularly noisy and Kit was tired, but she was so glad of the thaw in Tam's cool tone. She said she'd ask Wally if she could get off half an hour early in order to take the dog out.

'Oh, great.' Tam actually smiled. 'That's great.'

They walked back to the kitchen together with their arms full of dirty dishes, Kit almost melting with relief at Tam's changed attitude.

'So what do you think of Brendan and Gucci?' Tam asked with a laugh as she scraped the plates into the big plastic bin.

'What about them?' Kit said innocently.

'You don't know?'

'No.'

'Oh well,' Tam coloured a little, 'you've been away. I suppose I shouldn't spread gossip.'

Kit waited. This was not something she'd ever heard Tam say. They'd always told each other everything. Gossip wasn't a word they used. What happened in their lives was *life* and they shared it all. It chilled her to think that her best friend was thinking of holding something back.

'So what about them?' Kit asked finally.

'Well, they're sleeping together,' Tam said uneasily.

'But . . .' Kit was stunned. 'What about Calvin?'

'He moved out.'

'How do you know?' Kit felt like she'd been doused with a bucket of icy water. 'I mean, about Brendan and her. Who told you?'

'Well, he admitted it. I saw her coming out of his room in just a towel,' Tam whispered.

'A towel!'

'So I asked him point-blank. Weird, isn't it?'

'What did he say?'

'Kit, you look sick,' Tam laughed again, quite warmly. 'I know! Me too at first. It is a shock. Can you imagine a more unlikely couple?'

'No, I don't think I can.'

Kit broke one of Wally's finest vases that afternoon: the big blue patterned one, usually filled with loads of white lilies and fern, that greeted the patrons at the entrance to the restaurant. Then, while she was opening a bottle of red, it slipped from her grasp. Kit simply stood there staring as the wine spread out, like a huge puddle of fresh blood on the slate floor.

What game was Brendan playing? Brendan, who'd told her the

night before that he was in love with her. And it turned out he's been having it off with the Barbie doll upstairs.

'Sorry,' Kit said to Wally as he came out with a mop and bucket. 'I'm having a stupid day.'

But it was hard trying to concentrate when all she wanted to do was hit someone. Preferably Brendan, when she thought about it, straight across his big square head with something very heavy. A breadboard would do.

The phone was ringing when Kit got in after her long shift. She tore down the hallway, trying to remember where Tam kept Boy George's lead. He was barking excitedly, having heard her come in. Kit had a pang of sympathy for him, locked up alone all day in that cramped backyard.

'We'll go out in a minute, Georgie Boy,' she called, opening the door to let him in. 'Hold your horses.' She picked up the phone in the same movement. 'Just let me answer this.'

'Hello,' Kit said, cautiously patting the dog's head. 'Kit Quinlan speaking.'

'It's Martin Boylan here,' came the male voice. Slow-speaking and gentle, there was just a tinge of accent under the flat Australian tones. 'Is that Leonie's girl?'

'Yes,' Kit said shakily. 'I'm Kit.' *Martin Boylan?* Kit's tired mind flipped back to Leonie's notes. The young teenager who'd had his artwork torn all those years ago. *Yes!*

'Has your mother ever mentioned me?'

'Er . . . yes, she has.'

'I've just been talking to Annie,' he said.

'Oh! Have you?' Kit almost cried with relief. She'd left strict instructions for her Melbourne phone number to be passed on to anyone who called, but Annie hadn't rung her back and Kit had begun to despair that she ever would.

'Are you ringing from Ireland?'

'No, Sydney. I live in Australia now. I'll be in Melbourne next Monday. Could we meet?'

Kit didn't hesitate, even though she knew she was rostered on to work all day. 'Yes,' she said. 'That would be good.'

'Could you get into the city by six?' he asked. 'I have to catch an eight-thirty flight back up to Sydney, but we could maybe have a drink and a bite.'

'Yes,' Kit said again.

'I can help you,' he said quickly. 'I'll tell you everything I know and – '

'Well, I've decided I'm going to Ireland,' she burst out, 'just as soon as I can. I want to find my real father.'

'That's a very good idea.'

'You think so?'

'Of course. You should go as soon as possible.' He hesitated. 'What plans do you have?'

'I have to save the money first, and I have to find out his name.'

'His name is Eamon McCabe,' the voice went on. 'But he might go under another name, too. I'll check for you.'

'Oh.' Kit squatted down. Her legs were trembling. She hardly even noticed Boy George trying to lick her face.

Eamon McCabe.

What a name. What a wonderful, extraordinary, brilliant name. *Eamon McCabe!* Oh, sweet Jesus. She loved him already!

'Are you okay?' The voice sounded concerned, warmer now.

'I just . . . *thank you*,' Kit whispered. 'You . . . you know him?'

'Well, I *knew* him, yes.'

'What is he like? I mean, what *was* he like?'

Martin laughed. 'Well, he was a pretty extraordinary fellow back then. But look, why don't I tell you what I know when I see you.'

'Yes. Thank you so much.' She knew there were a million other things she should be saying. 'I really appreciate this. Taking the time to call me and everything.' She was going to burst out crying any second and that might seem particularly stupid to this stranger.

'Look, it's nothing compared to what your mother did for me. I want to help, okay? Go and book a ticket tomorrow.'

'A ticket?' Kit repeated stupidly. 'Tomorrow?'

'To Belfast. There are flights every day to London and connecting flights every hour or two from there. I'll have the money for you on Monday. I have a good contact there. I'll ring him over the weekend. He'll help you find Eamon. Don't bother with all the saving.'

'But . . .'

'You *must* go straight away.'

'God, I'd *love* to,' she whispered.

'Do you have a passport?'

'I've applied for one, yes.'

'Excellent.'

'So you're saying you'll lend me the money?'

'No,' he said firmly. 'I'll *give* you the money. Buy one of those student travel books. There will be enough money for you to stay in that kind of accommodation for a few weeks if you need to. It's the least I can do. Your mother was, she is a fantastic woman.'

'Was she?'

'Yeah. She was absolutely incredible. I owe my life to your mother.'

After the call Kit stood by the phone, shutting her eyes every now and again, clenching her fists.

Eamon McCabe. Her real father was moving out of the shadows and taking shape. He was coming alive. *I can tell you things*, Martin Boylan had said. *Everything I know.*

The problem would be waiting till Monday. *Eamon McCabe.*

227

What if she changed her own surname after she'd met him? Kit burst out laughing, making Boy George stop his sniffing to look up at her. *Kit McCabe.* Oh shit, there would be no stopping her with a name like that! She could be someone completely different with that name. She pictured herself in black tight suede pants and a big wide-brimmed hat, a fag hanging from her mouth and a silver gun at her hips. *Kit McCabe!* Hell. She couldn't wait. She clipped the lead onto Boy George's collar, still smiling to herself as she led him down the hallway to the front door.

Part Two

CHAPTER TWENTY-FIVE

The huge jumbo taxied away from the airport and Kit, cramped in her window seat, stared out into the blue sky and didn't know whether to laugh or cry. Until this point the trip had seemed unreal – an idea with as much substance as one of Lou's crazy spells. After all, only two weeks earlier she'd had no money, no contacts and, most importantly, no name for the mythical father she was so keen to meet. She was going to work all summer in the pub, go home for her twenty-first birthday, save the money for her fare, wait for Leonie to get better and, with luck, gradually find out what she needed to know. *Then* go.

But Martin had called, and changed everything. When he gave her the opportunity, she knew she'd have to jump at it.

So just six weeks before Christmas, Kit was on a plane to Ireland, with an open return ticket, an embarrassingly big heap of donated traveller's cheques and just two phone numbers. One was Leonie's friend Annie, who had been furious with Martin for giving Kit the money and had rung and told Kit not to come, that nothing good would come of her going to Ireland to look for her father. And the other contact was a man named Laurie who was friendly enough but cautious, too, making it clear in the brief phone call that he'd do his best to help her but couldn't promise anything. After all, he hadn't seen her father in years and couldn't even be sure he was alive. But Martin Boylan had insisted she go. Things will open up for you once you get there, he'd said. If he's alive, you'll find him. And if he's not, then you can visit the grave. He said this quite seriously, as though visiting a grave might well be as important as meeting the living man. So, although she wasn't quite sure what Martin meant by *things opening up*, she decided to take a punt and believe him.

The engines moved into full throttle. Kit fancied she could see the plane from above, poised like some huge edgy beast on the tarmac, waiting for the signal to begin its rush forward and up into the sky. She could feel its taut hesitation and was suffused with a sudden panicky hesitation of her own. No one except Martin thought she should go. Not her family or friends. The timing was all wrong, they told her. She had a family and they loved her and needed her at home.

She stared out the window at the flat concrete and almost moaned aloud. They'd been stuck on the tarmac for twenty minutes. *Why didn't this thing move?*

When the cheerful flight attendants began to explain the emergency procedures and exits, Kit clutched both armrests and shut her eyes tight. She didn't want to watch this. She didn't want to know about any of it. It felt too much like a warning.

Emergency landing positions? Oxygen masks? What the hell am I doing here? How do I get out of this one?

At last they were off, the enormous metal tube roaring its way up through the mountains of white cloud. There was no going back now. Nothing for it but to try to relax for the next twenty-four hours. Kit's mood lifted gradually as the plane slipped further and further away from earth. She fitted the headset, flicked on the radio, closed her eyes and lay back against the seat, fancying she could feel the last few weeks peeling right off her, like layers of clothing.

Johnny had picked her up from the Richmond house that morning, driven her out to the airport and seen her off. But he'd been pre-occupied. Kit had let him know that she was as nervous as hell and that she needed his support. Johnny had been the only one in her family who hadn't tried to talk her out of going. True, he hadn't said he approved of the trip, but he'd stuck up for her when Damien had raved on about Kit's 'natural but immature response to this highly charged peak emotional experience'. Johnny, God bless him, had more or less told Damien to shut up, that Kit had a right to make her own decisions.

But since that family discussion two weeks earlier, Johnny had seemed withdrawn and cut off.

Getting her luggage out of the boot, he made a half-hearted apology.

'Sorry, kiddo,' he said lamely, handing her the backpack, 'not much company, am I?'

'Ah well,' Kit, caught off-guard, didn't know what to say.

'Things haven't been so good for me lately,' he sighed. In spite of being keyed up with nerves about her own situation, Kit's alarm bells rang immediately. She'd never heard Johnny give away anything like this.

'What is it, Johnny?' she said as they walked through the car park towards the Qantas terminal. 'Has anything happened? Do you still like where you are?'

'The study is great.'

'What about the other guys?'

'They're great. Terrific.'

'The detention centre?'

Johnny was a qualified lawyer and worked in a voluntary capacity with refugees.

He turned and looked at her; a deep, strange look that she couldn't read at all.

'It's all okay,' he said softly. 'I just don't know – '

'Don't know what?' She was panicking a little. Johnny was her rock, her emotional springboard. If he didn't see a reason to be hopeful and positive, then there was none.

'You're helping people,' she said sharply. 'It's what you're good at.'

'Yeah. Maybe.'

'No maybe about it.'

Kit looked over at the swarms of people coming in through the automatic doors, and felt excited. Why the hell did Johnny have to have his angst attack now?

'It's just that . . .' he nodded miserably, turning to look at a baby who'd begun to wail loudly in the arms of its father, 'I've kinda lost the plot.'

'What does that mean?'

But he didn't answer her and they didn't have a chance to speak further for some time. After she'd checked her luggage through, Kit had to buy a couple of last minute items for the trip.

When the time came to say goodbye, he hugged her tightly and told her that he'd miss her.

'Look after yourself, Johnny,' she said fiercely, through a rush of tears because for perhaps the first time she realised that she was important to him, too.

'You, too,' he smiled. 'I hope you find him.'

'If he's alive, I'll find him,' Kit grinned and pulled away.

'Bring him home then!' Johnny laughed, letting her go. 'See if you can drag him back here. I want to see him.'

'I'll try.'

The automatic doors slid open and she turned for the last time.

Johnny stood, in his jeans and faded T-shirt, hair tousled, his eyes on her face, mouth tense, trying to seem okay.

A lump rose in Kit's throat as she waved.

'Bye then!' she called to him, 'and good luck.'

'Bye!'

Johnny. My brother. Always my brother.

Then she was off. Johnny was behind her now and she was onto the next stage of her life.

Kit pushed her seat back and tried to think about what might be bothering Johnny. But her mind couldn't stay on the topic for long. She had too much of her own stuff to think about.

Sebastian had called her a few days after the impromptu midnight visit.

'Just wanted to apologise for the other night,' he'd said straight up. 'Sorry you felt you had to leave so quickly. I was a bit distracted with Sara there.'

Kit had been pleased he'd rung, but embarrassed too.

'I shouldn't have come at that time. Er, who is Sara?'

'Oh, just a colleague. She's okay. A bit demanding actually. Thinks she owns me because we're in the same department. But how's the reading going?'

'Good, pretty good,' Kit had said slowly. She'd hardly had any time to read, she was so busy organising the trip, but she wasn't going to tell him that. 'Something exciting has happened, actually.'

'What?'

She'd told him about the call from Martin and the plan to go overseas. He'd been surprised and impressed, she could tell, and excited for her.

'That's great,' he'd kept saying, over and over. 'Really great.' Then he'd mentioned that he would be overseas himself for a few weeks over the Christmas period, doing research in Britain. Did she have a number where she'd be staying? Maybe they could meet up if it fitted into both their schedules?

'Well, yes!' Kit had given him the number of the bed-and-breakfast place she'd just booked for herself in Belfast. 'That would be great! If you can fit it in.'

After two hours, with the first of the airline meals out of the way, Kit pulled out a note-pad and pen. It would be better to get this over. Then as soon as she got to London or Belfast she'd post it back. She wanted Leonie to have it as soon as she was conscious enough to understand. The doctors were convinced she was on the verge of full consciousness. It was just a matter of days now, they'd said. Johnny had agreed to read it to Leonie in private as soon as he felt she was up to it.

How to begin? Dear Leonie? Or just, Leonie? Or, To my mother? Dear Mother? Nothing seemed right.

After a couple of minutes the answer came to her. Quietly, softly, like a heartbeat. Like the sound of a child's bare feet walking up stairs. As though it had always been there, thudding along underneath, waiting to be allowed to surface. The words written years ago, across the cover of a letter that she would never see. Kit knew exactly the right way to begin.

When you wake and find me gone.

She laughed quietly to herself as she wrote the words, but when she saw them sitting at the top of the page, in her own neat round letters, innocently waiting for what would come next, her eyes unexpectedly filled with tears and she had to concentrate like crazy to stop them spilling over and down her cheeks.

There was no point getting melancholy and sentimental about any of this.

She didn't look up for at least another hour. For minutes at a time she sat frowning over the next sentence, the pen in her mouth,

236

trying to work out how to put what she wanted to say. In the end, after all the effort, it didn't amount to much.

I've read some of the rough notes you were working on, presumably to give to me. (I found them in a little case that was given back to us from the car.) I know I shouldn't have read them, but then the fact that you were writing means that you were trying to work out how to tell me about my past.

All of which I have a right to know.

Why didn't you tell me years ago? So much misunderstanding could have been avoided. Anyway, maybe things will be better now that everything is out in the open.

Except there is still so much I need to know.

So here I am, on my way to Ireland to try to find my father. I don't know what to expect, except from what you've written and from some of the things Martin Boylan has told me. The accounts conflict. Nice, enigmatic, interesting . . . a mystery. I don't know. Anyway, whoever he is I want to meet him.

I hope you get better, Leonie. I'm sure you will. You were always a strong person.

Kit lowered her tray-table and nodded to the flight attendant who was asking if she wanted breakfast. Breakfast! Hadn't they just had supper? She'd been asleep for a few hours but she didn't know just how long. She poked at the plastic container of orange juice with one finger. Probably the last thing she should do was eat more airline food, and yet it smelt all right. And it broke the monotony of sitting for hours with nothing to do. She opened the silver foil that covered a minute portion of scrambled eggs and bacon, then picked up the plastic fork, looking out the window into the pink and yellow sunrise spread across the blue sky like streaky paint. The captain had just announced that they'd crossed Dubai. Only about eight hours to go until London.

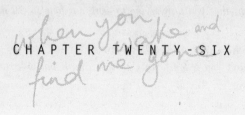

CHAPTER TWENTY-SIX

The excitement Kit had felt at finally arriving at Heathrow diminished somewhat as she waited her turn in the slow line that snaked through customs. Apparently there was some kind of staff dispute and the crowds of travellers were moving at a snail's pace. Still, Kit was full of anticipation. This was London. *London.* How could she not be excited? The city of Shakespeare and Dickens and The Blitz and a million other things she'd read and learnt about. Why not put off going straight to Ireland, and instead look at the Thames and the Houses of Parliament. Westminster Abbey. Why not go to a play in the West End? She had enough money! Or she could check out the place in Hyde Park where they used to have public hangings five hundred years ago. Why not stay here?

When the man took her passport and ticket asked her the reason for travelling, Kit looked at him in alarm. Surely he didn't want the real reason? He seemed to sense her confusion, and that she might be about to tell him something personal, so he cut her off with a faint smile.

'Holiday?' he suggested hopefully.

Kit smiled back in relief. 'Yes,' she said. 'Holiday.'

It was six o'clock in the morning by the time she got outside to wait for the bus that would shuttle her off to another terminal. Then she had an hour to wait for the plane to Belfast.

The flight from London to Belfast took a little over an hour. There was breakfast – yet more eggs and this time tiny sausages, plus a cold little roll, then coffee that tasted like dam water on a warm day. Kit watched the other passengers. They were mostly men in business suits. They were clean shaven, with sharp haircuts and shiny shoes. Every one of them looked like he knew exactly what he was doing.

Kit wanted to go to the toilet but felt too self-conscious to get up. It would have drawn attention to her lack of style and elegance, to her youth and apprehension. She had the feeling these men might not have ever seen someone like her. Or maybe it was that people her age didn't go to Belfast? Not at this time on Monday mornings, anyway.

She listened to the captain tell them in his nicely modulated British accent that they were now descending into Belfast, and could everyone turn off their mobile phones. They would be landing in a matter of minutes. Kit peered out the window at the multi-toned, criss-cross of tiny green fields, thinking how pretty they looked. They reminded her of a toy she'd had as a child: a complicated jigsaw that fell apart into small pieces if you weren't careful.

So I'm really here, Kit thought. This is it. Better hang on to myself or I might fall to pieces, too.

Kit waited outside the small airport for the bus that would take her into Belfast proper, the cold creeping up through her boots and the sleeves of her jacket.

After completing a half-hour journey through the most peaceful-looking countryside she'd ever seen, Kit arrived at Great Victoria Station. Where to now? But just as she'd been told, a row of huge black taxis was waiting outside the glass doors. She bought a map of the city and a packet of Minties from a kiosk, then pulled her backpack on again and made her way through the crowds.

The last leg of the trip was a short ride to the place she'd booked in Cromwell Road. It was a non-aligned area, she'd been assured by the travel book. No one would assume anything about you if you stayed in Cromwell Road. It was full of student digs and bed-and-breakfast places. Anyway, Belfast was a perfectly safe city for a new-comer. Kit hugged herself in the back of the taxi and wished the grey foggy air outside didn't make it feel like something menacing was hanging about. Her sense of being young, alone and unsure in a strange place was heightened by the crisp disinterested coldness of the driver's voice and the blanket of low white cloud that covered the sky.

By the time she pulled herself and her luggage out and paid the driver, it was eight-thirty. Kit felt better. A little spaced perhaps – a strange mixture of exhaustion and curiosity. A surge of excitement lifted her up the front steps to the brightly painted door of the old, three-storey Victorian building, Hanson Lodge.

Laurie had taken down the details of where she was staying and had promised to let her father know as soon as he was able to contact him. Laurie might have spoken to her father by now. Right at this minute, her father, Eamon McCabe, might be some-where in this very city, looking at the clock and thinking about her arrival.

Kit stared around the tiny room. It was more like a large cup-board, really – just enough space for a bed, a washbasin, a wardrobe and a wooden chair. A young man, who'd carried her case up three flights of stairs and through the winding narrow corridors, was handing her the key and telling her that breakfast was from eight to nine each day and that no food would be served before or after that time.

'So what floor am I on?' Kit could see he was about to leave. How would she ever be able to find her way back down those steep stairs and around the corridors again?

'Third,' he said grumpily. 'There are only three above-ground floors, and you're at the top on three west.'

'Okay.'

He left and Kit shut the door.

The room was furnished in an amazing array of different colours and cheap fabrics. The carpet was purple and gold, the curtains a pink floral cotton. There was fake shiny blond wood panelling halfway up the walls and then green flowery wallpaper above that, peeling off around each corner. The bedspread was orange chenille and the sliding door into the tiny toilet and shower alcove was covered in plastic printed with tiny roses. There was, however, a window, and it opened. Kit looked out into the cold grey air. Below her was a cobbled laneway that wound its way up to the main road. On the other side of the laneway, directly opposite, she could look down into a row of tiny backyards. The roof-line of the houses was so varied and disjointed, it might have been the painted backdrop for a movie set in a nineteenth century industrial landscape.

Kit closed the window. There was a TV sitting on top of the cupboard and, joy of joys, a small bar heater next to it. Kit pulled the heater down, plugged it in and then turned on the television. She folded down the bedspread and checked the sheets. They were clean and there seemed to be enough blankets. It was only just after eight-thirty in the morning but she felt too raw and nervous to go outside again. Still in her coat, she plonked herself on the bed, pulled the eiderdown up over her legs and clicked the remote control. A news program. Horse-racing. Well, she would just sit and wait for a while until she calmed down and worked out what she should do next.

Kit woke to the noise of a phone ringing and lay for a few moments, staring at it, completely disorientated. Her watch told her it was nearly four in the afternoon but outside the window it was already pitch black. That couldn't be right. Nausea welled up inside her. Where had the day gone?

'Hello?' she said cautiously.

'Outside call for you.'

'Oh. Okay.' Kit waited.

'It's Annie here, Kathleen.'

'Oh, hi,' Kit said warily. The last conversation she'd had with this woman had ended unpleasantly. And Kit hadn't mentioned staying at this place. How on earth had Annie found her?

'Were you asleep?'

'Yes.' Kit felt vaguely ashamed.

'It's a terrible long way,' Annie said sympathetically.

'Hmmm.'

'Will you be wanting dinner?'

'Well,' Kit stumbled over her answer, 'er, how do you mean?' Suddenly, she was aware that she was starving. She hadn't had lunch at all and breakfast had been at about six that morning.

'You've nothing planned?'

'No.'

'Well, I can pick you up at six,' Annie said, taking charge. 'You're right near the city. We'll go somewhere nearby so you get your bearings.'

'Okay.' Kit was glad of the invitation. It was now thirty-six hours since she'd left Australia and she'd hardly spoken to a soul.

'Annie, what time is it?'

'It's just on four.'

'But it's dark!'

'I told you,' Annie said, stifling a laugh, 'it's a terrible place. You should have stayed home.'

Once they were seated in the window table of the restaurant, Kit was able to get a good look at her mother's friend. Annie was well into her fifties – quite a bit older than Leonie. She was plump and plain but with bright eyes and, Kit had to admit, a very nice smile. Annie must have been assessing Kit, too, because she suddenly put down the menu and frowned.

'You look nothing like your mother,' she said crossly, as though this was a great disappointment to her. 'But I suppose you *are* like him.'

Kit smiled blandly, trying not to show Annie how pleased she was to be told this. She'd made a resolution not to bombard the woman with questions. She was going to simply eat, try to relax, and see if Annie volunteered anything.

'So you knew my father?' she asked casually.

'Oh, slightly.' Annie sniffed, then sighed. 'Haven't seen him in a long time, though. Are you ready to order?'

Kit nodded. She'd decided on the seafood chowder and bread, hoping it would be a generous serve. She didn't fancy trying anything more substantial like meat or fish. In spite of her hunger, she still felt queasy. The young waitress came over and they placed their orders.

'So this Laurie fellow,' Annie said, 'have you made contact with him yet?'

'I'm meeting him tomorrow,' Kit replied. 'I'm getting a taxi out there – he gave me the address.'

'He works out in Ledadoon, doesn't he?' Annie said, frowning and playing with the sugar bowl, 'in that big community centre?'

'Yes, I think so.' Kit smiled. 'So you keep in contact with Martin, then?'

'Oh, I did for years,' Annie said shortly. 'Now it's just occasionally.'

Kit waited. The woman had something on her mind. She could feel it. But she was taking her time. They talked of the weather, and the temperatures that Kit might expect. What kind of clothes she had and if they'd be adequate. The food came and to Kit's relief she saw that the bowl of soup was huge, the wedges of bread fresh and crusty. When Annie indicated she should start, she dived her spoon in hungrily.

'Will you be here for Christmas?' Annie asked suddenly, shaking salt slowly onto her steak and fried potatoes.

'I don't know.'

'Won't they be wanting you at home?'

Kit shrugged. What business was it of Annie's where she was for Christmas?

'Leonie will be missing you,' Annie went on.

'I doubt that,' Kit snapped. 'We don't really get on.'

'Even so,' Annie said quietly, 'she's your mother and she's very ill. She'll miss you at Christmas.'

Kit kept eating. The soup was delicious and the restaurant had a warm cozy atmosphere, but she wanted to leave as soon as she'd finished. She was sick of this bossy woman. She didn't need her, anyway. Thank goodness she was meeting Laurie the next day. He was the one who had agreed to help her. She said a fervent prayer that he'd come through with the information she needed. Martin had to be right, didn't he? Things had to open up for her, now she was in Belfast. *Shit, what was she going to do if they didn't?*

'I want to warn you, Kathleen,' Annie was saying, chewing on a piece of bread, 'you must try not to be starry-eyed when you meet your father.'

'What do you mean?' Kit said sharply.

'I've been a nurse most of my life,' Annie said slowly, 'and apart from two years in America, all of it here in Belfast. Twenty-five years a nurse.'

'That's a long time,' Kit murmured, wondering what the hell that piece of information had to do with being starry-eyed when she met her father.

244

'I ran the Accident and Emergency Department at the Royal for nearly ten years. And I've seen a lot.'

'How do you mean?'

'Violence is violence and it's all wrong, do you hear me?' Annie said abruptly. 'Totally *wrong*!' Her clenched fist came down hard on the table.

Kit stopped in surprise, the spoon midway to her mouth. People at nearby tables turned their heads. But Annie said nothing, just waited until the buzz of conversation around them rose to its former level.

'All those rebel songs,' Annie's voice was a low, caustic hiss, 'the brave young lads fighting for the cause!' She leant forward. 'If the ones singing the songs got to see what we nurses have to deal with, they wouldn't be singing so loudly.'

Kit felt foolish. What was this woman on about? All she'd come for was to see her father.

'The torn off limbs, the smashed knee-caps, the burns and the bullet holes,' Annie muttered through clenched teeth. 'We had to tell the relatives that their poor wee one had died. Did you know that a bullet from an armalite creates a flesh wound of ten centimetres around the point of exit?'

Annie cupped both hands to demonstrate. 'The bullets are designed to cause as much damage to flesh as possible.'

'No,' Kit murmured. 'I didn't know that.'

'Once, three bombs went off in the one day. We worked in that resuscitation room well into the night, up to our ankles in blood! Do you hear what I'm saying, Kathleen? Have you seen footage of those places where they butcher animals? It was like that. An abattoir. I had twenty-five nurses in there just trying to keep people alive. Every doctor in the province had been called in, and the floor was just a sea of blood.'

Kit shuddered and nodded slowly.

'Once, I had a poor young fellow, a British soldier, laying in front of me bleeding to death asking to see his mammy.' Annie's voice had become higher, and her plain face seemed to have transformed from within: it looked younger now, more alive. 'And only two beds away was a young lad from the Falls. All of eighteen if he was a day, and a Provo – Provisional IRA – and he was doing the same thing. *Dying*. He had both legs blown off at the hip – losing consciousness by the second, and asking for *his* mother. And it wasn't unusual, Kathleen. I've seen so much useless death. It's not glorious or wonderful in any way.'

'And you think my father is – ' But Kit didn't get to finish her question.

'Do you think that poor fellow's mother back in London or Manchester felt it any less than the Provo's mother?' Annie said furiously.

'I don't know anything about it,' Kit said, shaking her head.

'Nor did your mother at the beginning,' Annie snapped.

'So do you think my father – ' Kit began again.

'Don't talk to me about Eamon McCabe,' Annie cut in, her face glowering furiously. 'He ruined your mother's life. Absolutely. I don't want him to ruin yours.'

Kit gulped, put her spoon down and sat staring at the tablecloth.

'Go home, Kathleen,' Annie suddenly whispered. 'It's so *sensible* down there. There's the beach and lovely wide roads. It's coming on summer now, isn't it? Help your mother. She needs you.'

'No. I want to meet him.'

Annie gave a deep sigh, then pushed her plate away even though she'd only half finished. She fumbled around in her bag for cigarettes, then lay the packet and her lighter near her plate carefully without taking a cigarette out, brushing non-existent crumbs from the table.

'Don't think for a minute I'm not sympathetic to civil rights,' she said softly. 'I have been, all my life. I've been on marches. Too many

246

to count. God knows I had reason enough to march. I was virtually the only Catholic nurse in the place in the early days and I was discriminated against time and time again. I tell you I had to be twice as good as the other girls just to keep my position. I got where I did with the help of one man. A surgeon. A wonderful man. A Protestant, but not a bigot. Believe me, as mad as it sounds now, in those days that was something unusual. Anyway, he put my name forward for positions and looked out for me. As I said, I headed that unit for ten years. So I know what I'm talking about.'

They walked back to Annie's car through light steady rain, Annie apologising that she'd parked so far away. But Kit was glad of the chance to walk. The sea salt and the fainter, rustier smell coming up from the shipyards at Belfast Lough were invigorating. There was an odd confusing feel to this city, she thought, as she followed Annie through a narrow cobbled laneway and got into her car. Some streets had a new, almost brash tone about them – the cafés and pubs could have been in any Melbourne or Sydney suburb – and only just down the road or in the next street it felt stolid and proper, and sour, too. Like a bitter old relative, reluctant to smile at a family party given in her honour. Annie had told Kit earlier that the city centre had been bombed and rebuilt so many times that the place had no idea who it was any more. Although Kit thought this was an oddly emotional view for the plain-speaking Annie, she could see what she meant. The old sat up against the new, in a way that was disconcerting. Did a city have its own unconscious inner life? Could the individual buildings be about more than themselves? Maybe all that had gone on over the years had seeped into the stone. The idea intrigued Kit. She didn't realise she'd been so quiet until Annie spoke again and she flinched at the sound of a voice so near.

'That's the Europa Hotel,' Annie said, slowing down a little and pointing out the window. 'Take a look.'

Kit dutifully peered out at an impressive grey building with wide glass doors, all lit up like a castle.

'Very nice.'

'Infamous as the most bombed hotel on the planet,' Annie added dryly.

Kit said nothing. The place looked like any other sort of hotel for wealthy people. It was hard to imagine someone wanting to blow it up.

Annie pulled up outside Hanson Lodge.

'Let me know what's happening tomorrow,' she said warmly. 'If you've got some time before you meet Laurie, then I'll show you around.'

'Well, thanks.' Kit had expected Annie to wash her hands of her, now Kit'd made it clear that she was still as keen as ever to meet her father.

'I can show you the house where your parents met,' Annie volunteered, 'and all around the Falls and the Shankill and the docks, if you're interested.'

'I'd like that,' Kit said, and then suddenly, 'I would like to see the road all the people walked down when that hunger striker died, and the cemetery.'

'Bobby Sands?' Annie said in surprise. 'Falls Road, Milltown. Why?'

'I have a friend.' Kit's voice suddenly caught in her throat and she was unable to say Brendan's name. After a moment she went on. 'He was just a little kid at the funeral. He went down the road on his father's shoulders.'

'I see,' Annie said softly, and then more sharply, 'well we're very good at funerals here. There were another nine young men after Bobby Sands.'

'Yes, I know.'

'A lot of people turned out for the funerals.'

248

'Did you? I mean, did you go?'

'Oh, sure.' Annie smiled, then turned away as though she might be trying to get a grip on her emotions, too. 'So you'll ring me tomorrow?' she asked, fishing in her bag and handing Kit a card.

'I will, Annie. And thanks for dinner.'

They both got out of the car and at the bottom of the steps of the lodge, Annie kissed her cheek and again Kit was surprised.

'You look after yourself then. Leonie's little girl,' she said softly.

'You and Leonie were close?' Kit ventured shyly.

'Ah, she was a grand girl!' Annie laughed suddenly, fondly. 'In those early days she'd meet me outside the nurses' home after I'd worked all day. I'd be completely beat. And she'd say, "Come on, Annie, we'll just have one drink." And you know, with Leonie I'd perk right up. More often than not we'd end up dancing! After twelve hours on my feet at work, my legs aching, she'd take me dancing all night in someone's flat, and I just loved it!'

Kit smiled. Yes, she could believe it. That year when Kit was thirteen and Leonie had invited her down to stay in the city, they'd often ended up dancing around the lounge room of the little flat.

'Are you musical, Kathleen?'

'I play the flute,' Kit replied modestly, thinking of the instrument sitting at the bottom of her case. A last-minute decision to bring it had had her pulling everything else out to find space for it. Now she was glad she'd bothered, and glad too that she'd put in a little practise before leaving, although she was still nowhere near the standard she'd been at as a schoolgirl.

'Your mother had a great voice,' Annie said, 'and she knew all the old songs better than people who lived here. She only had to hear a song once and she'd be able to sing it.'

Kit nodded. Leonie had never learnt music formally but she could sing. She had taught Kit some old English ballads, some Irish and French songs. Brendan seemed to know a lot of them too.

Sometimes if there was no one else around, they sang them together.

'Bye then, love.'

'Bye, Annie.'

She watched as Annie walked back to her car. Kit took the first couple of steps up towards the front door but on an impulse turned back.

'Annie!' she called out through the rain. 'What happened the night you had dinner with Leonie in Melbourne? The night of the accident, I mean?'

Annie was unlocking the car. For a moment Kit thought she was going to ignore the question. 'Leonie called around to my house,' Kit went on. 'She was upset and angry, apparently. But I wasn't home.'

'Ah, well,' Annie's voice came slowly through the sleet, 'that's a long story now. One you'll probably find out for yourself before too long.' Suddenly, she came over to Kit, fumbling in her bag and taking out a large yellow envelope. 'I didn't know whether to give this to you or not.' She handed it to Kit with a sigh. 'Your mother was wanting to set the record straight with you. She was writing things down to give to you. I told her it was all very well writing things down, but she should tell you the truth, that you deserved to know. I had no idea she would go straight to your place that night. She gave this to me over that dinner. Wanted me to read over it. I suppose it can't do any harm for you to have it.'

'Thanks, Annie.'

'Your mother has the most terrible scrawling writing.'

'I know.'

'Goodnight then, love.'

'Goodnight.'

CHAPTER TWENTY-SEVEN

You probably want to know what attracted me to your father. Well, they were strange beginnings to say the least. I didn't believe anything about him at first and it took ages for me to accept that he actually fancied me but I suppose in the long term it was worth it. The slow, quiet progression towards each other was wonderful.

You're here and so am I and he is, well, wherever he is. I hope he has someone to laugh with, because he had a fine laugh, your father. When he laughed it was because everything in the whole world was ridiculous, or maddening, or just so hopelessly funny. He was popular with all kinds of people because his laughter included them, and warmed them right to the core.

Your father loved to talk and drink and dance all night, and he was generous. I'd never met a generous man before. He was always giving people lifts and buying them drinks and telling them they were terrific. All this was mind-blowing for me. When it finally dawned on me that he was for real, I felt like I'd been let out of jail.

I'd been complaining about never getting out of bleak stuffy old Belfast and so he'd offered to take me back to Donegal for the weekend to show me where he'd grown up. Storms were predicted right across the north of the island. As we drove west that Friday night, on small winding roads with the hail and rain whipping around the little car, the way we were being blown about made me very nervous. I remember sitting back and hoping like hell we'd get there alive.

I'd expected to meet a family; parents or the two cousins that he'd spoken about, but as it turned out, both parents were dead and the cousins were working down in Dublin. Still, he insisted, he would show me his country.

We stayed the first night with friends of his in Letterkenny. They were puzzled by me. Was I his girlfriend? And where was Australia, exactly? What was I doing there? I was glad when they put him in the spare bed in the room with their little boys and gave me the sitting-room sofa. I didn't believe I had it in me to begin something new.

But before long I was in love again.

I had no clear idea of exactly what your father was involved in. I knew he was a staunch republican of course, but I didn't understand much more than that.

I always think of that trip to Donegal as the one that sealed my fate. I will write about it at length sometime. But I can't quite bear it right now.

I was still living in the Falls with the Boylans, and the strain of living in that occupied area of the city cemented my belief that the British army had no business being there. That they were propping up an unjust regime, and the division of those six counties from the rest of Ireland was a figment of some idiot's limited imagination.

But I crossed the line into violence in my own way, for my own reasons. He didn't have to talk me into anything. I was living in the middle of it. I wasn't blind.

Before I go on, let me explain something. By February 1981, 360 Republican prisoners were 'on the blanket'. Margaret Thatcher was the British Prime Minister and she was adamant that they be treated as

252

common criminals. This 'dirty' protest had been going on for years, with various men involved with it over that time. You can imagine how the guards treated them. Or maybe you can't. It was brutal. Starvation, beatings and torture were widespread in the jails. And although there was enormous support for the prisoners in the Catholic areas of the province, somehow it didn't ignite much interest anywhere else.

There had been a hunger strike the year before that had been called off but by February things were worse, if anything.

Oh Kathleen, those days, those damned days of early '81 when you were just a tiny sea-creature inside me! For months before, there had been escalating violence. The Provos were planting bombs in London and pinpointing soldiers and individual policemen for assassination. The Ulster Defense Association was killing Republicans. Ian Paisley was unveiling his third force to a group of journalists. This was a paramilitary group of five hundred men who would 'stop at nothing' to keep the six counties British.

Then the hunger strike began. On March 1st, Bobby Sands refused breakfast. And by the time it was called off in August, ten men had starved themselves to death. Armbands were worn, and black flags and photos of the prisoners hung in the front windows of houses. There were demonstrations in the streets, fires lit, petrol bombs thrown and songs sung. Forty-five days, then sixty-three and then everyone was counting the days. Each day was like a rock around our necks. Each day a heavy stone weighing down our fate.

It felt like the whole community stopped breathing as we waited for them to die, one by one, hoping and praying that they wouldn't. The parents, you see, the mothers and the fathers, the sisters and brothers, were living amongst us. And from around the world and from the Unionists only streets away, we were told that it was a good thing that they were dying. That Margaret Thatcher sticking to her guns showed strength and purpose. That they were men of violence and they deserved to die, even if it was willingly and peacefully.

253

I'm writing this and at the same time trying to guess how much you know. What your attitude is. I can't write a history book for you. What I can tell you is what was going on inside my head. What happened to me.

I was still teaching. As the hunger strike proceeded, I began to feel like I was on a huge ship steaming towards an iceberg. There didn't seem to be anything anyone could do to avert disaster. Firstly, I was pregnant and I knew once the head of the school found out then I would lose my job. And, well, the whole province seemed to be at a terrible standstill. The atmosphere around me was full of wild rumours, incomprehension and hatred. Leading figures from around the world got involved, priests and politicians, even the Pope sent his man in! The men on the hunger strike were portrayed as either heroes or psychopaths, depending on who was doing the talking.

(If you take nothing away from all this, Kathleen, take this. Before you believe anything, know who is doing the talking, and why.)

While the Brits and the unionists called the Provos mindless psychopaths and murderers, to the Catholic population where I was living, the IRA were their brothers and sons, their cousins and uncles. Even if the ordinary Catholic people didn't agree with their tactics, they were not the enemy. The fact that some of them were mad bastards was beside the point. There are mad bastards in any organisation, including the British army. I tell you, in the Falls, the IRA was the only protection those people got. They certainly weren't protected by the British soldiers marauding through the streets and they most definitely weren't protected by the police.

Of course I was tempted to just go home. Believe me, I would wake and find myself nauseous with the pregnancy, but thinking all the time of the sweet smell of gum trees down by the creek, the smell of sun in the brown grass in summer . . . I loved Australia then, so fiercely that I could hardly believe that I willingly left it. Someone must have made me go, I remember thinking, lying in the Boylan's matrimonial bed, in an ugly stuffy room, full of icons to the Sacred Heart and the Blessed Virgin. But I only had myself to blame. There I was, in the middle of a terrible, centuries-old conflict, in love with a marked man, single and pregnant and about to commit a crime which would go against everything I had ever believed in.

It was a lonely time.

So who were these men? What made them do it? I thought I knew at the time, but thinking back now, I have doubts. The older I get, the more these doubts come to haunt me. All the reasons I thought I knew at the time seem now just clichés: like slogans you see painted on the walls of railway stations. But those ten men gave their lives, Kathleen, their very lives. Even Protestant Unionists not completely overtaken with sectarian bigotry had to admire their courage and sense of purpose. They starved themselves to death. And that is a terrible way to die. So I keep thinking that there had to be more to it than justice. Had to be more to it than a united Ireland. Had to be more to it than getting the Brits out.

But you know, in the end I don't think there was.

I don't know if this ambivalence I feel about it now is a good thing or not. Is it wisdom that comes with age or just cowardice? I do know that they saw themselves as part of history. There had been hunger strikes before, and martyrs before, and they were willing to be part of that continuum. This is such an alien concept to the modern-day Australian psyche that I hesitate to even write it down. As Australians, we're taught to see ourselves primarily as individuals and, apart from an allegiance to family, we are not encouraged to think we owe anything to anyone else.

Certainly not our lives.

Take Bobby Sands. He was twenty six (just a baby to me now!) when he went on the hunger strike. His background inside the IRA was not that notorious: he hadn't killed anyone or been part of any big operation. He was only a teenager when the Troubles broke out in

255

1969 but like so many others he'd had personal experiences that put steel into his Republican beliefs.

He grew up in Rathcoole which was a largely Protestant district in North Belfast. He and his family became the focus for sectarian hatred along with other Catholic families in that area. Shots were fired into his house, he was attacked with a knife and forced at gunpoint to give up his job.

You can read the words 'discrimination' and 'harassment' and think you know what they mean. But when you see a kid of fifteen being attacked by a gang his own age with knifes, when he can't get a job because of his name, when his family is burnt out of their house, when against the odds he does get a job but has to give it up because he is continually threatened . . . And, worst of all, there is no one to complain to. No police force to protect him. Then the words start to really mean something, don't they? Imagine how those kinds of experiences impinge on a young mind.

Anyway, he ends up in Long Kesh jail on a firearms charge at eighteen and in there learns Gaelic and Irish history and learns to play guitar and . . . he's out in three years. Within a year he's back inside for the possession of another gun. And he refuses to recognise the court, so he gets a long sentence and he goes on the blanket and he says the rosary with his fellow inmates, he writes poetry and sings songs. In prison he is cold and bored and tired and increasingly resolute.

And there were many more, so many more, just like him.

Anyway, I think I was in my second month of pregnancy and Bobby was in his second month of dying when the Brits lifted Martin again. Darling, skinny, seventeen-year-old Martin Boylan with his bad skin and bandy legs. I loved all the Boylan kids by this stage, but Martin was my favourite. A beautiful, gentle dreamy boy who constantly surprised me with all he knew. I think it was that he reminded me of our Johnny. None of them knew about the pregnancy of *course and I don't even know if they knew that I was 'seeing' your father. But I've learnt since then that kids know so much more than we think.*

Their mother was out of hospital by this stage and had gone to recuperate with a sister down in Clare. I was glad, in spite of everything, that she didn't choose to come home to her family because that would have meant me leaving to find some other accommodation. And by this stage I was committed to seeing Nuala and Martin through their exams. I think the children's mother was pleased for the opportunity to have a break. Women of West Belfast put up with a lot. As much as she might agree with the cause, no mother really wanted to see her son involved, because she knew where he'd eventually end up: in jail or dead. I had many women tell me that they were relieved when their boys were in jail because it meant they were relatively safe. My blood would run cold. How could they say that when they knew that conditions in the jails were so gruesome?

Anyway, it was just after exams and Martin had been out with a few friends from school. I was worried when he didn't come in at ten like he said he would. I told myself I was being a fussy old woman. He was a good kid, he wouldn't be in any kind of trouble. But I knew in my heart that he was in danger. It wasn't like him not to let me know where he was. And of course I knew that in Belfast sometimes all it took was for you to say your name to the wrong person for you to lose your life.

The next morning I went down to the local police station to report him missing. They couldn't have been less interested. I can still see that smirking officer, playing it up for his mates.

'Where did you say he lives, Miss?'

'Falls Road you say?'

'And his name is Martin Boylan? Would he be related to Pat Boylan by any chance?'

Pat Boylan, their father, was a well-known Sinn Féin member and it

257

was known too that he was in jail. I was so humiliated, so stunned that I almost walked out, but my need to find Martin was greater.

'He's not involved in anything,' I managed, my face red and getting redder. 'He's a very studious kid.'

'Oh yes, Miss,' the man said. 'Like so many of the lads down in the Divis Flats and the Falls, he's probably a grand student!'

I was crying when I walked out of that place. I'd never felt such hatred before. It was getting to me, I finally realised. The place was really getting to me.

Martin turned up two days later. He'd been picked up by the Brits and spent seventy-two hours in custody. (They were allowed to hold someone for this amount of time without charging them). After an initial interrogation he'd been stripped and put in a totally dark room. He was seventeen years old and no one came to tell him what he was being held for. As far as he was concerned they were going to leave him there forever. There was no light or heat in the room and only a bucket for a toilet. When they eventually came for him, he accidentally tipped over his bucket and had to clean it up, all the time being screamed at for being a fucking filthy Irish Paddy who probably wouldn't know how to use a toilet if he had one anyway.

When he got home he was completely traumatised. He couldn't speak for two days. When the story of what happened to him emerged, I was so shaken I could hardly speak myself. Of course I knew it happened all the time. Youngsters from the Falls, from Anderstonstown and the Ardoyne were always being picked up. Unemployment was so high and the kids committed a lot of petty offences. They pinched cars, ran roadblocks, gave out a lot of cheek. But the Brits picked up kids like Martin, too, kids who never got into trouble. They did this to intimidate the local population. People treated it as just an everyday event. But that first time it happened to Martin, I was deeply affected.

Just when he was getting over it, when he'd started to smile and see his friends and resume talking about applying for scholarships, it happened again. Only this time it was worse. They beat him viciously in the street. Then he was locked up naked for another seventy-two hours. When he came out this time he had black and purple bruises over his bum and legs. This time, he didn't want to talk about study or university. I could tell he'd crossed some kind of line in his head. They'd changed him. There was a sort of hard blankness in his eyes, even though he remained polite to me. Then I overheard him talking with two mates out the back and I could tell that they were toying around with the idea of joining the movement (the IRA). I freaked completely. Here I was sleeping with one of their leading lights but I didn't want that for Martin. Not in a million years. So I wrote to our cousins in Sydney and asked if I could send Martin out to them for a while. They said yes. Thank God.

I paid his fare and he went two months later. He never returned to Belfast.

Bobby Sands lasted for sixty-six days. He'd been given the last rites two weeks earlier. No one expected him to live so long. He was only twenty-seven and his young body didn't give up without a fight. Tension in the city was enormous as everyone waited for him to die. You see, there was the added factor that he'd been voted in as a Member of Westminster Parliament in the April. As the member for Fermanagh and South Tyrone. (An amazing turn of events that I won't go into here, except to say that people could hardly believe that Margaret Thatcher would let a legitimately elected member of her own parliament die of starvation.) Sick cruel jokes began within Unionist circles. 'Don't be vague, starve a taig' was written up on walls around the city; 'The republican weight-watchers', etc, etc . . .

But in fact you got the feeling that the Unionists were as freaked out by the whole situation as the Republicans. The world press hovered around like vultures waiting for his death. Of course no one realised that this scenario would be repeated nine more times over the next few months. Although the command within the jail were preparing for just such a scenario with deadly precision. The men's deaths would be strung out like little knots in a piece of string, a space of two to three weeks before the next one. For maximum effect.

I was in bed when the news broke. Like everyone else, I got up. I could hear the banging of dustbin lids, the whistles and drums in the street, and guessed what had happened. People all over West Belfast flooded out onto the street. They seemed shocked, in spite of the fact that they'd been expecting it for weeks. Huge barricades were hastily erected; cars, sheets of iron, wood, anything that people could find. A group of women huddled around on the pavement to say the rosary. Camera crews from all around the world filmed whatever they could.

I stayed in Falls Road and watched as a big saracan eventually arrived to break up the barricade. It was bombarded with petrol bombs and stones. Soldiers fired plastic bullets into the crowd. A full scale riot took place which lasted nearly an hour.

The next day, no one went to school or work. Francis Hughes was already a month into his fast and McCreesh was about to start. People walked around as though half asleep, stunned but trying to be hopeful. The Brits had let Bobby die. They'd made their point. Surely something would give soon, they all said. It couldn't be allowed to happen again.

It was on this day, the day after Bobby Sands' death, that I was approached by someone I didn't know. I was standing not far from the Boylan's house, staring into a street fire that some kids had lit, feeling so drained. I was worried sick about Martin, hoping they wouldn't pick him up again before I could pack him off to Australia.

An older man came over to me. He smiled and said that it was a sad day and I agreed.

'You know Viviane Ballard, I think,' he said.

'Yes,' I said, noticing that his accent wasn't the hard Belfast twang but a softer southern lilt. For some reason I immediately liked him.

Viviane was one of the senior teachers at school. She was a sprightly woman in her fifties, a bit pompous but basically okay. I didn't really know her well.

'Her husband is an RUC man,' the man said calmly. 'Works at Long Kesh.'

I nodded, surprised. Viviane was a Catholic.

'A mixed marriage,' the man said as though reading my thoughts. 'We need some information about him,' he added.

'Oh?' I said calmly, reeling inside. We? Who was I talking to? And what kind of thing did he need to know? I had a slightly sick feeling as I waited for him to speak.

'Do you think you could find out a bit about him for us?' the man asked softly.

'What kind of thing?' I felt cold, and moved in closer to the fire.

'Oh, just anything,' the man smiled easily. 'Perhaps he plays cards once a week, or goes to the pub on Saturdays?'

I knew then what he was asking me to do and why. I didn't speak for a while because I was trying to think clearly. I was afraid, too, because I knew if I agreed then I would be crossing a very important line and I had no idea if I'd ever be allowed to go back.

'If you don't want to, that's okay,' he said, bending down to feed tiny sticks into the fire.

Did I want to? I hated the police force now, with the same passion as most of my neighbours, and I particularly hated the guards at the jail. Stories of their savagery towards the prisoners came to me every day via kids I knew around the streets. And yet, did I want to harm an individual RUC man? No. The very idea sickened me.

'Well,' I said, 'I'll give it a go.' And to this day I can't tell you why I said that and not, 'No. I can't do it.' I had freedom of choice. I also knew that once I'd done something for them it would be harder to say no next time.

'Good. We'll meet here again in two weeks.'

'Okay.'

'Just see what comes up.'

Well, a lot turned up. And I turned out to be very good at this kind of work. I was a great little pregnant spy for the movement. Hardworking, meticulous and trustworthy. As an Australian and a teacher in a girls' school, I was above suspicion, too, which was probably why they asked me in the first place.

It was easy to cultivate Viviane as a friend. Under her slightly snotty air she was a kindly woman, just a little lonely. I knew all about that. I also knew all about sleeping with someone who you couldn't introduce to your friends. Not that I told her about your father. But she told me about her husband, Ken. What a lovely man he was. What a good father and how hurtful it had been that her own family and community had rejected her for marrying him. She let on that his position was dangerous. That he had to look under his car every morning in case someone had planted a bomb, and that he changed his route to work most days.

I surprised myself at how good I'd become at closing off. I knew that as long as I didn't meet the man then it would be okay, he would just stay RUC to me – someone like that red-faced bigot who'd laughed at me when I'd gone in worried sick about Martin. Not a person in any real sense.

I found out that Ken Ballard did have a card night and he went to the same pub every Friday night and that he went to see his unmarried bedridden aunt most Tuesday evenings. He left the house at seven forty-five sharp every morning and on Saturdays he coached the local twelve-year-old lads in football.

It was so easy to find out small things about the man that when the two weeks were up I was almost embarrassed as I handed over my three neatly written pages. My contact was delighted. 'Thank you,' he said. 'This is great. All this is . . . very useable.'

Within two weeks, Ken Ballard was dead: murdered by three

masked men outside his aunt's house on a Tuesday. Viviane took a month's compassionate leave and I signed the card that went with the flowers the staff at school sent her.

So how did I feel when I learnt of his death? Oddly enough, at first I didn't believe it. I was convinced that it had to be another Ken Ballard. Then, when it did finally sink in . . .

I've sat here for half an hour, Kathleen, trying to think how to continue – to describe how I felt when it finally registered that I was partly responsible. But I can't, somehow. Words can't be forced onto some situations. They will come when they are ready. That's all I can say. They will come of their own accord or not at all.

After Bobby Sands' funeral, I remember going with Annie to a bar in the city. How sad and useless we felt. The rain was pissing down, and we ran along under the trees by the river, getting soaked, scoffing down chips. We started laughing, hoarse as rusty drains. And crying. I was on the brink of telling Annie about what had happened with Ken Ballard. Of asking her advice. But I knew what her reaction would be.

Needless to say I utterly regret it all. I think I was on the wrong path altogether. Basically I allowed myself to be manipulated.

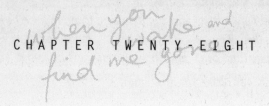

CHAPTER TWENTY-EIGHT

Laurie rang Kit the next morning, and put off their meeting for that day. He told her that he'd managed to locate her father. He was living in a place near Dungloe in far-west Donegal in the Irish Republic. Making personal contact was proving difficult. The local advice was that Eamon led a busy life. He travelled often and couldn't be contacted by phone. The place where he lived was remote. However, a local ex-fisherman who ran a small pub in the area told Laurie he was expecting to see Eamon back home any day now. He usually wasn't away for more than a week or two. Laurie apologised again but thought it would make more sense to meet when he'd spoken to Eamon.

'So he's alive,' Kit said into the phone, feeling her hands beginning to get clammy.

'Oh aye.' Laurie's accent was strong West Belfast. 'For sure. That's the good news, pet. I'm just sorry I can't be more specific about his whereabouts at this moment.'

'Oh, don't you be sorry,' Kit said with feeling. 'I'm so grateful!'

'Not at all,' he said warmly. 'I'll ring you as soon as I have more news.' He hesitated. 'Then, after we've checked out the lie of the land, so to speak,' he went on cautiously, 'then, things being well, I can help organise you getting over there.'

'Okay.' Kit knew he was alluding to her father's reaction. Would the news that his daughter had arrived from Australia annoy him, delight him or make him want to run a hundred miles? This was her third conversation with Laurie and each time she liked the man more. She hadn't even met him yet and he was going right out of his way to help her.

Kit rang Annie but got her answering machine. After waiting for a call back for nearly an hour she lost patience and decided she'd had enough of that poky little room. She would go and do a bit of exploring on her own.

She walked off towards the city. With travel book in hand, she went from one designated spot to another: the Town Hall, the Linen Library, the Museum. The crowds were buying up for Christmas. There were harried mothers and groups of busy office workers; young girls Kit's age dressed up in the latest fashion; mixed groups of young people hanging about the wet footpaths eyeing each other off. It was hard to think of this as a divided city. The cold of course was intense and so different to this time of the year at home, but the people *looked* like people from home. They smiled and laughed and greeted each other with hugs and wry comments about the weather and how busy they were. Groups gathered in pubs and cafés to eat and drink, just like anywhere else. There were clowns, musicians, and people selling hot food in the streets – not a policeman in sight, much less a soldier.

An older woman in a café where Kit stopped told her that everyone was desperate for the peace process to work. That it was such a relief not to have the army everywhere and the bombs going off and the fear and all the rest of it. Kit nodded and smiled, but none of what she was hearing really caught her interest. Her mind was churning wildly with her own predicament. Her father was alive! So what would happen when he was told the news? Did he even know of her existence? Yes, he'd have to. Even though he'd been in jail when she was born. She bought a delicious smelling mustard-covered hot-dog from a street vendor in College Square and then found she couldn't swallow more than the first bite. Waiting around for this kind of news was like being blindfolded and told to make your way out of a maze.

And of course there was Leonie playing at the edges of Kit's mind. *My mother,* she thought furiously. Trying to drag Kit into her long-ago life, forcing her into places she didn't want to go. *Keep all your Ken Ballards to yourself,* she wanted to scream. I don't want to know about your pathetic life. Or any more dirty little *murders.* It has nothing to do with me.

After a few hours, Kit felt crabby and impatient. Damn it. If she wasn't thinking about one parent she was thinking about the other! This wasn't natural. She was nearly twenty-one and she was obsessed with her parents! She'd read the handwritten pages that Annie had given her the night before, sitting up in bed at Hanson Lodge, the television news her only company. Again and again she'd read it. What else, she kept thinking. *What else?* This piece felt like only the beginning of a long line of crimes. What else had Leonie been part of?

By two o'clock in the afternoon, Kit was exhausted. And lost. She'd walked up the wrong main road leading away from the city, and found herself in a place called Sandy Row. Suddenly she was in another world altogether. This little estate, made up of blocks of cheap row housing, was like nothing she'd seen before. Deeply fascinating, and chilling. It had a small shopping centre down one street, and a number of little corner shops. People were quietly going around their business. But the kerbs were painted red, white and blue. There were Union Jack flags flying outside houses. Huge murals supporting the Protestant Unionist Militia were on every available wall. The paintings were of masked men with guns, along-side quotes from scripture. Kit stood before one, stunned, reading and rereading, trying to understand.

'And when the Lord thy God shall deliver them before thee; thou shalt smite them, and utterly destroy them; thou shalt make no covenant with them, nor show mercy unto them' Deuteronomy Chapter 7, Verse 2.

Next to this quote were three painted masked gunmen. And on the other side were the words, *Our glorious UDF.*

What would it be like living in one of these little houses? To come out every morning to get your paper and see that quote! It wasn't just an incitement to hatred. It was an incitement to murder. Kit suddenly understood that what her mother had been writing about was real. It was true. This was a world within a world. And one of the weirdest things about it was it was only five minutes away from busy ordinary Lisburn Road, which looked like Punt Road or Flemington Road in Melbourne. This place was no distance at all from the middle of Belfast.

She hurried back through the housing estate to Lisburn Road. Her sense of direction was completely messed up. She'd have to catch a cab back to where she was staying. Maybe Laurie would have left her a message.

But there was no message from Laurie. Not even one from Annie. Kit was disappointed. So much for the sightseeing tour. Still, she really didn't want to go out again. It was only three o'clock and beginning to get dark. Homesickness gripped her. *Why had she come?*

At about five, Kit carefully counted back the hours and put through a call to the house in Melbourne. Too bad about the cloud of bad feeling she'd left on. Maybe they'd had time enough to forgive her now. She would take a chance, anyway. She had to hear a familiar voice, or go crazy.

'Hi! It's me.'

'You!' Brendan's voice sounded tired, but glad enough. 'Kit, how are things? You got there?'

'You weren't in bed, were you?' Kit asked, then suddenly remembered with a pang that bed had a whole new embarrassing connotation now that Gucci was on the scene. 'It's so cold here,' she rushed on quickly. 'And everything is so different! I saw this weird place called Sandy Row just before when I was walking from the city. I got lost and . . .' she stopped suddenly, full of remorse for the nasty things she'd shouted at Brendan the day before she left. The fight had been huge and nasty. As far as Brendan had been concerned, Gucci had nothing to do with Kit, but Kit had refused to buy that. Their goodbyes had been strained, to say the least. 'Are you okay?' Kit asked.

'Fine . . .' There was silence for a moment. 'So, are you finding out what you need?'

'My father is alive,' she began, 'and last night this friend of my mother's gave me more stuff that Leonie had written. She really is . . . I mean, Brendan, this is real. My mother is a . . . I mean, she helped get people killed! Does that make her a murderer?'

There was silence at the other end of the phone and once again Kit began to rant nervously. 'Yeah, she spied on this policeman and then passed over the information. The guy got shot the next week.'

'So?'

'What do you mean, *so*?'

'The RUC were mongrels, Kit. Complete bigoted shits,' Brendan said calmly. 'Probably still are.'

'So they deserve to *die*?'

'Ah, Kit, you don't know anything yet.'

'I know a bit.'

'What do you know?'

'I know that if anything is worth anything then a human being's life has to be considered of utmost importance.' She knew she sounded prim and school-girlish but how else could she put it? She did believe this. She had to. If she let go of that, then what was left?

'Well bully for you.'

Kit's spirits slumped. This was not the conversation she wanted to be having with Brendan. She was too lonely for arguments about life and death. And he was so bloody stubborn. Part of her wanted to start screaming at him about Gucci all over again.

'So apart from all that, how are *you* over there? You feel Irish yet?' he added jokingly.

'Not really,' she said, and then stopped. 'But what is being Irish meant to feel like?'

'Completely fucked.'

'Ah, well,' Kit laughed, 'I guess I do feel Irish then.'

'Hey,' he said softly, 'it's hard when you first get somewhere strange.'

'Yeah.' The kindness in his voice made her want to burst out crying. 'So, Brendan, what's been happening with you?'

There was a pause, then Brendan began a Yeats poem without any warning.

'Out of Ireland we have come.
Great hatred, little room,
Maimed us at the start.
I carry from my mother's womb
A fanatic heart.'

'How the hell do you know that?' Kit was startled. 'You're an engineer!'

'So I'm not meant to know poetry, hey?'

'No, Brendan. You're not meant to know poetry!' Kit was laughing. 'I'm the one with the arts degree. Where did you learn that?'

'Jeez, Quinlan! My mother eats and breathes poetry. I swallowed it with the sour milk and stale Weetbix she used to feed us. She can hardly read, but she knows her poetry.'

269

'Lucky you!'

'Yeah, lucky me. It was a big buzz being brought up by two fanatics. We used to get belted if we didn't have our poetry quotations word perfect.'

'Ah, poor little boy!'

'You said it.'

'How's Tam?'

'She's . . .' he hesitated. 'Okay, I think. Lover boy has been around a bit. She's got a fresh black eye.'

'Ah, no.' Kit remembered threatening Robbie at the party. Loose talk. Showing off. That's all that had been. Just a load of crap. And he knew it. She was thousands of miles away now and her best friend was inside the terrible glass bubble that bastard had made for her. 'What do you think is behind it, Brendan?'

'Shit, who knows. Sex, maybe.'

'God! Really,' Kit groaned. 'So what's going to happen?'

'I dunno, Quinlan, but I think I'm getting your disease. I find myself wanting to smash his face in every time I see him.'

'Do it, Brendan, do it! Please. For me.'

Brendan laughed. 'I thought you didn't believe in violence!'

'I've changed my mind.'

On Kit's fifth day in Ireland, after a morning of sightseeing with Annie and an afternoon poring over old newspapers about the hunger strike at the Linen Hall Library, Laurie called with the news. He had managed to locate Eamon, had spoken to him in fact. Eamon was happy for Kit to come across to Donegal any time she liked. He sent his apologies for not being able to come and fetch her but his car wasn't reliable. He would meet the bus himself. She should ring first if she felt like it. He didn't have a phone but the pub down the road often took calls for him.

Laurie seemed almost as excited as Kit when he relayed the

news. They went out together that evening for a quick toast. It was great to finally meet him. His friendliness was really warming, but he couldn't tell her much more about her father's situation. Kit toyed with the idea of ringing her father straight away but chickened out. Laurie said he was happy to act as a go-between at this stage and she reasoned that the first time she spoke to Eamon McCabe she would like to look him in the eye.

CHAPTER TWENTY-NINE

The bus heading across to Dungloe left from the Europa Hotel every evening at five. The journey took approximately five hours. By the time Kit had settled into her window seat it was pitch dark outside. A shame, Laurie had told her, because the scenery she would be passing through was the most magnificent in the whole country. She'd hardly slept at all the night before. She'd come in about ten from her few drinks with Laurie. Just as she'd been brushing her teeth, Sebastian had rung. How was she going over there, he'd asked, in a polite, slightly distracted voice. Her knees had immediately gone weak. He would be in London himself soon. Spending Christmas there. How would she feel if he came over to Dublin before Christmas for a couple of days? Would she like to meet him there? Feeling as though she was in someone else's highly charged dream, Kit had simply said 'yes' to everything. And when she'd put the phone down she'd been virtually humming inside. Everything was working out at last. Everything in her life was coming together.

The bus pulled out from the kerb and began its torturous way out through Belfast's suburbs in peak-hour traffic. Kit stared out at the lights, then when they gave way to the steady blackness of open countryside, she lay back and shut her eyes.

'Are you Kathleen?'

Kit woke with a start. The bus had stopped in the middle of nowhere, and the driver was tapping her shoulder.

'Yes,' she said uneasily, shaking her head.

'I've had a call from Eamon. He says no point going through to Dungloe. He wants you to get out here. He'll pick you up.'

'But where are we?' Kit looked out the window at nothing but blackness. This bus driver was talking like he knew Eamon. What was going on?

'A wee place only an hour from Dungloe,' the man said matter-of-factly. 'But Eamon is on his way for you. He rang about an hour ago. You were asleep. I thought I'd let you be.'

Kit looked around in alarm and then scrabbled to her feet and pulled her coat and bag from the rack above. She'd never heard of someone ringing a bus driver before! Part of her didn't believe what the man was telling her but the other passengers were all turning in their seats, staring, waiting for her to get off so they could continue their journey. Hauling the bag onto her back, Kit headed down to the front door of the bus.

'So I just wait here?' she asked the driver.

'He'll be along any minute now. No need to worry.'

What else could she do? Kit stepped off the bus into the freezing wind and stood watching as it chugged on up the road and out of sight. Once the red tail-lights had disappeared around a bend and the engine sounds had petered out, the silence was overwhelming. It was after nine at night, freezing and spitting rain and she had no idea where she was.

'What am U doing here?' Kit muttered to herself half an hour later, rubbing her hands together furiously and stamping her feet to keep

273

the numbness at bay. The gloves were almost useless. She needed proper fur-lined ones for this kind of weather. Her coat wasn't warm enough either. Why hadn't she worn her wind-breaker and heavy walking boots? But she knew why. She'd dressed up deliberately. Worn her best clothes. Even make-up. After all, she was going to meet her father for the first time and she wanted to make an impression. Crossing her arms against her chest, she hunched over in the wind, toying with the idea of unzipping her case and pulling out the more practical coat. But what if all her other clothes spewed out in the mud? The wind was fierce. What if half her things got whipped away into the nearby fields? And just at the moment when she was trying to catch them all together in a pile, her father came along? Wouldn't that just be the end? The cold and wet was leaching up through her good boots that she'd worn especially, right into her bones.

All kinds of weird scenarios began to play out in her head as she walked around in the dark. This had to be his idea of a joke. Or, he was teaching her a lesson. God, she'd been a fool. Annie had tried to warn her. The man was a jerk. He wanted to humiliate her. Teach her that you couldn't just rush headlong into someone else's life, uninvited, without there being consequences.

One small window in a low building across the road gave off a tiny square of yellow light. Kit couldn't even see what kind of building it was, but guessed it to be a house. Well, she would have to go over there soon and throw herself on their mercy. Losing hope as the minutes passed, she was desperate. Her earlier elation that day seemed ridiculous. What could she have been thinking?

There was a noise coming from across the road. A woman yelling. Then the slamming of a door, and someone was running towards her.

'Are ye Kathleen?'

The accent was very different to the one she'd got used to in

Belfast. It was softer and more difficult to understand. Kit remembered vaguely crossing the border into the Republic a few hours before.

'Yes.' Kit gulped. The woman was thin, and wearing a coat, wide pants and a small beanie. Kit couldn't tell anything much else about her because of the dark.

'Will you come across then?' the woman said. 'Eamon's been held up. He rang half an hour ago but I didn't know that the bus had already been. I was thinking it was coming by about now. How long have you been out here?'

'Oh, well, a while I guess.'

The woman picked up her case. 'Come on in now and get warm. It's fearful weather, isn't it?'

Angry and humiliated and feeling almost sick with cold and disappointment, Kit followed the woman over towards the light.

The heavy stone whitewashed building was in fact a tiny pub – no more than a small room with a bar and a turf-fire. Three men were standing at the bar, drinking Guinness. Two were middle-aged and the other quite old. Another younger man was sitting behind the bar on a stool. A couple of children, babies really, were crawling around the floor. They all turned to watch Kit come in. She was immediately conscious of her city clothes. The men were obviously farmers, dressed in rough serge jackets, frayed jumpers and boots.

'How are ye?' one of the men said, nodding towards Kit.

'Okay thanks.' Kit was too freaked out to be anything but polite, but she wasn't feeling the least bit friendly. They were all looking her up and down like she was some kind of prize cow.

'Sit yourself down,' the woman ordered, pointing to the low chair near the fire. 'I'll make tea. Eamon shouldn't be long.'

'Thanks.' Kit did as she was told, holding her freezing hands out to the flames, the sudden heat making them tingle unpleasantly.

'From Australia, are ye?' one of the men said curiously.

'That's right.'

'Ah, dat's a big place,' the old man mumbled, shaking his head and staring dolefully into his drink. 'A desperate big place with all kinds of strange creatures.' No one made any comment about this but they all looked like they were thinking hard about what he'd just said.

'And you're related to our Eamon in some way?' the woman asked after a while.

Kit nodded. *Our Eamon!* Oh, give it a break. Kit wanted to run out of that place. If she'd had a bloody car she would have left! How did these people know everything about her?

'Well, it's a cold night outside and that's for sure,' one of the men said, slowly looking around at the others. They all mumbled in agreement, as though this was some kind of explanation for why Kit wouldn't tell them what her relationship to Eamon was. Kit found herself wondering that if they knew it was that cold then how come they'd left her out in it for so long.

'And what age would ye be, Kathleen?' the one behind the bar asked. He was a good-looking man, and probably, she thought, the young woman's husband. His dark hair stuck up on his head and his face had a pleasant rosy complexion.

'Twenty.'

The oldest man in the room, the one nearest to her, gave a sad little smile, then burped softly, and indicated with his glass that he'd like another drink. When it was in front of him he leant back against the bar, looking Kit up and down thoughtfully. It wasn't a lustful or lewd look, more as though he might be assessing a horse for purchase – checking it out for possible faults before he laid his money down.

'Are ye a married woman?' he asked at last.

'Er, no,' she said, gulping back her surprise.

'A boyfriend?' the one by the door suggested.

Kit shook her head.

'Now dat's a real pity,' the old drinker declared solemnly, 'because you're a fine lookin' girl and that's for sure! No one would deny it.'

Kit had to smile. This was, in its own weird way, turning out to be a rather funny conversation. Besides, if they were telling her the truth, then her father was on his way. Things might have been worse.

The door suddenly burst open, and a large man came blustering in. He looked around wildly. He was tall and solid with thick, curly grey hair. He looked to be about fifty, and his eyes were shining blue. When those eyes at last found Kit sitting near the fire, he stood still for a moment in the middle of the room.

It was him. She knew it immediately.

'Kathleen!' he demanded loudly in a thick, richly accented voice. 'Is it you?'

She stood slowly, her heart thumping, and took a step forward. 'Eamon?'

He gave a sudden roar of delight and rushed towards her, grabbing her in a huge bear hug, lifting her off her feet.

'Here you are then! And what a welcome to give a poor lass!' he yelled. 'I'm sorry I wasn't here for the bus, pet! I was on my way back from Sligo and I thought I'd save you the last hour. So I rang Harry. And there I was, driving like a maniac to get here and, would you believe it, I missed the turn-off! The roads out here are —'

'It's okay, it's okay,' she laughed, trying not to cry, loving the smell of his damp pullover and the warmth of his prickly face. He held her at arm's length for a better look, the blue eyes dancing in his broad, handsome, laughing face. Then he hugged her to him all over again, dancing her around the room like she was a doll.

'Ah, you're bonny! A bonny girl altogether! Will you look at her!' He held her out for the others in the room to see. They were all laughing now, the men raising their glasses. The young woman holding two babies smiled broadly.

'This is my wee girl come all the way from Australia! What a great lookin' lass!'

'Oh aye! She is!' The old man came forward. 'A grand-looking girl!' It was as though the fifteen minutes before hadn't happened at all and they were seeing her for the first time.

'You're welcome here, Kathleen!'

'Aye! You're welcome, lass!'

'Will you have a wee drink on us, Eamon?'

'Why not?'

The young couple began to busy themselves behind the bar.

'To McCabe's grand wee girl!'

'All the way from Australia.'

'So how's your mother?'

They were in the car, just the two of them, heading off along a winding road to the little village he lived in outside of Dungloe. The wee drink had turned into three and when a couple of new-comers had come in, they had to be told the story of 'McCabe's girl come all the way from Australia' and so there had been another round. It was now after midnight and Kit was beginning to fade. 'I only just heard about the accident,' he went on soberly. 'Laurie says she's going to make it.'

'She's slowly getting better,' Kit said, not knowing if this was exactly true but not sure what else she could say. 'She's beginning to wake up.'

'Well that's grand news,' he said distractedly. She took a quick glance at his profile in the dark. He was staring straight ahead, concentrating on the road.

Was he thinking of Leonie?

In spite of the tiredness, gladness rose in Kit. It *had* been the right thing to do. Even if there was nothing else but this. She would have this night as a memory, driving along a winding Irish road at night with her father. Eamon McCabe. Him having come to meet her, dancing her around that little bar, in front of those people, like he was proud. That would be something to think about all her life. Something to remember.

'I know a little about when you and Leonie met,' she ventured tentatively.

'Is that right?' he turned to her with a quick smile. 'Well, we'll have time to catch up on it all, so we will.'

She nodded. 'I hope so.'

She wondered how long it would be until they reached his house but didn't have the energy to ask. After a while, he felt herself drifting off to sleep.

'Kathleen, would you mind if we stopped to see the rest of them?' His voice jolted her awake.

'The rest of who?' she asked, sitting up straight. She'd slumped up against the door and cramped her neck. She began to rub it anxiously.

'Ah you know, the wife. And the wee ones.'

What? You've got a wife? Why hadn't she thought of this? Of course he'd have a wife! She was an idiot not to have expected it.

'But your wife won't really want to see me, will she?' Kit managed to say, panic rising like flood water. 'I mean, does she even know?'

'Of course she knows!' he said warmly. 'She's dying to see you. The girls, too.'

'The girls?'

'Rosalaind is our daughter. She's been jumping out of her skin since she heard she's got a sister now. But my wife has another three girls living there. Her sister died a couple of years back so we took them on.'

'Oh, I see.'

'Actually, you probably don't yet, pet.' He gave a laugh. 'Bridie and I don't actually live together. So I suppose she's my ex-wife but, well, I never think of her like that. She's a great woman is Bridie. We're still close, you know. We've got the girls and . . .' His voice trailed away a little sadly.

'Oh.' Kit was well and truly awake now. 'So where do they live?'

'Right in town. I know it's late but they'll never forgive me if I don't call in for ten minutes. It's not that far out of our way.'

'So the girls live with Bridie?' Kit asked, trying to get it straight.

'That's right,' he said easily. 'But we're all friends. There are no hard feelings. The girls give me hell, you know. I'm their father and their punching bag. The usual thing. So it is.'

'So they, the girls, know about me?'

'Oh sure! Since the moment Laurie told me you were here. They're dying to see you. Our Rosalaind is a real tiger, though. Beware of her. She'll give you a hard time, just to let you know who's boss.'

'How old is she?'

'She's fifteen, and a real handful. Praise be to God, she's into everything.' He turned and grinned at Kit. 'She told her mother a story about staying at some wee girl's place from school. Then she hitched down to Dublin to see Eminem.'

Kit smiled. 'And how far is that?'

'About two hundred kilometres, I'd say. Bridie had to call the guards out after her!'

A sister, Kit was thinking. *I have got a sister!*

'So your mother never told you about Bridie?' Eamon said conversationally.

'No.' *She never told me anything.*

'Well, I was actually married to Bridie when I was seeing your mother,' he confessed calmly. 'Which was not a good situation.' He turned to her with another fast smile. 'But all that is behind us now. And you're here. Which *is* good!'

Kit nodded. If it was such a good thing, then why didn't he ever contact her in Australia? And why hadn't Leonie mentioned that the guy she was falling in love with and seeing in the middle of the night all those years ago was in fact married to someone else?

Everything she knew about human nature told her that Eamon's reading of this situation with Bridie would be totally wrong. Men were often very thick about this kind of thing. Wives didn't usually have fond feelings for the offspring of their husband and his lover. And from what she could work out, families didn't like being disrupted, either. She thought of Tam and the bitter resentment she always expressed at the mention of her father's second family over in England. If Eamon had sons, it might be easier. But girls – they'd probably be catty and resentful. What in the world would she say to them?

'Now you're not to be worrying yourself about Bridie and the girls,' he said warmly, as though he'd could read her thoughts. 'Because there is absolutely nothing to worry about there.'

It turned out he was right. More or less, anyway. They stopped outside a small house on a narrow cobbled street and the rain suddenly began to bucket down. Eamon got out immediately, slamming the door. By the time he was around to Kit's side, the front door had opened and a small woman was hurrying down the path to greet them, a jacket thrown over her head as a shield from the downpour.

'Can you believe this weather?' she cried, holding both arms out to Kit and smiling. 'Welcome, Kathleen. We hoped you'd call. The girls have been waiting. I'm Bridie,' she said simply, hugging her. 'Welcome home to Ireland!'

'Thank you.' Kit shyly accepted Bridie's embrace. Her slight body under the coat felt soft and welcoming. But it wasn't until she got into the house that Kit could really see her father's former wife. She was small and finely built with an almost doll-like quality to her – tiny hands and feet and the sweetest expression that Kit had ever seen. Bridie must have been hitting fifty but her skin was soft and fine, very pale, with just a hint of pink in her cheeks. The lines around her eyes and mouth were barely visible. Her deep red hair, shot through with grey, was pulled back into a soft bun that looked like a nugget of burnished gold.

'We're not stayin' long, Bridie,' Eamon said firmly. 'The girl is wrecked.'

'Of course she is,' Bridie murmured, clasping Kit's hand and leading her down the passageway. 'You must be shattered after that bus ride?'

'No, I'm okay,' Kit said gamely.

She was led into a large warm family room. It was comfortably furnished with easy chairs and a wooden table. There were multi-coloured rugs over the two couches set against the walls, and all kinds of big and small embroidered cushions dotted over the chairs. Three red-haired young women stood in a line in front of the fire-place, one in jeans and a shirt, the other two younger ones in their dressing gowns and slippers. All smiling, all very pretty, all of them younger versions of Bridie: fine-boned, fair-skinned and with sweet smiles.

'This is Ellen.' Bridie pulled the tallest one forward with one hand. 'She's your age, twenty, and doing Accounting at the university in Galway.'

'Kathleen!' the girl said in the sweetest accent, shyly stretching out her hand to take Kit's. 'You're very welcome here.'

'Thanks.' Kit was moved by the genuine warmth of the greeting. The two younger girls were Ruth and Lily.

'You all look so much alike . . .' Kit said, and they laughed. 'And so like –' she looked over at Bridie, about to say 'your mother,' but remembered that Bridie was their aunt. These were Bridie's sister's children.

'Their mother was my twin sister,' Bridie explained quickly, smiling at the girls proudly.

'Oh!' Kit nodded. 'What was her name?'

'Rosalaind.'

The name reminded Kit that there should have been another girl alongside these three. Her very own half-sister, in fact. She gulped. God, this was almost too much to cope with, and it wasn't over yet.

Eamon must have sensed her anxiety. 'Is the wild one still awake?' he asked Bridie.

'Oh yes.' Bridie smiled at Kit. 'Our youngest was harping on all day about you coming. But she got shy at the last minute.'

'Well, I don't blame her,' Kit said with genuine sympathy. It would be quite a shock at fifteen thinking she was the only child of these parents, then a stranger from Australia turns up unannounced to claim almost equal billing. Eamon walked to the foot of the stairs.

'Rosalaind!' he yelled. 'Come on down!'

'No,' came the answer immediately. Sharp and definite.

'I've got your sister down here.'

'Well I don't need another sister, thank you very much. I've got too many already!'

Exasperated, Eamon was about to run up the stairs but Bridie held him back.

'No, Eamon,' she commanded. 'Let her come in her own time.'

Eamon shrugged and did as he was told. This Bridie was tougher than she looked, Kit decided.

'It's not very nice for Kathleen,' Eamon said grumpily, 'not to meet her sister tonight.'

'I'm sure Kathleen understands,' Bridie said with a smile. 'Rosalaind is just a little shy. Come on, Kathleen, sit by the fire and tell us . . .' she stopped only for a moment, the twitch around her mouth the only sign that what she was asking might play some deep painful note in her own life, 'tell us about how your mother is recovering from her accident.'

Ellen made cocoa and hot buttery crumpets with honey while Bridie and the other two nieces sat firing questions at Kit. Where did Kit live and who with? What was the farm like? How big? What was she studying? What did she hope to be? Kit tried to answer every question honestly but it was awkward. It had only been an hour since she'd met her father for the first time. It was too much, having to explain herself to an ex-wife who must have her own painful memories to deal with. The warm curiosity of the three sisters was intimidating in a different way. They were obviously so close; they teased each other loudly, laughing and poking fun, seemingly quite oblivious to the fact that it might be a difficult situation for Kit. Then Lily, the youngest, asked a question that made Kit reel out of control.

'So you grew up knowing that Leonie was your mother?'

'I've only known for about four weeks,' Kit unintentionally snapped. When they all looked so shocked, she buried her face in her hands, feeling utterly undone. She wanted to get away. Not because she was unhappy but because she couldn't handle any more.

The room had grown quiet around her.

'We had no idea, Kathleen,' Bridie said softly. 'No idea that this information had been witheld from you for so long. We thought you would have grown up knowing it.'

Kit saw that Eamon, too, looked shocked. 'Well, come on girl,' he said quickly, rising from his chair. 'Enough of this. I'll take you home.'

On her way out, Kit turned for one last goodbye and found she was looking at a replica of herself. Standing on the stairs was a girl in a thick white nightie with ruffles on the hem. Her long, dark, curly hair fell all about her face. So this was Rosalaind, come down to check things out at last!

'Kathleen is just going, Rosalaind,' Eamon said quietly. 'Will you come and say hello?'

'Will she be back?' The girl was looking at her feet.

'Oh, for sure she'll be back,' Birdie said with a warm laugh. 'Tomorrow probably, or the next day.'

'I'll see her then,' the girl said, suddenly turning around and running back up the stairs again.

Kit laughed, feeling for Rosalaind filling her chest and throat, making her eyes swim.

'Tell her I'm dying to meet her,' she said to Bridie, 'whenever she wants. I'm really looking forward to it.'

'Sure, I'll do that.'

'So we'll see you tomorrow?' Ellen asked anxiously.

'Yes, please bring her back tomorrow, Daddy,' Ruth chimed in. 'We've got to get to know her properly.'

Daddy? This one calls my father Daddy?

'We'll come soon,' Eamon said gruffly, putting his arm around Kit and ushering her out to the car through the rain. 'In the next few days, we'll come by again.'

CHAPTER THIRTY

Eamon's house, when they eventually got to it, was tiny. It was a cottage of just two rooms with massively thick walls, and a built-on bathroom and toilet out the back. The bedroom was divided in two by a thick red curtain hung from a rail that had been nailed to the roof. Eamon showed her to one side of the curtain.

'Will you be right here then?' he asked, putting her bags on the bed.

The space just managed to hold an old-fashioned iron bed covered with a patchwork quilt, and a small bedside table with a lamp on it.

'Sorry there's not much room,' he added.

'That's fine.'

Kit felt a pang of guilt. He'd had to divide up his bedroom for her visit. Still, this knowledge touched her, too. It was such a simple house and he was sharing it with her.

'Come and I'll show you the bathroom,' Eamon said. 'I'm afraid I'll have to get the fire going before we have any hot water. Will I cart some through for you when it's hot?'

'No. No, I'll just clean my teeth,' she said. All she wanted to do

286

was crawl into that little bed and get warm. The chilliness of the night air was eating into her bones.

When she got back from the freezing bathroom, Eamon was at the stove piling in wood.

'I asked old Cormac from down the road to come over and stick a hot-water bottle in your bed,' he said, looking up at her with a smile. 'Go see if he's done it.'

Kit went through to her side of the bedroom obediently and felt down into the bedclothes. Not one but two bottles were warming her bed deliciously.

'Yes,' she called through. 'He's done it.'

When she came back into the kitchen her father was standing with his back to the stove. The kitchen was small and basic, with just a wooden table, a small fridge, a dresser and sink.

'I usually keep the fire going all day,' he said. 'But I've been away a while.' He smiled. 'Now you get in there and have some sleep, Kathleen. I'll just sit up a bit.'

Kit slipped off her pants and jumper then crawled straight into the warm bed in just her undies and long-sleeved T-shirt. She couldn't be bothered trying to find the warm nightdress Therese had got her especially for the trip. Never had she been so thankful for flannelette sheets. And those hot-water bottles were wonderful against her legs and toes. She watched through the open doorway as Eamon's big shadowy figure moved around the kitchen, from the stove to the funny little fridge, then outside. After a while he settled himself near the stove, reading something up against a low lamp. Kit could hear sheep outside, and the occasional howl of wind against the window. Every now and again a splatter of rain hit the roof. Apart from that, there was nothing except the low hum and occasional splutter of the lamp Eamon was reading by.

'It's very quiet here,' she said.

'Ah, you're still awake?' he called over. 'Aye, it's quiet all right.'

Now she was finally in bed, Kit thought she would never sleep. This felt too odd and precious. The little house. Just Eamon and her. Welcome home, they'd all said. As though this was her place, too, somewhere she might have been all along if things had been different. She thought of the last few minutes of their drive up the mountain, and the fact that she hadn't seen many lights at all on the way.

'How many people live in this village?' she called.

'There's really just crooked old Cormac and me,' Eamon laughed. 'But there are others living around, you know. They come by at night to Cormac's and, you'll see.'

He got up and came over to the doorway.

'You're welcome here, Kathleen,' he said quietly. 'You go off to sleep now, girl, and I'll see you in the morning.'

Kit smiled in the darkness. It had all turned out. The trip, her father, everything was perfect. And this was just her first night. She had two weeks to get to know him before she had to head back to Dublin to meet Sebastian. *Oh, wow.* Kit's toes curled with delight thinking about what pleasures might be in store for her there. After Sebastian had gone back? Well, who knew what would happen? Christmas was coming. She wasn't sure where she'd be spending it but wouldn't it be wonderful if her father invited her to stay here? Maybe Sebastian could come back with her. The possibilities were endless. All of them delightful.

CHAPTER THIRTY-ONE

The next morning, Kit woke to find that Eamon had already left
the house. There was a note on the table and a roaring fire that
heated the whole cottage.

Back soon, the note read. *Sleep as long as you can. Eamon.*

She sat about for a while, enjoying the warmth and coziness of
the place. She filled the kettle and put it on the stove, looking out
the back window at a bare mountain that rose steeply behind the
cottage. She kept expecting him to return any moment. The low
sky and blustering wind and rain put her off going out on her own.
It was nearly eleven in the morning and she still felt dozy, deliciously lazy from her late night. She turned on the little radio above
the sink and began to wander around the cottage, picking things up,
studying them, looking for clues.

Peeping into his side of the bedroom, Kit saw it was very plain
and tidy. It held a narrow bed, neatly made, a small wardrobe with
a case on top, and a chest of drawers with a bedside lamp. On the
chest of drawers were a few framed photos: Bridie in a cap and
gown, getting a degree, Kit supposed; the three older girls together,
and a single picture of Rosalaind. Kit picked up another small

289

framed black-and-white photo from behind the others, and took it to the light of the window for a clearer look. It was her mother: Leonie as a young woman, leaning up against a fence, arms folded across her chest – looking confident, proud and sure of herself.

Kit had a sudden desire to go through all his things, to see if there might be something about herself. A birth certificate or a little baby's shoe, perhaps a photo? But she didn't, of course. It would be a terribly invasive thing to do and, well, what if she found nothing?

She wandered back into the kitchen and looked out the front window, her breath giving way suddenly with the stunning view. She'd had no idea that the cottage was positioned so high up. It seemed to be clinging to the side of a steep mountain. Right down below, through a deep valley of craggy cliffs, she could see the sea – a wide still blue plank merging into the sky.

Kit pulled a jumper over her T-shirt and stepped outside into the freezing air. There were sheep grazing about the house and nearby mountainside. Kit's farmer's eye judged the creatures to be doing poorly, half-starved they looked, ragged and scrawny as they wandered about sniffing desperately for grass. There was nothing much for them to eat. The land was brown-grey, the jagged hills barren, unforgiving and cold. Kit hoped someone around had enough money to hand-feed those animals soon. If not they'd die before the winter was through.

Yet her heart soared. The hills and cliff faces seemed to be whispering to her, welcoming her back.

She decided to go out walking and take a better look. As she stepped back into the warmth of the cottage to get dressed, she heard the whispers again. *Where have you been? Why so long?*

When Kit finally walked out onto the track that wound down from the cottage to what she supposed was a main road at the foot of the mountain, she wore hat, gloves, strong boots and a weather-proof coat. It felt good to be in the bracing air. Here I am, she thought, smiling to herself, staying with my father in Donegal. He wanted me to come, too. After all these years. He wanted to see me for himself. If only Johnny was here now. Or Tam, or Brendan. She began humming, wondering if Eamon was musical. Maybe she'd get to play the flute for him or they'd sing together, the way she and Brendan did sometimes.

She turned the corner, and a little further down the road was a low-lying building set into the hillside. It looked like a simple house. Kit walked closer and spied a rusted Guinness sign out the front. *The best drink in the world.* She hesitated. This was probably the man who her father had told her about. Cormac. But the place looked closed. Kit walked on, deciding she'd call in on her way back and introduce herself.

She'd hardly gone past when there was a banging door behind her and a man's voice calling out.

'Is it you, Kathleen?'

She turned around to see an old man limping towards her on two sticks. He was badly misshapen, hunched over to one side, with thin, stick-like arms, and bent legs that lurched forward at odd angles when he walked. As he got nearer, she saw some kind of big bone sticking out of his narrow chest. Crooked Cormac, she remembered Eamon had said lightheartedly the night before. So here he was, the man himself. The one who'd put water bottles in her bed. He stood before her, panting with the effort of having walked the distance and trembling a little, too, trying to catch breath. To her surprise she saw that he wasn't actually very old at all. His face, although slightly distorted as though he might have had a stroke, was quite smooth, without lines or haggardness. He was sizing her up curiously.

'I'm Cormac,' he said sharply. 'I'm well-known around these parts.' He flashed her a small smile, and pointed one of his sticks at her. 'Eamon has filled you up with all kinds of lies about me, no doubt. So, you got here?'

'I did,' Kit smiled back. How very nice his eyes were. A kind of weird, light, bright blue, like blazing gas lamps in that deathly pale face.

'Don't mind me,' he said unapologetically. 'I'm a desperate lookin' old freak but you'll get used to it.'

'Oh no,' Kit gushed with embarrassment. 'I was just going for a walk, then I was going to call in and say hello.'

'Well, all right,' he said, still panting a little, 'but be here tonight. Everyone will be wanting a gawk at you.'

'Everyone?' Kit said, looking around. There was not one other house she could see. She squinted. Maybe there were a couple on the faraway hills, but she couldn't be sure of that.

'Oh, they'll turn up,' he grinned. 'For Eamon's wee girl, for sure. They'll all be here.'

'Can I come in now?' Kit said, pointing at the pub and smiling at him. 'You've got a fire going?' She suddenly felt like company. Eamon would be back soon and she didn't want to be out walking too far when he returned.

'Oh sure, sure. Come in from the weather. Have a drink.' He led her back over to the little pub and pushed open the door. He winked at her. 'In a couple of hours there'll be hoards of them breakin' down the doors, but just now it's a fine time to come in.'

Kit stepped in and looked around. It was the oddest pub she'd ever seen. The room was big enough, with a bar in the middle and the rows of bottles and glasses behind it. And there were about five tables and chairs directly in front of it. But the place was packed with other produce as well. On one side of the room was a small greengrocer's. There was an open box of cabbages, boxes of eggs, a pile of green apples, and potatoes and beans. And on the other side was a supermarket, with dusty packets of toilet paper, dry biscuits and cleaning fluids all piled along the shelves. On that counter was a large plastic tray of bread: some packets and some whole loaves. A fire flickered invitingly.

'So do you live here with your family, Cormac?' Kit asked, stopping in the middle of the room.

'Oh, Lord, no!' he rasped. He headed to the counter, lifted the flap up, and hobbled to the other side. 'Sit down there near the fire and I'll bring you a whisky.'

'Well . . . okay.' Kit didn't drink much as a rule. Not in the daytime anyway, much less the morning and she virtually never drank spirits. 'Just a very small one.'

'Oh, be damned!' He waved his hand dismissively. "Tisn't the weather for small drinks.'

The fire was hot and Kit took off her coat. She felt already at ease, as though she knew Cormac. It was the oddest sensation.

'So you run the place alone?'

'Sure,' he said, struggling to get the ice out of the plastic container and dropping small blocks into two glasses. 'I had a wife once but she ran away.'

'Oh?' Kit was amused but didn't allow herself to smile. She didn't want to hurt the man's feelings. 'So how long ago was that?'

'Twenty years, now,' he said. 'Twenty years this Christmas. I still miss her but what can you expect? She was from Cork.' Cormac looked at Kit meaningfully from across the counter as though that explained everything.

'So, people from Cork, they run away a lot?'

'Don't tell me you've never heard!' Cormac seemed genuinely shocked. 'Don't tell me you don't know that women from Cork are a flighty lot. They just can't settle. The sanctity of the marriage vow means nothing to them!'

'No, I didn't know that.'

'Well, now you do.' Cormac slumped into his chair and raised his

293

glass to her health, winking again. 'To the girl from Australia.'

'To both of us.'

'Aye, that's good,' he grinned at her, and took a gulp. 'To both of us.'

And so the conversation continued easily. He asked her about her own family, showing keen interest in her brothers, their wives and livelihoods. And her taciturn father – most Quinlans are like that, he told her. They often need a cracker in their lunchbox to get them going! Cormac then told her about some of the people she'd be meeting that night. He mentioned forty-five year old Con, and the terrible old killjoy of a mother he lived with, who wouldn't let him out for a pint unless she came along. And a woman called Betty who (despite being English) had a lot more common sense than her husband, a local man who bought the garage repair shop the year before without having the first idea how to fix a car. At least Betty could make a decent sandwich in the local café. 'Whereas the whole countryside's littered with broken-down cars and all because of that idiot Sean Kiely!'

One after another the stories tumbled out, Cormac's eyes gleaming with mischief as he filled her in about his neighbours. She was to look out for a man named Jim Maloney who would be 'all over her' that evening, probably proposing marriage by the end of the night if her flute-playing impressed him. (Jimmy was a great fiddler himself.) But Kit had to resist his smooth talk because although he would be 'promising the world' he was a Maloney and that family were well known skinflints. She'd never have a shirt to her back if she hooked up with him.

'Right,' Kit said, shaking with laughter, 'I'll keep that in mind then.'

'You do that, lass,' Cormac muttered, swirling the whisky around his glass before taking another gulp. 'Keep him at a distance. It would be a shocking thing to be married to a miser. That it would!'

Kit gave up wondering just how much Cormac was exaggerating. Whisky was running down smoothly by this stage, so that might have been part of it.

'That bread smells good,' Kit called out. Cormac was going for their third drink and Kit, although she didn't feel drunk in the least, found herself slipping from her chair onto the floor, which should have been very embarrassing. But Cormac seemed to think it was the most natural thing in the world to fall to the floor when you were sitting talking to someone, even though she noticed he didn't seem to do it himself.

'Sure, I go into town every day to pick it up,' he said. 'I get up at five and I'm back by seven to open up. The people around here know they can rely on me for fresh bread.'

Kit accepted the drink and took a sip. She felt mellow and easy, as though she was on a big rolling ship and there was nothing else to do but sit around and pass the time.

'What are you smiling at?' he said, sitting down awkwardly in the chair opposite, his stick falling to the floor with a clang.

'I'm just thinking how good this is,' Kit said. 'I mean, who would have ever thought drinking whisky at this time of the day could be so good?'

'Well, of course it is!' Cormac burst out into a loud wheeze of delighted laughter. 'Of course whisky is good at this time of the day!'

Suddenly, the outside door swung open.

'In the name of Our Lord and Saviour and his Holy Mother!'

Eamon was standing in the doorway, roaring. 'And all the angels and saints. I might have known! You've got my daughter in here, Cormac O'Grady, getting her drunk no doubt, you old debaucher!'

'Ah, come in, McCabe! And shut your gob!' Cormac shot back sharply. 'We're having a civilised conversation in here. 'Tis mighty craic all right. She's got someone decent to talk to at long last! Isn't that right, Kathleen?'

'That's right!' Kit laughed as Eamon made his way over to the fire, holding out his hands to the warmth. 'Absolutely!'

Eamon wouldn't take a drink, but he seemed in no hurry to get away, either. He sat down in front of the fire next to Kit, joining in the conversation where he could.

Cormac did the bulk of the talking, but because he was good-humoured and witty, Kit enjoyed sitting back and listening. And to have Eamon there was doubly nice. The warmth of the little scene was only interrupted twice by people coming in to buy bread and having to be introduced. Then the phone rang.

Cormac got up grumpily. 'Probably some woman or other,' he winked at Kit. 'They won't leave me alone.' He hobbled over to the bar. 'I have to beat them off with sticks and dat's the truth, Kathleen!'

'Are you okay?' Eamon whispered to Kit, smiling.

'Yes, of course.' Kit was suddenly embarrassed. Her head had begun to swim. She couldn't tell how long she'd been sitting there and that meant she must be drunk. Who could have guessed it? Her first day with her father and she gets drunk first thing in the morning. What would he think of her?

'Kathleen!' Cormac called out from behind the bar. 'It's for you!'

'For *me*?'

'Aye, and from Australia too,' Cormac said, holding out the phone. Kit got up and immediately tripped over the edge of the square of carpet.

Eamon got up to help, putting one arm around her shoulders, more or less holding her upright.

'You feel okay to walk?'

'Yes,' Kit said, feeling her face heating up, 'I'm just not used to whisky.'

'Of course you're not,' Eamon laughed, helping her across to the phone. 'He's an old devil.'

'It's not his fault,' Kit mumbled.

She hoped it wasn't going to be Martin wanting to know how she was getting on with her father. She really needed to be sober for that conversation. At this point she wasn't sure what she'd say to anyone, actually.

It was Therese.

'Oh, hi Mum!' Kit's head cleared momentarily with the shock. It was imperative that she came across sober or there would be panic at home. Before she'd left, Therese and Gerard had threatened to send some creepy old cousin up from Dublin to check she was okay. 'I was planning to ring you tonight!' Kit added quickly. This was the truth but it sounded a bit weak. After the first phone call to tell them she'd arrived safely, Kit hadn't contacted her family, although she had sent two postcards. It was now, she thought guiltily, over a week since she'd left.

'We're all fine here,' Therese said a little stiffly. 'How are you getting along?'

'Good, good.'

'Where are you exactly?'

'I'm at a little place in Donegal. It's called . . .' for the life of her Kit couldn't remember the name of the town. 'How did you get the number?'

'Well, I was frantic,' Therese said sharply, 'so we contacted that Martin in Sydney and he rang us back with this number. Have you met . . .' Therese's voice petered out, 'the man you went to see?'

'Yes. Yes, I have, Mum,' Kit said quickly. 'Just last night, actually.'

'And is everything all right, Kathleen?'

'It's fine.'

'You sure there's not something wrong?'

'No, of course not.' Kit's head was swimming. She leant up against the wall. Nausea was coming in waves. Therese was going to start asking her all about her father and she didn't know if she'd be able to answer. The man was in the room for starters and Kit's thoughts were all murky and unclear. She'd had hardly any time to get to know him. It suddenly seemed quite unreal, quite preposterous that she was in Ireland at all.

'Well, I've got big news,' Therese was saying. Kit breathed a sigh of relief that the spotlight was off her for a moment. 'So you're going to have to pray about this, Kathleen. All of us are going to have to pray very hard about this.'

'Okay,' Kit said warily, her mouth going dry. 'Has something happened?'

'No, no.' Therese hesitated.

'What is it, Mum?' Kit managed. 'Is Leonie . . .'

'No, Leonie is doing well,' Therese said. 'Yesterday when Gerard brought her in some strawberries, she smiled.'

'Oh, that's good.'

'It's Johnny, actually,' Therese said carefully. 'He's left the seminary. And he's getting married.'

'Married?' Kit was so shocked that she let the phone go. It slipped out of her hand, knocking against the brick wall. She glanced down, thinking it looked like a dangling dead crow on the end of a bit of string. *Johnny*. All the time she could hear her mother's voice calling out sharply. *'Kathleen! Kathleen! Are you there?'* Kit forced herself to lean down and pick it up again.

'Sorry, I dropped the phone. What were you saying?'

'Johnny is getting married,' her mother snapped.

Kit suddenly realised what a blow this would be for Therese. She'd been so proud of Johnny training to be a priest.

'Oh, Mum, I'm sorry,' she said.

'Well, it can't be helped.' Therese gave a sob, and then pulled herself together again. 'Everyone has to find their own way in life . . .'

'Still, it's so disappointing,' Kit murmured. In fact the whole idea of Johnny leaving the priesthood was growing on her by the second.

'So who is he marrying?'

'Well, her name is Casey,' Therese said edgily.

'Have you met her?'

'Yes, very briefly.'

'When is the wedding?'

'That depends on you,' Therese said quickly. 'Johnny won't have the wedding until you come home.'

'Well, that's okay,' Kit said. 'I'll be home in a few weeks.'

'But when, Kathleen, *when*?' Therese implored. 'If you could just tell us because there is a baby to think of. And there's your birthday as well.'

'*Baby*?'

'Casey is expecting just after Christmas,' Therese went on. 'They say they don't care. But I *do* care! Johnny wants the wedding reception out at the farm. And I don't want her to go into labour on the day or to have a baby screeching blue murder during the ceremony.'

'You mean Johnny was having an affair while he was in the seminary?' Kit whispered.

'Oh Lord, no!' Therese cried. 'Goodness me, no. The baby is not his, although it will be as soon as they're married.' Therese suddenly began to cry. 'He's determined to look after Casey and the baby, and the little fellow.'

'Oh, God,' Kit groaned, the light dawning at last.

'She lost her husband in a work accident early this year. And she's got no family. Just one old aunt who doesn't seem right in the head. Oh, Kathleen, she's, Casey is such an ordinary little thing. She's so *ordinary* to look at! She's got these thin little bow legs! And her teeth stick out. I know I shouldn't say that, but Johnny is so handsome and –'

'So when is the baby due?'

'Casey has a little fellow of three already,' Therese said, 'and the new one will be born in the New Year.'

'Oh hell!' Kit groaned again. Typical Johnny! Why couldn't he just marry some reasonable single person? He always had to choose the most difficult thing! This was ridiculous!

Kit knew they were mean thoughts but she couldn't help herself. She was disappointed and drunk and she couldn't keep her voice down either.

'Why does it always have to be like that with Johnny?' she yelled into the phone. 'Who is she, Mum? I'll bet she's some ugly little pudding-faced toad who's leeched onto him because he's a soft touch. Remember the other ones! It's like he's got no defence against needy people. He just rolls over as soon as some blasted cot-case comes along!'

'Kathleen, that is not at all charitable!'

'But it's what you think, too, isn't it? I bet it's the case. Some needy little twerp. God, I'm going to ring him up now! If he marries her he'll never get out of it. It is absolutely the worst thing for him to be getting married so soon after leaving the seminary! He needs some time to think and work out what he wants.'

'Kathleen, have you been drinking?'

'No!'

'You sound like you've been drinking!'

'Well, I haven't.'

'Are you sure?'

'Mum, I told you . . .'

Eamon took Kit home after that. He insisted that she drink a lot of water and then lie down while he went out to see someone for an hour. When he got back they would go for a drive and see some of the countryside if she felt like it. Kit lay on the bed, full of remorse. *Why had she ended up yelling at her mother? Why hadn't she asked*

Johnny more questions at the airport? Why had she allowed herself to get drunk before midday?

Johnny had seemed strung out before she left but she'd assumed it was because he felt uneasy about her going overseas. What a complete clutz she was. Poor Johnny must have been going through his own turmoil and she'd been oblivious, concentrating on herself as usual. *Casey?* She couldn't remember him even mentioning that name. Then a conversation during the trip out of the airport came back to her. The detention centre. One of the volunteers. What had he said? That she was tough and determined. What the hell did that mean?

Kit doubted that she'd be able to sleep. Her head felt twice its normal size and her limbs felt heavy, like lead pipes stuck onto her torso. But she did sleep and when she woke Eamon still wasn't back, so she sat out the front of the cottage and opened up an envelope that Annie had given her as she was getting on the bus.

'Here's the rest of it,' Annie had said, just before Kit had boarded. 'You might like to read it on the trip.'

But Kit had been too excited about meeting her father to open the envelope on the bus. Now she began to read, the dread and the fascination building up inside her just like before.

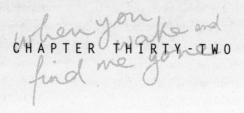

CHAPTER THIRTY-TWO

That weekend your father took me to Donegal. After we'd stayed in Letterkenny we drove for a couple of hours to the town of Dungloe, then up from there a few kilometres to a place called Killrose which was really no place at all. Just a bare landscape. We left the car at the base of a hill and went walking up a winding track to a small empty spot that looked out over the sea. I suppose it was about an hour's walk, and I was glad when he told me we'd arrived. It was a desolate place: the only building one burnt out cottage, and hardly a tree to break the unrelenting bare hills surrounding us. Further on stood the huge blue mountain. It was craggy, worn as an ancient face.

Miraculously, the weather had cleared. It was a bright, still, blue afternoon. We walked a little further. We were standing on a rugged track, with the Atlantic to the left of us, green and flat, almost metallic in the sunshine. Beneath our feet were moss-covered stones and about us some low tumbledown walls covered in moss, too, but fitting so snugly into the rest of the landscape that it took me some time to realise that I was standing where there had once been buildings. One small, stone end of a house, perhaps only six feet at the highest point with a tiny window hole in it, still stood.

Your father took my arm and brought me over to the wall. It had been part of a little public house (a shebeen) back in the middle of the 19th century, he explained, pointing out where the other end had been.

It was weird to stand inside that rough semi-square of stones, trying to imagine it enclosed, with people laughing and dancing and telling stories inside.

Your father told me he could trace his family right back to that desolate spot at the foot of the mountain. Well, back before the time of the Great Hunger. For centuries it had been a thriving village, with over a thousand people living around where we stood. And there had been other villages just like it. There had been a church in this place, two shebeens, shops, a well, places to tether horses and lots of small dwellings.

But when the blight took hold of the potatoes for two years in a row, and there was nothing to eat, it was in the crevices and caves of the nearby hillside that the people had starved to death.

I asked him how he knew all this. And he told me that he grew up in a house on the side of a hill only two kilometres from that place, not knowing much until he went to university. There he'd been lucky enough to get a professor who was researching the famine in that very region. An American, as it happened. He told me that the famine was only just starting to be studied properly – well over a hundred years and they were only starting to come to terms with it.

This puzzled me. I thought of the history of my own country, of all the books about different topics, like Federation, Gallipoli, the Depression, the Gold Rush, none of them as terrible and important as what he was telling me. More than ten per cent of the Irish population had starved to death. Why wouldn't they make a big thing of that in schools? But your father only shrugged and didn't say anything for some time.

After a little while he told me that the stories from that time were so terrible that people were ashamed even now and didn't want to admit it happened.

I didn't know what on earth he could mean by that. But I said nothing. It went very deep with him. I could see that. I didn't want to push.

He'd made a study of the area we'd gone to that day, back when he'd been in university. All along this track, he explained, waving at the peaceful road in front of us – which had suddenly grown ominous, full of terrible secrets – all along here were half-alive bodies, clustered, too weak to move, blackened with disease and swollen with hunger, lying by the roadside, eventually dying there. Some were buried. Some were eaten by dogs. Some managed to hobble back to a cave, to a crevice between two rocks, to die privately. Their shame hidden. Whole families were found like that, years later, their skeletal remains lying up against each other, away from prying eyes.

These were his people and they'd been let starve in their own land.

When they couldn't pay their rents, the landlords simply evicted them, put them off the land, and levelled the houses. The people had no food or shelter and nowhere to go. The lucky ones got a boat to America, while others ended up in the workhouse five miles from where we stood. Already weak from hunger and exposure, they tried to hack out some kind of existence in the sides of the hills, under trees and in caves, eating berries and bark and pinching fruit from the orchard of the big house, the remnants of which he would show me later. But eventually they'd had to make their way back down the track, meeting up with people like them from other villages.

'Ragged streams of them tried to escape on these roads,' your father whispered to me that day. 'Well over a million starved to death across this country. Old men and women and children were desperate with hunger, while the landlords stayed in their big houses, either here or back in England, and set about using the situation for their own advantage. Agriculture was changing. They wanted to clear the land for grazing. It suited them to be able to rid their lands of the indigenous Irish. So they sent in the bailiffs, razed the dwellings and turned

304

the people out. It wasn't actually a question of food, he said. Sure the potatoes were rotten, but the country had food. No, it was a neater solution all around to let them starve.

We kissed each other for the first time that day. Drawing close, our feet slipping a little on the moss-covered stones. Almost as soon as we touched, the sun went in and clouds began flinging themselves across the sky as though preparing for some big skirmish. By the time we walked back to the car, the day had become dark and gloomy again with only a thick streak of heavy yellow light bolting down between two blankets of cloud. For a while I didn't know whether I was filled with pleasure or dread. I felt the ghosts of the dead breathing down my neck as he started the car.

That night when I lay with your father for the first time, in a lumpy hotel bed just down the road from where his family had lived and died, I listened to the storm beating around the old stone guesthouse, rain pounding the slate roof, thinking about the ragged starving Irish on the road where we'd stood that day.

And I thought about the fact that they were my people, too. The same people who'd lain down to die by the road, or who'd ended up in the workhouse to eventually die there, some of these same people, the stronger ones, made it down to the ships, and got away. To America, to Canada, to Australia. Did you know that Dad's people, the Quinlans, came out in the 1860s, just after this time? And Mum's people, too – the Sullivans.

The storm blew all night. Your father slept fitfully, as though his dreams were full of unnamed terrors, too. I will never forget that night. The way the mournful wild sounds of the Donegal countryside played an echo inside my own heart. Something old had come alive in my bones.

Kit sat in the cold for some time. There were a few more pages in the package but she didn't want to read anything else. Mist swelled up in heavy clouds from the valleys below, closing down around her. She felt the bleak loneliness of the place enter her own heart. There are hidden things all about here, Kit thought, a flicker of fear teasing the back of her neck. So many secrets. *Something old had come alive in my bones*, her mother had written. It wasn't just the landscape. If Kit allowed herself, she could feel them too. In the half-light of the dying day, shapes and shadows of people long dead were shuffling through the blustering mountain air, gathering around her, clamouring. *For what?* If she listened very carefully she could hear the moan of their voices.

Kit forced herself to get up. It would be nine o'clock in the morning in Australia now. With luck she'd catch Johnny. She raced down through the darkening cold to Cormac's to ask if she could use the phone.

She tried home and got Frank who told her Therese and Gerard were in at the hospital and that Johnny had gone back to the city. So Kit rang the seminary number and was politely told that Johnny no longer lived there. Frustrated, Kit put the phone down.

'You'll be back later,' Cormac called to her as she made her way back outside again. 'There's a lot of people want to meet you, Kathleen.'

'Oh, right,' she said. 'Then I'll be here.'

CHAPTER THIRTY-THREE

When Kit and Eamon got home from Cormac's, it was after midnight. They walked up the track in the cold together, Kit pleased to be on her own with her father again, and in high spirits.

'They're good people eh, Kathleen?' he said, putting an arm around her shoulders. 'And you fit in well.'

'Oh yes,' Kit sighed, stopping a moment to look down the mountain towards the sea. Not that she could see anything much in the swirling murkiness of the dark night. But her mother's account of her first time in this place had been tugging at her mind all evening.

'So this is the place where you grew up?' she asked Eamon shyly.

'Well, it's the land where my people lived for generations. We grew up in another house down the road because this one had been burnt down.'

'What happened then?'

'We moved into Dungloe.'

'But this place?'

'This place was where my grandfather lived as a child and where his father lived, too.' Eamon smiled as he opened the door into the kitchen and switched on the light. 'I bought it back from a German, a few years back. He'd fixed it up a bit, put a new roof on.'

'Didn't Bridie want to come out and live here with you?' Kit asked. 'Was that why you split up?' She hadn't touched any drink that evening but she was feeling bold anyway. He'd been proud when she'd played her flute earlier that evening, she could tell.

'Ah well, it was more complicated than that with Bridie.'

'Do you remember bringing my mother out here?' Kit asked.

Eamon thought for a while. 'No,' he said, frowning. 'I don't remember doing that.'

'She wrote about it,' Kit said, 'about it being a very important day, with you and her.'

'Ah, well then,' he turned away, bending down to put more wood on the fire. 'Then I'm sure I must have, if she wrote about it.'

They'd had a great time that night. As Cormac had predicted, everyone had dropped by to check out Eamon's girl. There were half a dozen young families, along with middle-aged couples and some old people. A couple of bachelor farmers, regulars most nights, brought their instruments – a fiddle and a tin whistle. Someone else had a small drum. Kit was introduced to Betty, the sensible wife of the unpopular mechanic Sean who stood around looking awkward as though he was aware of all his shortcomings. Jim Maloney was there with his fiddle. He eyed Kit with great interest as Cormac thought he would, but there wasn't time for any 'smooth talking'. After meeting Kit and commenting on her likeness to Eamon, everyone wanted the music to begin.

Kit was intrigued watching them start to play. It happened so casually, almost like a natural phenomenon. There was no hushing to be quiet. The music seemed to simply erupt out of the chat and the laughter and the drink. When someone called for her to play, she did so with ease. (Eamon had urged her to bring her flute.)

She'd started off with some well-known Irish reels that Leonie had taught her years before. Delighted, the gathering of thirty or so clapped and sang snatches of the lyrics.

Then someone called out for Kit and Eamon to do a song together. To her surprise, Eamon immediately leant over and asked if she knew how to play 'The Wild Colonial Boy'. Kit laughed and picked up the flute again.

'Of course. It was one of the first things I learned.'

His voice was strong, and she knew that her playing sounded pure and light. It touched her that her father had chosen an Australian song. As she played, Kit found herself imagining what it would have been like for Leonie. It might have been a night like this that she'd fallen in love with Eamon for the first time.

Throughout the night, Kit watched her father carefully. People knew him and liked him, she could see that. And yet he held himself back. She could sense his reserve. She tried to fit this easy-going, genial person who had a kind word for everyone, with her mother's description of a passionate nationalist. Was all that outrage and passion still there in him? Was that why he'd bought back the family's cottage?

Who was he really?

I'm getting to know my father, she thought as she lay in her bed in the darkness. She could hear his gentle snores and was glad that he felt easy enough in her presence to fall off to sleep so quickly.

Only the curtain hung between them.

I'm getting to know my father, she told herself again.

But was she? Doubt gnawed away as she eventually dropped off to sleep. If this cottage and land belonged to Eamon, then surely it belonged to her, too? She wasn't just some little blow-in from Australia, here for a few weeks and then gone forever. It was her great-grandfather he'd been talking about. Her great-grandfather had been burnt out of his house. It was all very well singing an Australian song to welcome her. But how come he didn't remember bringing Leonie out to this place? It hurt Kit to think that what had meant so much to Leonie didn't even register in her father's memory. Could it be that he didn't want to remember?

CHAPTER THIRTY-FOUR

'So tell me about your life,' he asked her the next day. They were walking together in waterproof jackets, a fine sleet blowing in their faces. He'd driven her down to a spot on the coast between two headlands on the joking pretext that he was going to show her that Ireland had beaches too; maybe not as magnificent as Australia's but there all the same. It was perhaps twenty minutes away from the cottage, a wide sweep of bay surrounded by craggy cliffs, the mountains behind them. They'd parked the car just off the road and after they'd zipped up their hoods he led her down along a dirt track onto the rocky beach. A huge steel-grey sky hung low over the murky grey-green water, an occasional spit of white foam the only relief. 'Did you enjoy your schooling?' he went on. 'And what about university? What are you hoping to do when you finish?'

'School was . . . okay. Bayton is a big town so the school was reasonable.'

'You had friends?'

'Yes,' Kit hesitated, 'I had friends there.'

'So you liked growing up in the country?'

'Yes,' she said uneasily. His questions were matter-of-fact, almost impersonal. She had the feeling that his mind was on something else.

'It was good,' she added, wondering how to paint a picture powerful enough to catch his attention. 'Very free and easy.' Her inability to nail the words she needed gave her a sudden pang of homesickness for that place where she'd spent her childhood. How could she tell him about the smells: of dust and gum trees and horse sweat, of all the jostling warmth and good humour of days lived with her parents and brothers. And then the next phase. University. The house in Richmond. Brendan and Tam and Lou. She looked back to the mountains, blue now in the deepening wintry light of the afternoon. Patches of fine white mist were forming around the peaks. She could just make out the speck of her father's house not far down from the highest point. It looked defiant, perched near a jutting piece of rock the shape of a monster's nose. On the lower slopes of the mountainside were other cottages – little farms fenced by low stone walls and small intersecting roads.

'And Gerard and Therese were . . .' he hesitated, still looking out to sea. 'They were good to you?'

'Yes.'

'So you had a good childhood, Kathleen,' he said, calmly pleased. 'That's grand to know that.'

A twinge of anger surfaced in her head. *Why let him off the hook so easily?* Why not lie and tell him that she'd had a horrible, unhappy childhood? Would that shift him from this complacent polite stance? He was like a courteous stranger asking questions about something with which he was not intimately involved.

'Well, pretty happy,' she murmured, giving no hint of the turbulent undercurrent of feeling beneath her words. 'I guess I was lucky.'

What else could she say? *I had a great childhood. No thanks to you!*

What did she want from him? Just a million things. Some information would do for starters. What had been his reaction when he'd heard that he had a child? He was in jail, so perhaps he wasn't told straight away. She wanted to know if he'd been part of the decision to have her adopted out to Leonie's family. And there were loads of other things. But when she turned to him with the questions, she stopped herself. *Who is this person? I don't know him.* His face seemed as impenetrable as a block of granite. She told herself to wait and be patient. He had a strange reticence that she hadn't a hold on yet and she didn't want to get him off side.

'You obviously did well enough to get into university,' he said thoughtfully, bending to pick up a small stick that he threw into the water. They both stood, watching it bouncing along on a tiny wave.

'Leonie came back from overseas when I was thirteen.' The words rushed out of Kit. 'And then she left again after we'd become close. She stayed away for six years. Mum and Dad said she went back to France. Then to England.' Kit was almost breathless, waiting for him to turn and face her. But he simply nodded, frowning, and began to walk off again, his hands in his pockets. 'Did you see her at all then?' Kit called anxiously after him. 'I mean six or seven years ago? Did she come and see you?'

'I saw her . . . a few times, but we . . . Bridie and I were still married. And we had Rosalaind.'

Kit walked after him, waiting. She couldn't believe he was going to stop there. How in a million years could he think that would be adequate. *We had Rosalaind!* What was he saying? That Leonie didn't matter? That she, Kit, didn't matter? What sort of explanation was that?

'Did she . . .' Kit began stiffly, catching up with him, 'did she say why she left Australia?'

The rain was getting heavier, hitting hard into their faces. Someone else, in a red coat and with a big dog, was further up the beach heading their way. Eamon was squinting into the distance; he seemed to be watching the dog. But he suddenly took Kit's arm.

'Leonie told me,' he said quietly, 'that she had to leave Australia. That she couldn't cope with being a mother.'

Kit gave a short snort of laughter. 'But she wasn't my mother!' she protested angrily. 'Not then. She was my big sister and she was happy! I remember that year very well. She had friends and we had a good time. I used to stay with her. We used to go places and –'

'Kathleen,' he cut her off with a sigh. 'She was afraid.'

'Afraid of what?'

'Afraid of it all.' He paused. 'Of being a mother. Of being tied down. Of having to do it on her own.'

Kit waited.

'And,' he sighed, 'I think she hoped we, that is she and I, might resume some kind of relationship.'

'I see,' Kit nodded, then added coldly, 'but you had Rosalaind.'

'I was married,' he said simply. 'To Bridie. And yes, we had a child.'

'I see,' Kit said again.

But she didn't. She didn't see at all. The blustery cold wind now fell at an almost horizontal angle, slapping sharp bullets of rain into her face, making her cheeks numb. He suddenly grabbed her elbow, pointed at the thick low sky and indicated that they should go back the way they'd come.

'This will only get worse,' he yelled above the wind. 'Better get back.'

They turned around and quickened their pace, the rain driving into Kit's back now. It felt so persistent and unrelenting. An avalanche. Like a sudden teeming storm of memories that wouldn't leave her alone.

CHAPTER THIRTY-FIVE

'Have you any pictures of kangaroos?' was the first thing Rosalaind had said to Kit when they met two days after Kit's first midnight visit. When Kit said she was sorry but hadn't a single picture of a kangaroo, Rosalaind had sighed dramatically and stormed upstairs to her room. Bridie told Kit not to take any notice; that Rosalaind would come around in her own time.

Sure enough, she came sailing back downstairs minutes later, making her way around the back of the chairs were everyone was sitting talking about the party they were going to the next week. Kit was intensely aware of her as the conversation about clothes bubbled on, but tried not to show it. Rosalaind looked so much like Kit that it was almost funny. The same height and skin colour, the same wild dark hair falling down her back. Big blue eyes and shapely, slightly chunky legs. Even the way the younger girl moved her hands in that jumpy, awkward, impatient manner. It was impossible not to think that Kit was looking at a younger version of herself.

'Would you like to come and see what I'm working on?' Rosalaind addressed Kit across the top of the conversation. The others stopped talking, looking on amused, waiting for Kit to answer.

'Er, okay.' Kit got up from the table and followed Rosalaind to the stairs.

Rosalaind's bedroom was at the front of the house, overlooking the street. She held the door open for Kit and motioned her inside. Kit walked into the room and gasped in surprise. The walls were covered in drawings. All in sequence. Pages had been divided up into squares, like huge film strips with wide bare stripes of white at the top and bottom. The drawings themselves were all highly complex: fantasy land stuff. Castles and fairies, huge gnarled tree trunks, rainbows, goblins and giants, all beautifully executed. Some were in coloured pastel, some in ink and others in pencil.

Kit didn't have to pretend. She let out a low whistle of appreciation and moved in closer to examine them.

A queen-like figure in a red flowing dress was descending a staircase. She held a skull in one hand and a sword in the other. In the next drawing along, the same queen was threatening someone in a crowd. Then she was chopping off that someone's head with her sword. In the next, the queen was moving through a crowd of terrified people who were all cowering in front of her. She was holding the cut-off head in her hand, blood pouring down her arm.

'Who's that?' asked Kit.

'That's Maeve. The queen. And I'm going to do one about Cuchulain next.'

'You actually drew these?' Kit asked, wondering angrily at the others downstairs. With all their droll comments about 'the wild on' none of them had bothered to mention that the girl was talented.

'I'm not going to be an artist in the ordinary sense,' Rosalaind said, slumping down onto her bed and flinging both legs up high onto the wall, making her skirt fall down to her pants. She carefully tucked most of her skirt between her knees before continuing. 'I'm not actually even interested in drawing.'

'Oh?' Kit was amused by the casual confidence but didn't actually understand. 'Then what?'

'I'm going to be a film-maker. You see all these drawings? They tell stories. That's what I really want to do,' Rosalaind grinned. 'Tell bizarre and terrifying stories! In my deepest heart I want to direct horror films. These are my stills, until I can get hold of a camera.'

Kit nodded slowly. She did see now. It made perfect sense to draw if you couldn't get a camera to film your pictures.

'I have all these pictures and stories rushing around in my head,' Rosalaind said. 'One day they'll be a film.'

'I'm sure they will.' Kit sat down on the bed next to her, still looking around. 'They're fantastic. One day you'll be a famous film director.'

'You think so?'

Kit wasn't just being encouraging for the sake of it. 'I'm sure you will.'

'We look the same,' Rosalaind said suddenly. 'I'm already getting all these flashes about doing a film of two sisters who meet up after never having known each other. One of them wants to kill the other one because she is hell-bent on usurping the first sister's rightful place next to the father's throne.'

'Oh, shit!' Kit laughed, pretending to be nervous. 'I think I'm recognising this story. So what happens in the end?'

'Don't worry, I'm not going to murder you yet.' Rosalaind gave a low chuckle, delighted that Kit had got her meaning without being offended.

'Did you know about me?' Kit decided to change the subject.

'No,' Rosalaind said sharply, 'and I'm totally furious about it.'

'Well, I didn't know either,' Kit said defensively. 'I've only known that my mother was not my sister for about a month.'

'Hmmm. Will you be in my film one day?'

'Sure,' Kit grinned. 'You mean as an actress?'

317

'As a queen,' Rosalaind said dreamily. 'Queen Kathleen, flighty and mean.'

'She's ever so keen,' Kit added quickly. 'But not very clean!'

They giggled.

'So what do you think of our father?' Rosalaind asked, bringing her legs down and sitting up. A bit of a loon isn't he?'

'I like him,' Kit said slowly. 'But I don't really know him yet.'

'He's got a shady past, you know,' Rosalaind whispered dramatically, 'a shady, ferocious past!'

'Yes,' Kit sighed. 'Do you know much about it?'

Rosalaind shrugged. 'Didn't your mother tell you?'

'My mother is lying in hospital.'

'Oh God, I forgot!' Rosalaind jumped up, went over to the window, opened it and leant out. 'An unconscious queen and a bad king, with two fighting princesses. That might be even better!' She turned to Kit. 'Don't you think?'

'Well,' Kit laughed, 'maybe!'

They were quiet for a while, Rosalaind staring moodily out the window and Kit lying on the bed looking around at the drawings.

'The girls in my school want to be either models or lawyers,' Rosalaind said theatrically. 'I've got no friends.'

'I didn't have many friends when I was at school either.' This wasn't quite true. Kit had always had at least one or two people to hang out with. But as she got older she became less and less one of the popular, out-the-front girls that everyone wanted to be with. 'Have you got someone?' she asked gently, 'someone to talk to, I mean?'

'Not really.'

'When you start doing what you want to do,' Kit said encouragingly, pointing around at the drawings, 'then you meet like-minded people. I mean, when you go to film school, you'll have friends then . . .'

318

Rosalaind nodded moodily and went on chewing her nails. 'I don't want a house,' she burst out, 'or children. Or a husband. I want to live in a castle by the sea. A real recluse – that's what I want to be. Once a year I'll venture out, on a white horse maybe, and I'll make a film that will shock the world.'

'Wow!' Kit grinned at her. 'Yeah, I can see that.'

'Well,' Rosalaind said defensively, 'everyone has to have ambition, don't they? Kathleen,' she rushed back over from the window and grabbed Kit's hands fiercely, 'you haven't got any other sisters, have you?'

'No . . .'

'Me neither. So we should stick together. You and me. What do you think?'

'Definitely,' Kit smiled, delighted with the girl's passionate nature.

'Because,' Rosalaind stopped for dramatic impact, 'there is a lot of stuff going on. Weird stuff in this world. And we are blood sisters.'

'Yes,' Kit held her breath, 'okay. We're sisters. You're on!'

'No matter what they say,' Rosalaind added darkly, 'those three down there are not my sisters! I'm on my own and so are you!'

'So we'll be on our own together!'

'Yes!' Rosalaind slapped one hand hard against the wall, then stamped her feet. 'So we will!'

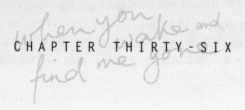

CHAPTER THIRTY-SIX

The days began to slide by. It wasn't as though Eamon avoided Kit's company or her questions. She could tell he went out of his way to talk sometimes, even when he didn't want to, and to make her stay as pleasant as possible. But after a while, she knew there were some things that he couldn't, or wouldn't, speak about.

But he put hot-water bottles in her bed every night, introduced her to people, took her places, made jokes about Australia, cooked for her. And of course in all sorts of oblique ways she did get to know Eamon. She knew he liked three cups of strong tea in the morning, along with a few strips of bacon between two slices of thick bread that he bought fresh from Cormac. She knew he liked to read. He borrowed most of his books from the library in town or from friends. There were two men in particular who came by occasionally: John, a big, cheery, dark-haired fellow from Tyrone who was about her father's age, and Sean, a good-looking young man, probably only in his mid-twenties and originally from Belfast. Sean had a strange blank look in his eyes that unnerved Kit; a hard, cold, curious look that made her think that he was attracted to her against his will. Initially, she tried to make it easier for him by making casual conversation. But after a while she gave up. With all her efforts, he never warmed to her, and was never anything more than civil. She guessed it was just shyness, but she wasn't sure.

Both of these men now lived in the nearby town. Together they were easy enough company. John always included Kit in conversation, although she had the feeling sometimes that he might have been talking about other things entirely with her father before she came into the room.

She knew, too, that her father didn't have another woman, even though he was separated from Bridie; and that he had a photo of Rosalaind in a small silver locket around his neck. He adored Rosalaind. She knew that much.

And Kit knew he liked to hear her play the flute. The nights when they sat together in front of the fire were the best. He would put down his book or newspaper, and ask Kit if she felt like playing a bit. She would pull the flute out from under her bed and begin with something simple. She was still rusty, but it didn't matter. Eamon would stand about listening, making cups of tea, offering encouragement and advice on how it might go, humming the notes and laughing at her mistakes and his own. If he knew the words to the song he'd eventually start singing along, or they'd make up their own words and it would turn into a patchwork of corny love song or soulful lament. Other times it would be a ballad with a story. They would break up with laughter at some of their weaker efforts.

Cormac struggled up from the pub most nights and cracked his stick twice against the door.

'Come in!' Eamon would yell, 'if you're handsome, or rich, or you have a cunning way with women!'

Cormac would crash in, grinning, pulling a bottle out from the pocket of his coat and thumping it on the table.

'Have ye a glass in the house, McCabe?'

'You know where they are, man!'

Drink in hand, Cormac would fall into the nearest chair, grumbling about the rain and cold, and begging Kit for some kind of decent tune 'to get his blood flowing again.' Eamon would smile at Kit with those incredible blue eyes as she played. Kit had no idea where that smile came from. Yet the warmth of it blazed right down under her skin, into her bones.

Sometimes, when his back was giving him trouble, Eamon lay flat on his belly between them on the floor. He'd fold his arms in front of him, cradling his head, eyes closed, just listening, a half smile on his face as Cormac and Kit bickered about which songs were good, who wrote them and who sung them first.

The two men would occasionally ask Kit about Australia. Were all the farming properties measured in square kilometres? How high did kangaroos really jump? What about Ned Kelly – were people still interested in him? They would often all end up laughing at some of the strange ideas that they had about her country.

Then Cormac would begin the same plaintive Van Morrison song each night when he'd had enough and was at the point of heading back to his bed. Eamon would join in immediately.

'Oh won't you stay, stay awhile
with your own ones.
Don't ever stray, stray so far
from your own ones.
This old world is so cold.
Don't care nothing for your soul
you share with your own ones.'

Listening to Eamon and Cormac sing that song always put a lump in Kit's throat because it felt like they were singing it for her. For those brief minutes, she felt as though everything about her life there with her father was in place. She was part of him and he of her. Nothing needed to be said and nothing else needed to happen.

Kit never found out exactly what her father did for a living. Nor why he and Bridie split up.

'What do you do?' she asked him one night after they'd eaten and before Cormac came in. 'I mean, what's your job?' He'd just told her that he had to be away for most of the next day and that he'd drop her at Bridie's so she could mess around with the other girls.

'Well,' he said lightly, 'my needs are not great.'

What kind of answer was that? The week before, she would have let it pass, but by this stage Kit was feeling more confident.

'But everyone needs money,' she persisted, laughing a little. 'You run the car and you eat.'

'Damn,' he grinned. 'You noticed. I do eat. Quite a bit actually!'

'So?'

'Well . . .' he frowned, 'a bit of this and a bit of that. It's not like a regular job. I work for an import company, I suppose you could say. I help manage the distribution of goods through the west of Ireland.'

'What kind of goods?'

'Oh,' he shrugged, 'lots of different merchandise. Tinned food . . .'

'And where –'

But Kit didn't get to finish her question about where the goods came from because there was a sharp knock at the door and Cormac's face was peering in the tiny window.

'The wrestling is on in ten minutes,' he called, 'if you both want to come and see.'

'Oh, right!' Eamon yelled back, going for his coat. 'I forgot. I'm coming.'

Wrestling? It turned out that they were both big wrestling fans and because there was no television in the cottage they watched the matches in Cormac's tiny kitchen behind the pub.

'I don't really know much about wrestling,' Kit said, amused, when Eamon encouraged her to come along. 'Who's in it?'

'What!' Cormac pretended to be outraged. 'It's the European finals, girl! Don't tell me you haven't heard!'

'So who's going to win?'

'I've got my money on The Bolt Cutter,' Cormac frowned. 'He's a mighty little cut-throat from Slovenia.'

'Don't listen to him!' Eamon laughed, as he tied his shoelaces. 'The Barfly will win. Nothing surer.'

'So where's he from?' Kit wanted to know.

'The Ukraine,' Eamon said. 'You coming, lass?'

Cormac had already begun walking back down to the pub. 'Come on down with us, Kathleen,' he yelled, 'I promise you'll love every minute of it.'

So she put on her coat, too. And much to her surprise, in a crazy way she did enjoy the wrestling. Within five minutes she was barracking for The Bolt Cutter because he was smaller and seemed in need of support. When he eventually won, she found herself slapping palms gleefully with Cormac and wishing she'd put money on him too.

Kit didn't get around to pressing Eamon for details about work again because he seemed almost bored talking about it.

'Ah, you don't want to know,' he said once, after coming back from a long trip to Donegal. 'Believe me. I waited around all morning for something that had already arrived yesterday. Those idiots don't know their arse from their elbow!'

Nor did Kit ever hear in detail what had happened between Eamon and Leonie. Just the odd comment here and there that had her pecking like a hungry bird for more.

When Eamon suggested over breakfast that they take a trip out to Arranmore for the day, Kit was pleased. There was a ancient fort there, he said, and a lot of stories and history she might be interested in. As well as spectacular views.

'I'd love to come, if you can spare the time.' She was conscious of him trying to juggle a busy life around her. He often had to head off for a few hours, a morning here and an afternoon there, sometimes a whole evening. Time was slipping away for her, too. The following week she was due in Dublin to meet up with Sebastian.

'We don't want you going back to Australia without having something grand to tell them about,' he said with a smile.

Kit went for her purse and waterproof, trying to ward off the fresh pang of unease in her heart. *Did he even want her? Was he looking forward to her going away again?*

They were travelling down the mountain on a dirt road when Eamon began singing. The fast, flying clouds came at them in swirls of menacing white as his deep voice reverberated around the little car. The song seemed to have a double function of filling up the silences between them as well as holding the little car down in the blustering wind.

'D'eirigh mé ar maidin dhá uair roimh an lá
'gus fuair mé litir ó moo mhile ghrá.
Chuala mé an smolin 's an londubh á rá
gur ealiagh mo ghrá thar sáile.'

They were driving through a turf bog, a lonely deserted place that Kit loved in an aching, instinctive way, in spite of the fact that, combined with her father's song, it caused outbreaks of goosebumps on the back of her neck and down her arms. There was not another car in sight. When at last the song was finished, he asked her if she knew any Irish and when she said that she didn't – not even a word – he began to sing the same song in English.

'I walked up and walked down.
I walked Cork, and Dublin, and Belfast towns,
but no equal to my true love could I find.
She's the wee lass that's left my heart broken.
I got up two hours before day

And I got a letter from my true love.
I heard the blackbird and linnet say
That my love had crossed the ocean.'

The nostalgic mood of the song lasted well after he'd finished singing. In the silence Kit fancied she could feel Leonie with them in the car. Leonie at twenty-three or four: at the height of her beauty with her long red hair, her wide smile and her passionate heart.

And all along that empty ribbon of road, brown loaves of earth were stacked up on either side like funeral pyres. Kit shivered, wondering if this might be the place people came to after they died. The hard flat sky; the dung-coloured tubes of earth like so many dead souls piled up. A halfway place, like limbo, perhaps, where dead people came to wait until their ultimate fates were decided.

'I remember the day you were born,' Eamon said, cutting through Kit's meandering thoughts.

'You were in jail,' she said.

He nodded. 'One of the other men handed me a note when I went past his cell to empty my bucket.'

'What did it say?'

Eamon stared ahead, both his hands gripping the steering wheel intently. Yet his voice sounded vague, like he, too, was in a state of dreaminess.

'It said, You have a daughter. Born at five a.m. yesterday. Both well.'

'No weight, or name or anything?'

'No, no,' he said kindly, shaking his head. 'Nothing like that.'

'So what did you think?'

'I was pleased,' Eamon said, 'and glad it was a girl.'

'Why?'

'Well,' he shrugged, 'my mother had always wanted a girl, apparently.'

Kit knew from a previous conversation that his mother had died giving birth when he was ten. That the dead baby had been a girl. And that Eamon had grown up with his father, as an only child.

'Was there any celebration?' she asked.

'Not really, although someone managed to get me a smoke.' They were driving gradually out of the bog and into farming country.

'A smoke?'

'A cigarette was very precious,' he explained with a smile. 'Then they all yelled out, "Congratulations, Eamon!" And they sang me a song. I think it was the "Star of The County Down". Something like that. An old song anyway. In Irish. Some of them had real voices, you know. It sounded grand. So there was a bit of a celebration.'

'And then you had the smoke. On your own?'

'I had to wait the whole day before I could have it. When everything was quiet, I took it out from under the mattress and lit up. All the time I was enjoying that fag I was thinking about the fact that now I was a father, that I had a wee girl. I kept wondering what her name would be.'

'You never discussed a name with Leonie?'

'No. And then I got to wondering if I would ever hold the baby in my arms,' he added.

'Did you . . . ever?' Kit whispered.

'No,' Eamon said again, shortly. 'No, I never did.'

Me! Me! You're talking about me! A voice inside Kit wanted to yell.

'Why isn't your name on my birth certificate?'

Eamon looked surprised. 'I'm not there?' he smiled.

'No.'

'Well, Leonie probably thought it wasn't worth her while. I was married, remember, and in jail.

There was a moment of quietness between them.

'What else do you remember?' Kit asked.

'I wondered what colour eyes she had,' he continued, 'and I felt sad for Bridie because she wanted a baby so much.'

Kit bit her lip and looked away. Bridie was his wife. Of course it was natural that he wanted her to have his baby.

I was not planned. I was an accident. My birth was not intended. Get used to it. Get over it. Face it. Grow up.

'What else?' she whispered again because she knew he was telling her the truth. And even if it was painful it was better than lies.

'When I finished the cigarette,' he said, 'I knelt down in the darkness and thanked God for the baby.' He paused. 'I prayed for my daughter. That her life would be good.' He turned and looked at Kit in surprise, as if only then making the connection that he was actually talking about her.

'For *you,* I mean!' he laughed. 'I prayed for you.'

'Yes,' she murmured, looking away. She didn't know what to say to that.

'It was the first real prayer I'd said since I'd been inside,' Eamon continued, 'and from that point on, I felt lighter. A burden off my shoulders. Doing my time in there was easier after you were born.'

They were quiet for a few minutes.

'So do you still pray? Do you believe in God?' she asked.

'Oh, yes,' he said softly. 'Don't you?'

'No,' Kit muttered. 'Not really.'

Eamon nodded, but her admission seemed to trouble him.

'Well,' he sighed, sadly matter-of-fact, 'I'm from a different generation, I suppose. Do you think that's it?'

'Maybe.'

The next afternoon, Kit walked all the way down to the sea and stood on the cliff, waiting for Eamon to come and pick her up in

328

the car as they'd arranged. It had taken her nearly two hours to walk down. She stood on the rocky edge for ages, her arms held out, the wind making her face ache with the cold. The sea, rolling and furious beneath her, was intoxicating. What would it matter, really, if she stepped off into it; part of her almost believed that she could glide down slowly like a bird into the spray, then sit bobbing on top of the churning waves. *Why not?* When the warm car arrived, the ache inside was harder to deal with than her cold hands and wet feet. But on her way back to the cottage she said nothing except to answer him when he'd asked if she'd like pie for lunch.

'Oh yes, please,' she said, smiling, faking it. 'I love pie.'

Back at the house, Kit stood warming her hands by the fire, watching through the little back window as Eamon piled turf into a barrow outside. She remembered applying for her passport, and her birth certificate arriving by post. The coldness that washed over her as she read the words, Father: Unknown.

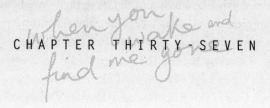

CHAPTER THIRTY-SEVEN

'What was it like in jail?'

Kit was sitting cross-legged on the floor reading the one Irish history book she'd managed to fit in her suitcase. Soon she'd be meeting Sebastian in Belfast and she wanted to have at least read something when they met. It was ten in the morning and Eamon looked up in surprise from the paper he'd just brought in from Cormac's. 'Were you on the blanket with the hunger strikers?'

'I was. For a short time.'

'Was that hard? I mean . . .' Kit stumbled over the words because he was looking at her in such a strange cool way. 'It must have been terrible.'

'I wasn't on it for such a long time,' he continued. She could see him forcing himself to relax. 'So it wasn't so bad. Some of them were on it for years. But for me it was just a few months. The hunger strike started and the blanket protest was called off.'

'What were they like, the hunger strikers? I mean the ones who died?'

'They were ordinary men,' he said slowly. 'Ordinary men doing the right thing.'

330

'Surely they weren't ordinary?' Kit gave a laugh. 'I mean it's a pretty extraordinary thing to do!'

'They were ordinary men,' Eamon said again. 'That was – *is* – the whole point.'

Kit looked away. Anger flared in her. She wanted to scream, *Tell me!* But he'd answered her questions, hadn't he? Maybe the past was painful for him. Maybe he hated remembering? What right did she have, digging around in other people's lives? *But she did have a right, didn't she? He was her father, after all.*

'Leonie did things for the IRA,' she said suddenly.

'She told you that?' His voice was non-committal; he'd gone back to the paper.

'I found some of her writing. She was going to tell me things,' Kit said.

He looked up slowly.

Glad that she seemed to have his full attention again, she asked, 'Can you tell me about it?'

'What particular aspect?' he said.

'Well, why were you in jail?'

'I killed two men,' Eamon said without hesitation, 'two members of the UVF who'd burnt five Catholic families out of their homes and were planning more. The authorities knew I did it, but they didn't have enough evidence. So they got me on a lesser charge of firearms which' he smiled wryly, 'I actually didn't have anything to do with. Not that particular haul, anyway.'

Kit nodded, refusing to acknowledge the chill that had slipped into her bones. He would never speak frankly again if she went all emotional on him now. Eamon seemed to sense her shock because when he next spoke it was more gently.

'It's hard for outsiders to understand, but in a war people get hurt, people die. He stopped for a moment, frowning. Do you think that the Brits didn't know what they were doing sixty years ago when they decided they didn't want Germany ruling England? They killed millions of people – civilians, too – just so they could keep their country. This is just on a smaller scale. In the end we were soldiers fighting for our country. Do you see that?'

Of course she did, in a way. Hadn't a lot of her political studies over the last year involved reading up on armed conflicts all around the globe? South Africa and Indonesia were just two that came to mind, and there were heaps of others. The big essay that she had planned to write, about African independent states, was all about this. People get hurt, people die. She repeated the words to herself. Blood is spilt. *But this is my father. And he murdered two people. And he believes that's okay.*

'What about the Unionists? The Protestants?' Kit mumbled edgily, wanting desperately to keep the conversation going. 'They want to stay part of Britain, don't they? Haven't they got a right?'

'They live on this island,' Eamon said, standing up, 'and Republicans have never had anything against a Protestant who calls himself Irish. In spite of all they go on with, they've got nothing to fear. We're not going to make them do jigs or stuff the Pope down their throats. This is their country too.'

'But violence?' Kit looked up into his eyes. 'The bombs, and the rest of it. I mean we're talking about human beings. Maybe there's another way to change things.'

'Violence works,' he snapped. 'You know it. I know it. And every government in the world knows it.' The cold sureness of his tone was terrible. 'Why do you think this British Prime Minister is talking to us now? Only because we made a lot of trouble, because we were tough, and violent. It's not because we had a few marches in the street.'

Kit gulped and nodded.

'Leonie wrote that the guards were brutal,' she mentioned.

'Some of them were all right,' he said, 'but it was hard for the families coming to see us. Very hard for mothers and wives and the wee ones. Our hair was way down past our shoulders, our nails were long, our teeth yellow, and we stank. Sometimes I think that the people on the outside suffered more than we did.'

'Really?' Kit was moved by his empathy for the families.

'Sure. We had each other. It was brutal, but we had each other. We were brothers. But a lot of the wives, the girlfriends and the kids, well, they were on their own. And there was all the worry for them. And the harassment, too.'

'Would you do it again?'

'Oh, I would. I regret nothing. Nothing. I'm part of history.'

Another wash of coldness went through Kit. *What did that mean?*

'Did Leonie come and see you?'

'She did.'

'Did she freak out about the way you looked?'

'No. She did not,' he said softly. 'She . . . your mother was always very strong. She knew her own mind.'

Kit wanted to ask about Bridie. Did she visit Eamon in jail? Did Bridie and Leonie know about each other? But she had a distinct feeling that he'd given her enough for that day. Try again tomorrow, she told herself.

As the days progressed, Kit knew something fundamental was missing. She felt like one of those little birds that used to fly up to the windows at home, pecking away at the glass, again and again, not understanding why it couldn't fly into the room. As the stay with her father came to an end, she'd become just like that bird, able to see quite clearly through the pane of glass to where he was sitting, but unable to get in. Unable, in the end, to peck at his plate or sit on his shoulder.

'So will this latest peace plan work?' Kit asked one morning over breakfast, thinking that general topics might be easier for him to talk about.

'The peace plan will work if there is one, independent Ireland at the end of it,' Eamon said shortly. 'That is the only thing that will bring peace.'

'What chance is there of that?' she asked. 'I mean in the near future?'

'You ask a lot of questions.' He smiled and got up. 'Come on, get your bag, girl. Aren't I dropping you off at Bridie's?'

She went to pack her bag, vaguely humiliated to have been so casually dismissed. She was going down to Galway with the three older girls for a party that night. Their cousin Brian was turning twenty-one and they'd all been invited. He went to university with Ruth and was apparently a hunk. The three sisters breathlessly told Kit that every girl in Galway had already fallen in love with him and so she'd better watch herself. Kit was tempted to tell them about Sebastian, about her plans to meet him in Dublin the following week. But she didn't. It was something she needed to hold to herself, some private hope that she could pull out every now and again and examine with pleasure when things got too difficult.

Eamon had to go away for a couple of days, so it worked out perfectly for her to go with the girls to Galway. When he dropped her off, the three girls came rushing out immediately.

'Hello, Daddy! Hello Kathleen.'

'Hello, my lovelies!' Eamon kissed them all warmly. 'Where is your mammy and the wild one?'

'Down the shops. They'll be back any minute.'

'I have to go now,' Eamon said, 'tell them all goodbye from me.' He turned to Kit with a smile. 'I'll see you on Sunday night then.'

'Okay.' Kit accepted his kiss, wishing she felt as easy with him as his three stepdaughters did. But she didn't have time to think too much about it. Ruth had one arm around her shoulder and was tugging her to come inside.

'We've been waiting for you, Kathleen!'

'Have you decided what you'll wear?'

The three girls were good company, even if sometimes their level of hilarity and enthusiasm was too much. Kit particularly liked Ellen, the eldest, who had a more thoughtful edge to her, especially when she was away from her sisters.

'So Bridie hasn't changed her mind?' Kit asked hopefully, looking around the little kitchen. There was still no Bridie and no Rosalaind.

'No,' they chorused, sensing her disappointment. 'She couldn't be persuaded Kathleen, sorry.'

Kit had only met Rosalaind twice but she already loved the girl and wished she was coming with them down to Galway. It wasn't just that she was her half-sister. The girl was a genuine eccentric. Rosalaind had apparently been invited to the party but Bridie had put her foot down, declaring the fifteen-year-old was too young. After the initial wails of protest, followed by a full-blown temper tantrum, Rosalaind had accepted her fate, declaring that parties were a bore anyway and she had better things to do with her time.

'But we could all look after her,' Kit tried again when Bridie came back carrying rolls and bottles of drink for their trip.

'Ah, no,' Bridie smiled kindly. 'That wouldn't be fair on you all. She'd get herself into some terrible scrape for sure and ruin your night!'

Rosalaind had sidled in after her mother, but after throwing a sour nod at Kit, she retreated to her room.

'So we're all ready then?' Ellen was the driver and she was anxious that they get going. Kit followed the girls out to the car, looking up at the window for any sign of her half-sister. Yes. There was a small face peering out from behind the curtain. Kit grinned and waved frantically. Rosalaind gave one small wave, then disappeared. Kit would have preferred to spend the couple of days at Bridie's place with Rosalaind. Parties where you didn't know

335

anyone were often boring. But the others were so enthusiastic about her coming with them that she hadn't known how to politely refuse.

Ellen started up the car and they all waved to Bridie who was standing on the cobbled footpath calling out last minute instructions on how to get to their aunt's place in Galway where they'd be staying the night, and not to be driving fast, or dangerously, or with drink inside them.

The girls in turn were yelling that they'd see her soon, and not to be too lonely without them, and don't trouble herself too much about the wild one. Needless to say, no one was listening to anyone else.

Before long they were on their way, heading south along a pretty winding road to Galway. The mood was up and the chatter loud and cheery. Lily began a song and the others joined in. After a while, Kit sat back staring out the window, enjoying the good humour around her, but easing herself away from it, too. Trying to think. The last days had begun to shift about in her memory. Was she learning anything new at all here? Was this what she'd come for?

CHAPTER THIRTY-EIGHT

No one had any appetite for the meal Bridie had ready when they arrived back at about five the next afternoon. The girls were totally exhausted. The party had not wound up until six that morning, so they all decided that it wasn't worth going to bed. Ellen had insisted that Kit change her clothes and they go out walking in Galway.

It was a wonderful city. Small ancient cobbled streets that were, by the middle of the morning, alive with music. Groups of school children singing carols and playing the flutes and drums, lone guitarists and lively Celtic bands. Kit had forgotten her tiredness for those few hours, listening to the music and the stories of the city. The narrow streets, the stone and wooden shopfronts and the bustling pubs delighted Kit. By the time they had got back to the aunt's place around two in the afternoon she wished she could stay longer. But Ellen had to be back for her part-time supermarket job the next day, so in spite of the aunts begging them to stay one more night, they all dosed up on coffee and got back into the car.

'So how was it?' Bridie wanted to know eagerly, letting them in through the front door. Rosalaind was there too, looking on

resentfully as Kit sat quietly amongst the other three, who were all
yawning, groaning and complaining, giving Bridie only the barest
of monosyllabic answers.

'So you all enjoyed yourselves?'

'Yes.'

'So it was good?'

'Fine. Good. Okay!'

No one wanted to go into details, least of all Kit.

'So was there good music?' Bridie wanted to know.

'Sure.'

'And dancing?'

'Of course. It was a party!'

'And did you all have someone to dance with?' Bridie asked
slyly, looking from one to the other. They were sitting around the
kitchen table, eyes downcast, picking disinterestedly at the food in
front of them. Kit put a fork of mash in her mouth and tried to
remember if she'd had any food the night before.

'We told you what would happen,' Ruth said blithely, 'and it did.'

'What's that?'

'Kathleen fell for Brian!'

'No I didn't,' Kit said hotly.

'Well there's no harm in that,' Bridie laughed.

'You were dancing with him all night,' Lily said sharply to Kit,
ignoring Bridie.

'Is that a sin?' Kit snapped. 'There was no one else I knew and
he kept asking me!' It was true. Kit had flirted and danced with
Brian, although she had no real interest in him at all.

'You were dancing up close,' Ruth said, 'for absolutely ages. Like
you were very involved.'

'No I wasn't!'

'Will you leave her alone!' Ellen exclaimed furiously. 'She's a
visitor here. She can behave how she likes!'

Ellen's defence wasn't all that reassuring. What an idiot Kit had been. Why hadn't she taken heed of what the girls had told her? It seemed that every girl in Galway was after Brian. But it wasn't until the end of the night that she'd realised how resentful they'd been that he'd picked her out to dance. *If only* they hadn't seen her kissing him goodnight under the trees! Even his mother! She'd come over with a bright tenacious smile plastered over her face, holding a plate of hot party pies.

'Now you two look like you need something to eat,' she'd said loudly. Giggles had broken out around them. Oh, the humiliation! Kit had taken one of the pies, hoping the woman would go quickly, but she'd been determined to break things up. 'Now, where in Australia do you come from, dear?' she'd asked Kit. 'Do tell us what the weather is like at this time of the year.'

Suddenly devoid of all gallantry, Brian had given his mother a snarling look then sloped off back to the party, leaving Kit to talk with her about Melbourne! She knew all this would be officially part of Galway party history. *Oh, shit!* It was something they'd talk about for years to come. The night the little blow-in from Australia swept the lovely Brian off his feet at his own twenty-first.

'Kathleen,' Bridie said, beginning to clear the meal, 'Eamon rang earlier. He's unable to pick you up tonight. He asked that you stay here if it's all right? He'll come by for you tomorrow.' It was just Kit and Bridie in the kitchen at this stage. The other three were up taking showers, fighting over the washing machine and calling insults to each other on the stairs. Rosalaind was in her room.

'Okay then,' Kit said, getting up to help Bridie, secretly depressed by this turn of events. She'd been dying to get back to the little cottage on the mountainside with her father. To the gravity and the quietness, the mystery of being alone with him.

'I've made up a bed in Rosalaind's room,' said Bridie.

'Does she mind?' Kit said anxiously.

'She suggested it.'

CHAPTER THIRTY-NINE

'They didn't want you to come.'

Rosalaind was lying on her side, facing Kit in the semi-darkness. The spare bed had been put right under the window, and there was not much space between them. 'Mammy cried all day after Daddy said you were coming.'

'Did she?' What a good actor Bridie was then! Kit was devastated, but felt some sympathy for Bridie, too.

'Daddy said he couldn't refuse,' Rosalaind went on, 'that you were his daughter.'

'Oh.'

'Don't be sad.' The younger girl held out her hand and Kit took it briefly. 'We're all glad you're here now. Mammy, too. She really likes you. I can tell.'

'Thanks,' Kit said dully. Rosalaind was being totally honest. After the awkward preliminaries, a real closeness was growing between them. So what point would there be in not knowing the truth? Yet part of her dreaded discovering anything more.

'Did you feel anything odd a few weeks ago?' Rosalaind asked. 'Any pains in your chest?'

'No,' Kit tried to think back. 'I don't think so. Why?'

'I had a doll,' Rosalaind said darkly, 'and I was trying to do voodoo on it. I was up here sticking pins into it pretending it was you. That was the first night I heard you were coming.'

'Oh!' Kit burst into laughter. 'You're a spooky little witch, aren't you!'

'But after a while I started thinking it might be good to have a *real* sister,' Rosalaind continued thoughtfully. 'I get so sick of those three *imposters*, so I stopped doing it.'

'I'm glad about that,' Kit whispered.

There was quietness between them for a while. Kit was beside herself with tiredness from the party but unable to drift off to sleep.

'So they didn't want me to come?' she said at last, in a small voice.

'They started to talk about your mother,' Rosalaind went on. 'They were down in the kitchen yelling at each other. They thought I was in bed. But I crept downstairs and I heard.'

'What did they say about her?'

'My father said that he didn't love her. That he had never loved her. That the whole thing was a figment of her imagination. As far as he was concerned it had only been a brief fling that had meant nothing to him. And that he'd always been sorry it had happened.'

'What else?' Kit forced her voice to sound normal.

'He couldn't believe it when she told him that she was pregnant and was going to go through with having the baby,' Rosalaind whispered. 'I can't remember much else after that. Except that he said he only saw her a few times after he came out of jail. And only because she wanted to.'

Somehow this was the saddest thing that Kit could have been told. Far more sad than the fact that she hadn't really been wanted by these people herself. Tears flooded her eyes and she began to sob. *Poor Leonie*, she kept thinking. She had only been twenty-four, not much older than Kit now. And she could tell by those letters that

342

she'd been totally in love with Eamon. But he was married to Bridie. He was the love of Leonie's life and she meant nothing to him.

When Rosalaind heard Kit's sobs, she crept out of bed and came to comfort her.

'Kathleen,' she whispered, 'I'm sorry. Don't be sad. I'm glad you came. Mammy and Daddy too. We're all glad you came! I'm sorry I upset you.'

'No . . . no, I'm glad you told me,' Kit sobbed. 'I'm just thinking of Leonie.'

They clung to each other, fiercely, both crying.

Kit went to sleep and then woke around two in the morning. The gentle sound of Rosalaind's deep even breaths was comforting. She got up and went to the window, pulling the curtain back. It was very cold, so she took a blanket from her bed and wrapped it tightly around her shoulders, then propped herself against a bookcase and stared out. There was a thick frost. The street lamp made a wide yellow halo that spread out in a long fading wash to the end of the street. Across the road were two huge bare trees, coated in whiteness, their branches standing out against the houses like etchings. The cobbled street itself seemed covered in the most fragile white glass. All of it seemed strange and holy.

She woke again with bright sunlight pouring through the window. Rosalaind was edging through the doorway with a tray holding two steaming cups and a plate of toast.

'Daddy's downstairs,' she said to Kit. 'Come to pick you up. But he says take your time, he's in no hurry.'

Kit sat up.

'They're telling him all about you at the party,' Rosalaind said, sitting on Kit's bed, her eyes bright with amusement. 'Is it true?'

Kit groaned furiously. Couldn't those three keep their mouths shut about anything?

343

'Is what true?' she snapped, pulling the dressing gown around her shoulders and accepting the tea.

'You were kissing my cousin Brian?' Rosalaind laughed, 'making everyone wild because he should have been kissing someone else?'

Kit sighed. Somehow this kid sister of hers always managed to make her see the funny side.

'Oh, that's grand!' Rosalaind went on, her eyes dancing.

'No. Not grand, actually, Rosalaind.'

'Yes,' Rosalaind insisted firmly. 'It's totally grand!' She lowered her voice. 'Did you end up *doing* it with him?'

'Rosalaind!' Kit took some toast and stuffed it in her mouth. 'No, I did not.'

'Hmmm.' Rosalaind was thoughtful. 'Just as well. Sounds like some of those girls would be after you with guns if you had.'

'If you say so.' Kit took another sip of tea and tried not to smile.

'So have you got a boyfriend at home?' Rosalaind wanted to know, her whole face alive with curiosity.

'I'm going to meet him next week in Dublin,' Kit said, deciding on the spur of the moment to spill the beans. It wasn't a criminal offence. 'He's not actually my boyfriend yet,' she confided, 'but I'm hoping it's going to work out that way.'

Rosalaind picked up more toast and took two huge bites, looking at Kit intently the whole time. 'He's coming over to Ireland?' she said in wonder. 'Just to see you? How romantic. I want to know everything. What's his name?'

When Kit finished telling Rosalaind about Sebastian, she felt better. It was good to talk about things. Hoarding hopes and dreams only got everything out of proportion.

'But you're going to be back here for Christmas, aren't you?' Rosalaind wanted to know.

'Well, I don't know yet,' Kit answered honestly.

'Oh *please*,' Rosalaind was looking at her imploringly, '*please* be

344

here for Christmas. It's such a mighty time! There's snow and ice. We have a huge tree. There are lots of presents. All our cousins come and they're boys. Great craic! Much nicer than those three *imposters!*' She wrinkled her nose with distaste, making Kit laugh. 'Then we all go out to Daddy's place in the afternoon. Pine-cone fires and hot puddings. There's Cormac and all the funny old geezers around there. It goes on for days. You'll love it!'

'Does it really snow?'

'Yes!' Rosalaind shouted. 'It often snows. But even when it's just cold and icy, it's grand. Please say you'll come back for Christmas? This is your family now.' She grabbed Kit's hand.

'What if I brought a friend?'

'He'd be welcome. For sure!' Rosalaind was jumping around the room with excitement, clapping her hands. 'You've got to come!'

When Kit got downstairs an hour later, fresh from her shower and in much better spirits than the night before, Rosalaind had already told them about her planned trip to Dublin to meet Sebastian, and they were adamant that she should come back for Christmas and bring him with her. Ruth and Lily seemed to have forgotten her party misdemeanours, or at least forgiven her for them. But it was Bridie's warmth that won Kit over in the end.

'Kathleen,' she said seriously, taking her hand, 'it just won't be Christmas without you. You're part of us now. Please say you'll be here.'

'You know, I think I will,' Kit said. 'I'd love to, actually.'

'We'll have to bring our dinner out onto the beach,' Eamon joked. 'Buy a big bright beach umbrella so Kathleen feels at home!'

But apart from the one reference to beach umbrellas, no one mentioned Australia. Or Leonie. Or Kit's family back there. Kit herself was so overwhelmed by the warmth of the moment that even she forgot them. Christmas in the northern hemisphere seemed like a wonderful idea.

On their way back to Eamon's cottage, he asked her if she was happy in Ireland.

'Yes,' she said, immediately confused.

'So you enjoyed the party?'

'It was okay.' She hoped he wasn't going to grill her about it.

But he only laughed. 'Those girls are gossips, aren't they?'

'They are,' Kit agreed, smiling at him, 'but really nice, too. I particularly love Rosalaind.'

'She's great, isn't she?' He looked at the road. 'Such a grand kid.'

Kit gulped. It was the way he'd said it. So passionately. *Would he ever say that about me?*

'You and Bridie waited a long time to have a baby,' she ventured tentatively.

'Ten years,' he said. 'Poor Bridie. She had so many miscarriages. Two babies went to full-term and were born dead. We thought it would never happen for us. I didn't mind so much. Only for her. She wanted a baby so badly.'

Kit sat back silently. Did Bridie know at the time that Leonie was having his baby and giving it away? It must have made her feel bitter. Then again, bitterness wasn't something you easily associated with Bridie.

She would have loved to ask him more about Leonie. Tell him what Rosalaind had told her and then hear him explain it from his side. But in the end she kept quiet. Maybe he would open up of his own accord.

'Would you mind bringing something down to Dublin when you go?' he asked when they were getting out of the car back at the cottage. 'It's just a small parcel.'

'Sure,' Kit said. 'Will I post it when I get there?'

'No, I'll have someone pick it up from where you're staying.'

'Okay.'

'Just a few bits and pieces for an old friend of mine.'

'I could probably drop them off if you gave me the address,' she said.

'You don't want to be worrying yourself about that. I'll have someone come and collect it from you.'

The conversation threw Kit a little. She would have liked to meet her father's old friend. But she didn't quite know how to say it.

Kit woke up the next morning glad of the quietness. When she walked out to the kitchen, Eamon wasn't there but he'd left one of his notes. He'd be back at around midday and suggested she go down and have breakfast with Cormac. Donning her hat and coat, Kit made off down the icy hard track. After her first drunken morning, Kit had formed a special affection for Cormac.

'I've heard about it,' was the first thing he said to her. 'Every last detail, so don't bother with excuses. A young floozy I had with me all along!' He gasped with the effort of his walk from the kitchen, and was standing behind the bar, smiling broadly. 'When I thought I was entertaining a lady.'

'Bloody hell!' Kit threw her bag down and leant across the bar, pretending to clip him over the ear. 'Who told you?'

'Nothing goes on around these parts without me knowing about it!' he wheezed and settled the last glass back onto the rack. 'I know most of what's happening in Donegal. Now, will it be a whisky while you tell me your sins?'

'No thanks,' she laughed, looking at the grimy face of the ancient clock sitting on a ledge above the bar. It was nine o'clock in the morning. 'A cup of tea would be great, and could I have some breakfast?'

'Good God!' Cormac exploded, obviously pleased, 'as long as McCabe knows he's footing the bill!'

'He knows!'

'Well you're in luck. I was just about to cook my own.'

'So I am in luck,' Kit smiled. 'Double everything. I'm starving.'

She knew the food wouldn't go on any bill. Cormac liked getting people meals and he seemed almost put out if anyone suggested paying him.

'Right you are.' He motioned her to sit in front of the blazing fire as he headed for the kitchen. 'Eggs and bacon and my special fried-up tatties do you?'

'Anything. Thanks.'

'So you're going to Dublin to meet this young fellow from Australia,' Cormac said, coming over to the fireplace with a tray, 'but what I want to know, is he a Catholic?'

'So you know about that too?' Kit said, 'and I only told the rest of them yesterday. I don't know if he's a Catholic. I never asked.' She eyed the food hungrily as he settled it on a small table between them. Toast, eggs, bacon and tomatoes. It smelt wonderful. 'But I'd guess he's probably not.'

'Get with your own kind, Kathleen,' Cormac muttered, shaking his head dolefully, pouring two mugs of tea. 'The mixed marriage isn't much chop when it comes down to it.'

'I'm not going to marry him!'

'Well, what's the point then?' Cormac looked shocked. 'Why won't you marry him?'

'Maybe one day I'll marry,' Kit said hurriedly.

'Sure, of course you will.' He looked relieved. 'And all I'm saying is: stick with what you know. There is more understanding between people of the same faith.'

'What about those girls from Cork?' Kit teased. 'They're your own kind and they run away!'

'Oh, you're in a cruel and heartless mood today,' he growled, 'and that's for sure. No feeling for an old man in his loneliness, have ye?'

'Not a bit,' Kit said happily, tucking in.

'Have you a nice hand, Kathleen?'

The food was almost finished, and they were sitting in front of the fire, sipping their tea. Kit held out her right hand for him to look at.

'No, you foolish girl,' he laughed. 'I mean can you write with style?'

'Yes, I can,' Kit said simply, surprised. From the time she was little, people had always told her that her handwriting was lovely. She'd even been employed a couple of times to write out wedding invitations in black ink.

'Well, McCabe has got one hell of a nice black fountain pen up there in the house. Next time you come down, could you bring it and I'll get you to write a few invitations for me.'

'Sure. Are you having a party?'

'Well, not exactly a party, Kathleen, my dear, but an *occasion*, if you like.'

'Sounds like a party,' Kit smiled.

'You're right. In a manner of speaking. I suppose you could say, at a pinch, that it's a party.'

When Kit got back, Eamon was home. She told him about the request for the pen. He was reading the paper at the table.

'It's in the dresser,' he said, pointing. 'Somewhere in either of those two drawers.'

Kit went to the drawer and began to rummage about. At the same moment as finding a lovely old-fashioned fountain pen, she turned over an ageing, yellow envelope. Across the front scrawled Leonie's untidy hand.

When you wake and find me gone

Kit's heart began to thump. She looked across to Eamon. He was still reading.

Kit's hands were shaking. She turned the envelope over and saw it was sealed at the back. How was it that *he* had it? She carefully

349

replaced the envelope, slipping it down to one side. Why keep a letter for twenty years without opening it? Maybe he had opened it and sealed it again. That letter was meant for her and yet she didn't quite trust his response if she asked for it. She would have it though, she decided. And soon, too.

Cormac was delighted with her efforts the next day.

'That's a fine hand there for a girl,' he muttered, taking her first effort over to the window for a better look. Kit could see the pleasure in his eyes as he turned the paper this way and that. Being able to help him gladdened her. Apart from all his other disabilities, Cormac's poor hands were crippled with arthritis. He was going to be giving a special party two weeks into the New Year: a proper dinner and by invitation only.

'What if everyone around here expects to come to the pub?' Kit ventured, wishing he'd tell her exactly why he was giving the party. 'What will you say to them?'

But Cormac was unapologetic. 'I'll put a sign on the door saying Private Function,' he replied shortly. 'Let them go somewhere else. It's only one night.'

The invitation read: *A Special Event. Please come and celebrate with Cormac O'Grady.* Then the address and the time. There were about sixty invitations, and to people all around Ireland, north and south. Half a dozen were addressed to people in England and there were even a few being sent to America. By the end of it, Kit's arm was aching. She smiled when she saw that the very last invitation was to herself and Eamon. She wrote the words and held it out for Cormac to blot.

'I was sweating on that last one,' she said. 'I thought you might have forgotten us.'

'Ah,' he muttered, 'a star like you! And why would I leave you out?'

The phone was ringing. Kit got up and stretched. 'Do you want me to get that?' she asked. Cormac nodded and she went behind the counter to pick it up.

It was Brendan, and he sounded like he was in the next room.

'I've been thinking about what you said last time,' he announced cheerfully, getting straight to the point as usual.

'What about?'

'About human life being important. I've been thinking a lot about that.'

'And?'

'I think you're right,' he said. 'I think you've got to have some ultimate value, some line in the sand that you won't step over and that's it . . . life. Thou shalt not kill. It makes sense when you think about it.'

'So you're a pacifist now?' Kit teased him. 'The Nazis are coming and you just lie down and let them walk over you? Oh yeah, I can really see you doing that, Brendan!'

'God, you're a cantankerous bitch,' he said with a dry laugh. 'I had it all sorted out and you stamp back in with your big boots, mucking up my new, neatly organised philosophy.'

'I'm not!' she laughed. 'I've been thinking about it too since we last spoke and I was starting to come around to *your* point of view. I mean —'

'Don't do that, Kit. Please!' Brendan interjected. 'I need someone to fight with.'

He hesitated before speaking again. 'Will you be home for Christmas?'

'I don't think so,' Kit said slowly. And for the first time, she really thought about what that meant. Therese would be so disappointed. And there was Leonie to think of, too, and the rest of the family. Kit was weighed down suddenly with all she'd been avoiding.

'We'll miss you,' Brendan said.

'Yeah.' Kit was touched. 'I'll miss you, too.'

Brendan gave a rueful laugh. 'Me and the dog and Tam. What'll we do without you? This place has turned into a brothel. No kidding. No one even tries any more. The food-scraps tin is overflowing, and there are flies, now that it's hot.'

'Spare me!'

'The stove's covered in last week's meat sauce and there's rubbish everywhere,' he went on. 'The mice are starting to behave like they own the joint.'

Kit began to laugh.

'Just this morning,' he went on, 'one of them stopped on the sink and looked at me like I was the houseboy. I thought he was going to ask me for fresh towels for the bathroom!'

'Keep going, Brendan,' Kit was laughing, 'and I'll never come back!'

'Okay, okay,' he groaned. 'I'm joking. The whole place is just like an operating table. Ajax, White King, you name it. We bleach down the benches every day. You'd be proud of us.'

'Does Tam still hate me?'

'Yeah, of course.'

'You're a bastard!' Kit laughed again. 'What has she said?'

'Why don't you talk to her yourself?'

'I'm too scared.'

'Gutless, Quinlan. In the extreme!' Brendan's voice softened. 'I went to a movie with her last night. She was okay. Said she was looking forward to seeing you again.'

'She did? Well, give her my love, will you. Don't forget, okay? I . . .' Kit paused, swamped suddenly by a mass of feeling she didn't understand. She wanted to tell Brendan that she was sending her love to him, too, but didn't know how. How could you tell what someone was feeling when there were thousands of kilometres between you? She wanted to grab a fist full of his hair, squeeze those big shoulders between her own two arms. Then she remembered Gucci and felt sick. Desperate to ask him if he was still sleeping with her, the words stuck in her throat. Just the idea of them together was hideous. What if he told her they were really close? Kit closed her eyes and shuddered. *Never* would she accept Brendan with that little twerp. It made her angry even thinking about it.

'Have you spoken to your brother?'

'Johnny?' Kit asked guiltily. 'No, I haven't. Did you know he's left the seminary? He's going to get married.'

'Yeah?' Brendan said shortly.

Kit had only tried to contact Johnny once, although she did think about him a lot – usually during the day when it was the wrong time to ring.

'Tell me, have things worked out with your father?' Brendan asked.

'I guess so.'

'What does that mean, Quinlan? You don't sound sure.'

'Well, I'm not sure.' She hesitated.

'So what's he like?'

'He's great,' she sighed, 'in lots of ways. He's got a great smile. A great laugh. He's big, like you, Brendan.'

'Like me, heh?' Brendan laughed.

'Right!' Kit was on the point of tears, but she didn't know why.

'You can't expect to know someone in a couple of weeks,' Brendan added encouragingly.

'I guess not. That's what I've been telling myself.'

'So what are your plans? How long are you going to stay?'

'I'm going to Dublin in a couple of days,' Kit said, and then stopped herself, thinking about whether to tell him about Sebastian. She didn't want to, but withholding the information wouldn't be right either. 'I'm meeting up with Sebastian,' she added stiffly.

'What?'

'Yeah.' He's over in London for work so he rang and we're going to meet up in Dublin.'

There was silence.

'Brendan? You still there?'

'Yeah, I'm here.'

'So how are you?' she asked brightly, desperate to keep him talking. Brendan had this wonderful grounding effect on her. Just by asking a few questions he'd got her thinking about things she should have worked out long ago.

'I gotta go now, Quinlan.'

'Don't go!' she begged. 'Please, Brendan. How's the dog? When is Lou getting back? Tell her to ring me when she does. I've got things to talk about.'

'Yeah, well fuck it,' he sighed angrily. 'I've got to go. Bye.'

CHAPTER FORTY

Eamon had booked Kit on a bus to Dublin. This time of the year was very busy and she'd been lucky to get a seat. As soon as Bridie saw how tight the bus situation was, she insisted Kit contact Sebastian immediately and invite him back for Christmas. If he was coming, they'd book the seats straight away. Kit rang the hotel in London for three days without success. Yes, she was told, a Mr Sebastian Davies had checked in but he wasn't in his room, would Kit like to leave a message? She didn't want to do that. There was no phone connection to Eamon's cottage and because she was out a lot, either walking the hills or at Bridie's house, then ringing Cormac's place didn't make much sense either. But where was he? What if she left a message and he didn't return it? Would she be game enough to ring again? She hadn't spoken to him since leaving Australia. Maybe he'd gone off the idea of meeting her.

To her relief, they eventually made direct contact three days before she was due to leave for Dublin. He seemed pleased to hear from her and was still enthusiastic about coming over. He had an aunt to stay with in Dublin, but wanted to know where Kit would be staying. If they both arrived on the same day they could meet up straight away. She told him the name of the hotel, slightly embarrassed. It was a big one in O'Connell Street, and very expensive compared to all the bed-and-breakfasts listed in her guide book. But Kit had her own secret plans for what might ensue over their couple of days together. She certainly didn't want to invite Sebastian back to some seedy little hole like the one she had in Belfast. She wanted a bit of space, with a king-size bed and a decent en-suite. Breakfast in the room if they wanted it. She was hoping for big things.

'Will you be staying with your aunt for Christmas?' she began tentatively.

'Oh no,' Sebastian replied easily. 'I'll be going back to London.'

'Do you have relatives there?'

'No,' he laughed, 'I'll be having a lonely Christmas on my own this year. But I've come over to do work and so I've just got to get on with it.'

Kit took a deep breath. 'Well, I'm coming back here for Christmas,' she said quickly, 'and they said, I mean, my father and the rest of them are very happy for you to come back, too.'

There was a pause.

'Well that's a very nice offer,' Sebastian said slowly, obviously surprised and turning the proposition over in his mind.

'We could come back from Dublin together on the bus,' Kit burst out, suddenly almost sick with joy at all the possibilities. 'Apparently Christmas is great over here. Lots of fires and singing and drinking,' she laughed. 'It would be so great if you could come! The little church is beautiful. We could go to midnight mass in the cold . . . sometimes it snows . . . and . . .' Her voice died away. She was embarrassed. Midnight mass? God! She'd been staying with her father a little over two weeks and already she was forgetting how the rest of the world thought about these things. The whole idea of going to church at Christmas might seem ridiculous to him. Why would she think he'd be even remotely interested in that? Why did she have to wear her heart on her sleeve all the time? Why couldn't she be cool like other people?

'Hmmm . . .'

Kit bit her lip and closed her eyes tightly. She was determined not to speak until he did.

'You know, Kathleen,' Sebastian said at last, 'there's something absolutely lovely about you.'

'There is?'

'Yes,' he laughed. 'There is! You're so sweet. I really like it when you get breathless with excitement!'

'You do?'

'You were like that the whole time we were doing the play. Breathless. Like everything was so exciting. Sometimes I felt my main job as director was to calm you down.'

'Did you?' Kit gulped.

'I hope I didn't repress you?' he joked.

'No . . . no . . .'

'Listen. If it's okay with them, I mean your family, your father, or whoever, then I'd love to come to the West of Ireland for a few days over Christmas. By the way, you've got to tell me all about meeting up with your father when we get to Dublin.'

'I will.'

'So when does your bus get in on Tuesday?'

'Four in the afternoon.'

'How about I meet you in the foyer of your hotel on Tuesday evening?'

'Fine. That would be good.'

'Shall we say six, then? We'll go and eat and . . .'

'Yes. Six o'clock.'

Kit put the phone down, looked up and caught sight of herself in Cormac's grimy mirror. She moved over slowly, staring intently.

Her hair bounced out in dark curls and her cheeks were flushed with vitality and good health. But her eyes seemed different somehow, darker and more moody than she remembered. Did eyes ever really change colour or was it just the light? It was something she must remember to ask Brendan.

So much of her life was on hold. Eamon. Leonie. Johnny. Brendan and Rosalaind. Where did they all fit in? She turned away from the mirror. So what did it matter? She was going to Dublin and Sebastian was coming too. It would work out. Everything would come together in its own good time.

CHAPTER FORTY-ONE

Eamon had dropped Kit off at Bridie's the weekend before her Dublin trip. She'd had a great evening with Rosalaind and the others, playing cards and talking. Eamon himself had business in Sligo and wouldn't be back for two days.

But the next day one of those headaches had descended. It crept up on Kit gradually and by two o'clock she couldn't ignore it any longer. Since she'd been sixteen she'd had a migraine every few months, but they were easy enough to manage and she knew what to do. She had to lie down. The trouble was, it was impossible to rest at Bridie's place. There was nowhere to be quiet. No one seemed to know the meaning of the word. Even Rosalaind, supposedly sympathetic to her 'real sister', kept barging into the room where Kit was lying down, with new ideas for film sequences and questions about Australia. In the end Kit had to ask Bridie if she would drive her out to Eamon's place.

Refusing Bridie's offer to come in and make her a cup of tea, Kit kissed her goodbye and went into the cottage, closing the door behind her. She went through her backpack to find the strong tablets she'd brought from home. After downing a couple, she made straight for her little bed behind the red curtain and crawled in, relishing the darkness, listening to Bridie's car puttering off back down the mountain, and feeling glad to be alone at last.

Kit lay on her bed in the darkened room and waited for the tablets to do their work. She was quite happy at the prospect of spending the night alone in that quiet wild countryside. The little cottage with its thick walls was now deliciously familiar. By the time her father got back the next day she'd be feeling well again. Eventually, she drifted off.

She awoke to sounds in the kitchen and immediately recognised her father's voice. Kit shook her head. What time was it? Five in the evening. Something wasn't right. Eamon wasn't due back until the following day. Then she recognised John's voice, and there were at least two others, but Kit couldn't make out who they were. About to call out that she was there in the bedroom, Kit slumped back on her pillows. It wasn't a conscious intention to eavesdrop, she was just a little groggy and didn't feel like meeting new people and being polite.

'So, the travel documents are all in order?' Eamon demanded.

'Yeah,' a younger voice answered. *Was that Sean?*

There was the sound of paper shuffling.

'Hmmm. Looks okay. So tell me again. What's his route?'

'Dublin, Canada, Brussels, into Edinburgh on the twenty-third and then down to London for the twenty-forth.'

'It's tight,' Eamon muttered.

'It has to be tight,' John's voice boomed. 'But no one will pick up that track.'

'Especially this time of the year,' another voice cut in.

'Yeah,' Eamon sighed, 'just a bit worried by the Canada/Brussels connection. It's been used before.'

'Not for a while.'

'How does he get to Whitehall?'

'Morning train to Westminster.'

360

'Should be okay,' said Eamon. 'So, reason?'

'A sales conference in Vancouver. Totally legitimate, then a couple of girlfriends.'

'We'll have to spruce him up a bit,' John laughed, 'so they'll believe it's possible.'

'Hopefully that won't be necessary,' Eamon said dryly. 'What about Scotland?'

'A relative.'

'Good. And Micky?'

'Paris for five days, then straight into London. He'll be on the first morning train to Charing Cross.'

'No connection with Sean until –?'

'Until they get there . . .'

'Why so simple?' Eamon asked.

'He's got an old school-mate in Paris.'

'Okay. So he'll stay there?'

'Yep.'

The talk went on, and Kit's curiosity grew. They were planning something. Something important. Three men were to come into London all via different routes, on Christmas Eve. But what for?

'So, the other?' Eamon asked suddenly. 'Any word?'

'Nothing to report at this stage.'

'But the gear will be ready? No point unless it is.'

'It'll be ready.'

'Everyone knows what to do. Right? The way in. And the way out?'

'No stuff-ups this time,' John said matter-of-factly.

'If for some reason the operation goes past nine o'clock, then it's off,' Eamon said firmly. 'One minute past, and we close down.'

There were mutters of assent.

'The unit must understand that.' Then came words that sent a shiver down Kit's spine. 'We don't want another Omagh.'

'A nice early morning job,' the young voice piped up cheerfully. 'A Christmas present for the Brits. A reminder that we're still here.'

'Can't wait to see that fucking thing go up,' Sean continued fervently.

'Forget about it,' Eamon ordered sharply. 'You have a job. So do it. Time enough later to celebrate.'

Everything in Kit was trying to believe that they were discussing something legitimate and ordinary.

'So who'll call the plodders?'

'I will,' Eamon said. 'I'll call from here. Good sticky trace through Donegal.'

'We could get Pete in Derry.'

'No,' Eamon said firmly. 'I want to make sure.'

'What about these documents?' someone asked. 'How do we get them down to Dublin command? Can't risk the post at this time of year.'

'My wee girl will take them,' Eamon said immediately. 'She's leaving Tuesday. It'll work out well.'

'She knows?' Sean asked incredulously.

'Christ no. She's taking some things to an old friend of mine.'

'So will Pete pick up?'

'A woman would be better. Someone like Marion or Claire Dockety. I'll have the name of the hotel tomorrow.'

'Okay.'

'Will you see to Claire? Or if she can't, Marion?'

'Yeah.'

Soon after that, they moved outside. Kit could hear them talking out the front, bits of their conversation coming to her but none of it now making sense.

'Good luck, then.'

'And you'll contact the unit?'

'Aye. So I will.'

'You'll pack those passports right for the girl?'

'Sure. She'll never know. It'll be okay.'

But Kit knew enough. She lay in bed going over what she'd heard.

My wee girl will take them . . .

The headache was gone, but Kit felt as if she was drowning. She was flailing around, trying to take hold, gulping, trying to catch her breath, spitting out the vile salty water. And trying to stay afloat.

The casual way he was going to use her!

Kit lay still, listening as two cars started up and went away. She was going to have to get up and confront him, but somehow she couldn't move. She felt like she'd been beaten. No bruises or weals, yet her whole body seemed damaged. My life, she thought, is no better than an onion. I peel off one layer and there's another just underneath, waiting to be scraped at, torn open and pulled apart. How long am I meant to go on with all this? What does it mean?

She thought of Johnny and the plain little-wife-to-be that she'd never met. The children, not his own, that Johnny was going to care for. Tears came to her eyes. What sort of sister had she been to Johnny? Well, she wasn't his sister, but what sort of friend, anyway? And what about Tam. What sort of friend had she been to her? To Brendan? She hadn't cared a rat's arse about Rory. Not seriously. And what about Therese and Gerard? They'd been so good to her all her life. How was she repaying them? By running away to another country when they needed her most.

Kit forced herself to stop crying. She got up, buoyed with a sudden determination to have it out with him.

I will not be used. I will not.

She shivered as she pulled on her warmest sweater.

But he wasn't in the kitchen or the bathroom. Kit put on her hat and coat, grabbed a torch and went outside. His car wasn't there, so she ran down the track a little way to see if he was with Cormac. There was no car outside the little pub. And when she peered through the window of Cormac's there were only three patrons, none of them her father. He'd obviously left with the others. She was all alone.

Kit waited for hours for Eamon to come home. She sat by the stove, every so often pushing more turf into its bright red fiery mouth. She fell asleep a couple of times, but she was still too angry to go to bed. Over and over again, she heard Annie's words.

'Don't talk to me about Eamon McCabe! He ruined your mother's life. I don't want him to ruin yours.'

No risk of that, Annie. No one is going to ruin my life. Especially not him.

And yet, if he'd asked her. Explained things. Confided in her. Would she have done it? Would she have willingly taken those false passports down to Dublin, so that three men might secretly meet in London at Christmas time to cause havoc? Maybe carnage? Death and destruction? The frightening thing was that Kit didn't have an honest answer to that question. They were going to put a bomb in central London. She was sure of it. The fact that her father didn't want innocent bystanders involved or hurt was beside the point. They might be. If you want to be sure people don't get hurt, you don't put bombs anywhere.

At around three, Kit went over to her tiny bed alcove and packed her bag. She lay down, fully clothed, pulling just one thick blanket over her, thinking that there was no way she'd fall asleep because she was so churned up. If he came back that night, then she would confront him. After that, she would leave.

It gave her no pleasure to admit that she loved her father. Eamon McCabe, with his open face, his kind, generous manner. The one who could sing and make people laugh. The blue eyes. Eyes he'd

364

given her. She was his daughter. His blood ran in her veins. She was closer to him than Leonie had ever been.

But in the end it was a bitter realisation. The fact that she loved him made her decide she couldn't risk staying. She couldn't risk being dragged into his net because, well, she was already halfway there. And perhaps the deepest part of her longed for exactly that to happen. To stand alongside her father. To see it out in the way her mother hadn't. To join in a just cause.

To be part of history.

Kit woke from a deep sleep and stared at the green fluorescent hands of the small clock near her bed. It was half past four! Then, to her amazement, she heard the soft easy sound of her father's snores. He had come in quietly without her hearing. Should she disturb him now? Or wait till morning? Kit slid out from under the blanket and stood stretching and yawning, conscious all the while of her father on the other side of the curtain and also of the need, growing in her steadily, to simply escape. *Damn him. Damn everything.* The anger had gone and a tired hurt had taken its place. What would she say anyway if she did wake him? What effect would it have? Nothing. She was nothing to him. She was just some 'wee girl' he hadn't remembered, who'd turned up after twenty years, someone to use and manipulate. She would go. Simply slip away, out of his life, the way she'd slipped in. No warning. No fanfare.

Kit reached for her coat and picked up the two bags by the side of her bed. The talk with her father, if she ever got to have it, would have to be at another time. And somewhere else. She would catch Cormac on his bread run into town.

She pushed her way past the red curtain and stopped by the door to take a last look around the little kitchen. The fire gave muted light to the room, washing the old table, the dresser, the tap and sink in a soft red warmth. A surge of grief broke open in her chest, and she was drowning again, trying to keep her head above as the raging sea pushed and tumbled her against sharp rocks. This place belonged to her. This was where her great-grandfather, where all the generations on her father's side, had been born and died. They'd spoken to her that first morning. It was their voices welcoming her back. A wild sob rose in her throat. *History?* She was part of history too! He wasn't the only one. It was wrong that she was leaving like this. As though she was guilty. As though she had no right to be here.

Will I ever see this place again?

Then she remembered Leonie's yellowing envelope at the back of the drawer. Kit put the bags down and hurried to the dresser, hitting her knee against the corner of the table, making a loud scraping noise. What did she care? If she woke him, let him come out of his warm bed and see what she was doing. She dug amongst the bits and pieces until she found the letter, then slipped it into her bag. She stopped again, listening for any sounds of stirring. All was quiet.

Should she tell him she'd taken the letter? He wouldn't miss it. It was meant for her, anyway. She thought of the small black-and-white photo of her mother on the chest in his room and toyed with the idea of taking that, too. How dare he tell Bridie that Leonie meant nothing to him! He kept her picture, didn't he? Would you keep a picture of someone you cared nothing about?

On a last impulse, she snatched up a piece of cheap lined paper from the dresser. Fumbling in her bag for a pen, she leant over the table and wrote.

Eamon,

When you wake and find me gone, don't come looking for me. I waited most of the night wanting to speak to you, but I have to leave now.

Your daughter,

Kathleen.

CHAPTER FORTY-TWO

It was three in the afternoon before Kit struggled into the warm palatial reception area of the Excelsior Hotel in Dublin with her two bags, the strap of the heavy one digging into her shoulder. But she was told that no, she couldn't have the room a day early. She had booked for the following day for two nights, but she wasn't to even think about coming a minute before midday because the cleaning staff were run off their feet.

'The whole city is booked out,' the receptionist said. Kit would be lucky to get in anywhere at this time of the year.

'Oh. I see.'

It was all Kit could do not to scream. She stood at the desk, taking in the pretty girl's smart uniform, the sleek expertly styled curly hair, the pert confidence and easy indifference. It had taken Kit seven hours and fifteen rides to get where she was at that moment. Fifteen 'thanks for stopping'. Fifteen 'how are you?' And fifteen 'where are you going?' In short, fifteen new relationships, with nice people on mainly short rides, who thought it great craic to give a travelling girl a lift just on Christmas. Then as soon as they heard her accent, well, what part of Australia was she from? Why was she travelling through Ireland during the worst part of the year? By the time a ride was over they were usually asking her back to stay with them and checking she had enough money for a cup of tea and a bun in Dublin, because the place was full of gangsters and shameless thieves and she'd do well to watch herself.

'Are you completely sure?' she asked the receptionist.

'Absolutely! This time of the year is always bedlam.' She ran her wide, mascara-lined eyes over Kit's bedraggled appearance, 'You'll have to wait till tomorrow.'

Kit turned away. If there really was nowhere to stay in Dublin, then where would she spend the night?

'There are a lot of bed-and-breakfasts out along Cabra Road,' a friendly male voice called out behind her. 'Would you like us to try for you?'

It was the young guy who'd been sitting at a computer behind the receptionist. Plain in appearance, with spotty skin and badly cut hair, he had flecks of dandruff over his shoulders and grey watery eyes behind thick glasses.

Kit fell in love with him on the spot.

'Oh! That's kind of you.'

'It's a fair way out.'

'It doesn't matter. I'll get a taxi.'

By six, she was ensconced in her room way out of Dublin proper, along a busy road that led to Cork. Hers was the third in line of about a dozen almost identical brick box-like bed-and-breakfast establishments, built cheaply for the burgeoning tourist trade.

Kit laid out some clean clothes and took a long shower. The big road sign just outside her building, pointing to Cork, made her well up with tears, thinking of Cormac and his runaway wife. Of his little bar and the turf-fire. Of drinking with him, singing and joking, and listening to his stories. She knew, too, that she wouldn't be at his 'special event' in the new year – the party that wasn't exactly a party that she'd been so keen to attend.

After dressing in clean jeans and a light shirt, Kit lay on the bed and flicked on the television. The letter was sitting there in her bag, but she felt too fragile to read it. She could hear the traffic outside, and noises of other guests as they made their way up and down the stairs.

She watched the news without taking it in. The Middle East conflict was reaching a new level of animosity. America's 'war on terror' was still going on. Catholic children in the Ardoyne were being spat on by their Protestant neighbours on their way to school. Rocks were being hurled. Some American billionaire was opening beauty parlours for dogs right across the country.

Kit lay back, glad that she had this time. She needed to calm down before meeting Sebastian.

But time hung heavily in Cabra Road. At nine-thirty, she went downstairs to put a call through to Bridie's house, hoping to catch Rosalaind. She had no idea how she was going to break the news that she wouldn't be there for Christmas. But she was going to try because, well, she'd promised, and Rosalaind would be so disappointed.

Kit stood in the foyer and punched in the numbers. How could she be doing this to that girl, *her sister*? She was only fifteen. It struck Kit with an awful clarity that she was going to clear out on Rosalaind in much the same way that Leonie had cleared out on her seven years before. Kit listened to the phone ring. She wasn't that kind of person. There had to be some other way to look at it.

But she could not go back to her father's place. If she was going to become part of his scene, then it had to be on her own terms. *After all, what was the point of all that stuff Leonie had written, except as a way to show her that?*

But it was Bridie who answered the phone – Bridie's sweet

369

voice, which showed no surprise when Kit told her breathlessly that she was already in Dublin.

'Well, sure, Kathleen,' she said easily, 'I've heard you left a day early. But we're all keen to know that you'll still be coming back for Christmas.'

Kit opened her mouth and shut it again, a flood of hot tears pouring down her cheeks. Bridie sensed her distress straight away.

'Ah, Kathleen, love,' she murmured, as Kit fought for calm. 'Don't you be upset now.'

'But I want to come,' Kit managed to gasp at last. 'It's just that . . .' Kit didn't know how to go on.

'There's no need to explain,' Bridie said.

'But I just . . .'

'There's no need to say anything. I understand.'

'Do you?'

'I know,' Bridie said simply.

It was then that Kit understood that Bridie did know. Everything. That she had had to make similar decisions herself. Except hers would have been a lot harder. After all, she was married to Eamon. They shared a country, a history and a child.

'Will you explain to Rosalaind and the others?' Kit said.

'I will, and if anything changes or you want to come, just give us a call.'

'I will but I don't know if . . .'

'There will be other times, Kathleen. You're always welcome here. Next year. Or the year after. You know that, don't you?'

At ten o'clock, Kit turned the lights off and prepared to sleep. But light and noise flickered through gaps in the heavy curtain and she lay awake for ages, eventually turning the television back on.

She tried to work out how long it had been since she'd spoken to anyone from home – it was difficult separating days from each

370

other. Then she went over her stay with her father yet again. How come she had more unanswered questions now than when she'd first arrived? At midnight, she wrote herself a note to ring home the next day. It was appalling that she didn't know what kind of progress Leonie was making. Tomorrow she would definitely ring.

The hours passed very slowly. It was well after two before Kit fell asleep.

The next day she was back at the Excelsior's reception area at five past twelve. The same girl was at the reception desk but pretended not to remember Kit, who was dressed more carefully this time, in her freshly dry-cleaned coat. Her hair was pulled off her face with a thick velvet scrunchie. She'd managed to dry her boots, scrape off the mud, and polish them, too. Maybe the girl genuinely didn't recognise her.

She had a few hours to kill before she was due to meet Sebastian and so, after settling into her lovely big room, Kit headed out, down past the post office towards the river, enjoying the cold and the crowds, the pretty Christmas lights that hung along the streets. She had her map with her and was suddenly imbued with a rush of delight when she remembered that she was in James Joyce's city. Some of the most difficult but rewarding study at university had been Irish literature. Damn everything else. She wanted to see a bit. Drink in the atmosphere. Try to forget everything. She would start off with a fast walk to St Stephen's Green then head back up to the museum.

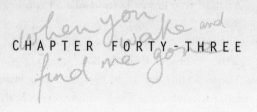

CHAPTER FORTY-THREE

Kit saw Sebastian before he noticed her. He was sitting in the lobby on a plush couch under a big mirror. Crowds of people were walking past him on the marble floor, back and forth through the glass doors that led out onto the street. Couples and work groups, fine-suited business men and well-dressed ladies, talking, smiling and laughing like there was no tomorrow. *Sebastian*. He was the one still point within it all.

It was five past six. Kit stood by the lift she'd just come down in, looking at him. She was dressed in her long maroon crushed-velvet skirt, a white lacy shirt and a tight small black beaded cardigan. She carried her good coat over one arm and her bag was slung over her shoulder. Her hair hung down her back, pulled back from her face with a wooden clasp. She was wearing mascara, and a deep, plum-coloured lipstick.

She was ready for the rush of excitement to hit her. How long have you waited for this? she asked herself. *Nearly six months and here he is!* All those weeks working on the play. How she'd longed for a moment alone with him, a close intimate word, or one of those smiles that sent her heart racing.

But no rush came. He looked ordinary, sitting there. Slightly built. Average height. Hair in need of a cut. Simple clothes. Just an ordinary young man. What had all the fuss been about?

Kit rushed over to him before the disengagement could set in, determined not to sabotage herself again.

'Hello!' she smiled, looking down at him. 'I'm here. Sebastian! Hello!'

He shoved the paper to one side and got up quickly. 'Kathleen,' he smiled eagerly, putting his hands on her shoulders and pulling her towards him, kissing her lightly on both cheeks, 'it's great to see you!'

They caught a taxi down to Temple Bar, and sat together in the back seat, holding hands. The driver let them out just over the bridge and they began the short walk down to all the bars and cafés.

'So, what have you been doing?' He took her hand again as they edged their way along the narrow footpath through the crowds.

'No,' she laughed, 'you first! What have *you* been doing?'

He began to tell her about the last week in London: his dodgy little hotel where the hot water ran out after a couple of minutes; the delicious greasy breakfasts that he couldn't resist even though they stayed with him rather unpleasantly all day; the wonderful central London library, where the staff had been so helpful. He'd not done much else but work so he was glad to take a break in Ireland. His mother's funny old aunt who'd invited him to stay had turned out to be delightful. She was nearly eighty-five but still very sprightly. As soon as she saw him she'd started talking about 'putting a bit of meat on his bones' before he went back home!

How good it was to be walking hand in hand. Neither of them knew quite what kind of place they were looking for as they roamed the narrow, cobbled, newly renovated streets of the trendy Dublin precinct. They stared into café windows, read menus pinned up outside, and made jokes about the weak Australian dollar, and what they could afford to eat.

In the end they settled on a small pub because it was promising a live band of traditional music later on and the food prices seemed reasonable.

The atmosphere was warm, with groups of people standing at the bar chatting and drinking. When they were shown to a table near the window, Kit looked out at the busy street, feeling the last few days peeling off her like dead skin. She turned back to Sebastian and found him watching her carefully, a warm smile in his eyes. Kit blushed and grinned back, delighted, thinking how lucky she was to have a man look at her like that.

He wasn't all that good-looking, she suddenly decided. Not in the obvious sense. His eyes were too small, his nose too sharp. But what did that matter? He added up to more than all his parts because of who he was. His manner was lovely, his smile warm and genuine. And those hands! When he suddenly slid one of them over the table and gripped hers, she shuddered inside, a nervy, bouncy bubble of delight spreading down her legs.

'What will you have to drink, Kathleen?'

The young waiter was standing by their table.

'Oh.' Kit was caught off guard. She hadn't even looked at the wine list. 'Yes!' she said, suddenly feeling excited. 'Let's drink!'

Sebastian and the waiter laughed.

'Okay. Do you like wine?' Sebastian asked.

'I do.'

'Then pick a bottle.'

They settled on a South Australian red from the Barossa Valley because it was cheaper than the others and Sebastian had had it before and said it wasn't too bad. The waiter brought it over, poured them each a glass and stood waiting to take their food order.

'Are you hungry?'

'I am,' Kit laughed.

'Me too!'

374

Kit picked a meat dish at random. She had no idea what she felt like eating, only that she wanted the ordering over with, for them not to be interrupted again. Sebastian took more care, frowning as he went down the list of specials, eventually deciding on the fish. He said he'd heard that Ireland did most fish dishes well.

'Where did you hear that?' Kit teased.

'I don't know.' He immediately laughed at himself. 'Probably from my aunt! A great source I must say, seeing she told me last night that she hasn't had a meal out in ten years!'

'Ten years!' Kit exclaimed without thinking. 'God, you'll have to take her out!' Then she remembered that he was hopefully going to be spending all his time in Dublin with her. 'Or perhaps when you're over next time,' she added.

Sebastian nodded. 'I asked her to come with us tonight,' he said casually, taking a sip of wine, 'but she refused. Said she had better things to do than waste someone else's money when she could be enjoying herself at home watching her favourite TV shows.'

Kit laughed with him, underneath wondering nervously what it would have been like if the aunt had said yes. How would she feel if he'd bought an old lady along with them? *What could he have been thinking to even ask?*

'So tell me about you,' he said again, smiling at her. 'You haven't told me about meeting up with your father.'

'Haven't I? Well, there's not that much to tell, actually.'

Something in Kit knew it would be disastrous to begin talking about Eamon, so she warded it off by describing the countryside of Donegal.

'It's poor land for farming,' she told him, 'very rugged and wild.'

'Did you walk a lot?'

'I did. Nearly every day. Up and down the mountains.'

She went on, telling him about the walks and the landscape,

375

making him laugh with her descriptions of the farmers she met, and their roundabout directions when she got lost. When she saw that he was pouring her another glass of wine, a warning sounded in her head. *Be careful. Stay light. Don't tell.*

After describing Donegal, it was easy to run off in other directions. They spoke of the weather, of Christmas presents sent and not bought and of his plans for producing a play in the new year. All of the talk was warm and enjoyable and, for Kit, full of promise.

But the food took ages to come. By the time it was put in front of them, Kit was more or less drunk. She'd only had three glasses of wine, but on an empty stomach it went straight to her head. When she picked up her knife and fork, she was suddenly aware that she'd been rambling on for ages about some play she'd seen a long time ago which she could only vaguely remember. Had she really been urging him to produce it when she hadn't even been able to remember the title? He hadn't seemed bored but maybe . . . she was being an idiot. She held her hand over the glass as he went to pour her another wine.

'No. Thanks, I've had too much already.'

'You know you've been very evasive tonight,' Sebastian said, bringing a forkful of food to his mouth.

'I have?'

'I want to hear how it's been for you in Donegal.'

'You do?'

'Yes!'

'Can we eat first?' Kit tried to giggle easily.

'No.' He smiled at her. 'I want to know about this father of yours while we're eating. Seeing as I'm going to be spending Christmas with him.'

Kit sighed. She was going to have to tell him. There would be no family Christmas in Donegal. No turf-fires and snow and warm puddings. No midnight mass at that little stone church. No Bridie, no Eamon. No Rosalaind.

She was wretched with grief about it all over again. Eyes down-cast, she didn't trust herself to look up or speak.

'Kathleen, I've upset you.'

'No, no.' Kit put her knife down, biting her lip, appalled because her eyes were filling with tears. 'I'm okay.'

'Then what?'

She looked up, hardly able to see him, her eyes swimming. She was furious with herself for drinking too much. This evening was about her and Sebastian. She desperately didn't want it to slide into an angst-filled night about her father.

'It didn't work out?' he said sympathetically.

'No,' she gulped, 'it didn't. Not really.'

Kit described how good it felt to be there. The way her father was close but enigmatic at the same time. She told him about Bridie and the girls. Sebastian listened carefully. And he was sympathetic, she could feel that. He wanted in particular to know all about Rosalaind. He was amused at the idea of Kit meeting up with a sister who looked so much like herself at a younger age. About Rosalaind's hopes to be a director of horror films. About her wild ideas and beautiful drawings.

But it was when she got to the overheard conversation in the cottage that Sebastian's interest intensified. He was a politics lecturer, after all. This was his passion. He became quite still. She could feel him sitting across the table, watching her closely in a dry, almost disengaged way. And when she came to the end of it, his comments and questions were dry, too. And, just as she knew it would, some-how the whole thing took over. There didn't seem to be anything else worth talking about.

'So Whitehall?'

'Did they stipulate Christmas Day?'

'Was it mentioned who forged the passports?'

She found herself telling him about what else she'd learnt from her mother's outpourings. Then about Annie and her assessment of Eamon. Within the space of half an hour she'd blurted out the whole damned lot.

Their food lay half finished on their plates and Kit sat back in her chair. There was some satisfaction in having unburdened herself, but she felt flattened, too. Emptied. As though she'd given everything. And for what? Sebastian smiled at her kindly, then leant forward with the now empty bottle of wine.

'I think we need another one of these?'

Kit shrugged. 'Okay.' She didn't feel like more wine but on the other hand, why not? It might make her feel better.

They were both quiet for some time. The pub was beginning to fill up. The buzz of talk and laughter ebbed and flowed around them, filling in the gaps of their silence. They watched as the band came in and began to set up on a small stage near the bar. Sebastian called the waiter over and asked for another bottle, and Kit turned back to the window.

'So, what do you make of it?' She picked up the fresh glass of wine that had been poured for her and took a sip, trying to sound light and easy. 'What do you think about what I've told you?'

'Well, I'd say he's almost definitely a member of a splinter group.' Sebastian frowned as he played with the small container of toothpicks. He picked up his wine glass and took a deep swallow. 'A commander, probably. A few of these groups have blossomed since the Good Friday agreement. The Real IRA perhaps?'

'I don't know much about them,' Kit mumbled, mentally kicking herself. Here she was, back in the position of being a student again. Why hadn't she made it her business to find out about all this before she came? *Because there wasn't time. And because she hadn't really wanted to know, had she?*

'Your mother probably knew it,' Sebastian went on thoughtfully. 'About him still being active. And that might be one of the reasons why she's found it so difficult to tell you everything. She'd know that you'd want to meet him.'

Kit's attention was immediately galvanised. She sat up straighter. God, his mind was so sharp! He was making all the connections. Piecing things together. He'd forgotten nothing she'd told him. It was almost frightening.

'She's not going to be very pleased to learn I'm over here then,' Kit mumbled with a dry laugh. 'That I've been staying with him.'

'No,' Sebastian agreed. 'How is she, by the way? Does she speak yet?'

'I'm not sure.'

'Is she fully conscious?'

'I don't know.'

Kit saw the surprise on his face and turned away, embarrassed, remembering the note she'd written herself. *Ring home!* Why hadn't she done that?

They got up from the table. Sebastian insisted on paying, which Kit, although she protested, found touching. When they walked out into the cold air, he put his arm around her. She was filled with a new rush of optimism. Maybe it would be okay after all. Maybe they'd be able to leave Eamon and Donegal back there with the loud talk, the music, the stuffy, noisy, smoke-filled atmosphere. The cold was biting, but invigorating too: a great excuse to put your arm around someone.

'Will we walk back to my hotel?' she asked shyly.

'Yes,' he said. 'I feel like walking.'

They were quiet but it still felt good to Kit. Arms entwined, they pushed their way through the crowds, across the River Liffey into the brightly lit shopping district.

At a red light, Kit moved in closer. She put one hand around the back of his neck and then, laughing a little, she leaned up and kissed him on the mouth, putting her other hand up to caress his hair. He was obviously surprised, but kissed her back. This was better, Kit decided. Drinking too much had its advantages. It had given her courage, anyway. Once across the road, they walked on and then, in front of a shop window displaying toys for Christmas, they kissed again. This time it was longer and more lingering. Bliss. In his arms, Kit felt outside ordinary time. The feel of his mouth and the lovely roughness of his shaved face made her limp with desire.

When they eventually got back to the hotel, Sebastian stopped just inside the glass doors and stood with both hands resting lightly on her waist. He kissed her again.

'You're coming up,' she smiled. It was almost an order. 'You have to,' she added, laughing.

'I'm sorry, I can't,' he said, pulling away from her a little, but holding both her hands in his own.

Kit came crashing down to earth in an instant. 'But why not?'

'I have to get back,' he said.

'But it's early,' she wheedled, looking at her watch.' Only ten-thirty.'

'My aunt's just bought a new video,' he said. 'I promised that I'd be back to set it up for her. Apparently there's some film on at three a.m.' He gave a short, half embarrassed laugh. 'She's desperate for me to tape it for her.'

In any other situation, Kit would have burst out laughing. What an excuse! It was so ridiculous it almost had to be true! She buried her face in his neck, slipped her arms inside his coat and began caressing his back.

'Sebastian,' she murmured, 'she'll live without it. I promise you.'

'Sorry, I can't,' he said, kissing her forehead lightly and extricating himself from her arms. 'I promised I'd be back about now.'

'Then just come up for a while,' she said desperately.

'Sure,' he sighed as though he'd been talked into something. 'I'll see you up to your room.'

When they got up there, Kit threw off her coat and went immediately to the fridge.

'Drink?' she asked, as though the awkward little scene down in the foyer hadn't happened at all.

'No, thanks.' He stood by the door with his coat still on. All the way up in the lift they'd held hands but he'd been distracted.

Kit motioned to the plush chair near him. 'Sit down!' she ordered. She could hear the hysteria in her voice and was immediately embarrassed. 'Please, sit down and relax,' she added in what she hoped was a more casual tone. She got two glasses out of the fridge and poured orange juice into one of them.

'Are you sure?' she said, holding up the empty glass. 'It's nice, actually. I had some before.'

'No thanks.' He shook his head and smiled, but didn't move. She sat down on the bed, leaning up against the pillows, her confidence evaporating by the second.

'Actually, I'd better go,' said Sebastian. 'Shall we meet again tomorrow?'

'I want you to stay with me now,' Kit said quietly from the bed. 'Please, I've been longing for it. I really want you to stay.'

There. It was out. She was offering herself to him in the only way she knew how. Directly. But part of her felt ridiculous, too. This wasn't the way other people did it, she was sure of that.

Sebastian came over and sat down next to her on the bed. He picked up both her hands and kissed her lightly on the forehead and then the nose.

'Kathleen,' he whispered, 'I can't stay with you tonight.'

She looked away, on the point of tears, wanting to scream.

'Please don't think *anything*,' he said suddenly. 'Dinner tonight was great. I've really enjoyed being with you, but I'm afraid I'm very preoccupied at the moment. I can't stay.'

'Okay,' she said. But it wasn't okay at all. What did him coming to Ireland mean, if he wasn't interested in her? What did all the kisses mean? She wanted to cry and beg him, and she wanted to yell at him too. But she just sat there stony-faced, dully watching his hands as they gently let go of her own.

'I'll see you tomorrow,' he said again, getting up and moving to the door.

'Right.' Kit nodded numbly and stayed where she was, half lying on the bed.

'So what time will we meet?' he asked from the doorway.

She shrugged.

'I'll ring you in the morning then,' he said. 'We'll meet for breakfast.'

'Okay.'

Sebastian quietly let himself out of the room.

Kit waited for about three minutes, then sat up and began systematically chucking every cushion, every pillow she could find, around the room in a mad rage. Never had she felt so angry and humiliated. She ground her teeth, punched the wall and screamed under her breath, making her face red and blotchy. There were no tears, though. She was too furious. The plush hotel room was mocking her. The king-size bed. The stupid little frosted glass lamps on each side of it that she'd liked so much when she'd first walked in. The nifty little fridge, full of drink that he'd not wanted. All those fantasies she'd had of what they might do in this room! She picked up her glass of juice and threw it hard against the wall. The crash was disappointingly muted. *Damn*. She fell back down on the bed, clenching and unclenching her fists, watching the orange liquid running down the wall. Her heart was racing. She wanted to kill someone. Here she was, twenty years old. In Dublin. Having come all the way to meet the man she'd wanted so badly for months. He'd acted like he wanted to be with her. Then, at *ten-thirty*, he chooses to go back to some dozy old aunt to work her fucking video player!

Kit picked up the other empty glass and threw it at the TV. Smash. That was better. A much more satisfying sound. If only she had a dozen glasses to smash! She felt like destroying the room and everything in it.

What was wrong with her? Was he gay? Didn't he find her attractive? *Shit!* She didn't even want him now! She hated him!

Then, because she couldn't stand the look of broken glass, she got some toilet paper and began to collect the pieces. She didn't take enough care because she was still too angry, and cut her right hand. She stood, holding her hand up high, watching the blood run down her fingers and arm into the crook of her elbow, like vibrant little rivers. She had no Band Aids and there was nothing in the bathroom. Weighing up whether to call reception for help, in the end she was too embarrassed. So she stood for ages, in the lovely marble bathroom, with her hand under the tap, waiting for the blood to stop, staring at her flushed face in the mirror. No way was she just going to bed. *No bloody way!* Let him go and watch videos if he wanted! It didn't mean she had to.

With her face washed and the cuts bound up with tissues inside her leather gloves, Kit slipped her coat back on and made her way down in the lift and into the lobby. The pretty receptionist was behind the desk again. She looked at Kit with a mixture of envy and curiosity.

'Out again?' she asked, all fake friendliness.

'Oh yes,' Kit smiled sweetly. *As if it's any business of yours, sweetheart!*

Kit buttoned her coat and wrapped her scarf tightly around her neck, then took off on foot in the same direction she'd come from with Sebastian. Down towards the river. She had no idea where she'd go. Only that she was full of energy and couldn't stay another minute in the hotel room.

She ended up back in the pub she'd left a little over an hour before. The place was crowded with drinkers and revellers. Some were there for the music, sitting in groups, watching the band, and even singing along. But most were just there for a good time. The music was background for the more important tasks of schmoozing and socialising.

And around it all the flutes, the fiddles and drums played, the music's circular rhythms getting faster and faster with each number, as though infected with a kind of madness. There were no breaks. Each tune seemed to career off into the next, losing its thread in a fresh pattern of rhythmic mayhem. Kit let the wild sounds stir her own blood into a thumping state of excitement. The band was really good, she decided. The music was hypnotic. There was no time left in life for anything else!

She spied a few spare seats in the corner of the room, then lined up at the bar. When she had a glass of the thick brown stuff that everyone else was drinking, she made her way over. Within minutes, a man named Joe and his friend Peter were chatting her up. Then when they had to go off to some mate's party and she decided not to join them, a tall, good-looking fellow called Andy sidled in.

'This seat taken?' he asked politely.

'No.' Kit smiled at him and moved up.

'Band's not bad.'

'They're fantastic.' She beamed at him again.

Kit accepted his offer of a drink and they began to exchange chit-chat amiably. He reminded Kit of Brendan. She liked his direct and friendly manner. His brother was in Australia and Andy was thinking about coming out the next year to see him. So he asked questions, some of them quite practical. She told him about distances and weather. He was a builder on a construction site, and he told her that he'd wasted a few years messing around at university without finishing anything. And, now he'd found what he wanted to do, he planned to set up his own business with a mate. Contract themselves

384

out. They had plans and loads of ambition. Now was the time to make it big in Ireland if you had a mind for it.

'One day,' Andy boasted in his soft lilt, 'I'll be in charge of a whole outfit. I'll be a millionaire.'

A millionaire? Hmmm. Kit figured that she could do with one of those. She liked his thick accent, the way he paused before he spoke, like he was in no hurry to do anything. He liked to talk and was quick to laugh.

After half an hour, Kit decided, Why not? She was tired of hanging around waiting for love to arrive. She'd be twenty-one next month. She could feel herself turning into someone else. Someone boring and semi-hysterical. Andy would do. He was nice. She could tell. As good as anyone. She'd invite him back to the hotel. They'd sleep together. She'd tell him she hadn't had much experience. And he'd be the sort who wouldn't mind. Maybe he'd be touched. They might even have breakfast together before he headed back to the building-site . . . Damn Sebastian.

When Andy came out to Australia next year, he might look her up. Who knew what might happen?

An hour into their conversation their hands brushed together and it made both of them pull away and then smile. Kit liked the fact that he wasn't too cool to be a little embarrassed, too. Then after a couple more drinks, in the middle of a conversation about the Australian beach, he took hold of that same hand, looked into her eyes, and told her she was gorgeous, that she reminded him of his older sister before she turned into a smart-mouthed, hard bitch. Kit giggled, seriously pleased. They sat there for maybe an hour longer, holding hands. Then, by mutual agreement, although nothing was said, they both stood up.

'I'll see you back to your hotel,' Andy said gallantly.

'Okay,' Kit nodded, hoping he meant what she thought he meant. 'Let's go.'

When they were just outside the door, chaos broke out. A small, sleek car pulled up. Two older women, well into their thirties, got out and walked towards Kit and Andy. As they got closer, Kit could see that the blonde one, dressed in bright pink leotards and high-heeled shoes, looked furious. Kit instinctively stood aside, thinking that the women were going into the pub. But they were heading straight for Andy, who suddenly let go of Kit's hand.

'What do you think you're doing, Andrew Kelly?' the blonde yelled at him. 'As if you aren't in enough trouble. You come out drinking to make more. That's your plan, is it?'

'Ah, come on, Ruth!' Andy said shiftily. 'Give us a break now.'

'I'll give you a break all right.' The blonde lifted her arm and smacked him hard across the mouth. 'There's your break, you feckin' dolt!'

'That's right!' The other woman said smugly, poking Andy in the arm with one long painted fingernail.

The slap had Andy reeling backwards. He put a hand to his cheek. 'There is no need to get nasty.' His voice petered out.

'Who's this?' the woman sneered, motioning towards Kit with her thumb.

'Er, a friend,' Andy said gamely. 'Kit, this is Ruth.'

'I don't want to meet your *friends!*' Ruth screamed.

'If you want to know what's good for you,' the other woman said more calmly, taking Ruth by the elbow, 'then get home right now.'

By this stage Kit's eyes were wide, her mouth hanging open in shock. Who were these women and what did Andy have to do with them? A few other men were watching from the sidelines.

'A fair couple of bitches!' a voice mumbled. The blonde spun around and took a few steps towards the group of men. In spite of how tense the situation was, Kit almost laughed when she saw them all take a step backwards.

'If I want to know what any of you feckless morons think,' she snarled, 'I'll ask!' She turned back to Andy. 'Now get your skates on, you dolt.'

Andy turned to Kit and gave a weak apologetic shrug. She saw that he was quite a bit older than she'd originally thought. Thirty at least. Maybe more.

'I'm sorry,' he said. 'I just wasn't thinking.'

'It's okay.' Kit was still amazed. She was dying to ask who the woman was. A wife? Girlfriend? Or perhaps it was the hard, mean-mouthed sister? But if she said something out of turn she might get a smack across the mouth, too.

Kit walked back to the hotel alone, but in much better spirits than when she'd come down earlier. Every now and again she broke into a smile, thinking of herself and Andy, and the look on his face when he realised he'd been caught. The pity was, she'd probably never know just who they were.

Back in her room, she put through a call to the Richmond house. It would be eight in the morning. Brendan would be awake and she had a sudden longing to talk to him. She wanted to tell him about the incident outside the pub. It would have him cackling across the distance that separated them. It would be great to have a laugh with Brendan.

But no one answered. She let it ring and ring, then she tried again. Kit went to bed after that, a little down but very tired, too. And surprisingly, she slept well.

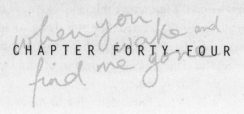

CHAPTER FORTY-FOUR

'The thing is, Kathleen, how would you feel if that bomb went off and someone was killed or maimed?'

Sebastian spoke quietly and intensely, his arms folded, the cup of tea and toasted sandwich sitting on the plate untouched in front of him. 'I really do think you must tell someone,' he went on.

Kit was sitting across from Sebastian at a small table in the glassed-in breakfast room of the hotel. It was cozy, with a brief warm burst of sunshine shining in from outside. She was drinking from a large white cup of strong latté and fiddling with the croissant she'd just covered in jam. She'd dressed for the breakfast date in jeans and her good pink shirt. Her hair was washed and pulled up into a loose bun. Until they'd begun this conversation she'd been feeling okay, considering her mood the night before.

'Even if they call it off now, they'll plan something else. Probably they're doing it already. He and whoever he works with should be at least watched.'

'So who?' she asked. 'I mean, who would I tell?'

'The Police. Special Branch. MI5. There are any number of tracks to go down. I'll help you.'

Sebastian was making Kit feel like she had no choice. She under-stood now why he'd had to leave her the night before. How worried he'd been by the information about her father. As soon as they'd sat down and ordered breakfast, Sebastian had told her that he'd gone back to his aunt's place very troubled, worrying about what was the best thing to do. He was sympathetic to her position: Eamon was her father and it was a terribly difficult situation for her. But after much thought, he'd come to the conclusion that family ties had to be crossed and possibly broken. She owed it to the rest of society.

Kit bit into her croissant grimly. While he'd been deciding all that, she'd been out boozing, trying to pick up men! How come she'd barely considered the wider relevance of what she'd heard in that cottage? Until now, she'd thought that the whole thing was only about her and her relationship with Eamon.

Sebastian picked up his cup and took a sip.

'But how do you go about finding the right person?' she asked, stalling for time. *Could she possibly do what he was asking her to do?*

'That's the easy part,' Sebastian said, and then looked away to the small family group entering the room. There was a tall, olive-skinned father of about forty. Then two young children of perhaps six and eight, and a baby in the young mother's arms, squirming around, chortling and grinning at its siblings. 'Just think. It could be people like that,' he sighed. 'Complete innocents just walking past.'

Kit looked over at the noisy little family, feeling a chill spread right down into her legs.

'But my father was very concerned that there wouldn't be people around,' she said lamely. 'Remember I told you he said: "We don't want another Omagh".'

'Bombs often don't go off as planned,' Sebastian said sharply. 'In fact Omagh is a good case in point. They hadn't intended to kill all those people. Your father might have the best intentions in the world and still something happens, someone is there and they get hurt or killed.'

Kit nodded. She took another bite of the soft buttery croissant, not meeting his eyes.

'Kathleen, would you willingly help blow anything up? Even if it was just bricks and mortar?'

'No!'

'Then you must speak up.'

'But they'll keep me here,' Kit said childishly. 'I need to go home soon. I've got my brother's wedding.'

'It won't take that long.'

'But it will,' she said, panicking. 'They'll want to question me. Maybe I'd have to give evidence or –'

'So you do it anonymously,' he said quickly. 'They work on tip-offs all the time. As long as the information is sound.'

'How do you mean?'

'Write it out,' he said, 'in as much detail as you remember. Names, places.' He looked at her anxiously. 'Do you think you can? They would already have a dossier on him because he's been in jail. But whether they know where he lives now or not is another thing. They may be aware of him already, but you don't know that.'

She sighed. How strange that they were sitting like this over breakfast, her and Sebastian, plotting against her father.

'I'll try,' she said at last. He leant across and squeezed her hand. 'But I need some time to think,' she added miserably.

'Okay. Fair enough,' He took out pen and paper and quickly wrote out a number. He looked at his watch. 'It's ten now. This is my aunt's number. If you have any problems, then call me. I'll help in any way. You don't have to sign it. I'll give it to the authorities. If that's what you want. We'll do it any way you want.'

'Okay,' Kit said dully, taking the piece of paper from him.

'How long do you think you'll be?' he asked.

'Give me two hours.'

He smiled kindly and squeezed her hand again. 'I'll expect a call from you in a couple of hours, then?'

'Okay.'

CHAPTER FORTY-FIVE

Kit went upstairs as soon as he'd left. She walked around the hotel room feeling dazed.

Eamon is my father. My father. And I'm expected to hand him over to the police? No. I don't think so.

But in the end, Kit decided that Sebastian was right. He had to be right. Innocent lives might be at stake here. Eamon was just one person. That he was her father was beside the point. She took a small writing pad out of her backpack, and stuck it in her handbag. Then, putting on her warmest clothes, she left the hotel room and caught the lift down to the street.

Besides, she didn't want to turn into another Leonie.

Kit sat in a grimy little café on Capel Street, writing for perhaps an hour. One rough draft and then another one, more carefully. When she was satisfied, she went back up towards Parnell Square where she remembered seeing an Internet café in a side street. When she got there, the place was buzzing with activity but the friendly proprietor showed her to a spare computer down the back. She paid her money and sat down to type it out. When she was finished she printed it, folded the two neatly typed pages and slipped them into the envelope she'd bought. On her way back through driving sleet, she passed a police station. She stopped and then walked up the front steps.

I don't need Sebastian to hold my hand. This is my business. My father. I'll do my own dirty work.

But at the top step she peered in and saw a whole lot of uniformed men standing around. They were talking about something serious. She lost her nerve and walked back down onto the street again, heading for the hotel, deciding she needed a little more time.

At the line of phones in the foyer of the hotel, she looked up the Central London Police Department. Then she put a call through and asked to be connected to Special Branch. There was a long wait. Kit's mind began to play tricks on her. *Where was she again? What was she doing? What did this mean?* The little cottage loomed up in her head like a mirage. She could remember every detail inside the kitchen. The yellow stain in the old sink. The one worn brass tap. The slightly rotting wooden door to the cupboard. Even the things on the sideboard. There were four yellow eggcups with a silver line around them sitting on the second shelf. She watched herself being danced around the floor of that little pub when she'd first arrived. How long ago was it? Around and around they'd danced. How glad she'd been to look into his face at last.

And will you look at her! All the way from Australia.

What a good-looking lass!

'Hello, Special Branch,' a female voice said. 'Sergeant Moore speaking. How may I help you?'

'What is your address there please?' Kit asked in a flat voice. There was a moment's pause before the woman gave out the information. Kit wrote it carefully on the outside of the envelope.

'Is there anything else I can help you with?'

'No. Thank you.' Kit put the phone down, picked up her bag and began to move off.

Then she saw Sean. Or thought she did. A young man hovered just behind her, before walking past towards the hotel doors. For an instant, their eyes locked. Or had she imagined it? Those same blank eyes that had unsettled her in Donegal. Kit stopped and tried to think. Shock was coursing down her backbone like an icy river. She suddenly bolted after him, wanting to get a proper look, to make sure. But once she'd got through the glass doors and out into the cold again, the young man had disappeared. Kit shrugged. It was easy to get paranoid if you got too tense. *Would her father send that little stooge after her? No way. Not possible. What a crazy thought.*

On her way down towards the city, Kit passed two Santas ringing bells and giving out lollies. Around them children gathered, the young ones smiling shyly, the older ones interested only in the free sweets. Kit walked into the strong wind. Heavy sleet fell in great blustering splatters into her face. She clutched at her hat with one hand and pulled her scarf tightly down into the collar of her coat. When she saw a postbox, she stopped. If she sent the letter today, it would be picked up in the evening. It would reach London either the next day or the next. There would be time to alert the police. To stop the bomb . . . just. If she sent it now.

But she didn't do it. She couldn't bring herself to slip the envelope into the box. And walking past another city police station, she found she was unable to leave it there either. She did try; she made herself go in and take her place at the end of a long queue. Out of the corner of her eye, she saw the same young man who'd been hovering near her in the hotel. *Sean.* Was it him? His face was turned away and he had a hat on. She couldn't be sure.

When her turn had almost arrived, Kit left her place and sidled out towards the wide swinging doors. She didn't want to go back in there again. Never. She was furious with herself, and weirdly elated. *She couldn't do it. It was asking the impossible.*

This is what it must feel like to be a terrorist, Kit thought. None of them know that I am walking around with this *bomb* in my pocket. What am I going to do with it?

Tired and disorientated, Kit sat down on the police station steps to watch the first soft snowflakes of the season cover O'Connell Street. So pretty. Around her, people slowed down, some of them stopped to watch. Delighted children held out their hands to catch the flakes, giggling at the magical white blanket that was gradually beginning to cover the grey roads and footpaths, the gutters, the shop window-sills. The adults watched on, smiling.

Kit knew she'd have to move soon or her bottom would freeze on the step. She searched in her bag for a hanky to wipe her dripping nose, and her hand brushed up against the letter that she'd taken from the cottage. It was still sitting in her bag, sealed and unread. She pulled it out. The words on the envelope seemed to scream at her.

It was Leonie, her mother, who'd written those words. Calling out to her now from twenty years ago. Kit's hands began to shake. Now was as good a time as any, she told herself. She stood up. Walking around under the shelter of the pillars, she began to read.

My little one.

When you wake and find me gone, you will be in the arms of your grandmother. She will be the one holding you, comforting you. She'll have a bottle of warm milk ready for you even before you want it. I know that. That's what steadies me. That's what keeps me sane. She'll keep you dry, she will coo and whisper in just the right way. I smile just thinking about it. I'm remembering her taking my cousin Sharon's new baby out of the bassinet a couple of years ago. So tenderly. So full of joy my mother was, holding the baby up for all to see. That's how a baby should be touched. Gently, lovingly, by someone who knows that they're doing the most important job in the world. A baby doesn't need an anxious, neurotic, ambitious heart-worn misfit for a mother.

I smile again, thinking of where you're going. About the brothers who I know will adore you. Johnny is only ten. And such a gentle boy. He'll love you to bits!

I haven't yet been to sleep since giving you away but already I'm dreaming of the little patch of dark hair on your head. The nurse told me that it might change colour. Will you end up with my wild red masses I wonder, or will you keep your father's colour? I hope you have his dark good looks. He won't be able to deny you then. He won't be able to spin some tale about it all being a misunderstanding on my part. When you're five or ten or fifteen I'll take you to see him and he'll know then that the whole thing was real all right.

Real. Real. Real.

One day, I'll tell you all about all this. I'll come clean about it all. I'm trying to think of how you will grow up. And thinking about what I'll say when you ask me questions. The truth is, I have no idea what I'll say.

If I was a true believer I would have you with me now. If I was as strong as some of the others, I'd want you here, growing up part of it all.

But who would ever want this for a child? These bleak rainy days, the row housing, and ancient disputes. When I was tempted in hospital, I remembered the warm blue skies of home. The summer days spent down by the river. I didn't want you growing up filled with tribal hatreds the way the kids around here grow up. You, my daughter, will have everything important. That's what I thought. A good mum and dad. Plenty of fresh air and sunshine. Good food, and room. Room to grow, room to be silly sometimes, room to make mistakes.

Of course I'm comforting myself. The reality is, as the minutes pass I'm missing you terribly and feeling more and more bereft, as though some part of my body has gone or been chopped off. I turn around suddenly as Annie comes in the door with the tray of food. The creaking floorboards sound like a baby's cry.

I remember deciding finally that I would give you up. I was seven months pregnant and visiting a friend in Andersonstown when I saw a group of young kids playing with an old car tyre. They were having a great time with it – giving each other rides, falling off, just messing around happily in the street. It was quite unusual to see such prolonged, simple, childish happiness. A few of us women were watching, as were a couple of old men. Then a skinny kid of about fourteen came along and pushed those kids away, making two little girls fall on the road and skin their knees. He began to play with the tyre himself. Casually, only a short distance away from the younger ones, as though he'd just thought of the game himself. A couple of us protested but he just grinned nastily and sloped off with the tyre, hardly even bothering to give us the finger.

The thing was that none of the little kids was surprised. No one cried out: 'That's not fair'. The bully boy wins every time. The kids here don't learn about waiting your turn or seeing life from someone else's point of view. You want something, you take it – if you can. And expect the same to happen to you. I went back into the house that day, my mind made up. I thought, I hate this place. I hate what it has done to people. I don't want my child cowering to other people's rigid demands. I want her to have a chance.

I want her to grow up into whoever she wants to be.

They've gone! Gone.

My parents. Back home with you.

I've just had a long bath and I'm sitting at Annie's rickety old table in her messy little sitting room, next to the spluttering gas heater, waiting to find out what I feel. Relieved? Yes, I suppose I can say that. The long front window is partly covered by a thick red curtain, but I can see the front post covered in ivy, and a bit of that bleak old Belfast sky. I cried myself sick in the bath, filled up with the sadness and tension of the last few days – few months, really. But I don't actually trust tears. What did my sobs mean? That I was sad? Yes. That I *regretted giving you away? No. I regret a lot of things but I don't regret giving you away.*

I'm sitting here, my breasts swollen and sore, leaking milk meant for a little one who is no longer here. How did I land in this situation? Annie is so good. I can hear her pottering away in the kitchen, making something for us to eat. She knows this is traumatic for me, that I'm a little mad at the moment, so she doesn't talk much. She doesn't press me to talk, either. What would I do without her?

When I found out Eamon was married I thought I would die. Literally. I thought nothing could be worse than that. I'd fallen so passionately in love with a married man who loved his wife. He told me this, firmly and carefully, the night before he got picked up.

'I don't know why you're going through with this, Leonie,' he said, 'and I'm terribly sorry about it. But I'm not leaving Bridie. And I will never leave her.'

But there are worse things. Of course there are! This is worse, for a start. This baby business is much worse than finding out your lover will never be yours. Your tiny pink hands and perfect feet. The little creases of fat around your neck. Mouth like a rosebud. It took me three days but I did fall in love with you. I named you on the third day. Kathleen – after Eamon's dead mother. I don't know why but as soon as I felt sure of your name, I fell in love with you.

Bridie's been trying to have a baby for years, so this has rubbed her nose in it. I'm sorry for that. I am.

But could I honestly say that I wouldn't have got involved with him if I'd known about him being married? Maybe I would have been more careful. Less willing to open the door to him in the middle of the night for a 'chat'. More circumspect.

Did I seduce him? No.

Did he seduce me? Not really. But he didn't tell me he was married until it was too late. So I suppose that was a form of seduction.

I was interested in him. Before anything happened between us I

398

was interested in what he had to say. In who he was and what he was doing with his life. Not that he told me everything. Or even half of it. But there was so much talk. About politics and history. About what was possible and why. Still, talk is only surface between people who are attracted to each other. It's the excuse to be together. I was wildly attracted to him and I let him know. Underneath the talk was a river of other stuff.

That stuff is life! I refuse to deny it. I refuse to belittle it. I refuse to say it doesn't matter, even though I know it is often the cause of much suffering and confusion. Put a lid on the pulse of attraction between people, clamp down on the joy of love, repress the spark of Eros and you are spitting on God's creation. That's my honest view!

I have no job any more. No husband. No boyfriend. No baby.

Why am I writing about love?

That was it. Kit slowly folded the pages and pushed them back into the envelope. The letter seemed truncated. Leonie had stopped in full flight. Why? Kit stood still, quite disorientated, back with Leonie at the time of her own birth, staring out into the snow-covered street, wondering what was happening to her.

The dilemma she'd been living through for the past few hours suddenly seemed ridiculous to her. To report her own father to the authorities as a terrorist seemed like someone's bad joke. *As if I'd betray my own father.* Sebastian was too bookish. Too much the academic. He'd got carried away. Maybe he wanted some excitement in his life to show off about to the other lecturers. And he wanted to use her to get it. *Stuff him.* Who said you were responsible for someone else's actions? Her father wasn't some twenty-year-old out to randomly kill people. He knew what he was doing.

Kit took the letter to the police out of her coat pocket, pulled the two pages out and tore them up into tiny pieces. Then she threw the pieces up into the air and watched them come down slowly and get lost in the snow. They' looked for those brief moments like tiny birds – little white fledglings on their first flight.

Then she hurried back to the hotel.

CHAPTER FORTY-SIX

Brendan.

Back at the hotel, Kit had to talk to him about all this. He was the only person who would understand. She looked at her watch. Midday. So that made it nine o'clock that evening at home.

She put a call through to the Richmond house. *Please.* She began to pray as the phone started ringing. *Please pick up the phone. Please, Brendan.* But no one did. There wasn't even the answering machine. Just the dull persistent sound of the phone call ringing out.

Kit rang the farm and Therese picked up immediately.

'Mum, it's me!'

'Oh, thank God!' Therese said, as though something miraculous had just happened. *'It's her! It's Kathleen. Oh, thank the Lord!'*

There was an excited clamour of familiar voices behind Therese.

'Mum, I'm really sorry I haven't called,' she began. 'It's just that I've been –'

'We were so worried!' Therese cut in immediately, on the point of crying. 'I called that number in Donegal, and the old chap there. What was his name? Corey?'

'Cormac.'

'Yes!' Therese said breathlessly. 'Well, he was very nice. But he said you'd gone and no one knew exactly when you'd be back, although he'd given you a ride into the nearby town. Is that right? He seemed quite upset. Oh Kathleen, where are you?'

'I'm in Dublin.'

'Dublin!' Therese cried, her mood changing immediately. 'How wonderful. I had visions of you being whisked away to a terrible foreign place in the Middle East!'

'Mum,' Kit smiled, 'why would you think that?'

'Is Dublin lovely? Are you enjoying yourself? I've heard the people are very nice. Is it cold? Have you got enough warm clothes? Gerard saw on the news that the temperatures in Europe are very low. That it's very cold and oh, Kathleen, I'm talking too much. Are you all right?'

'Yes!' Kit laughed. Therese was being her usual self. But somehow it was endearing rather than annoying.

'Casey's had the baby,' Therese said suddenly.

'Already? I thought it was due in the new year.'

'Yes, well she got her times mixed up, poor little thing. Anyway, a lovely girl was born last week in the local hospital.'

'Is there still going to be a wedding?' Kit hesitated. 'Is he still going to marry her?'

'Oh, yes,' Therese said brightly. 'We're all looking forward to it, now that the baby's born.'

'So what date?'

'We were waiting to hear from you,' Therese hesitated. 'Johnny wants you to be here for it. Would you have even an inkling of when you might be back, love? It's not that I'm trying to tie you down but we have to set a date so that the invitations can be sent out. There's so much to be organised. But I don't want you to be thinking I'm pushing you.'

'I'm getting on the first available flight,' Kit cut in quietly. 'I'm coming home, Mum.'

'Oh!' Therese seemed stunned. '*She's coming home on the first available flight!*' she whispered excitedly to whoever was in the room.

'It'll be really difficult to get a seat though,' Kit added, 'being Christmas and all.'

'But you'll try and come soon?'

'Yes, I will. I'm about to ring now to try and get a seat.'

'Oh, that is great news. We're just dying to see you. You'll miss Christmas. But it will be wonderful to see you just as soon as you can get here. Will you be back by your birthday?'

'Mum, I'm not even thinking about my birthday. We'll celebrate it later, OK? How is Leonie?'

'Oh, she's coming along. Very slowly. You'll see a great improvement. She has the most wonderful people helping her. The physio and the speech therapist are marvellous.'

'So she's completely conscious?'

'Oh yes.'

'Can she speak?'

'Well,' Therese hesitated, 'she is trying to speak. She says your name, often.'

'Does she know I'm here? Did Johnny read her my letter?'

'I believe he did,' Therese said warily. 'Yes. It was a shock for her.'

'Tell her I'm coming home.'

'I will. She's home from hospital. She's out on the verandah having a little rest now. But I'll tell her as soon as she wakes. She'll be very pleased.'

'Tell her I . . . that I . . .' Kit couldn't finish. Her voice cracked and she began to cry. 'We've got a lot to say to each other.'

'I will, love. I'll tell her that.'

Kit put the phone down in complete shock. She hadn't known beforehand that she'd decided to go home. She hadn't thought

403

about when she'd be going home at all. There'd been too much business here. She sat down on the bed, her hands trembling. But she did want to go home. Desperately. She'd had enough. There were people she needed to see. Leonie and her family and . . . Brendan. It was time to get on with her own life.

She rang the airline and after nearly half an hour they found her a seat on the 'horror flight' leaving London late on Christmas Eve. There would be a ten-hour stopover in Dubai and another twelve hours in Singapore. It was going to take her three days to get home.

'It's this time of the year,' the girl said apologetically, 'there's just the one seat available. Do you want to take it?'

'Yes,' Kit said immediately. 'And I'm in Dublin now. Can you get me a flight over to London as soon as possible?'

'Dublin,' the girl murmured. Kit heard the click click of the computer keys in the background. 'Now, just let me see. There are a couple of seats on a plane going at three. Could you make that?'

Kit looked at her watch.

'Book me on it, please.'

CHAPTER FORTY-SEVEN

Kit rang Sebastian the next day from London. She had another five hours to wait until her plane left and although she was nervous she decided what the hell. She was in another country, and on her way home. Nothing he said could touch her now.

'Kathleen!' his voice was both relieved and annoyed. 'What's happened to you? I've been ringing the hotel and –'

'I'm in London,' she said simply.

'I see. Can you tell me why?'

'Why? Because he's my father!' she suddenly blurted out. 'There is no way I'll . . .' Her voice had risen and she knew she was bordering on hysterical. 'I came over here to meet him. For the first time. He was good to me. He talked to me, showed me around. Anyway, what do you know about it? How come you're so sure of yourself? He's not a thug or a gangster. He's a soldier, fighting to free his country!'

'Okay. Okay,' Sebastian cut in sharply, 'I understand. Will you let me have the information, then? Give me his full name and exactly where he lives. Then I can at least make a call.'

'No!' Kit cried. 'That would be worse! I can fight my own battles. I can do my own dirty deeds.'

405

'But you're not going to, are you?' Sebastian replied coldly. 'You're not going to tell anyone.'

'No, but not because I'm scared. It's because . . .' Kit's mind suddenly went blank. She was arguing, with this lovely man. This quietly intelligent, gifted man who loved theatre and acting. Who knew a lot about world politics because it was his field. This guy whose only crime was that he didn't want to see people blown up. It didn't make sense. She stared around her, at the crowds waiting for flights, bored and restless.

Then she saw him in the next booth. A tall young man in a coat. No hat. Sean. It was him. *Listening to her*. He had been following her around, spying on her.

'Hang on, Sebastian,' Kit interrupted, edging out of the booth. 'I've just got to . . .' But the young man turned and caught her eye, then immediately began walking away.

Kit leant out of the booth, still hanging onto the phone with one hand, about to yell at him. But he'd already disappeared, merging in with the crowd.

About to tell Sebastian she'd call back, that she was going to go chase after a little stooge, Kit's legs suddenly seemed to have lost their strength. She could hear his voice still talking into the phone, going on in his quiet, insistent way but she couldn't hear what he was saying. Eventually she crumbled, squatting in the phone booth, hoping she wasn't going to vomit over that shiny pristine floor.

'Are you okay?' a nice-looking American girl, with a blond ponytail, wanted to know. 'Can I get you anything?'

'No. Thank you.' Kit took the girl's hand, stumbled to her feet and picked up the phone. 'I'm just . . . in the middle of talking to someone.' But when she put the phone to her ear there was no one there. Just the insistent ring of the engaged signal.

Sebastian had hung up on her.

CHAPTER FORTY-EIGHT

The news came two days into the trip home. She'd got through the ten gruelling hours of sitting and waiting at Dubai. She'd read newspapers and drank so many cups of terrible coffee. She'd talked to people to pass the time.

Then there'd been the Singapore stop. And shopping for presents in the airport. In Singapore she realised it was actually Christmas Day. She was in between time zones, in a kind of limbo, travelling on to somewhere else. It was black outside. It didn't seem possible that only eight hours away people she knew were opening presents, laughing and wishing each other well, sitting down to traditional dinners and cracking open bottles of wine. The knowledge was so disconcerting. But was it only the oceans and the time zones cutting her off? Never before had she felt so fragile and disconnected.

Finally, she was on the last leg. As she settled into her seat, there was some relief knowing that she wouldn't have to wait in any more airports. The next stop would be Melbourne.

The news came on as she was opening the silver foil covering her meal. The newsreader was a young woman dressed in a blue suit. Her image flickered throughout the plane on half a dozen elevated televisions.

'*A bomb went off in Central London early this morning,*' she said coolly, '*destroying the Cenotaph, Britain's major monument to the war dead, in Whitehall.*'

Kit stopped fiddling with her package and stared. Images appeared while the woman spoke. Firstly of the Cenotaph as it had once stood. A close-up of the words *Our Glorious Dead* and poppies strewn around its base. And then the pile of rubble. The mound of smashed stone and marble.

'*Her Majesty Queen Elizabeth is said to be deeply saddened by the senseless destruction of the magnificent monument that means so much to so many people,*' the newsreader went on. '*A spokesman for the Prime Minister declared that all decent people will abhor such a vile deed . . . and the monument will be rebuilt as soon as possible.*

'*Although police received a warning twenty minutes before the bomb exploded, they were unable to completely clear the area. One young woman, out walking her dog, sustained an injury to her right eye when a piece of flying debris hit her. She was operated on this morning and remains in St Margaret's Hospital in London in a stable condition. Doctors will not know for several weeks if the operation will save her eye.*

'*Although no one has yet claimed responsibility for the explosion, police are investigating a number of leads.*'

Kit stared at the screen in disbelief. She continued to stare, long after the news bulletin had finished and the movie had begun. *So he went ahead with it.* She handed her meal back uneaten.

The eight hours from Singapore went by in a tangle of shifting emotion. Kit seethed with anger and at the same time felt a deep sorrow, way beyond tears. Sorrow for the hurt girl out walking her dog, for the destroyed monument, for Sebastian and herself . . . the relationship that finished before it had even had a chance to start. What good would they be to each other now? Lovers were meant to start off showing each other the best sides of themselves. But Sebastian had seen the worst of her. A cowardly hysteric who didn't even have the courage to confront him when she found she couldn't do the right, the brave thing. She ran when she should have stayed.

Numb, Kit sat wide-eyed in the darkness of the plane while everyone else slept. She'd run from Sebastian, like she'd run from her father, from Rosalaind, just as she'd ran from her mother when she couldn't face the circumstances of her birth. I'm just like Leonie, she thought cynically.

When you wake and find me gone? What a joke. So who was she really? How come she'd always thought of herself as someone not afraid to speak her mind or stick up for what she believed in? Where was the evidence of bravery of any kind?

At one stage she fell asleep, probably for a couple of hours, then woke with what must have been a loud cry because the man next to her asked if she was all right. The hostess had been passing and asked Kit if she'd like a drink of water.

A drink of water? Yeah, right. That should fix everything!

She'd been dreaming of those bits of paper. The ones she'd thrown away into the snow. In her dream, she knew they were going to explode when they hit the ground. She'd been out in the freezing snow trying to catch them, desperately clawing at the air as they floated down in front of her. Stuffing them in the pockets of her coat. So much paper! Her pockets were bulging. Millions of tiny bits of paper. I shouldn't have done this, she'd kept saying to herself in her dream, I shouldn't have thrown them up into the air. I have to catch every single one of them, or *someone will die.*

Of course Eamon was tangled up in all her confusion and sorrow – living by himself in that house on the mountainside, alone with his memories and savage ideals. Eamon was as emotionally remote as a monk and would probably remain so. He had to be like that because he was a soldier, and that was his reason for living. And she,

Kit, was simply an inconvenience that had arrived unannounced from another part of the world. Bridie and Rosalaind were the only two he loved. And yet they didn't live with him. He couldn't even love them properly.

But some satisfaction that the attack went ahead as planned had sprouted in her, too. It meant her father trusted her, didn't it? He knew she'd keep her mouth shut. How could this spark of pride and pleasure live alongside the revulsion she felt; for the useless destructiveness of blowing up a war monument. It sickened her that she actually cared about what he thought of her after that.

Kit was waiting numbly in a queue to go through customs in Melbourne when the next piece of news came on. A TV screen near her had been broadcasting local news bulletins for perhaps twenty minutes, and Kit was barely watching as she inched her way along the line.

'And before we close, news has just come in from London. The bomb that went off in Whitehall yesterday, destroying the monument to Britain's war dead, has been claimed by a splinter Republican group calling themselves Easter Rising.'

Kit shuddered, and wondered whether Sebastian had gone to the police.

After the long wait, her bags went through without a search. Still dazed, she pushed her way into the main part of the airport. She'd forgotten to ring Therese with her flight details. Now that at last she was back in Australia, she felt childishly sad that there would be no one to meet her.

Expectant faces lined both sides of the walkway, a few people were holding up signs with names written in Texta. As Kit moved further out, groups of people stood around hugging each other. Some were crying and others laughing and calling out. But, as she'd expected, there was no one waiting for her.

Kit headed for the automatic doors that led outside, then stopped to relish the blessed relief of fresh air. She had been cooped up inside planes and airports for over three days. She stood for a few moments breathing it in, and looking out at the car park and the straggling early morning crowds. Above her the sky was a clear pale blue. She fancied she could smell eucalyptus in the air, even though there was hardly a gum tree in sight. But that other crisp, cool smell of an early Australian morning before the heat settles was definitely there and made her spirits rise. She went to the end of the taxi queue and stood in line. This would be over soon. She'd sleep and then be able to think. There was no point trying to work anything out now. She hoped someone was home at the Richmond house because she didn't have a key. Later she would ring Bridie and see if Eamon was around. Or in custody. Slowly the line snaked forward as one taxi after another pulled up and people got in.

'Hey, Quinlan!'

Kit was the next in line when she heard a voice behind her. She turned. There was only one person who sounded like that. Only one voice with that peculiarly flat Australian tone, edged with a hint of something else. Now that she'd been there, she could hear the tinge of Belfast twang. *Brendan*. Kit's heart began to bang against her ribcage as she looked around, searching for him.

He was some distance away, one arm raised waving, the other one restraining a leaping Boy George who was pulling at the lead and trying to jump up on people as they hurried past. A uniformed man was talking to Brendan and pointing crossly at the dog. They weren't allowed in airports. Didn't Brendan know that? Kit grinned. Brendan was fobbing the man off and edging his way towards her through a large crowd. She picked up her bags.

They finally met in front of the poster promoting safe sex when travelling. Kit was in a kind of shock. I love this person, she found herself thinking. I always have. I love the bulkiness of him: his

411

shoulders, those big square knuckled hands, the tough sad mouth that looks like he could laugh or cry any minute. But of course that wasn't what she said. She didn't trust those thoughts at all.

'Brendan!' She dropped the bags in front of him. Boy George jumped up and tried to lick her face.

'How did you know?' she demanded. 'I mean about me getting in today? I didn't tell anyone!'

Then she burst into tears.

Brendan laughed. 'I'm psychic,' he said, lifting her up off her feet in a big hug, then kissing her briefly on her forehead. 'Your mum rang me. She was worried. Told me you were coming, so I did a bit of ringing around. Not that the airlines would tell me much. Security. You know,' he laughed again and continued to hold her, 'I might have been a terrorist!'

'Right,' she sobbed.

'Hey,' he said softly, cupping the back of her head in his hand, his cheek against hers, 'what the hell has got into you?'

'You don't want to know,' Kit managed through her tears. 'You just don't want to know.'

'Try me,' Brendan grinned.

'No way,' she laughed, fumbling around for a tissue. 'No bloody way.'

'Okay.' Brendan handed her the dog's lead with a smile. 'But you get the mutt.'

'So Lou still not back?' Kit took hold of the lead and Brendan picked up both her bags easily, slinging one onto his back.

'Next week,' Brendan grinned. 'They had car trouble and then they got sued.'

'Sued?'

'Yeah, some venue got wrecked and they're being held responsible. Something like that.'

'Hell.'

About to head off, they paused to look at each other: a quiet look that ignored all the airport chaos around them; the furtive smokers out for a last fag before take off, the whining kids running ahead of their frantic parents, the businessmen and the perfumed superwomen all rushing to and from their flights and jobs and families.

It was a deep, straight, painful look, right into each other's eyes.

'I thought about you a lot,' she said quietly. 'You were never far away.'

Brendan smiled. He held out his spare hand. Sensing that the gesture was, in some way, a serious invitation, Kit stopped a moment before slowly taking it in her own.

They walked off together, hand in hand, the dog pulling and yapping in front of them.

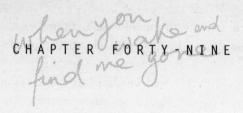

CHAPTER FORTY-NINE

Everyone said that they'd never seen Johnny looking better. On his wedding day he glowed with a confidence that he'd rarely shown before. He shook the guests' hands and accepted their good wishes, his beautiful eyes dancing with delight and pride as he turned every now and again to introduce his bride.

There were over a hundred guests and most of them had never met Casey before. So there were more than a few rubber-necks as she came up the aisle in her simple cream cotton dress, that – it had to be said – looked more like a nightie than a wedding dress, holding a bunch of flowers freshly picked from Therese's garden.

Who was this odd freckled little creature with the crooked teeth, the cropped dark hair, the mother of two young children already? And was she going to be worthy of Johnny?

The ceremony, officiated by Simon, one of Johnny's best friends from the Jesuits, was at five in St Joseph's. It was as lovely as it was simple. And wasn't it a blessed relief to have no photographers, no video cameras and no pop songs! No one arrived in big fancy cars either, much less hired suits or expensive dresses. It was exactly Johnny's style. And judging by Casey's dress, her simple bouquet and broad smile, it seemed to suit her as well.

Not that the ceremony was austere in any way. There were candles all over the altar, and vases full of cut summer flowers from local gardens. A group of Johnny's friends from the seminary sang beautiful hymns. Moya played the organ. Gerard, who had a very good voice but hadn't sung in public for years, sang 'I Know That my Redeemer Liveth' during the Communion because Johnny had asked him to. Once outside, everyone was full of praise, and the old man was duly chuffed.

The only flashiness was Casey's son Jordan who at three years old saw the nuptial mass as a great opportunity to show off in front of a crowd. He skidded about the polished floor in front of the altar and called out and waved to the congregation while the ceremony was in progress. But he was easy to forgive with his mass of blond curls and big cheeky smile. No one really minded. After ten minutes or so, Eileen and Det managed to entice him back to their pew with a few sweets and a colouring book they'd brought especially. The new baby was being minded by a lady in the town, but would be coming out to the reception later because she was still being breastfed.

Kit, in her new mauve dress, hair pinned up loosely at the back, stood next to Brendan and tried not to cry as she watched Johnny and Casey moving through the crowd outside the church, laughing and kissing people as they dodged clouds of confetti.

Contrary to the family's first impressions, Casey was quiet, but not shy. She had an almost gruff manner and a low chuckling laugh that, once you got used to it, was rather appealing. She was older than Johnny and shrewder, but she wasn't hard. And anyone could see she adored Johnny as much as he did her.

Leonie was one of the last to come out of the church. Kit watched her slowly negotiate the steps with Frank and Pete on each side, gripping her thin arms. The whole right side of her body still dragged and her movements were stiff. But she was so much better

415

than she'd been, even two weeks before. The doctors held out great hope for a strong, if not complete, recovery. Each week there were gradual improvements to her speech and movement. She'd put on weight and her lovely red hair, tinged around the temples with grey, was growing back. For Johnny's wedding it was covered in a little black straw hat that framed her pale face. She was wearing make-up which gave her much needed colour, and the simple green linen dress that Aunty Moya had insisted on buying her suited beautifully.

Of course, apart from Johnny, Leonie was the other star of the day. Everyone wanted to tell her how well she was looking and wish her luck for further recovery. And to a lesser extent, Kit, too, was a focus of attention. People were keen to let her know of the change in Leonie since Kit returned home. Leonie was brighter, more optimistic, more *herself*, they all said. This was humbling for Kit because she had to admit privately that she didn't know what it meant. Leonie was more *herself*?

And yet, of course, in some ways she did know Leonie. And so much better than any of them. Even so, it was still very confusing.

The family and friends wanted to know about Kit's trip, too, the more openly inquisitive asking directly about her father. But Kit didn't say much. Life since she'd been back had taken on dramas of its own. The big one was herself and Brendan. What they had going was making her happier than she'd ever been. But there were other things, too. She'd turned twenty-one. It'd been hard convincing everyone that she didn't want to celebrate just yet. Maybe she'd have a party in a few months. Tam had moved back to her mother's while Kit had been away. Kit had only seen her once and it had been pretty strained between them. And Rory had moved in to the Richmond house more or less permanently. Kit hadn't said anything to Brendan yet, but she didn't know if she wanted to live with a fourteen-year-old drug dealer. She was going to have to find out about getting her place back at university, too. She'd probably have to grovel to some

Dean or other. And she'd just received a terse note from Sebastian to say he'd be back in a week and wished to meet with her, *to talk*.

What the hell were they going to say to each other?

There was Ireland and all that had happened to think about as well. Her little sister was still over there drawing film-scripts and seething about Kit running off on her. And there was Eamon, gone to ground in Donegal since Christmas Day. Kit rang Bridie soon after getting back and was told that no one knew where he was, but that Kit shouldn't worry because, 'he goes away a lot and always turns up when he's least expected.'

Did Bridie know about Eamon? Of course she did. Did she know that Eamon had been part of organising that bomb? Was that why they didn't live together any more? But how could Kit even begin to ask Bridie questions like that?

Apart from a few short tortuous conversations with Leonie, she'd confided in no one but Brendan.

She supposed it was all going to get easier as time wore on. It had to, didn't it?

Leonie smiled when she caught Kit's eye on the way past, still on the arms of her brothers.

'Your turn next,' she teased, her voice still very slurred. Kit smiled and looked at Brendan. 'I keep asking him,' she joked, 'but he says I don't come up to scratch!'

'You know how it is,' Brendan shrugged and gave Leonie a wry look. 'Some people just don't cut it.'

Kit gave him a sharp nudge and Leonie moved on to another group of well-wishers. Most people were heading for their cars, out to the farm for the reception, so Kit and Brendan began to walk off too.

'Thanks for all your help, Brendan.' Therese stopped to kiss him, and Kit could tell from her smile that she was able to relax at last. Kit and Brendan had come up two days before, to help put the finishing touches to the decorations. The whole family had been there working like beavers. But Therese had done the bulk of the work. She'd slaved solidly on the wedding for the three weeks since Kit had arrived home. A huge marquee had been set up in the front garden. The tables were set with linen, crockery and flowers. All the food, the drink and the music was at long last organised. The champagne was on ice. The only thing that remained was for people to enjoy it.

'You've got that look on your face, Quinlan.'

Two hours later, Kit was looking around at the other guests. The meal over, most of them were now getting up and moving towards the polished wooden dance-floor. The band was warming up. Kit and Brendan were the only ones left sitting.

'Have I?' Kit laughed, trying to shrug off a feeling of melancholy that was creeping up on her. Brendan was looking so handsome in his white shirt and tie. He was regarding her quizzically, waiting for her to speak.

For a couple of minutes, Kit had been back in Ireland with Cormac. His big day would be starting soon, too. It was being held at around the same time as Johnny's wedding: Cormac's own special occasion, which she wouldn't be going to.

'Let's have the happy couple out here!' the fiddle player shouted into the microphone. 'We'll start with the Bridal Waltz.'

Kit and Brendan joined the crowd swarming around clapping as Johnny and Casey began to dance. When they'd done one turn of the floor, other couples joined them.

'Let's dance,' Brendan said, holding out his hand. 'You and me, babe.'

Kit joined him on the floor. They were in close at first, just rocking together, Brendan's hand on her back, holding her.

'So?'

'So . . . nothing,' she said. But Brendan was a hard one to fob off. He was the good-natured, simple guy that everyone liked because he was funny, but he had all kinds of other layers to him as well. All these different skins lying just under each other. He was both very tender and sharp. Sharper than Kit had ever realised before. They'd had a couple of amazing rows over the last couple of weeks.

'Bullshit, Quinlan.' He raised one eyebrow and gave her a grin that said: *It will keep . . .*

She laughed, not minding at all. She knew it was early days, that real problems were sure to arise, but at the moment they were making each other very happy. There was so much talk and discussion between them, and so much passion, too . . . *What more could you want?*

Kit giggled as she watched Aunty Moya glide past in a stately manner in the arms of an old neighbour. She'd forgotten that Moya never smiled when she was dancing. All three aunts took formal occasions very seriously.

'There is just one thing,' Kit whispered into Brendan's ear.

'Yeah?'

'Something I want to say.'

'Here's trouble,' Brendan said dryly, pushing her away from him, making her spin around where she stood. The band had picked up a bit. Kit gasped, the exertion making her face go pink.

'I can't believe my luck!'

'How do you mean?'

'I thought I was going to end up knitting or something.'

'What are you talking about?'

'Both sides of my family are full of single women.'

'You've told me that fifteen times, Quinlan!'

'So I thought I was destined to live alone, into old age.'

Brendan pulled her in close again and grinned down at her, pushing his fingers through her hair.

'So I came in useful after all?' he said, kissing her.

'Yeah. You did. Very useful.'

CHAPTER FIFTY

On her way back from the toilet, Kit cut across the house and into the back garden, making for her favourite place, a huge peppercorn tree which had been planted by Gerard's grandfather. She took off her shoes and sat under the lowest branch, leaning her back against the trunk. She looked up through the canopy of branches, and saw that stars were beginning to appear. What a lovely night for a wedding! Streaks of yellow light from the house cut across the lawn in a complicated pattern of waving ribbons, as the caterers moved about in front of the venetian blinds inside.

She'd rung Cormac the day before to say she wasn't going to make it to his special occasion. It was the first time she'd spoken to him since he'd dropped her in the town three weeks earlier. She hadn't told him then that she wouldn't be back for Christmas, although something about the way he'd said goodbye, clasping her hands in his old arthritic ones and looking into her face before waving her off, told her he knew something was up.

If he was surprised by her call, he didn't show it. His voice sounded exactly the same, making her feel that he was just down the hill, and that she might easily have put on her hat and coat and

420

walked down the slippery track to meet him in front of the turf fire.

'Kathleen, you will be sorely missed,' he said formally. 'I'll be thinking of you.'

'Oh, God, don't do that,' Kit said impatiently. 'I want you to have a great time. Cormac, I'm sorry. You know I really wanted to come.'

'Ah sure, I know you did,' he sighed. 'But life catches us out sometimes.'

Kit wanted to ask him if he'd heard anything of her father. He was close to Eamon. But how close?

'We had the wild one as mad as a stuck pig out here on Christmas Day,' Cormac said wryly. 'When you didn't show, she was turning up the ground with her feet!'

'But I told Bridie!'

'Ah, but Rosalaind thought you'd turn up anyway,' Cormac chuckled. 'She thought it was some kind of conspiracy and that you'd win through in the end.'

A stab of shame hit Kit. She'd let her sister down.

'So she was really mad?'

'She was ropeable!' Cormac yelled gleefully. 'Screaming at her mother, shouting at those other girls, calling them imposters, and chucking things about. Your father threatened to tie her to the tree outside if she didn't get a hold of herself.'

'So he was there?'

'Sure, he was here for Christmas,' Cormac replied. 'We have a big crowd out here every Christmas.'

'Well, I've written to Rosalaind,' Kit said carefully.

'Aye, I know,' Cormac wheezed. 'Sure, she's been quieter since then.'

'Is she going to write back?'

'Aye, she will.'

There was a moment's pause and Kit heard the painful rasp in his breathing.

'Can you tell me now why you're having the party?' Kit asked. 'What is the special occasion?'

'Oh sure,' Comac said blithely. 'I'm dying soon. And I wanted to see everyone before things get too bad. You know how it is.'

'Dying?'

'Sure I am!' he chuckled. 'Now don't you be telling me that I look the picture of health! I had that Mrs O'Haire in here earlier picking up her bread and she was so enthusiastic about how well I look that I started thinking I might have to go in for the next Olympics like!'

'But Cormac,' Kit laughed, even though part of her wanted to cry, 'has something new turned up? I mean, how do you know you're dying?'

'Jesus, Mary and Joseph!' he exclaimed. 'You haven't got all day. I won't bore you with the details, Kathleen. But I am dying very soon. And I'm not at all bothered about it, what's more. The sooner the better, in fact! I've had a grand life and now I'm going. It's as simple as that.'

'So when?' Kit said, her throat tightening.

'Ah well,' he said, 'I don't have a hot line to Our Saviour, but let's just say I won't be here in a couple of months. You could put it like that.'

'But you feel okay now?'

'Ah, sure. I feel on top of the world!' he wheezed. 'You know, girl, you're going to be missing something special here. I got the best caterers up from Galway. I got French Champagne and fresh trout. And that's just the beginning!'

'How many people?' Kit said longingly. She could imagine the pub all set up for them. The cold outside. The fire going. The noise. The music. The warmth and the laughter.

'Fifty-three people,' he said proudly. 'Now, that's not bad, is it? For an old codger like me to pull in over fifty people at a few weeks notice?'

'It'll be great,' Kit said enthusiastically.

'Sure, it'll be great. Two are coming in from the States especially.'

'So, who'll run the pub when, when you've . . . gone?'

'I'm leaving it to my sister's boy, but you know he probably won't last out here. Too quiet for a young person. Then again, I've been telling him he should hang on. The way things are going with all the tourists now, he'll probably end up selling it to McDonalds. Next time you come, Kathleen, you'll be heading down the hill for a hamburger!'

'God!' Kit groaned, 'I can't wait.' She paused a moment. 'Cormac?'

'What is it, girl?'

'Have you heard from my father?'

'Not a word,' he said matter-of-factly, 'but you're not to be worrying yourself about him, Kathleen. He comes and he goes. And he always turns up again.'

'Right,' Kit sighed. She wanted to ask Cormac something that had been on her mind since she got home.

'Cormac?'

'What is it now?' He was only pretending to be impatient. Kit knew he was enjoying the conversation.

'There is something . . .' she began tentatively.

'Out with it!' he snapped.

'Do you think,' she gulped, 'do you think that Eamon . . . Do you think my father is . . . a *good* man?'

There was a moment of hesitation while she listened to his intake of breath.

'A good man?' Cormac repeated quickly. 'Well, of course he is a good man . . .'

'I mean *really*,' she said.

Cormac sighed. 'It's a hard question, Kathleen,' he rasped eventually. 'It's a hard question to answer about anyone. You see, I've known him all my life.'

'But what do you think?' Kit persisted.

'Well,' Cormac said after a while, 'some people have to fight the big battles for the rest of us.' He hesitated. 'But I don't know whether that makes him a good man.'

Kit waited for him to go on.

'You should ask your mother,' he added quickly, 'she's someone who'd have an opinion on the subject.'

'Yes,' Kit sighed. 'You're right. I'll ask her. But can I ring you again?' she stumbled on, trying not to sound sentimental. 'Will it be okay? For me to call every now and again?'

'Sure,' he said, 'and if I'm here I'll answer it. If I'm not, then you'll know I've headed over the hill.'

'Oh, God.' There was a raw miserable feeling of loss going right through Kit. 'I'll miss you.'

'One thing, girl. You're to come back here. You hear me?'

'Yes,' Kit said uneasily. 'I hear you.'

'This is your place,' he wheezed. 'Your father is here and your sister. And you're to come and see everyone, and visit me . . .'

'You?' Kit was puzzled.

'I'll be right up the far corner under the big conifer tree. By the time you get here it'll probably have a stone on it. But just in case, remember *the conifer tree*. There's only one of them in the whole place. I'll be right in front of my mother, Brenda. On the other side of her are my two brothers, Patsy and Kieren.'

'Okay.'

'You'll come and see me?'

'Yes, I will.'

'You never know,' he said, quiet seriously, 'I might be in a better position to answer all your questions then.'

'Okay,' Kit said. 'I have to go now, Cormac.'

'Bye, Kathleen.'

Kit continued to sit under the tree. She could hear the buzz of voices, the occasional shout of laughter and the music bouncing away through the darkness. The air around her was still and heavy with the perfume of Therese's garden.

Kit watched the shape of a women come slowly around the end of the house, and stand just outside the arch of ribboned light from the back window. Too small for Therese or the aunts, although they were the only ones she could think of who would come looking for her. Some old person, probably. Kit stood up and fitted her shoes back on. She really should be getting back. It was a wedding, after all. No one should sit away from everyone else at a wedding.

The shape began to shuffle forward, and Kit's heart was suddenly in her mouth because she realised that it was Leonie, without her walking-stick.

'Leonie?' she called, concerned as she hurried over. 'Be careful.'

Leonie stepped into a stream of yellow light from the kitchen window. Kit saw that she was looking tired.

'I've come to find you,' Leonie said, slowly, in her slurred voice. 'For the speeches. Johnny doesn't want to do the speeches without you.'

Kit held out her arm. 'Here, walk with me,' she said simply.

They went slowly back around the side of the house, arm in arm under the bright star-studded sky. Back to the wedding party. To the lightness, the gaiety, the laughter. Kit wondered what Leonie would think if she told her she'd been praying. To who, she wasn't quite sure, but praying anyway. For forgiveness. Forgiveness for her father. For her mother. And herself.

Then, as they passed under the strings of lights that had been draped around the surrounding trees, she prayed for courage.

Don't let this have all been for nothing. Don't let me settle down to all the ordinary stupid easy things. Make me a fighter, too.

Courage. It was what she needed more than anything, because she knew that it was a good time to begin again.

GREG

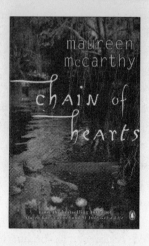

Chain of Hearts

I always shiver when I think of the painting hanging above the fireplace in the old house. A girl in a red dress is floating face-up in the river. My Aunt Fran did the painting when she was seventeen ...

At seventeen, Sophie is a mess. Her best friend is dead, her boyfriend has gone, and she's dropped out of school. Then her family dumps her on an aunt she doesn't know in a country town where she'll be a complete stranger. She's bored before she even gets there ...

But Sophie is about to embark on the strangest journey of her life. It will take her back into her family's past, to the origins of the bitter rift between her mother and her aunt, to her Uncle Jimmy and the Vietnam War, and finally to the girl in the painting and the story haunting all their lives.

Shortlisted for the Ethel Turner Prize in the 2000 NSW Premier's Literary Awards.